I0609372

HEROES &
MARTYRS

DOMINIC LACHANCE

Dear Boys,

This book is dedicated to you three, Liam, Anthony and JP, you who are always there to make me feel like my life has a noble purpose. Thanks, JE VOUS AIME!

Dear Nicaraguans,

This is my homage to you, you have welcomed me with opened arms and made me feel good about myself. Thank you Martin, the only character in the book whose name could not be changed, without you, I wouldn't have lasted a week. Finally, thank you to the people of Cinco Pinos for treating me so well. I have travelled in 38 countries in this world and you guys will forever remain my favourites.

Dear readers,

This book has taken many forms over the years and you are about to read my favourite one. Everything is true, except the story. It would be like painting on a fake canvas with real colours. I have worked two summers in Nicaragua, travelled around Central-America and also six countries in South-America. My story was born from actual events that have happened to me over these two unforgettable summers.

As always (since it is pretty much the same as in my first book THE UNDERCOVER TREE PLANTER... cheap plug), hope you enjoy the story, laugh from time to time, and learn a few things along the way. Again, I feel like I should also apologize for the price of the book, it is self-published and trust me when I say I don't see much of what you paid for it. Sorry, for you and for me.

Thank you so very much for buying and reading it; it truly means the world to me. And if you borrowed it, well thanks for reading but remember to return the book to its rightful owner.

Don't hesitate to write!

Dominic Lachance
dominic_lachance@hotmail.com

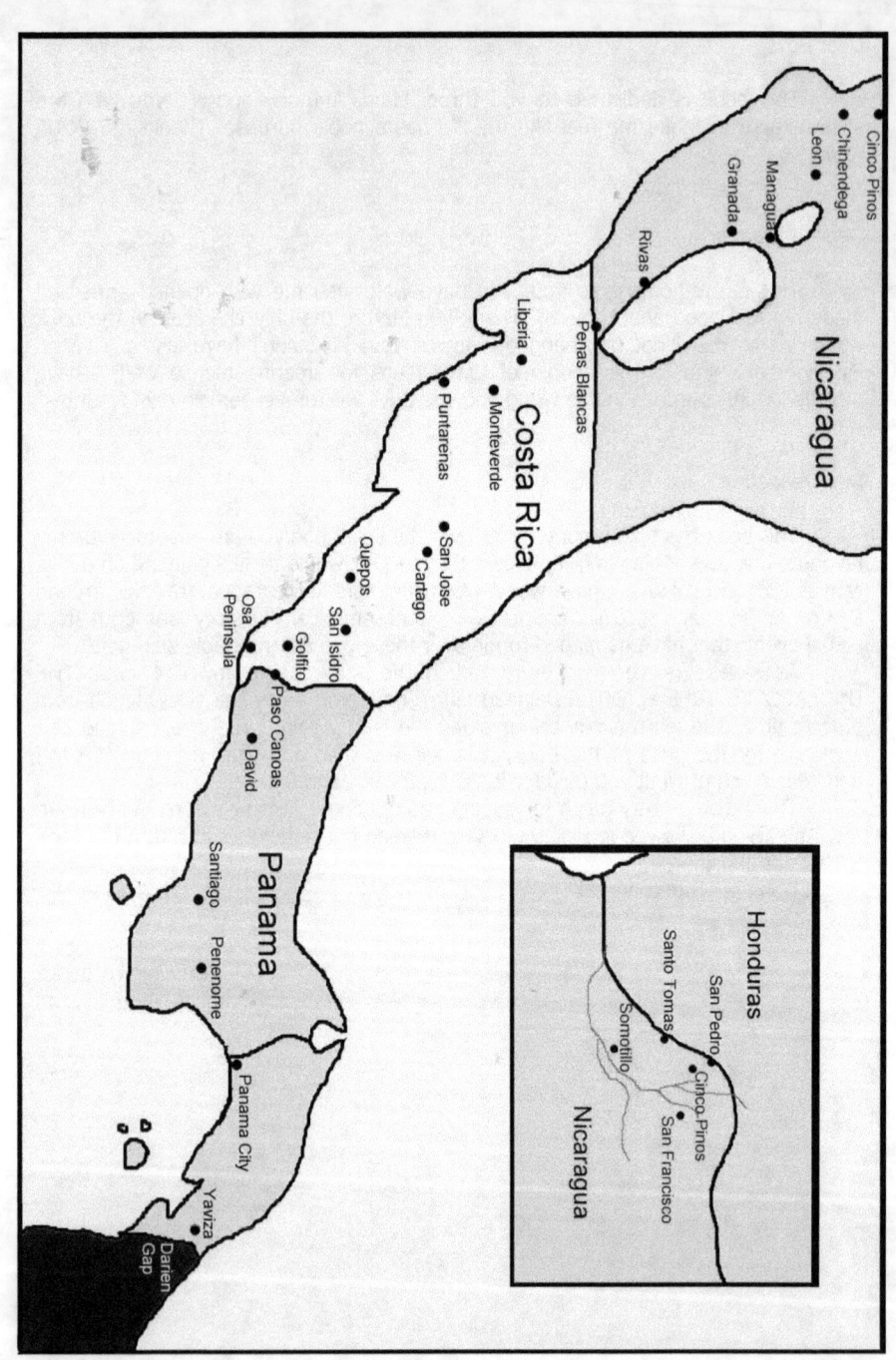

4

PREFACE

An imaginary friend of mine once told me to write a book about what I had gone through. I am not sure about the idea, but I decided to give it a go anyway. I mean, how hard could it be?

It was a heck of an adventure. My parents were on vacation in Rome and since no one was available to drive me to the airport, I had hitchhiked. It took me about fourteen hours to travel four hundred fifty kilometres and a total of twelve drivers offered me to share their vehicle.

Every single time I waited for a car to stop, I always went through the same emotions. First everything was fine; the excitement was there when I expected the car. I just wanted to have a ride. Then, I started to feel angry. The drivers became enemies; they had the power to help, but refused to use it. I was rejected and it made me feel sad. I felt lonely, standing by myself on the side of the highway, waiting for a ride that would not come. Later, these two emotions were transformed into light insanity. How could I feel angry or sad when I had no clue why? This lack of understanding made me go nuts. I sang, danced, screamed, imagined weird things, and laughed uncontrollably. Luckily for me, this period was very short. Once these three phases were totally over, I simply wanted to be at peace inside a moving vehicle. Strangely, a car would then stop and pick me up. It was always the same thing. I could not fake the stages. I had to live them fully, completely, and honestly.

CHAPTER 1.1

I was standing in the doorway of Emmen airport in Luzern and I did not really know where I was going. I did know the name of the country, it was on my flight ticket, but I had no clue *where* it would lead me. I tried not to worry too much, the future was never set, and control was only an illusion. After all, I had always managed to do pretty well in life; this trip would not be different.

For me, travelling seemed like a good way to escape reality. People incapable of leaving their homes saw a trip like an act of courage. In my view, it was a pause from everything that tied me down, monotony, the usual routine and the folks who filled it with boredom.

I walked to the counter. "Good morning sir. May I have your ticket please?" The lady behind initiated.

Of course I handed it to her; was I going to refuse? I held back not to ask her why prices seemed to have doubled in the last few years. Maybe because overweight people were costing airline companies nearly three hundred million dollars more per year in fuel. Still, it was ridiculous that I should be the one to be penalized.

She asked for my passport, if I had been the one to pack my bags, if I had left them unattended? I positively answered nonchalantly to all her questions.

A few moments later, she tagged my big bag and gave me a little ticket for my small one. "There you go, enjoy you flight." She said in a fake, but very sexy tone of voice.

I was off to my gate.

I sat down and my eyes closed. I had gotten up very early this morning. I dozed off for a bit. I dreamed of an apple that I took a bite in, then I ended up at an opera located on a giant bay, I did not get anything that was going on, but luckily I was holding a map in my right hand.

Things changed in a flash, I had millions of dollars, unlimited money. I had a huge mansion with over sixty bedrooms. I had an ocean view and a beach that was all mine. In my yard, I had an Olympic swimming pool, a golf course, and four tennis courts. In my garage, I had about twenty cars and thirty bikes. I had a huge gate around my property and I had a lot of fans with cameras on the other side of it. There was even a tour bus that stopped and a bunch of Japanese tourists came out to take pictures. I walked in front of the crowd and signed my name on a few pieces of paper. Later, I went back inside and saw a lot of different people. I had a butler, a maid, a masseuse, a cook, a physical trainer, and a personal adviser. I had walls made of white marble. They had some stones carved into them, kind of like the Taj Mahal.

Wham! I woke up. A flight that was not mine was called on the overloud speaker. In a yoctosecond everything had vanished, I had lost it all and was left empty-handed.

CHAPTER 1.2

I waited two and a half hours, surrounded by many people, but really felt alone. Thankfully, none of them were conversing with their neighbours and I was no different: I preferred to read my book and listen to my music.

Shortly after I turned the fourth page and started the second song, a man came to sit beside me. Unfortunately, I could tell that he would start speaking very soon. My book was interesting and I did not feel like talking, but how could I tell him that nicely?

"Do you speak French by any chance?" He began.

"Of course, I speak French." I answered, I felt like sarcastically returning the question. After all, this was Switzerland, anybody who mastered less than three languages was considered inferior.

He stopped for a while and did not say anything else. The suspense was far from killing me. Supposedly, there was always a reason for people to cross our path; I simply did not see one in this case. I went back to the lines of my page. The man replaced his shirt collar and looked at his watch. "Is it here for the flight to Paris?" He asked.

Was that all? He had come to see me just because he was too lazy to look at the board? The futility of his question really gave me the certainty that he simply wanted a conversation, a way to kill time. I looked at his greyish hair and I answered his question with a nod.

"So, where are you heading?" He questioned expectedly.

"Nicaragua." I simply replied.

"Wow! That's great. I'm going to London on business; I've an interview with Lloyd's insurance company." He bragged. "Will it be your first time in Central America?"

I wanted to tell him to leave me alone, but I did not dare articulate it. "Yes." I answered without concentration.

"Are you going on business or pleasure?"

"Both." I said. When the word came out, I realized that my sentences would have to be longer if I wanted to get rid of this guy any time soon. I continued with business details, it seemed to be what he was mainly concerned with. "I'm going to work as a consultant on a coffee plantation."

"Well that's good. Did you study commerce at University?"

"No." I answered and before I could develop about my studies, he asked me a new question.

"Then how did you get that job?"

"I spent a summer in southern Italy and worked on a farm where the proprietor grew coffee, it gave me some experience."

"Where did you apply to get the position?"

This guy was starting to get on my nerves with his interrogation, but I kept on answering. "Nowhere really, earlier this year, I helped the friend of a friend renovate his house. He worked for an international organisation." I explained.

"You're good with your hands as well, that's why they gave you the job?" The man questioned.

"Not really, I think I simply made him laugh at the party we all had when the renovations were finished." I admitted. "The friend of a friend was alright. Over the evening, I was able to fill his head with half-lies about how I could do a great job helping villagers to set up their plantation."

"You were lucky, but what about the organisation, the boss said yes without fully testing your qualifications?" The man interrogated.

"By the time the company board interviewed me: I had done a lot of reading on the Internet and had learned quite a bit about coffee. Next thing I knew, I was offered a well-paid contract, airfare and living expenses." I thought that he would appreciate that I included some monetary information.

"And how much money an hour do you get?"

Who was this guy anyway, what made him so special and deserving of my personal details, why was he even talking to me? I wanted the curtain to fall on this horribly irritating show. Luckily, just when I was about to reply with another vague answer, my flight was called and we were, to my great delight, forced to split up. He was travelling in first class and naturally I was not. I would be safe from now on.

We waited on the plane for a bit and it allowed me to calm down. Why did I even bother to get angry with this idiot?

During that time, I tried to know which type of plane it was, it would surely be the first question my father would ask. For my part, as long as the pilot got me where it said on the ticket, I did not care if the plane had one, two or three engines: it could be a glider for all I cared.

CHAPTER 1.3

In this new airport, I had about two hours before my connection so I shopped around the stores. I had forgotten suntan lotion and it seemed like a good thing to bring with me. I was slightly taken aback when I arrived at the cashier. Usually when monopoly settled in a building, prices went high, but I did not expect it to be sky-scraping high. It was not really nuisance, it was the good old capitalist way and I had brought more than enough money not to be concerned about it. My parents had given me a sufficient amount to guarantee my financial safety until I started work.

I went to sit in front of my gate after making a small detour by the book store. The people around me all seemed to resemble the ones I had left in my previous airport. They all looked like they were so proud to be able to use the most expensive means of transportation. I could easily separate the people in two classes: business and pleasure. On my right hand side, there was a man in a suit reading the Wall Street Journal on his portable computer. On my left hand side, a man in shorts was standing with three kids running around him like there was no tomorrow. I noticed that both men were wearing the same kind of very expensive watch. I could easily see the two of them switching places, depending on the time of the year.

Later, a man came to sit by my side; I could use the word at the plural because he literally kept changing from one seat to the other. Inevitably, he engaged a conversation. "Where are you going?"

"My next flight will stop in Miami, but I'm going to Nicaragua" I answered. I was expecting many other questions, but none came.

To my great surprise, he started talking about his own personal life. "I just got divorced, stopped working and I'm retiring in Florida for a while." He quickly began.

"You seem a bit young to be retiring." I dared.

"You're right; I'm only thirty-four."

At my age that seemed to be pretty old. "Why are you leaving, how can you afford it?"

"I'm a retired police officer. They gave me my pension."

"How come so early?"

"I suffered what some call a severe mental breakdown. So they had to give it to me for mental disorder." He explained.

"What happened to allow you to deserve such a title?"

"I was on the job about four months ago and I saw a guy get killed while his own brother was watching, doing nothing."

"You'll have to go on, because I don't know how that can be so immensely traumatic. Don't you guys see that kind of stuff everyday?"

"You see they were Siamese brothers. I watched them both go down. The one who hadn't even tried to get his brother out of the way just fell on top of the wounded and he died a while later, unable to live without his twin. It was an unwilling suicide, a revenge coming straight from above. I couldn't take that image out of my mind: the look of betrayal on the victim's face." He paused. "I took a short break and tried to get back on the job, but all I thought about was these falling bodies. I was no good to anyone. I took my pension right away and left for the Sunshine State." He concluded.

I felt for that man, his story was a sad one. "The summer's just beginning; shouldn't you wait for winter to go down south?"

"I have to leave right away; my friend offered me a job in his hotel."

"Really, what will you do, will you be like a manager?"

"Not really." He answered in a tone of voice that made me believe he would never tell me.

"Okay. I prematurely give up, what will you be? If you don't want to tell me it's fine, but remember: sharing is good." I said.

He laughed a little. "I'll be a gigolo" The ex-cop told me.

"What?" I exclaimed.

"A gigolo! These grand hotels are full of lonely women who wait for their husbands to return from work. Some men leave their wives all day to go to meetings or play golf. My job will be to chat with them, cheer them up, make them feel sexy again. My buddy guaranteed me some good action and great money as well. All this with room and board included, plus an ocean view. How could I have said no?"

"It's a tough one I admit." I replied as the voice from the speakers announced that my flight was now boarding. I got up. "Well good luck and be sure to wear a condom." I advised with a grin.

He signalled for me to bend down as if he was about to give me the location of a great treasure. "My boy, the secret of the female orgasm is trust and comfort. Don't ever forget it and you'll have a long and healthy marriage." He whispered in my ear.

"I guess you learned it from your wife?" I surprised myself to ask impudently.

"Actually, she learned it from her lover and explained it to me when I discovered about their little scheme."

There was nothing for me to add. I felt bad for this guy, he looked unhappy so I held back and did not ask him how he planned to gain the trust from these old women he would be paid by. Surely he was right about the trust and comfort part; although, I did not think the concept only applied to relationships with women. What a sad man he was, even his gigolo adventure was depressing and yet he did not see it that way. How could he enjoy sleeping with these old hags? The announcer repeated the message and got me out of my thinking state of mind. I ran to the gate as quickly as possible.

CHAPTER 1.4

When I arrived at the next airport, English was now the official language and Spanish the second. Luckily, when I was young, we had a satellite dish and my Dad had always forced me to watch the American version of *Sesame Street*. After a few courses in school, Spanish was a fourth language that became like a second one to most people.

In Miami, as I waited for my last connection, there was a girl, who for some reason, changed places when I arrived and came to sit directly in front of me. I could not believe my luck. What was I to do? She started to read a book that seemed pretty boring if judged by its cover. She had blond hair and blue eyes, female characteristics that would unquestionably become a rarity in the next few weeks. The young woman was almost certainly from the high rank of society. She was chewing gum and that, in my book, was a luxury. It was not like it would feed you or you could appreciate your own breath. As for the girl, she coughed and even said pardon out loud. I could smell the pretentiousness in the air. Strangely enough, over the years, politeness had almost become synonymous with snobbism. I still had my last conversation with the retired cop in mind, so I figured she could cheer me up, help me pass the time. I tried to initiate a conversation but nothing came to mind, or out of it. She must have realized it because she started things going. "Hi!" She very simply said.

It was such a brilliant introduction, why had I not thought about it? "Hello!" I pronounced all crookedly. It sounded Parisian so I decided to continue and fake a French accent. In my way of thinking, I would sound a lot more interesting. "How var yu?"

She barely looked at me. "Good." She answered awkwardly.

"Ham fyn, yu see, I yam goingue to Nicarragua four a spezial misseeon." At that very moment, she made such a face, it made me feel like a complete idiot. I got up and quickly escaped to the bathroom. What was I thinking? I sat on the porcelain chair and stayed for about ten minutes. I stared at the blank pages of my passport and wished it was filled with more stamps.

When I returned, she had gone back to her original place. I sat as far from her as possible and buried my face in a book and shut my ears off with my music. Why had I pulled such an insane stunt?

The last plane ride took me out of my misery. On the way, there was a superb sunset out the right window. There was a bed of cotton balls in the middle of a yellow sky. Because of a huge hole in the cumulus, the sea could be seen and reflected the light of the flaming star. It was like a great abstract painting, everything was topsy-turvy. It made me think of my trip. There would probably be some highs and lows, but something was telling me it would be unforgettable.

CHAPTER 1.5

As I got out of the plane, the heat hit me unbelievably hard. I had left a cold Swiss freezer and I was now entering a real Central-American oven. I purposely decided not to think about what the high-noon temperature would be like tomorrow.

I got in line and prepared all my documents. Behind the glass, I saw a tall young white man staring at me. Without a doubt, it was my contact who went by the name of Martin and that was, pretty much, all I knew about him. The man had been living in the village for the last six months, setting everything up. The big smile on his face gave me a good first impression.

I went for the other line-up in front of the customs people. "Where are you going?" The agent began.

"A village called Cinco Pinos." I replied. I was sure he knew it was a village, but I felt I had to be precise.

"Why?" He continued with the same awfully serious tone.

"To help out on a coffee plantation." I thought it sounded better to say the word *help* instead of *make a financial killing*.

As the agent read my passport, his eyebrows came down in the middle of his face and his serious tone became more interrogative. "Why do you have a double citizenship? Where do you live?" He questioned.

"I lived in Switzerland almost all my life, but I was born in the USA." I made clear.

Somehow he became even ruder when he realized about my birth country. I wondered why, it was not like that could be a bad thing. The man asked me four more questions, way too rapidly for me to understand properly. I gambled and answered positively to the first three and then negatively to the last one. I mostly sensed the intonation. Luckily, that was enough for him to give me a nonchalant *move along* signal with his right hand.

It was weird how I had started the day not wanting to talk to anyone and now I was truly anxious to meet Martin. I had endured the annoying insurance salesman, had been tamed by the sad police officer, and had acted like a nut in front of a beautiful girl. Luckily this custom agent had put everything back in order in my mind. I was here, I had touched down, and I felt like the first circle was complete.

CHAPTER 2.1

Martin looked like me physically: he was a tall dark handsome man; of course, not as handsome as me. I mean, how could he be? Was that pretentious? Unquestionably.

I got closer and he initiated the discussion. "Hey Kristian, how are you?" He questioned.

Since this was probably a rhetorical question, I did not answer. "Hey!" I greeted. "You've been waiting for a long time?" I asked.

"Not really, about an hour, but it's probably nothing compared to the day you've had."

Judging from that sentence, he seemed like a thoughtful enough fellow, but again I chose not to comment. "You can say that again." I whined.

"It's good to finally meet you. The villagers are great, but it's not like we have a lot to talk about, yet."

"How's everything coming?"

"Honestly, we're ready to begin. Your expertise's the only thing missing." He said and looked around the room, seeming to be looking for someone. "So, do you know anything about coffee?" He asked.

"Of course!" I bluffed.

"Go ahead!" He invited.

"First appeared in Ethiopia over a thousand years ago, a farmer noticed his goat was on a high after eating some little red fruit. The Middle-East people started eating it."

Martin seemed pleased. "Go on!" He challenged.

"Evidently, monks called it the devil's plant. It was Pope Vincent III who decided to baptise coffee and not leave it only for the infidels." I said; Martin's facial expression seemed to be asking for more so I continued. "During the seventeenth century, the drink became popular in some European countries and it was known as Arabian whine."

"Whine without raisins hey?" He interrupted.

I needed to keep going quickly. I was on a roll and could not lose my train of thoughts. "Frederik the Great of Prussia attempted to ban coffee, he recommended his people to drink alcohol instead." Martin tried to cut me off again, but I did not let him and continued. "Later it came to America, in the North by John Smith and the South by some French guy called Gabriel Mathieu de Clieu. Anyway, it's now the most famous drink in the world, and since technically coffee beans are fruits pits, it means it's also the most popular fruit in USA." I recited as quickly as possible, before I would forget.

"Is that all?" My new partner teased.

"And I'll help you guys to put some more in ground." It had taken me two weeks to learn all of it from the Internet and memorize it. Hopefully Martin was impressed and satisfied, because I definitely could not afford to repeat it again. "Do *you* know anything about coffee?" I kept our conversation going, confident.

"Sure, I know some things." He answered.

"Like what?"

"People who drink a lot of it, never kill themselves." He alleged.

"Is that right?"

"Proven fact!"

"Is that all?"

"Well, I do know that Lloyd's insurance company started out as a little coffee house by the London docks." Martin said.

"What are you talking about?" I asked for clarification.

"Yeah, there were so many insurance brokers selling policies to sailors that the coffee shop's owner decided to change businesses." Martin made clearer.

Was this guy a joker or an idiot, was he just testing me? Since, most my knowledge was already forgotten, I decided not to push it. I did think about the guy I had met at the airport who was going for his interview, it would have been a great ice breaker. "Okay, what's going on now?" I shortly inquired.

"Cinco Pinos is located about five hours up north, we won't go right now. We'll spend the night in Managua. I made reservation in a small hotel I know."

With a name like *Cinco Pinos*, I was wondering why we were not planting pine trees instead of coffee. "That's sounds great to me." I lied. "Lead the way!"

He picked up my backpack from the floor before I could and we headed for the door. The place was noisy, full of people. Men all looked alike, but girls were extremely beautiful, dark skin, black shinny hair, brown-eyes. This country was a pure feminine delight.

The heat struck me, once again, full blast when we stepped outside. Martin unlocked my door and I rushed quickly to have time to unlock his.

"Thanks for the door!" He acknowledged.

"Ain't no thing!"

"If you hadn't, you would've ridden in the back." He replied with a smile and a serious tone.

"You're nice, if you hadn't returned the favour to me, you would've just stayed there." I assured him.

We both started laughing, happy that we saw things the same way. Deep inside, I was glad to notice that Martin had the same style of weird questioning as me. Coming here, I was afraid to be forced to work with a bunch of unpleasant snobs. Coffee was a simple thing, but could sometimes be demanding. Luckily for me, this new colleague of mine would be able to let loose and relax. Hopefully I would be up to the task; I would truly dislike being under qualified. By principle, I would hate to be renamed *Peter.*

We drove in the city for about fifteen minutes. Everything was hell; there were so many people everywhere. We kept quiet; Martin was probably letting me getting use to it all. "You don't buckle up?" I asked to break the silence.

"No, not really, no one does around here and I guess I just follow their bad example." Martin retorted.

"*No one* buckles up?"

"Well, I don't know about *no one*, but most people don't. They just find the seatbelt too containing."

I was shocked by the silliness of that last statement. "It's definitely less containing than a wheelchair that's for sure." I concluded in a *Duh* tone of voice.

We arrived at the hotel around ten o'clock. A big black iron gate was opened for us by a man standing guard. We went inside and people saluted Martin by his surname. It certainly was not his first time here. He then asked for the room, without an *S.*

"Are we staying in the same room?" I had to enquire.

"Oh, I'm sorry; I thought we could save some money this way." He answered nervously, uncertain of my reaction.

"Don't we have paid expenses?" I retaliated.

"Yes we do, but there's nothing in the contract that says we can get bargains and save up the rest."

"I know, but if you don't mind, I think I'll take a room for myself."

The man behind the counter, who was following our every word, stepped in our conversation. "No problem Señor, there is one right in front of Don Martin's room."

"That'll be perfect; I didn't want to be far." I replied. "Thank you." I added to be courteous.

We settled in our rooms and decided to go out for a late dinner. All the airline food I had gobbled down over the day was not sufficient anymore, I was hungry again. I took a quick shower and applied a double coat of deodorant. How could it be this hot at this time of the day? I walked naked around the room. Even though, it had probably ruined the good first impression I had given, I was glad to have my own space. I did not feel like sharing everything with my new partner. After all, I hardly knew him and was getting money for accommodation, why not use it?

I lay down on the bed and closed my eyes for a short moment. Oddly, I had time enough to have a swift weird nightmare. There was a caterpillar, with one single eye right on the edge of a cliff, suddenly a bomb exploded. Then everything vanished, the only thing left was a badge, laying there at my feet.

Things changed again, I was coming home from university, but instead of taking my car; I had decided to walk. I was looking through some house's windows, checking things out. Then, I saw a couple in the middle of an argument, more like a fight. Since the thought of going home was not appealing to me, I was almost glad to have found a reason to slow down. The two participants were throwing angry words at each other. Suddenly, the man struck the woman in the face. She fell and hit her head on the wooden floor. I witnessed everything too clearly. I hated that curtainless bay window. The husband got closer to his wife slash victim. I thought he would give her a hand to get back up, feeling guilty, but instead, he gave her a kick to the stomach. I got closer to the window and knocked on it, but the aggressor did not stop. I turned around to ask for help uselessly. Inside, the man kept hitting. I screamed my heart out, banging the window with all the strength I possessed. Nothing happened. I searched the ground for something solid. I picked up a rock and began hitting the glass. The window was unbreakable. I was powerless and this maniac kept on with his assaults. A tear of rage fell down my cheek. Unexpectedly, the husband stopped and moved away. Subsequently, a little girl in a red pyjama appeared at the bottom of the stairs. The curly golden haired infant went to see her mommy. The colour of her clothes made the blood vanish from my mind. I pushed out an ultimate silent scream that no one heard.

Knock, knock, knock!

I woke up to the sound of Martin knocking on my door. He came into the room. "Wake up, if you wan to eat!" He warned.

I was still in half-asleep and confused as to how he had gotten in. Did he have a double of my key? Evidently, after what I had just dreamed, I was not able to articulate these thoughts.

I went back in the bathroom and splashed water on my face. I stared at myself in the mirror. What horrible dream, a good meal would sure help to clear my mind.

Once inside the restaurant, glancing around the room at the other noisy costumers, we decided to eat outside on the empty terrace. "How come no one eats outside on a beautiful night like this?" I asked.

"I think what's a beautiful night for you is just ordinariness for them. Remember, they don't come from the same place you do. This heat isn't a novelty to them. It's so hot during the day, they had enough. It's a lot cooler inside. This place might even have a bit of A/C running."

"That makes sense I guess." I admitted.

At that moment, the door opened and a waiter brought us the menu. There were a lot of dishes I did not know what they were and Martin realized it. "So, you have any clue what you're you going to order?" He asked.

"I think a lasagna sounds pretty good right now."

"You don't feel like trying something new? They have a traditional dish called *Bajo*. It's a mix of beef, ripe plantains and some other stuff."

Though I did not tell him, it sounded absolutely disgusting. What the heck were plantains anyway, was it those weird looking green bananas? Not knowing what to say, I just stared at my partner with a dull expression in my eyes.

"There's also the *vigoron*, a combination of cassava served with pork skins and coleslaw." Martin said, with such a serious tone of voice that it was hard for me to say no.

The second meal with its pig skin sounded even more repulsive than the first one and I did not need to know what cassava was to form my opinion. Still, I had to answer something. "Sounds good, but I'm sure I'll have the opportunity to try some new dish later. I'll stick with lasagna, for now." I went with a half lie.

"Perhaps you're right. Give your stomach time to adjust. Enjoy this meal though, because when you see where we eat in the village: trust me, it's nothing like this."

I obviously could not know what he meant. "That's fine; I'll just shop at a grocery store." I replied.

"Well, there's a convenience store in the village, but you won't find much grocery there. Don't worry though; the restaurant's right next door to my house. You can cook for yourself if you want. Personally, I don't. It's about a dollar and a half for a meal. It's worth it, especially with the money the organisation gives you per day. If you don't mind paying for a hotel room, you won't mind paying for food."

"You're probably right. I guess there's nothing wrong with encouraging the local economy." I said.

"That's why I have a maid, a carpenter, a gardener and a woman to wash my clothes." Martin expressed without shame.

"Does the restaurant serve a good breakfast?" I questioned.

"Yes, but don't kid yourself, Nicaraguans don't eat the same food we do. They usually have eggs, accompanied with *gallo pinto*, a mix of rice and beans. The cooking water from the beans is added to give the rice some colour."

It sounded so horrible. "Holy smokes, can I get cereal?" I asked.

"You'll be able to get some in Chinandega, a city nearby. It's tricky though because we always lose power when it rains, and we're in the rainy season by the way, so milk doesn't keep very long."

I did not know what to answer, every time I thought of a solution, something was crushing it into pieces.

Martin noticed the expression of worry in my eyes, a flash of uneasiness quickly passed in his. "So really, what's your story, how did you end up here?"

I just shook my shoulders and stayed quiet.

"Personally, I studied sociology and I have a master's degree in international relations, what did you do? What do you really know about all this?" He then questioned.

I did not feel like filling him with BS. I thought I should play fair from the beginning. "Honestly, I spoke to the right person at the right time. At university, I studied English; mostly because it was the only subject I was ever good at in school. I do have a little experience with coffee, but it's mainly practical. In theory, I know very little, but don't be afraid I know how it has to be done." I tried to sound confident.

Martin did not seem too worried. "You'll have to take this very seriously. These villagers want to earn a living, be able to feed their family. I don't think you realize how important what we're doing here is."

"I guess I don't, but if coffee doesn't work for them, they can always go do something else." I unconsciously blurted.

"You see that's the thing; there isn't anything else for most of them. Some of these people sometimes get up at four in the morning, walk for three hours just to go work in different villages, all this to earn about three US dollars a day."

My eyes almost popped out of their sockets. "They only earn three bucks a day?!" I replied in total shock. "Why do they even bother?" I questioned.

"I told you before: I don't think you know what you're getting into. Earlier, when I asked you what you knew, I didn't only mean about coffee, I meant about this country." Martin asked and then waited for my response.

"Well, honestly, I know even less about Nicaragua than I do about coffee."

He looked around, as if he was searching for the right words. "That's fine; Nicaraguans are very nice in general. Although, there are some idiots everywhere you go on the planet, be careful. Just go easy with them at first. The villagers, especially this far up north, don't see many foreigners. It'll take a certain time for them to decide if you're worthy of their trust. As long as you know about the Sandinistas revolution and show them respect for carrying it out, you know enough for now."

"When was that?" I interrupted. I had no idea that there had been any other revolution than the one in Cuba or somewhere like that.

"In nineteen seventy nine, but it wasn't the end of it. The village where we're staying is right on the border of Honduras and there was a lot of damage done there. Some of the people are very hesitant to trust anybody who looks American." Martin explained.

I had no clue about any of this, I did not know what the word *Sandinistas* meant and did not even want to ask. When he was talking, I realized I had not mentioned that I was not born in Switzerland. I hesitated for a while, but decided to keep up my fairness deal and tell him. "You know, I was born in the USA."

He made a weird face, his eyes definitely got bigger.

"Yeah, like the song." I added to be funny.

His expression stayed the same. I did not know if it was because of his learning about my birthplace of his misunderstanding of the song reference.

"If you want my opinion, I don't think you should tell the villagers right away, not if you want to have a chance of fitting in anyway." He finally advised.

I did not understand Martin at all. Why and how could my origins be a bad thing? All my life, I had always wanted to go back to my native country. It was the promise land to me and I had been ripped off of it when I was just a toddler. I had spent my childhood with Swiss people,

22

totally different from me. My parents knew very well about my intentions to return. "That's alright; I'm used to not fitting in." I admitted.

"What do you mean?" Martin inquired.

"My parents gave me an American background. Swiss were interested in different music, books and TV programs. I had no subject of conversation while I was growing up. I never belonged where I was. There was always something somewhere to remind me of my origins and I decided long ago that I would not want to feel like an alien for the rest of my life. The States accepted everybody and since I was now over twenty-one, I would use my dual citizenship to get back in." I explained.

My new friend hesitated. He did not seem to share my opinions. "So what's your life story?" He asked me.

Although I was still young, I was not sure we would have enough time. Regardless, I could not avoid his question. "I was born in the state of Louisiana, in the French quarter of New Orleans, some street called Chartres by the Mississippi River."

"What brought you guys to immigrate to Switzerland?"

"My mother was born and raised in Lézin and had always wanted to return. My Dad agreed to move during the Vietnam War."

"He deserted?" Martin inquired accusingly.

"No, he didn't flee or anything. He's always told me he had even left his coordinates, just in case."

"Was he called?"

"Never." I replied, but I could tell he was not really satisfied. Martin had his doubts. I wanted to develop more, defend him, but the waiter arrived and we ordered our meals. Things in this restaurant seemed to be moving very slowly. Even though I was enjoying the moment, my stomach was beginning to complain a little too much.

"Go on with your story: what did you parents do when they moved?" Martin asked.

I tried to make it as interesting as possible, as hard as that may be. "My father was an extremely talented musician and lived for music. I mean, this man could vacuum the carpet in complete synchronisation with Strauss' waltzes. He had headphones on for half the day and he talked to us about it for the other half. So trust me, I know about music, even the words to the song *YMCA*, and I don't mean just *young man*."

The food appeared a little while later. We ate rather silently. My lasagna was great, similar to the ones back home. I figured it was Martin's turn to open up. "What about you?" I questioned.

"Mine's too boring. I was born in Vernon, a small town located between Paris and Rouen. I don't remember anything about my early childhood. Basically, I grew up, saved up my money and went to University so I could get a job as far away from my family as possible. If you don't mind, I won't get into details. You're a lot more interesting."

No one had ever qualified my life as interesting before. "I guess, that's why you're comfortable working in that village, in the scorching heat." I jokingly said.

"In a way yes, but make no mistake about it, what you will see tomorrow, you have never seen anything like it." He assured.

That made me a bit nervous to hear. Would there be two headed donkeys or something?

When we finished our dinner, I looked at my watch and decided I had told enough. "If you don't mind, I'd like to go to bed. We have to keep some conversation for tomorrow's drive anyway." I alleged.

"I agree: Vamos!" Martin replied.

"What?" I inquired, knowing full-well this was an easy one.

"Vamos! It's a Spanish word like *let's go*." He clarified. "By the way, how good is your Spanish?"

"Obviously, it isn't as good as yours. In the last few years, it has been all grammar for me. I need to have conversations. It'll take me a few days to get comfortable so don't go too far." I answered as we started to walk back to the hotel.

"Don't worry; I won't leave you alone at first. But even if I do, in the village there are many beautiful young girls who will fall for the new white boy. It'll be easy to practice with them."

"Girls make me nervous." I quickly joked.

Martin seemed a bit confused. Perhaps he never expected that answer. "I don't know, talk to children then."

"I don't like kids."

"Okay, if they make you nervous, well there are also a lot of dogs. I'll teach you how to say *fetch*." He concluded with a smile.

We walked back to the hotel and then went our separate ways. I had had a good time with this new guy. He was alright, worthy of sharing a room with after all.

"You better take a shower and enjoy it because it'll be your last real one in a while." Martin shouted as he knocked on my door in the early morning.

I woke up. His shower threat was not a huge deal to me. I had been raised in a house that did not use washcloths, where short and curlies were never even an issue. Still, I knew that heat around here would push me towards perspiration city; a good shower would surely be appreciated. "Do you mean I'll be so busy I won't have time to wash?" I dozily shouted back to Martin.

"I don't know about that, you'll almost certainly have time to wash, but only with an old plastic bucket." He answered with discernable laughter.

I got out of bed and took his advice. It lasted about fifteen minutes and I came out as clean as a Latino whistle.

Later, around five thirty A.M., we climbed in the vehicle and got on our way. The air was fresh and quite enjoyable. We stopped in a small convenience store and grabbed some food for the road. The city was different than what I had seen last night. Yesterday's darkness had stopped me from living the cultural shock I was going through at the moment. Everything was beyond words. "What's up with all the junk laying around? Don't they have laws against polluting?" I asked Martin.

"Of course they do, only they're neither followed nor applied. They do have a garbage dump though. I'll show it to you once we are a bit outside of town." He slowed the vehicle down to let some old man walk in front of us. "In the villages, they don't even have a sanitary system."

"Why not?" I questioned.

"The money just isn't there." He replied.

Everywhere I looked, things were financially bad, there did not seem to be an economical situation to discuss. Maybe there was a rich neighbourhood somewhere in this capital. It must have been south of town though because we clearly did not pass it on the way up north. Even the animals I saw were very thin. "How the heck can these dogs be that bony and be able to stay alive? Don't they have any owners that feed them?" I had to ask.

"Most of them have owners yes, but they have a hard time feeding themselves and their family, dogs just come after. Animals here have to find their own food." He told me in a *don't you get it yet* tone of voice.

Perhaps Martin was right. I should slow the question rhythm down and try to think for myself. I wondered how the village could be any worst than this hell hole. "How can Managua be so bad, is it really the best city in the country, has it always been the capital?" I interrogated.

"No, it was created to put an end to the conflicts between the cities of Leon and Granada. The first city was liberal and the second conservative. The government just had to come up with a neutral territory." He answered with a tone that meant to leave him be for a while.

As we got out of the city and went up a hill, Martin turned to me and broke his silence. "Remember the sanitary dump I said I would show you? It's over there on your right hand side." He said.

"Where? All I see is the lake."

"Exactly, but if you look on the city shore, you will see a big pile of garbage advancing itself into the water."

I scouted the scenery and found what he was describing. "You mean, they just push the garbage in the lake!?" I blurted in disbelief.

"Careful, this is not just a waste disposal site; it's home to many poor people trying to survive off the scraps from the capital."

"At least they live by the water." I joked with poor taste.

"The colour of the water is so grey anyway, no one can notice." Martin answered with a non-caring attitude. "Speaking of water, did you bring any purifier?"

"Yes, I did. I bought myself an eighty-dollar iodine filter. According to the salesman, it's the best thing on the market." I declared with pride.

"I know the type and he's right, it's good stuff."

This was definitely not the kind of place where you could flush the toilet after throwing in a paper tissue. "What happens when you drink untreated water?"

Martin did not give me an immediate reply; a strong look answered my question instead. "Have you ever tried to pass liquid knives through your anus?" He then asked.

I did not think I really needed to respond. "Uranus the planet?" I retorted anyway.

"Funny guy!" Martin whispered as he gave me another look.

Doubtlessly, I was now in a territory where flatulence would have to be done with great prudence.

We passed by Leon and it seemed like the most important city if I compared it to the others I had seen. My chauffer looked like he was about to fall asleep. "Do you want me to drive?" I had to ask.

"No thanks, I'll be fine."

"I can drive you know."

"Good for you, but drivers do things differently here."

"What do you mean?"

"Notice that every time you overpass a vehicle, you have to beep the horn a couple times." He explained.

"Why is that? Don't they have flashers on their cars?"

"They do, but they don't really use them, they'd rather honk the horn."

"It's kind of the same as most drivers at home, except they do it silently." I said.

"Yeah you're right, but what can we do?"

"Drive defensively I guess." I concluded.

The mountains of the area were a little strange. Most of them were full of green trees, but some had long lines of sand cutting through them. "What's up with all the sand on the mountains?" I asked.

"These mountains are actually volcanoes." He corrected.

Great! I had never seen one before in real life. I always pictured them in eruption, with a group of indigenous people dancing around, throwing somebody in the lava.

"And the landslides are souvenirs from Mitch." He started again.

"Who the heck is Mitch?"

"My gosh you weren't kidding when you said you had no clue about anything that went on in this country. Mitch is the name of a hurricane that killed about ten thousand Nicaraguans."

"Geez, when was this?"

"At the end of nineteen ninety-eight. A year's worth of rain fell in a single week. It washed out roads and bridges. You'll see, just before we arrive in Somotillo, the army set up a temporary bridge until the old one can be fixed."

"Was Nicaragua the only country included on Mitch's path of destruction?"

"Of course not, a hurricane that size touched about every country in Central America. Even when the storm calmed down, the rain continued for a long time and did some damage of its own. There was a mudslide on the Casita Volcano that buried several communities."

"That's too bad." I said and paused for a bit. "You know when people say there's always a reason for everything; well it's pretty hard to see one in this situation." I added to be caring.

"You could say that there's one though. Following the disaster, some nations decided to cancel Nicaragua's debt. It gave the country a chance to rebuild itself."

"Isn't it strange how hurricanes always seem to hit poor countries? You never see them in Europe or North-America."

Martin waited before answering, he seemed to wonder if I was joking or not. "That's because they can only be formed in warm waters. Plus, with the way the earth rotates, these giant storms always head north-west. There's no way a typhoon could cross all of Asia and hit Europe." He explained.

"Did you study geology?" I questioned.

Again, he simply answered with a disapproving look.

The side of the road was full of peasants standing around, probably waiting for a bus. Most of them were carrying huge bags. "These sacks are full of fruits, or vegetables. They're surely going to sell them in the city or bringing them back home." Martin explained.

As he said these words, some people started to move their right hand up and down. "Why are these folks waving at us?"

"They're hitchhiking. Here, the thumb isn't used to ask for a ride." He clarified. "Do you want to stop?" He offered.

"Well if we do, about fifteen'll climb in the back box and that's going to slow us down." I retaliated.

Just as I finished my sentence, some lady almost got in front of the pickup. "I guess sometimes we don't have the choice." Martin said with a smile.

"Hey at least, they're only eight and not fifteen." I mockingly retorted.

Martin got out of the vehicle and helped them load up their bags. When we went on our way, I realized that I was right: we were a lot heavier and slower than before.

They all got off about ten kilometres later and they thanked us many times. The old lady, who was definitely in charge of the group, handed me a few orange fruits from a bag. "Muchas Gracias!" I smiled.

Martin noticed my expression of interrogation. "They're mangos Kristian." He clarified.

"Really, I wasn't sure. They don't look like the ones I have seen at home." I wiped the fruit on my T-shirt and took a huge bite. The juice splattered out, fell on my chin and chest. It was all very sticky.

Martin started laughing. "So, what do you think? Good isn't it?" He implied

"I don't know. It's like eating a peach filled with strings." I complained. "I'm definitely going to need dental floss." I added.

"Don't worry, I got some at home."

I took a few more bites and just chucked it out the window. Who could eat such a messy fruit?

We arrived in Somotillo and went to get some stuff at the general store. I plainly could not believe how high the temperature was. This town was almost certainly one of the hottest on the planet. Everybody was walking so slowly. How could these people tolerate living here?

Inside the store, there was a little girl that looked at me like she had never seen a white man before. She surely was impressed by the pure colour of my un-tanned skin. She was about nine years old, so tiny and short. Her clothes were shinning with poverty. She stared at me with her begging eyes and it made me feel uncomfortable. I was happy to be financially well off and thought about helping her, but then again, I could not save them all. Why should I give her and not the others? Perhaps she simply needed to look upon me. I decided not to worry about it and go about my business. The girl's eyes never detached themselves from my body. I passed by Martin. "Is there something hanging from my nose?" I whispered to goof around.

My partner took everything he wanted and had it put on his tab. We both went back to the vehicle. As I passed the little girl I swiftly bent down right in her face. "Boo!" I loudly blurted with a smirk and brutal eyes.

She got a fright and started to laugh nervously as I climbed inside the pickup.

Martin looked at me disappointingly. "What was that for?" He asked.

"She kept staring at me." I replied trying to explain my action. I wanted to have some peace, was that too much to ask for?

"You'll have to get used to that. You said earlier that you felt like an outsider at home, well here: you truly are one."

Martin was right. The villagers would certainly look at me like an alien. One thing was for sure; here curiosity was too much in the open to be considered a fault.

CHAPTER 2.2

The village of Cinco Pinos was surrounded by green mountains. It was very small, there were only seven streets, four oriented north and south and three in the opposite axe. Only the main one was paved with stones, the others were covered with loose pebbles.

"The school was back there, this is the general store and on the other side is the pharmacy. Like I said before, the restaurant is right beside my house." Martin explained.

"Is this all I need to know?" I asked.

"Pretty much! You think you'll need anything else?"

"Police station." I named half-jokingly.

"There isn't one." He answered with a cocky smile.

"What!" I almost shouted. "How can that be?" I questioned with astonishment.

"There's just no need for it."

"How do people keep the peace?"

"The whole community does it." He said and since I stayed quiet, he went on. "Do you know about *e-bay* on Internet?"

"Of course."

"There's no one upholding the law on the site. If somebody screws another, he gets a bad review and buyers start to lose faith. The more bad reviews he gets, the less people do business with him. It's the same thing here. It's a tiny village. No one can mess with another person and get away with it." He explained and smiled. "But don't worry; I was joking with you earlier. There might not be a police station, but there's a sheriff. He's just not that busy, that's all." He concluded.

Martin parked the truck in front of his house. "What are those two donkeys doing on your front porch, are they yours?"

"Of course they aren't!" He said and laughed. "Don't worry; I'll easily chase them away." He explained with a smile and stretched his neck out of the window to yell a few French insults. His head came back in and his mouth went on. "By the way, speaking of animals; be careful with the truck. Try not to roll over anything bigger than a chicken."

"Why, is it bad for the wheel alignment?"

"Course not, but there's a lot more meat into a pig for example. A decent size hog will feed a whole family for two dinners."

"Feel safe. Alive or dead, I still haven't crashed into anything so far in my life and it's not in my plans to start doing it now."

"Good! Because, they say that there's supposed to be almost twice as many chickens than humans on the planet, well a lot of them are in this area." He said.

"Don't worry, I won't squish one." I concluded as I killed a mosquito on the dashboard. I was getting tired of this poultry conversation. I had never seen a guy care so much for chickens.

My new partner was renting a house on the main street for about fifty US dollars a month. We entered and he dropped his bag. Technically, there were only two rooms in the house. His bedroom was the only one separated really. The rest was the kitchen, dinning room, office and locker all together. "Where's your TV?" I asked.

"I don't have one." He quickly retorted.

My face went blank: no television, how did this guy live? "What do you mean?" I had to question out loud.

"I just don't want one. I feel I don't need it, that's all."

"What do you do during the evenings?" I asked intriguingly.

"I go out, see people, go for a drink next door, and take walks. I sometimes, but very rarely, work. Often, I read a novel." He listed. "Why do you need TV so much?"

"Information, entertainment." I stopped to calm down. "I guess I'll get use to it." I said, trying to sound okay about the whole thing.

"Television's very poorly used anyway, too much TV reality and not enough authenticity." Martin said and before I could tell him he was full of crap, he continued talking. "Would you like to live with me?"

"Sure!" I answered hesitantly. Although I would have preferred to go to the hotel for the first few days, maybe they had a TV, I felt like staying close to Martin even if his idea of accommodation was to put a mattress on the floor beside his desk-slash-dinner table.

Some old man knocked on the door. "Come on in Señor!" My friend invited. "This is Frederico, he works miracle with wood. He could build you a nice bed if you were willing to spend a few cordobas." Martin explained in French.

"Don Martin, what can I do for you?" The owner asked only to my partner, barely looking at me, like I was not even there.

"My friend Kristian will work with us in the coffee plantation and he needs a bed." Martin explained.

"I do have a decent one left. It's three hundred thousand Cordoba." He answered with a triumphant tone of voice, as if he was so happy to be able to make some money off me. I did not care; three hundred thousand was the equivalent of about thirty US dollars. He still had not looked at me yet. "Is he Americano?" He asked Martin in a condescending way.

"No, he's from Europa, like me." My partner replied embarrassingly.

This exchange got me pretty upset. What was wrong with these people? Suddenly coming from the greatest country on the planet was something to be ashamed of. I felt like bursting out my dual citizenship. Where was this colossal hatred coming from? I stayed there in silence, boiling inside. I did not desire to give this guy any of my money anymore. "Wait a second; let me see your mattress to see if I really need a bed." I said to Martin without looking at the guy. After all I had come here to become a man, what were a few nights without an official bed.

Martin took out the mattress and it was just fine by me. "Why would I need your help, you can just get out of here." I said to the man, looking at him straight in the eyes.

Martin seemed ready to dissolve with shame. He came close to me and pushed me aside. "Please, be careful not to mess up the good relation that I established with these people for six months. This is a very small village and everybody knows everything that goes on. You've insulted this man so make it right. This man has succeeded a lot better than most other villagers. He's not easily intimidated. Just say thank you and tell him you simply prefer save up your money." He said in French with lightning coming out of his eyes. "Mostly, remember that in his business, he's the boss." He added.

"No, no, Bruce Springsteen is the boss. He's just a crummy carpenter." I sarcastically replied with a smile that admitted I knew my co-worker was half-right. I looked at the Nicaraguan. "Sir, please take no affront, I am not thinking straight." I apologized. I then took out a five US dollar bill and continued with the most submissive tone I could possibly take. "Please accept this for your troubles and forgive my arrogance. I just arrived in Nicaragua. I'm exhausted because of the time difference."

The man took the money and smiled at me. "Thank you. Please feel free to come and see me if you change your mind." He concluded nicely.

Martin waited for the man to leave. "That was a hell of an apology. I'm amazed at how quickly you changed your mind."

"What do you mean change my mind? I haven't changed my mind at all. This guy's an asshole. You wanted me to fix it; I did what you asked for, plain and simple. I paid him off and let him think he was king of the world. Don't be fooled Martin, I still think he's an ignorant baboon." I blurted out.

"Wow, you should be a diplomat then. I truly believed your request for forgiveness was sincere." He said with disillusionment in his voice. "But why are you so angry?" He carried on.

"Isn't it obvious? This brainless twit didn't even look at me at first 'cause he thought I was American. Well, guess what Martin? I am American and they'll have to get used to it and like it." I exploded.

My friend looked at me a bit disappointingly. "Please, keep this a secret for now. You could screw it all up. With some of these people you'll have no chance of establishing contact and it's essential to work with them."

"What are you talking about? The people at the Managua hotel knew where I was born, they saw my passport. Why would these villagers be different?"

"We're no longer in Managua, things aren't the same here. This area was badly wounded by the war. Trust me on this. I'm not asking you to burn the flag; just avoid the subject for now. Please." He spoke in a way that meant he wanted to end our discussion.

"What happened here? As far as I know, the States were never at war with Nicaragua." I said.

"I'm sure you'll find out soon enough."

The rest of the day went well. We simply walked, drove, biked around the area. Martin wanted me to know my way around. He would mostly have to stay at the house and work in his papers. I would have to be able to go on my own.

The next morning, we woke up really early, way too early. Fortunately, the mattress I slept on made it very easy for me to get up. All night, my back had felt the hardness of the concrete floor beneath. Furthermore, the temperature was incredible. I was so glad when at two o'clock I had felt chilly and had put the sheet over my legs.

The workers started to arrive about three hours after I awoke. I wished I could have slept longer instead of standing around.

The first meeting took place right in the centre of the main road. Roughly fifty men were present and waited to hear what Martin and I had to say. They all looked alike: dark skin with the little moustache. They seemed generally happy, most of them smiling and laughing. Before the meeting, we chatted with some of them. My colleague thought I had to establish a good relationship; an investment for the future. I was introduced to many villagers, all of them very nice indeed.

They were very curious and anxious to know how things were going to go down. "Isn't there too many people here? I thought we only needed three teams of ten." I turned to my partner and commented quickly.

"You're right, but you see this project is huge news. The excess is probably men who are curious or looking for work. Regrettably, we'll be the ones that will have to turn them away and break their hopes."

"I'll do it." I coldly exclaimed.

"You absolutely will not!" He directly replied as he stared at me.

Minutes later, I noticed some guy in the crowd wearing a t-shirt with the soviet hammer crossing the scythe. The letters *CCCP* were strongly written underneath the sign. I walked to Martin and took him aside. "Did you see this guy's t-shirt? Is that why you didn't want me to tell about my birthplace?"

"Well, that's a part of it, but that's not all. You'll have other surprises later." He predicted with a smile.

"I don't have time to play games. Are these people Communists?" I interrogated.

He sensed I was getting irritated so he answered. "Well technically no, they're Sandinistas. I told you that before, didn't I?"

"Alright I admit it, I had and still have no clue what that word means."

"Well, it's kind of the distant cousin of Communism." Martin explained.

"You're joking, how distant?" I immediately questioned.

"It's definitely an opposite of the Capitalism you fully support, if that's what you're asking."

I was shocked. How can I be working in a communist country? A big reason for my coming here was money. I did not want to have to share it. Would I now be getting three dollars a day as they did? I was glad to have negotiated my contract before coming here. There was no way the company could get out of paying me.

Martin noticed my inner panic. "Hey, before you start tripping, I'll tell you that a lot of the clothes these people are wearing were sent by humanitarian organizations. You'll see it's mostly leftovers from past sporting events or outdated music groups. I honestly think that this guy has no clue what is written on his T-shirt."

This just proved my theory that humanitarian aid was a load of crap. It was poor people from rich countries giving to rich people from poor countries. There was always somebody somewhere screwing someone else. That communist T-shirt was definitely given as a symbol, not as a piece of clothing. "Those four letters symbolises the worst enemy that we ever had." I declared.

"Be careful Kristian, *we* doesn't include the people around you anymore, not even me. Let me repeat, you're the alien here. Remember it and you better stop acting like one if you want things to change."

"How can you work for these Communists?" I insisted, when the discussion probably should have been stopped.

"Are you from the seventies?" Martin questioned to make fun of me.

"Hilarious! I'm serious, how can you work for them?"

"I don't work *for* them, I work *with* them." Martin clarified. "And what's so wrong with that Kristian? They're still people you know, just like you and me. You think we should kill them because of their economical system?" He asked accusingly.

"I can't believe what you're saying. What kind of Western European are you?" I answered and also asked. "Check your facts, Capitalists and especially Americans are the hardest working people in all the industrialized countries. How can you not believe in their system?" I added.

"Capitalists compete against each other. They want to be the best, regardless of who they hurt. As for our economical system back home, newsflash Kristian: our countries are not capitalist. We have anti-competition laws, laws so no one will sell gasoline, beer or even milk cheaper than the next guy. Do you really think consumers get the best deal possible?" He paused, but continued since I remained silent. "Here people all want the same, everybody equal. Isn't that the American way? It doesn't matter if they're Sandinistas or Communists; they're human beings, Kristian, and so are we." Martin concluded his preaching with authority.

He was full of crap. "Do you know anything about Stalin who killed over seven million of his own people, Mao Zedong who's responsible for the death of thirty million Chinese, Pol Pot who exterminated close to two million Cambodians, or Milosevic in Yugoslavia?" I enumerated with pride of my knowledge.

"You're just naming people, leaders that have nothing to do with their economical structure. Not all dictators are communists: think of Pinochet or Idi Amin, and yet they still killed a whole bunch of their citizens." Martin said in a very firm tone of voice. I stayed quiet, giving him the opportunity to continue. "You're so in love with North America. Did you know that in the forties, there even was a Communist officially elected at the Canadian Parliament?"

"That can't be." I frowned.

"Check your facts. Some guy called Fred Rose, I think." He argued unsurely.

There was something telling me he was playing dumb and was hiding something. Martin seemed like Political history machine, I was surprised he was unsure. "Seriously, how did that guy do once he got elected?" I pushed.

A smile appeared. "He got busted and was sentenced to six years in prison." He laughed.

"Why did he go to jail?" I questioned, glad to see that he was arguing on good faith.

"Espionage for the Russians." He admitted.

"Your honour, I rest my case!" I yelled. My new partner surely was a good debater, even though he had proven me right with that last argument. Could Communism be seen as a step between Capitalism and dictatorship? Martin was about to go on, but some guy came to talk to us and we had to cut our discussion. My partner took care of him and I started to walk around, looking at all these Commie bastards like my Dad used to call them. Where was Roy Cohn when you needed him?

Unexpectedly, I heard Martin shouting words I did not have time to understand. He was standing on his front porch and all the men came towards him. "Do you see those two men over there?" He asked as we waited for the flock to gather around.

"Of course."

"They're cousins."

"Well, I'm happy for them. I do see a resemblance."

"Funny guy. The one on the right is called Diego and the second one is Raymondo."

I was a bit stressed with all the people here and I did not understand why he was telling me about these cousins, as if I should care.

"They were born only four months apart you know." My partner went on.

My God this guy knew how to drag a story. "Please! Oh please, get to the point will you?!"

"Do you see the scar on Diego's forehead?"

I was really annoyed now. "Yes! It's pretty big. What happened to him, he had a bicycle accident when he was ten?"

"Actually, he had to serve in the army." Martin said. He saw the expression on my face change and went on. "The Revolution ended in seventy-nine. About a year later, soldiers came down from Honduras to try to stir things up again. It's what was called the *Contra*. All the villages in this area, including the one we're in right now were severely affected." He had noticed I was felling pretty stupid with my bicycle comment so he paused for a short while before he kept going. "You see Raymondo's forehead?" He did not wait for my reply and simply said. "It's fine, he didn't have to serve. He wasn't sixteen when everything happened. It wasn't guerrilleros anymore, but an official army. There were rules to follow, not all kids were freely welcomed to join the fight. Raymondo now has a house with a wife and two kids."

"And Diego, what's he doing?"

"Diego has nothing; he lives with his parents and starts a decent job today for the first time." Once more he stopped and stared at me. I did not know what to say, so my partner continued. "I told you before; what we're doing here is more than just dealing with coffee. These people, Communists or not, depend on us, on you." He finished.

We both started to explain how things were going to work over the course of the contract. What happened after was pretty simple; these people were farmers so they basically knew how to plant stuff, coffee would not be a problem to them. The most complicated part was to organize it all, tell foremen where they would go everyday. There were three teams from three different villages. When I was speaking, every man looked at me in his own way. Some eyes were full of compassion and curiosity, others filled with suspicion and even aggression. It felt weird to talk in front of them, especially in my fourth language. I was becoming their leader on the very first day of our acquaintance. There was a lot of intensity in my mind while the Spanish words were hardly and stressfully coming out of my mouth. I talked about the ripe cherries that were picked up in another village and would be delivered directly to the loading sites. They would already be fermented in small containers, ready for the real ground of the mountains. I told them about the best place to plant and how the soil should not be too compacted. Hopefully, my explanations did not last too long for them to lose interest. It seemed clear to everyone and not many workers asked questions. The speech ended after less than an hour.

"We will later go on a piece of land for a practical demonstration, just to make sure we were all on the same page." Martin concluded to the crowd.

I stayed alone and Martin went to talk with some men. I started to look at them carefully, with a different eye. I observed that many of them had scars. It was deplorable to learn that most of these people had personally lived the harsh reality of war. Their heads were probably full of hideous memories. They must hate being forced to live beside a country that attacked them. I wondered why they were at war with their neighbour. There had to be a reason, even if it was a stupid one. I had, of course, never heard of this conflict. I felt weirdly upset, like from out of the blue sky a huge cloud of ignorance had become visible over my head. For unknown reasons, I was getting really nervous about this practical demonstration.

I unconsciously strayed from the others. Suddenly, I could almost say in a blinding flash of light, a man appeared beside me. "Buenas Días Señor!" He said with a low voice and a slow joyful tone.

"Don't call me Señor please." I replied on a more serious one.

"Okay! May I call you Don Kristiano?"

"Sure if you want." At that point, I honestly thought he was going to leave, but he kept on talking. "How did you end up around here?"

"Don't worry about it: it's a long boring story."

"No story is boring if it teaches somebody something about someone." He replied with a smile that allowed me to see that his two front teeth were covered with gold. There was something about this man that was telling me he was different. His height was average, but he was a bit more muscular than the others. It was absolutely impossible for me to guess his age. Evidently, he had a moustache, but strangely no hair grew right below his nose. His clothes were very ordinary, again probably some North American leftovers. It seemed like this man was the first one who had forgotten to judge me. "Who are you?" I asked intriguingly.

"My name is Pedro Sanchez. I will be working for the San Pedro team." He replied.

"Are you from San Pedro?" I had to enquire.

"No, but since Cinco Pinos already had too many people, I was given the privilege to work in a different village."

"How will you get there, do you have a car?"

He smiled at my question. "I will walk every morning."

There was no way he could do that; it would take him half the day. "Maybe I'll be able to give you a lift sometimes." I offered.

"It would be great, but don't worry about me. I am the one who is here to help you." He kindly said with all honesty.

How could this worker help me? He probably just meant that he would be at my service in the fields. I then clicked on a detail; I took out the papers from my pocket to double check. "It's funny because I have the crew lists and your name isn't on any of them." I said before I could properly verify. I thought my comment might embarrass him, catching him on his lie, but it did not.

"It is probably written Angel, it is my first name." He calmly clarified.

I very quickly looked, but did not even find it on the paper. I was curious so I went on. "Why do people call you that? What does it mean?"

"Nothing really, a lot of Latinos are called Angel. I was not born quietly or peacefully, so my mother said; I do not remember much of it."

I laughed at his joke. "Does your forename suit you at least?" I asked.

"I don't think I help people more than they help themselves. It is just my name, a common one." He repeated and paused. "Actually, my father wanted to call me Juan Pedro, but my mother figured it would be too many names for me to write." He concluded.

Martin had started some huge discussion with almost everybody. My partner could do without me for a little longer. "Do you know anything about coffee Don Angel?" I felt like I needed to ask.

"Maybe not a lot." He said and saw my face fall down. He figured he had to say more. "I can tell you why Columbia is the biggest coffee producer though." He added.

"Why's that?" I asked for precision.

"It is because of the priest's demands after confessions. Instead of being asked to recite prayers to compensate for their faults, the villagers were told to plant coffee. A nation filled with sinners became a nation full of coffee producers." He narrated.

Really? "That's a great story, but I doubt it'll help you for the job you're about to begin." I shortly retorted.

At that moment, Martin joined us and asked me to come with him, ignoring my new acquaintance in the process. I quickly nodded to Angel Pedro Sanchez and left with my friend. Why would a person use two names? I had so many new faces to remember, so many names to learn. As if it was not enough, I would now have to associate Don Angel and Pedro to the same person.

Martin and I walked a while. "You really have to meet someone." He told me.

"Who's that?" I retorted.

"An important man that just needs to be known. Don't bother him with too many questions. Let's make it short." He added.

It felt like annoying public relation to me. "Why's that?" I asked.

"He owns a lot of the land our cooperative will be planting the coffee on."

I had no use of meeting a man in a suit and tie, but when I first saw him, I realized it was not the case at all. Basically, he had a thick moustache and fluffy greyish hair. He wore a short-sleeved shirt with buttons, no T-shirt for this chap. The way he was physically built demonstrated that he had not been born in a manor. I had never seen more nerves and veins coming out of forearms. He had a wooden cross that fell at the bottom of a gold chain around his neck. "Antonio!" Martin called.

The man waved to us and walked our way. "Who's this boy?" He questioned.

"Señor De La Vega, meet Kristian Imbeault. He will be working as a consultant on the project." Martin explained.

"Hi, how are you?" I boldly enquired.

He hesitated a second or two, looking at me in an analyzing way. "Good enough." The new man finally answered.

"Do you live in the village?" I dared to ask.

"Antonio is from San Pedro del Norte." Martin clarified in a way that he assumed I knew where every tiny village was.

I stared at him with an annoyed look. "Where's that?" I demanded exasperated.

"About thirty kilometres away." My partner said.

"On the border with Honduras." Antonio added.

"Antonio's lending us his land and has also invested financially. He's helping us a lot with our project." Martin continued.

"That's great. Are you a farmer or do you have some interest in coffee?" I asked.

"You could say I was forced to find an interest in farming. I inherited many acres of land in the past. You people are looking for some good land, well I have some to lease."

"How did you get to have so much land?" I questioned.

Martin looked at me with angry eyes. "You don't have to answer, Don Antonio, if you don't want to."

"It is okay Don Martin, do not worry. When the dictator was overthrown, the new government gave some land to the commoners. I was lucky enough to get a share. I was also unlucky enough to lose my father and two brothers during the following years. They gave me their land and I can now help you guys, plus my community at the same time." He said.

"That's great, we appreciate it." Martin brown-nosed.

Then, the Nicaraguan shook my hand without looking me in the eye and walked into the crowd.

My partner got closer. "He's a good man, very money centered, but a good guy nonetheless. Did you notice the long scar on his right arm? You don't think it was a bicycle accident, do you?" He sarcastically raised his eyebrows.

"You mean to tell me that man also went to war?"

"You did hear where his village is located, right? Believe me, Antonio was a prime target for mercenaries."

I was taken aback. "Before, you called them soldiers, now they're mercenaries."

"So?"

"If they were what you say they were, who was paying them?"

"Good question, I'll tell you later... if no one else tells you before."

I could tell he was dying for me to find out though and it bugged me.

"I admit: I'd love to be there when you do find out." He added and then left.

I was tired of playing games. "How come I've never heard anything about this country and those Sandinistas?" I asked.

"Well, you'll be happy to know that the Sandinistas are no longer in power and that's probably why we never hear anything about Nicaragua in the media. Since nineteen-ninety, a US supported candidate shocked the whole Latin-American world when she won the election. The former Sandinistas leader Daniel Ortega accepted defeat and peacefully handed over the controls. He's still at the head of his party, but many say he should quit politics. So why would the United States make a fuss about the Nicaraguan government when it's now in favour of free-marketing and profit?" Martin questioned. "As for what happened here in the past, I'm sure you'll find out soon enough." He said and left.

His attitude of knowledge, laughing at my ignorance was ticking me off. Back home, the international segment of the news report was so short, you could miss it if you blinked.

I was glad to learn that at least most commies were locked up in their mountains, but I still wanted to find out what had happened around here. Since I could not see Pedro anymore, I decided to walk towards Antonio. I made my way through the crowd and found him sitting on the sidewalk of a perpendicular street. He was not actually sitting on the ground but rather on his calves. He was quietly smoking a cigarette, listening to two guys talking to him about the rainy season. I probably should have also discussed the weather to put the man at ease, but I did not feel like waiting. I wanted to have my answer. "Martin told me you served in the army, when?" I straightforwardly asked. I did not care about involving my friend in this. I would not be here now if he had just told me what I wanted to know.

He hesitated. "I fought for too long, and not long enough ago, amigo." He answered softly.

"Did you participate in the Revolution that put the Sandinistas in power!?" I said joyfully.

He looked at me like I was from another planet. "Yes I did."

"Why?" I exclaimed out loud, but regretted it as soon as it was out of my mouth.

"It was the only way for us to decide who would form our country's government." The man replied.

It made me realize that I had not voted in the last election, never in my life actually. "It must have been tough." I stupidly implied to keep the conversation going.

He, again, looked at me with disbelief. "Yes, but it was the Contra-Revolution that truly killed me." Antonio answered.

I knew he was speaking figuratively, I know a dead guy when I see one, in the movies at least. "Yeah, I bet a revolution can be a hard thing to do." I clumsily said.

"No, I said the *Contra* Revolution." He paused when he finished his sentence and studied the ignorant expression on my face. "I guess it is normal that you have not heard of it, it was never an official war. It was a *secret* war, a strategy of terror as some called it." He added.

"Why did the Hondurans come down to attack you?" I asked.

Once again, the same look of incredulity appeared on his face. He must have thought I was the most uninformed person on earth. At that moment, I understood what Martin had told me about being an alien. I truly had the impression to be one. Although I felt bad about my state of ignorance, it also made me angry. "You have absolutely no clue about anything that happened around here?"

"No, not really. Well, not at all I should say."

He looked right into my eyes. "Sit down, I'll tell you a part of it. I will keep it short because this is not the place for it." He said.

"Thanks a lot, I appreciate it." I said to be polite.

He took a breather and started. "You see after we won the Revolution, we went back to our homes. As for our defeated enemies, many went into exile; most of them went to Honduras. They organized themselves, found funding and came back to our land to restart the war. They joined forces with Nicaraguan peasants who did not believe in the new Sandinistas government. They were out for blood, any person, from any nationality caught in the war zone would be treated as an enemy. Even foreign volunteers were warned not to come to our country or they would be killed on sight. The Contra army attacked and slaughtered people, kidnapped children, burned down houses and schools." Antonio stared at the distant crowd and carried on. It was obvious that he was getting emotional. "I had given enough during the first Revolution and my old demons were hard enough to bear. I was now well established and even if I did not want to go through it again, I could not stay away and decided to enrol myself as a medic. I felt like these invaders had to be pushed back. We could not let them advance in our lands." A big black bird flew right in front of our faces and forced Antonio to stop talking for a second. "After a while, we realized what their plan was. They always came for short attacks and retreated to Honduras. It was clear they wanted us to follow them up there. We knew it was probably a trap and we never fell for it."

I cut him off. "But why did the Hondurans come here? What did they want from your land?" I asked.

He did not answer my question, but ask one of his own instead. "Who do you think financed this army? Who did not want to see a Sandinista President in power?" He waited and with a facial expression, insisted on me answering.

"I don't know!" I admitted angrily.

"The mercenaries were paid by the US government, Don Kristiano!" He said and paused, waiting for a reaction, but I could not speak. "The CIA was financing these men to murder our families and burn our villages. They wanted to instigate a war. US troops were waiting for us in Honduras, probably begging for us to cross over the border so they could get involved."

"Why?" I asked shortly.

"To stop Communism." He answered in a way I could tell he was finding the idea absurd.

I could not believe that story. The entire crowd beside us had seemed to vanish. I wanted to call him a liar and spit in his face. I was listening to Antonio's personal version of these events. Even though he really seemed to be telling the truth, he had to be wrong. I wanted to ask somebody else, right away if possible.

"Don't worry." He started again. "The fact that you are not a Unitedstatesian makes you totally innocent. I know, and all the other villagers know for sure, that your family and friends had nothing to do with this secret war. We are confident that the blood of our people is not on their hands. Do not be troubled."

I stayed quiet, not knowing what to answer. Still, I had to say something. "What do you consider a Unitedstatesian?" I questioned.

"People from the United states of course."

"Aren't they called Americans?" I sarcastically commented.

"By themselves maybe, but why should they be the ones to have the right to be called that? We are just as Americans as they are, us all, Central, South and North America." He answered.

I shyly smiled and finally fully understood why Martin wanted me to keep my birthplace a secret. I still was not entirely convinced about this story, though; I would need to ask other people and sooner better than later. Even the thinnest medal has two sides. "We should go. They're probably ready to go to the demonstration." I said.

"Vamos!"

We got up and marched back silently. His fairytale disturbed me. As I walked, I analyzed every face I crossed. It felt strange to be in the presence of these smiling warriors. What did I know about war?

We joined the others. Antonio got on his horse and decided to come with us. I was surprised he did not have a car. He was definitely not as rich as I thought he was.

I finally got my chance to drive the pickup truck. Martin was sitting in the passenger seat, four were squished in the back seat and about twelve climbed into the back box.

On the way up, Martin and I discussed the *Contra*. I initiated the conversation in French and spelled out the main subject. I did not want anyone else to understand. I carefully chose my words so no one could have the slightest idea about the conversation's subject. "Tell me honestly, were the States really just coming back to kill everyone?" I questioned.

He looked surprised at the directness of my imprecise question.

"Do you seriously think that this is the right time?"

"Is there ever a right time to talk about war?" I argued. "I need to know!" I exclaimed.

"Do you always need to know everything right away?"

"These people hate Americans, Martin! I think it's pretty important for me to know why." I blurted.

"They don't *hate* Americans. You're exaggerating." He replied.

"Antonio said I had nothing to worry about because I wasn't one. What would happen if he knew?"

"Nothing would happen, and remember Antonio's only one individual. Most villagers like Americans. Perhaps the government is another story though, but what do you expect when more than half of the elected presidents were once lawyers?" He stopped to allow himself a little laugh. "As for Antonio, I'm pretty sure he lived traumatic experiences. Trust me on this, you can't blame him."

"No, I'm not blaming him. I don't even know what he went through." I replied with sympathy. I knew how I had felt when Antonio had told me the story. I saw the pain in his eyes, the revenge he wished he could have. If he had known, he probably would have killed me on the spot. "Did the States really pay off those mercenaries to exterminate people? I'd like to know, please." I demanded in a serious tone.

"You didn't like what you've heard. I told you to wait, didn't I?" Martin retorted.

"Yeah, yeah, you were so right and I was so wrong. Now answer my question and we'll be done."

He waited a bit, until we were passed the curve. "Well, I've heard different versions. Although many, and I do mean many, were horrible to the States, there was one that said the rich people of Nicaragua thought that Sandinistas were too radical and called for the return of the US influence." Martin admitted.

"I knew it. I knew there had to be more." I joyfully said.

"What makes you so sure *this* version is the truth? This is just the one you want to believe. Be careful my friend, I've just heard it through the grapevine, Antonio lived it."

"I don't care; I knew there had to be more behind it all. How come I never saw anything about it in the news?"

"How old were you in the early eighties? Do you even watch the evening news? So you had never heard about the Nicaraguan revolution before, does that mean it never existed? I mean I'm sure you had never heard that oysters could change sex depending on the water temperature they live in, but that doesn't make it untrue."

"What?"

"What makes you so knowledgeable from watching a media that decides what you will know and ignore?"

"What are you talking about? It's the land of the free!" I said.

"Be careful, the only freedom that the States give you is the one to think like they do." He alleged. "If it's the land of freedom, then why does the government ban certain songs from radio stations during war times? Why aren't artists allowed to say out loud whatever they want without fear of being boycotted? Check your history, during the first

World War, how many Americans were jailed because they dared to oppose the war out loud?" He questioned, but before I could answer, he started again. "Why should the States have the right to intervene in other countries' affairs?" My partner asked again.

I was discovering a side of Martin I did not know before. Was he a communist as well? I decided to answer his question and worry about him later. "Someone needs to do the job, if the other countries' way isn't the right one, why not?"

"But what makes you think the American way's the right one? Maybe it's the right one for them, but they don't know anything about other cultures. Do they know what people want and need in other countries?"

"If the United States is the most powerful country in the world today, they must know the proper way to do things." I said.

"The proper way for them and that's just great, but what if other people want to do things another way? Does it have to mean that it's better or worst, could it simply be different?"

"Anyway, as long as they are fighting for peace, I'm on their side" I exclaimed, thinking it would shut him up.

"You're joking right?" He questioned and then stopped. "Jack and Bobby wanted peace and they were both assassinated for it. Their whole economy is based on guns, weapons, war. End of story." He added.

I felt like I was arguing with a teenager: Martin always had something to reply and unfortunately, it was usually something good. I was about to say more when two or three people banged on the pickup roof and the rest of them whistled.

During the pre-work, I realized that the workers here were very slow. I understood that the heat weighed heavy on them, but I did not think they would be this unhurried. Looking at them moving, I was not sure they deserved more than three bucks a day. If they wanted to have more like I did, they would have to work harder for it. If only Martin would allow me to crack the whip and tell them to go faster.

Thanks-be-to-God, some workers seemed to go at a decent pace. There was a guy named Carlos, he could make a fortune working in America. Even with his crummy salary, Carlos wanted to be the best he could be. The amazing thing was that he had a huge hole in his left elbow and he still wanted to go faster. Evidently, if I believed what I was hearing and knowing where his wound most likely came from, I doubted he would want to go up north. Still, it was the land of opportunities; he could have his shot at the big leagues. He did not need a perfectly functional body, his heart was fully loaded. The most excellent part was that he was doing the job really well, not many people could combine quality and quantity.

By the end of the afternoon, I had already taught everything that needed to be taught. The rest could easily be done by the three foremen. Obviously, I would only have to keep an eye out. My job from now on would mostly be to supervise the activities. The men seemed to have understood the principle and even though I was not the one doing it, the work was under my responsibility. I needed to be alert. These crew leaders had no real experience with coffee; they could not be trusted.

I was on my way back to the vehicle when I saw Antonio beside his horse, waving at me. He was merely signalling goodbye, probably about to go home. I wanted to ask more questions, I was unsatisfied with his communist version. As I got close to him, I noticed him touching a long scar on his neck. "Is that the only one you have?" I asked.

He stared at me. "The worst one is here, amigo." He answered with passion as he pointed to his heart. He kicked his horse's lower belly and went on his way.

Wacko!

Once the work was done for the day, I had time to reflect on Antonio's description of the war. It was surely crap! It had to be. Martin and I relaxed in his home. "It'll be a lot longer than I'd expected." I started by saying.

"It's only the first day, they'll get used to it." He answered, knowing fully why I was worried. "And so will you." He added.

"I don't know. I wasn't impressed today."

"Let's face it Kristian, you're a hard man to impress." Martin replied.

I thought it was weird for him to say, he barely knew me. "Maybe you're right." I admitted nonetheless.

Later, Martin went into his room and put on fresh clothes. To my great surprise, he appeared with this guy Che on his front side. "What are you doing with that Cuban Communist on your T-shirt?" I shockingly asked.

"He was no Cuban, he was Argentinean." He replied.

In my mind, the man remained a symbol of Cuban Revolution. I never liked that country, never, not only for the Bay of Pigs, but also because they were the last ones to abolish slavery in all Americas.

Retarded Communists! "What was he doing hanging out with Castro then?" I questioned.

"He was a born revolutionary, just like Simon Bolivar."

"Like who?"

"Didn't you study history in school?"

"Obviously not enough." I admitted. "Just tell me about Fidel's castrated friend." I pleaded.

He looked at me strangely. "Ernesto Guevara was a rich man's son, a medical doctor, who decided to travel across South-America and the more he travelled, the more he realized that the poor were oppressed by the rich. He decided to help those people against corrupted governments." Martin said.

"Was his first name Ernesto or Che?" I asked.

"Che simply means *man*. They gave him the nickname because, like all Argentineans, he used it a lot when he spoke. Be careful when you talk about him, he's the hero of many Nicaraguans. For them, he is the man: *El* Che." Martin warned.

"No wonder, with all those revolutionaries hanging around this village, but I don't get why *you* like him. Let's face it, you're no revolutionary." I boldly teased.

"Maybe, but I'm against all corrupted governments that believe they can impose their way of doing things, thinking they're better than everybody else."

"Are you saying this for the United States?" I irritably demanded.

"Partly, they had no business in a tiny country like Nicaragua."

"Who's to say they did?" I interrogated ignorantly.

"I mean check your facts. In the American budget of eighty-six and eighty-seven, there was eight hundred million dollars injected in the destabilisation of Nicaragua and its Sandinistas government. Now that's a lot of money for a country of three million peasants." He said.

"Why would they do that?" I asked.

"To make sure the country couldn't spend money on important things like education or health. Defending yourself costs a lot and doesn't leave much for essentials." He paused. "But relax, earlier when I talked about arrogant governments, I also meant the Persians, the Greeks, the Romans, the British, the French, and the Germans." Martin listed.

"You do know your history, I'll give you that." I paused and decided to end our first conversation. "Whatever happened to Guevara, is he still alive today?" I questioned.

"No, he died fighting in the Bolivian civil war."

"Oh yes, the Bolivian war." I pretended to look like it was all normal stuff to me and prepared my next interrogation, but Martin cut me before I could ask it.

"By the way, the CIA is responsible for his death." He blurted out and then looked away.

I was left there with my mouth wipe opened, reflecting on my retaliation, but again, Martin cut me off before I could even start.

"On a different subject: There's going to be a huge celebration tonight." Martin told me.

I decided not to get back to his CIA allegations. Perhaps because I was glad that Martin knew who the man on his T-shirt was, unlike so many little ignorant punks back home who just wanted to look cool. "Why's that?" I questioned.

"Don't laugh, but I'm not sure yet, might be the National Day or something, I'll tell you later." Martin admitted without shame.

"Do Nicaraguans know how to party?" I demanded.

"Of course! They first start the celebration with a big horse race and then they have a party with dancing and music."

Then, some street kid appeared on the door steps. "Don Martin the race is about to begin!" He shouted and went away.

"Come on, the duck's about to get it!" Martin announced with a smile.

I had no clue what he meant, but I got up and put my shoes on. My partner went to get his motorbike from next door and we both jumped on it.

We arrived at the sight and saw a few men hanging a rope over the street. There was a crowd filling both sides of the road. There also was a bunch of people on horses about a hundred meters away. Then, the cable was lowered and some guy appeared with a black-necked turkey and tied it by its legs, up side down. The rope was pulled back up to its original height. "Why is that turkey's neck black?" I asked Martin.

"It's full of grease." He answered. "By the way it's a duck. Remember the one I told you about back home?" He added.

I ignored his question. "It's a turkey." I replied annoyingly. "Why full of grease?"

"Well you see the riders have to go full speed and try to tear off the duck's head. It's a bit disgusting isn't it?"

"A turkey." I countered, not yet taking notice of his last remark. "Yeah it's kind of disgusting."

"I'm glad you don't think it's terrible. I was worried you might go out there and try to save the DUCK!" He insisted.

"What do you mean save the TURKEY, turkey like at Christmas and Thanksgiving? Why would it need saving?" When I finished the question, I saw the bird flapping his wings. I then realized what everybody else already seemed to know: it was still alive. "You mean the turkey isn't dead!?" I exclaimed for every nearby person to hear.

The first rider came by and could not grab any part of the poultry. The crowd gave a desolation sigh and turned to look for the next horseman.

"Calm down." He advised. "It's a duck." Martin went on.

"I really don't care what kind of bird it is: it's cruel."

The second rider was able to catch a wing and pull strongly on it. Clearly this winged fellow now had a broken limb. Kids looked on and enjoyed the show. Everyone was smiling, the scene was absolutely normal to everyone else but me. "You know Martin, these villagers are lucky that people from animal rights have no knowledge of what's going on here." I said.

"Well, maybe they do know, but unlike some, they understand it's in the country's culture."

"These turkeys definitely need a kind of Diane Fossey or something." I said.

"Diane Fossey was for the chimpanzees." Martin replied.

"I said a *kind of*, not her personally." I corrected. "By the way, she was for the gorillas. It was Jane Goodall who was with chimps."

"Are you sure?"

"Listen, I don't give a hoot if it was Brigitte Bardot, Ric O'Barry, or Joy and George Adamson, these TURKEYS could use a hand."

"You're making a big fuss over nothing. I'll have you notice that you're the only one who sees a turkey being killed."

"What are you saying?" I questioned frustratingly.

"Well, everybody else thinks it's a duck." He responded with a smile. After that comment Martin could see how totally ticked I was getting and he knew he had to calm me down. "I understand what you go through, but you have to realize where you are. You aren't on Lake Lucerne anymore." He added as the third rider passed by and missed. "At home, no one comes to tell you how to yodel."

"Yodeling doesn't hurt anyone does it?" The fourth rider came without notice. I knew that deep down Martin was on my side. He was only trying to get me to understand the way things were done here. On the wire, the bird was hanging motionless with his head towards the ground. The fact that it was in one piece did not mean it was still alive. A fifth rider passed by, grabbed the neck and tore it in half. I barely saw it; it was mostly the roar of the crowd that made me realize it was detached from the body.

"The other riders at the back now have to try and catch him before he can reach the end of the street." Martin explained.

It was mainly to make the race more interesting because, catching up to the leader was almost impossible. The spectators all started running to see the end result. I did not follow them, I slowly walked behind. I could not tell who won, I did not care. All I knew for sure was that the turkey, or duck for all I cared, had lost.

Once the race was over, there were some hundred-meter sprints. There were not any ducks or turkeys anymore, only bird-brained riders who would try to go faster than their opponent by sticking spurs into their animal's belly. It was unquestionably not a good day to be an animal in Cinco Pinos. These cowboys were far from deserving the title of horse whisperers.

I walked back to Martin's home by myself, our conversation was never finished. Perhaps, it was just fine the way it had stayed. I knew my new partner thought as I did, he was just more used to these things than I was. In a way, he was right: I needed to accept certain things. I was not here to change anything.

During the evening, there was a great celebration. I did not like dancing so I stayed alone, enjoying the unidentified drink that was offered to me. Some girls came to chat, but they did not stay very long. As for Martin, he was dancing the night away. I even saw him getting down with two girls at the same time, sexy ones too.

As time passed, there were a lot more men than girls swinging to the rhythm of the music. There were even some men dancing together, way too close to my liking. The villagers seemed to appreciate each other very much. Maybe that was a Communist thing; you had to like your people if you were willing to share your wealth with them.

I always hated going to any gathering of any type, especially family reunions. Get-togethers back home lacked in depth, like a deep frozen lake, but with thick ice that constrains us on the surface.

The Nicaraguan party was going well. Martin interrupted his Travolta swing to come and chat for a little while. "You like the Latino music?" He asked.

"Not bad." I blurted. "I'm just glad there not playing any Dean Reed songs." I declared.

"Who's that?" Martin questioned intriguingly.

"He was also known as the red Elvis, a big star in the Communist music world."

"Funny guy!" He laughed. "By the way, we're celebrating Saint-John the Baptist." He informed me to change the subject.

"Cool!"

After discussing which girl was the hottest, he started talking about the weather. "In the evenings of the rainy season, it's not abnormal for the power to cut. We're very lucky." My friend said. For now, the village generator creating the electricity was holding on and that was supposedly a rare thing.

"The electricity stops because of the rain?" I asked.

"Yeah, a couple months ago, it stopped for two weeks." He paused and looked at the expression of disbelief on my face. "You know it's not that incredible when you think that forty percent of the world doesn't even have any electricity." He added.

How could he remember that fact in his drunken state? Was this guy ever relaxing?

"You don't seem to be in a party mood; don't tell me you're still upset about that duck?"

"The turkey you mean?"

"Whatever." He gave up. "Don't you have some kind of old ritual back home?" He asked.

I thought about it for a while. "I guess in Sursee, there's the Gansabhauet."

"What does that mean?"

"The beheading of the goose."

"A goose hey?" He looked at me with accusing eyes. "Give me more details." Martin insisted.

"Happens every year on November eleventh, a *dead* goose is hung by the neck."

"Are you sure it's dead?" My partner interrupted teasingly.

"Yes." I answered shortly.

"Well that's no fun." He joked. "What's going on next?"

"Young men with blindfolds try to find the goose and cut off its head with a sword."

"Well for such a civilized country, it seems pretty similar to what we witnessed here."

"Except that our goose is already dead." I countered.

"Really, and does it die of old age right before they tie it up?"

Silence. "I don't know." I faked.

52

"Face it Kristian, the only difference is that your goose's execution is hidden and this DUCK's is public." Martin made a strong point. "And here we party for the night, so get off your butt." He encouraged as he got up to go to the dance floor.

"We party back home as well." I defended the Swiss honour.

The music was loud and I was getting tired. I needed to go to bed, be on my own to reflect on the events of the day. Around here, darkness fell around six o'clock and even if it was only about nine thirty, I felt like it was eleven. So, I took a last glance at the party scene and went to my mattress even though I knew that the heat and the *boom-boom* of the music would keep me awake for hours. These people could dance all they wanted, as long as they would be up and working tomorrow at the proper hour.

CHAPTER 2.3

I woke up at four thirty with a bad taste in my mouth, not like I had been drinking, but more like I had eaten a full bag of salt-and-vinegar chips the night before. "Today you'll go spend the day in San Francisco de Cuajiniquilapa." Martin told me a few seconds after I opened my eyes. "Half the team was missing yesterday at the pre-work; it would be good for you to check them out."

"Are you coming with me, I have no idea where it is?" I questioned as I sat up on my mattress.

"No, I have to stay here. Just drive to the *T* in the road and Don Garcia, the foreman will meet you there." He instructed.

"I've to admit, Martin; all these people look alike to me. I don't remember at all what that foreman looks like."

"Don't worry, he'll be there. You'd have to be Ray Charles to miss him." Martin added.

I looked at him with wonder. Was his last sentence a little politically incorrect? It was strange to hear it coming out of Martin diplomatic mouth. "Wait a second. I thought the San Franciscan foreman's name was Carlos?"

"It is, but we call him Garcia."

"Is that his last name?"

"Not even, his last name is Cortez. I don't know how he got that nickname."

"These people seem to pick out their nicknames out of a big black hat." I finished with.

I took a quick breakfast, composed of an entire pineapple and packed my daily stuff in a small backpack. "Seriously, where exactly is this village?" I stopped on the doorsteps to ask Martin.

"About thirty kilometres from here. Take the east road." He answered with an exasperated tone of voice.

"Why did I wake up so damn early if it's only thirty klicks away?" I replied while I was holding my hair with both hands.

"It's not the distance that matters; it's the state of the road."

"What do you mean?"

"It's just windy and in bad condition, full of holes. You most likely won't be able to go faster than forty. There are also three waterways to cross."

I hesitated for a second. "By waterway, you mean little creeks right?"

"Nope, they're rivers, but usually they're really shallow. You shouldn't have any problem with the truck, unless of course it rained during the night, now that could become a different story." He joyfully answered.

It bothered me the way my uncertainties constantly seemed trivial to him. "Did it rain last night?" I enquired nervously.

"I don't think so, but I'm a heavy sleeper. You'll see when you get there, if the level of water is okay or not."

"I've never seen those rivers, how am I supposed to... and come to think of it, I've honestly never crossed a river with a vehicle in my life so, again, how am I supposed to know if it's acceptable?"

"My Gosh! Just go and stop stressing so much. I mean there's a bus that goes there everyday, it can't be too bad."

Why had he not mentioned that before? "Really and what happens to the bus when it rains for two days?" I felt like asking.

"I guess it gets stuck or plainly doesn't go." He answered exasperatingly. "Keep it simple, will you."

I did not come back with anything. I only picked up my bag from the floor and left.

I got in the truck and went on my lonesome way. The village was silent. There were surely some people already up, but they were indoors, quiet. The sun was about to rise and was showing me the path to follow. I started rolling slowly. A dog unhurriedly got up and moved out of the middle of the street. I had rarely experienced such quietness.

About three hundred meters further, I saw Pedro walking alone through a petite mist. He had a little knapsack and crossed the street to take the turn that lead towards the hill. I stopped and rolled down the window. "Buenas Días Señor!" I greeted.

"Please don't call me Señor Don Kristiano!" He answered with a pleasant tone and his already usual smile.

It was true that I had the choice between two names already for this man, Pedro and Don Angel; I did not need Señor as well. "So you're off to San Pedro already?" I questioned.

"Si!"

"You don't mind walking so far?"

"Not really, the walk is very soothing. It is perfect before a day's work, calms me down." He kindly replied.

Strangely, I thought all about the early-bird drivers in traffic back home, they certainly did not relax on their way to work. "Well, I'm off to San Francisco for the day." I carried on.

"Good! You will like it. It is where I was born."

"Really, why did you move out?" I asked.

His facial expression changed. "Circumstances forced me out." He replied.

I thought about the reasons why someone would move from one tiny boring village to another and I could not find any. "Did you leave because of the war?" I then felt like asking.

"In a certain way, yes." He answered distantly. "In San Francisco, you will be working with Carlos. He is a very good person and once a good friend of mine. You will like him a lot." He added to change the subject.

It was strange that he had used the past tense to say he was *once a good friend*. I would definitely keep this interrogation to myself. "Well, I'm off!" I simply said.

"Drive carefully!" He advised.

"Yes, I heard about the road. Do you think it'll be okay today?" I asked.

"Do not be concerned with the rivers; it did not rain during the night. I can guarantee you will have a safe journey." As he finished, he gently smiled and turned to his right. He started to walk up the small mountain overlooking the village. The hill was actually called *El Cero*, which very simply means: the hill. I have to admit that these Communists possessed a wonderful simplicity. No one in my country would call a mountain: *the mountain*. It would have to be a name paying tribute to some supposedly successful man. I myself made a hundred and eighty turn and headed east.

The road was not as bad as I expected. I had to take it slow, but it did not matter, I was in no hurry. Once at the first river, I stopped the vehicle and got out. I took a few rocks from the ground and threw them in the water. Pedro, or Don Angel, was right. I would not have any trouble crossing today, although relatively wide, the waves were barely covering the shallow bedrock. I got back in the truck and started to cross. I felt like Jesus moving on the surface of water, except I had a four by four to do it with: different times called for different measures.

After about a forty-minute drive, I safely made it to the *T* in the village and Carlos came to welcome me right away, this guy was trustworthy after all. "Buenas!" He greeted.

"Hello Sir!" I said. "Are you alone?"

"Yes, the workers only start at six-thirty." I looked at my watch and realized that it was not even six, soon, but not yet. "I thought we could go to my house for coffee. Are you interested?"

"Sure, hop in!"

We drove in the village. His house was close to a nice little park where a guy was already shooting some hoops. Carlos saw the look of astonishment on my face. "Some men choose to wake up early to be able to do most of their activities before the real heat comes crashing on us." He explained.

We went inside the house and he quickly introduced me to his wife. We sat down at the table and two cups of coffee were brought to us. "I can only offer sugar. We do not have any milk for the moment."

"That's perfect. I never liked milk in my coffee." I decided to lie to make him feel better. A couple of children's voices were heard from the backyard. "You have kids?" I asked.

"Of course!" He replied. "I have only three so far though."

I had to laugh at the word *only*. "In my country, it's rare to have more than two."

It was his turn to laugh. "Here, we are considered to have a small family." He paused and looked at his wife far away in the kitchen. "Honestly, I may have more that I do not know of." He whispered as he took another look and timidly smiled. "I just did not want to be like my father."

"Why, how many kids does he have?" I asked, or should I have asked how many mistresses did he have?

"He has forty-two. Obviously, they are by different women, but still, I do not think children are like cattle. They require and deserve much attention."

"You have forty-one brothers and sisters! That's a lot of people at the Christmas party." I exclaimed. "Do you even know all of them?"

"I think I have seen most of them at least once. My father moved to the capital a long time ago. He left when I was ten years old. We rarely contacted each other over the years." He admitted.

Then some guy came in the door. It was one of the workers. He was tall and slim. When he waved to us, I noticed that he had only three fingers on his right hand. I turned to Carlos. "Was the war fought in this village as well?" I naively questioned.

He simply looked at me with a surprised gaze in his eyes. He did not say anything for a few seconds. "Yes it was, but if we really must talk about it, I would prefer it to be a little later if you do not mind.

There are some things I do not like discussing during breakfast. I can even show you some evidence if you would like."

I nodded simply to acknowledge my understanding.

Three more men arrived and minutes later we were all in the vehicle ready to go. More people joined us as we drove through the village's streets. I brought all the workers to the site and the foreman came to see me. "The water pump at the well is broken. If you do not mind I would like to go set up the new one. Come with me." He stopped and stared at me. "Or you can stay here if you want." He seemed to be embarrassed that he had tried to tell me what to do. He did the right thing; I would take no order from any of those Commies that was for sure.

"I'd rather the both of us stay here for awhile and then *I* will go fix it myself. The workers need to be supervised at all times." I replied in a severe voice.

We spent about two hours on the land, walking up and down. The work was progressing slowly.

After Carlos explained where the pump was, I said goodbye and jumped in the truck. No plantation of any kind could survive without water. I was heading for the *Bomba*, on my own.

It took me about three hours to get everything settled at the site. The guard there had helped me as much as he could, which meant not much in my book. I left the well's site and drove back to check on Carlos. I parked the truck and walked up the hill. The different pieces of land had all been prepared during the last month. Men using machetes had cut down all the standing trees and had pilled them on the ground, making long fences across the slope. There was not really much wood left; villagers had come to pick it up to burn it in their stove.

I found the crew; about half of it was sitting for a break. I was not going to say anything. Evidently, they would answer that they had only sat down two minutes ago. I ignored their laziness for the time being. "Where's your foreman?" I asked.

"He is up in the mountain, checking our quality." The worker replied.

Was he only saying that? Maybe Carlos was just taking a nap somewhere in the shade.

I climbed up the mountain and when I saw him, he really was checking the plants, making sure everything was okay. "Hey, how are you?"

"Good, I think my people are doing a good job. Would you mind telling me if you agree?"

When he asked, I realized that I had not even checked anything on my way up. "Yes, it all looked fine. Let's walk together for a while, see if we have the same standards."

We strolled around for about an hour and discussed many trivial subjects at the same time. Over the course of our discussion, I received permission to call him by his inexplicable nickname of Don Garcia. My primal desire was to ask his opinion about the war, but I could not do it, not straight away. He had been very clear at breakfast: it had to wait. He seemed like he had things to teach me. I still wanted a second opinion; one that would hopefully contradict Antonio's and approve Martin's version.

Then, it started to rain. "We will stop working for the day now." He timidly declared.

"There's still an hour left before quitting time." I opposed.

"We can not work in the heavy rain, Don Kristiano." He whispered embarrassingly.

"What do you mean?"

"The rain, we do not want to be sick."

I could not believe what I was hearing. At that moment, we arrived at the bottom of the slope and the crew was already packing up their stuff. These people were afraid of a little rain, as if they would melt or something. "Wait a second." Some guy started to walk away, totally ignoring me, so I repeated louder with a more severe tone. "Wait a second I said!" The man stopped and looked at me and then at Carlos. He was now listening. "Why are you scared of these tiny drops?" Right at that point the rain intensified itself and made a liar of me.

Carlos came to me. "We have worked hard all day. Our bodies are very hot. If we get wet and cold now, we could get very sick. Maybe even get pneumonia. We need to get out of the rain now Don Kristiano. Please." He said in a begging tone.

"I don't get it, Don Garcia."

"I don't know how it is in your country, but here if we get sick, we can not go to the hospital easily. We do not get paid when we stay home in bed." He clarified in a more commanding way. "Please!"

I felt I needed to give up on this one, even though I did not understand at all. So, I did. I would definitely talk to Martin about a pay cut. My decision was appreciated by the crew and their leader. I think it got me in the foreman's good book, he was happy to see I had a heart, sort of.

We all walked to the truck and I drove them to the village.

We stopped in front of Carlos' house. Even if the rain had diminished a lot, everybody went straight home to take cover. The leader and I were left alone. "So! What about the war? Is this a good time for me to be educated?" I had to ask.

He simply looked at me. "If it is truly what you want, come with me." He peacefully said. He started going up the road. Evidently, I followed even if there was a part of me that knew I could regret it. I might hear things that I may wish to be able to un-hear. Still, I was curious, as always and needed to have this knowledge. I silently walked behind the man, listening to him telling me insignificant details about his village.

We came to a fence, surrounded a small building with a big yard. "Wait here a second please." He told me as he went to knock on the front door of the opposing house. An old man answered and greeted my acolyte. He put his head back inside for three seconds and came back out, handing Carlos a key. The man was thanked and went back to whatever he was doing before the banging sound on his door.

The foreman unlocked the gate and we stepped in. The rain stopped falling. I had absolutely no clue why we were coming here. There was a house in the middle, surrounded by red and black concrete blocks. Actually, everything within the gates was painted with the same two colours. I had no idea why, for me it only reminded me of a beer my father used to drink.

"What's up with the red and black?" I inquired.

"They are the colours of the Sandinistas' FSLN."

FSL... what? "Why did you bring me to this place?" I questioned.

"At the house this morning, you asked me if the war had been fought in this village. Well, this is it. This site where we are standing now is where our most infamous moment occurred. This is the place where what is now known as the San Francisco massacre happened. The date was the twenty-fourth of July nineteen eighty-two." He paused. I stayed silent. He knew I wanted to know more so he went on. "One sunny morning, mercenaries decided to come here and have themselves a bloodbath."

"Why this village?"

"I heard that some commander of the opposing army was born in Cinco Pinos. Our village is the second biggest in the area, perhaps this is the reason. Honestly, I prefer not to know how they decide these things. How a person choose who deserves to be wiped out."

I sensed then that he would only solidify Antonio's version of the story, but I still chose to listen carefully.

"You see a group of people, including myself, were standing where we are. We barely had time to see them coming before they started shooting. My father-in-law and I were teasing my friend about his wife being pregnant. I remember us discussing the future of the baby, picturing what he could someday become and then bullets started flying over our heads. The noise was unbearable. I immediately threw myself on the ground. I thought my father-in-law had done the same, but a few seconds after, I noticed his shirt was full of blood. I heard the voices of other people, they were in pain. The roaring sound was ever present, like an unstoppable clapping thunder. I panicked when I saw the blood's colour on his shirt. I turned him over and begged him to talk to me. I wanted him to tell me it would be alright, like he had done so many times before." A tear discreetly dropped from Carlos' eye.

I felt horrible about asking him to remember all this. This site was surreal; it was like I could see those soldiers coming up the street, dressed in the green of the jungle. I pictured them holding their machine guns. "I'm sorry. You can stop if you want." I said, but he ignored my sentence and kept going.

"My friend was still standing, frozen, unable to move and then a split second later his head exploded. It was amazing how a man who had never in his life thought about committing an act of violence could die in such a way. All my friend had ever talked about was having a family and enough money to raise cattle on a small farm. He was barely twenty years old. Seconds later, farther away from us, his own brother was also shot dead." Carlos stopped.

"What happened after?" I very shyly asked.

"As I told you before, my own father left when I was young. My father-in-law had sort of replaced him. He had been the one there for me, the one I could always turn to when things were going badly. This time it was different, it was the time where I needed him the most. I wished I could have relied on him. Unfortunately, it was my turn to take over. I went closer to him and he tried to speak. I could barely hear the sound of his voice. I only heard one word: water. He was thirsty and I was absolutely petrified. We were face to face. His eyes were wide open, full of conflict, full of pain. I saw five men being killed in about a minute. I could not move. I wished I could have had water with me." He paused for a bit a looked around the yard. He seemed to be searching for something. "Do you see that block over there?" He asked me.

I acquiesced in silence.

"When my father-in-law was asking me for water, I saw a man being gunned down at close range. It was right at that spot. He did not even have time to scream."

"I'm so sorry." I could not believe how opened he was. I never wanted so many details.

"I had decided to stay with my father-in-law until he died, but then on the right side, I saw three mercenaries coming straight for me. I closed his eyes and kissed his forehead. I started running and never looked back. I heard the bullets whistling, flying around me. I kept my head down and ran for the mountains." Carlos stopped when he noticed I was close to tears. He put his hand on my shoulder. "It's alright." He consoled me. "I stayed up in the jungle for the day and carefully came back down at nightfall. The murderers had gone and the bodies had been put in a big pile." He added.

"How many were killed?" I asked with the most respectful tone I could take.

"All you have to do is to count the tombs." When he pointed at them, I felt pretty stupid. The fifteen concrete blocks were actually graves. "Which one is your father-in-law's?" I questioned.

"It is the one over there and my best friend is the one next to it." I got up and went to see them properly. His name was Reymondo Garcia M. When I read it, a little light of association went on in my head. "This is why they call you Don Garcia!"

He smiled at me, he seemed like he was proud of me for figuring it out. "Yes it is. When he died, I inherited most of his properties. In a way, I sort of took over his place in the village. I looked after his smaller children. His friends became my friends. I turned into a respected man. My presence at the massacre made me renowned all over the area. That day, I was the only one in the square to survive; only me could tell how our people had died." He paused. "I come here often. Legend says that the souls of the unprepared are still hanging around, like angels. I like to walk around and ask them for advice." Carlos said.

We walked to a brick monument in front of the house. I had seen it when we had gotten in, but the signification was now different. I was saddened by this man's story. This time, I did not feel angry at my own ignorance towards this country. How could I have known about this? We knelt in front of the block. Carlos touched some of the names. Then, he kissed the tip of his fingers and placed it on his father-in-law's name. My throat was all chocked up. My nose was tingling; I had to scratch it quickly to keep the tears from coming up. The main writing said: "Héroes Y Mártires". There was also a patriotic slogan that said that dying for your country was not really dying, it was sowing the seeds to victory. It was the kind of partisan motto I used to believe in, but today it felt like a load of crap.

Finally, Carlos softly read the inscription at the bottom. "Patria libre O Morir!" He whispered. "This was the national rallying-cry during the Revolution, ending every Sandinistas meeting. It used to be the slogan of Augusto Sandino, our original leader." Don Garcia explained.

"I understand." I shortly replied, it was the same saying as on the New Hampshire licence plate, as if a comparison could ever be made.

Carlos got up and started to walk around. He looked up and smelled the fresh air coming with the breeze. Maybe as time passed by, he had had time to make peace with himself. Hopefully it was the same for the souls of the victims. Was there one hanging around me right now?

I also got up and we both started to march out. He locked the door and gave the key back to the old man. Then, we returned to the house and had coffee.

I decided to go home for dinner, regardless of Carlos' invitation to stay over. As I stepped out of the house, a man of imposing stature ran right into me. I apologized and picked up my cap that had fallen at some point during our collision. It was the mayor of the village, a good friend of Carlos, probably because he would never want to compete against him. "Are you the new coffee boy?" He started.

"Yes I am, Señor." I thought he would appreciate being called Senor.

"Are you Americano?" He asked as he lowered his eyebrows.

A part of me felt like saying yes, but with all Carlos had just told me, he surely would have seen it as treachery. Although, come to think of it, his version had been absolutely non-political. Maybe, he did not think the US were responsible, perhaps, he did though. One thing was for certain, after hearing his story; I sure was not going to ask him. "I am from Europa, just like Don Martin." I smiled and went straight for the vehicle, praying he would not ask me again.

The fat man spoke with Don Garcia while I checked the oil in the truck. A bit later, he quickly said good-bye to both of us and left. I got closer to Carlos. "This man seems to be quite a character." I alleged.

"Most village mayors are." He replied. "That is why I never wanted to be one, regardless of everybody who has asked me to be."

"Why do you say that?"

"I will not talk especially for this one, but in general mayors are elected by the people and do not return much to their voters. The position is simply a big front for money transactions and other dishonest schemes, a total abuse of power."

"You have any example of what you're saying?" I pushed my luck.

"Well, I know for a fact that the mayor of Cinco Pinos has a wife who lives in Chinandega and a mistress in his own village."

"Who told you all this?" I questioned.

"His second mistress, she lives in our village, beside my step sons' house." He said with a smile.

"Is it just me, or it seems to be normal to cheat on his wife for people around here?" I enquired.

"What do you mean for the people *around here*? It is probably the same thing all over the planet. Men physically and mentally can not be faithful. They do not have the strength, or the will to use that strength." He replied convincingly.

With a sentence like that, I was not going to ask him if he was faithful. I had learned enough about this man, I wanted to keep parts of him secret. It would disappoint me to learn that he had mistresses as well. I had had enough for today. "Thank you very much Don Garcia for today and good-bye for now." I said and smiled.

"I hope to see you again soon." He put his hand on my shoulder.

On the road, I thought about many things, but I mostly I reflected on these tombs and also all the women who were deprived of the right to feel special, unique. I felt slightly depressed. I needed to get back to Cinco Pinos, get a decent meal accompanied by an uplifting conversation with Martin, take it easy during the evening and sleep for a long night.

CHAPTER 2.4

The day started off really well, we left around six. I could almost say that I was allowed to sleep in if I compared to yesterday. The men walked to the field since Martin and I had to go get some posts. We had to build fences around the plantations because farmers were letting their cows wander around and eat everything they wanted. My colleague took his motorbike. I was alone in the truck and blasted the music way up loud.

I felt a bit weird in the morning, as if there was a wind of change in the air. My last two days had been emotionally full. It was like I knew that today might be the same. Something was coming for me; I simply did not know how far it was.

I spent the day in the mountains of San Pedro. The foreman was a very strange man. He rarely spoke to his men and was worst with me. He greeted me when I first saw him, but he did not say much for the rest of the day. I mostly talked with the workers; they were a funny gang. To my great surprise Don Angel was not around. "Where is Pedro?" I asked the leader.

He seemed bothered by my question, hesitated and looked at the horizon. "Obviously not here." He finally responded.

The man had a weird look in his eyes. I could not tell if he was confused about my question or simply confused in general. Nonetheless, I decided not to insist.

I walked around for the rest of the morning, going from one plantation to another and sitting down wherever I would find a decent spot.

On the way home, I stopped in a gathering of houses called *El Chaparral*. We had some working sites in the area and I had decided to go take a hike. I spent about two hours checking it out. It all seemed like decent ground, but it was as hard as steal. Unless it rained a bit more, it would be very difficult to plant anything.

I made my way back down, there was a little convenience store where I bought myself a few tiny bags of chips and a Fanta. I ordered my bags in French and the clerk looked at me strangely. It was not a facial expression of misunderstanding, more like he was telling me to stop being an idiot and speak properly.

I quietly sat in the vehicle to eat and drink. The school bell rang and all the kids came out, wearing blue and white uniforms, the same colours as the country's flag. All of a sudden, a kid noticed me and called half of the school to come and join him. A minute later, about twenty kids appeared, staring at me. They did not even say anything. They just stood there, some were silent and others giggled. The only thing that could make them look away was when I stared back into their eyes. It lasted for about three minutes, until I got tired of giving them the evil eye. I started speaking, telling them to bugger off, but it only made them laugh. I decided to speak German, French, Italian and English to them. I even quoted Sioux lines from an old Indian movie I had once loved: nothing worked. They probably thought I was rich and waited for me to throw them a few coins. I took off my sandal and showed them my pinkie toe. It was right on top of its neighbour. I wanted them to figure out that I had not been born a rich kid. I too had suffered from poverty and undersized shoes. Evidently, they did not understand my point of view from watching my crooked toes so I put my shoe back on. Then, I got up, danced around and pretended to hit my head with a stick I had picked up from the ground. I got reactions, some ran away and others laughed, wanting more. It was useless.

I re-entered the truck and finished my drink. I was getting ready to leave when I heard a man's voice screaming. "Wait please!"

I thought I had been busted by some local authority, let's face it; my kid show had been pretty weird. I did not move. At that moment, listening for a second sentence seemed like a good thing to do. I looked in my rear view mirror and saw a tall man coming my way. He looked unfamiliar. Behind him, three odd men were coming along. "We want your vehicle Sir!" He quickly demanded.

I thought he meant to steal it. I was petrified. "You want me to just give it to you?" I dared politely, choosing my words properly. After all the violent revolution stories I had heard, I knew these people should not be messed with.

He shook his head. "No, I cannot drive. I need you to drive it as well."

"What's wrong?" I interrogated truthfully, because really I had no clue what was happening.

"We have a sick person in the house over there." He was pointing toward the tavern. "We need you to take us to the San Pedro." He added.

I did not feel like driving some inebriated fellow home just because he could not walk anymore. I had not come to Central America to carry on Jean-Marie De Koninck's mission and play *Opération Nez Rouge*, after all if it had failed in Switzerland, why would it work here? "What do you mean sick, what kind of sickness is it?" I asked again, but this time with less concern. I mean, these Hispanics use the same word for *waiting* and *hoping*, was the same word used for *drunk* and *sick*?

Then all four men, who had been joined by three more, started speaking at the same time, with their hillbilly accent to top it all off. My Spanish was good, but not that good. I could not understand a single sentence. I got ready to tell them to go to hell. Then, I thought about Martin and his public-relations crap. He would be really angry if I did not help these people. I had to give in. "Vamos!" I finally said.

The man tapped my shoulder and gave a loud whistle towards the drinking hole. I stepped out of the vehicle and saw two men carrying a hammock using a massive branch. To my great surprise, they came out of the house beside the tavern; it was no drunken fool after all. When they got closer, I had one of the biggest shocks of my life. I saw the roundness of a pregnant woman's belly sticking out of the hammock. She was moaning in pain. These crisis situations usually happened in movies, not in real life and certainly not to me. I was out of it, almost in an altered world. When they opened the back door, the woman let out a mighty shout and it made me pop back into reality. All of a sudden, I had a moment of inner panic. The other back door was opened and the lady was placed inside. I kept my head forward. Her screams were stressing me out, and these idiots expected me to drive suitably. There was actually a foetus involved in the story. Regardless of the reason that had brought this woman here, the baby was surely not responsible. Things were bad. Some clueless looking man came to me. "The little one is like this." He put his two indexes on top of one another in the form of a cross. "Normally, it should be like this." He then said as he put his two indexes side to side.

I could not believe what was happening. Was this woman going to give birth right now, she did not seem to be big enough, but what did I know about it? What did this cross-fingered man know about it? How could this ignorant farmer know the baby was not placed correctly? Hopefully, the baby was smart enough to know that this was unquestionably not a good time to come out.

They finally settled her in properly. I was mentally getting ready to transform myself into an ambulance driver. The initial man started to speak to me so fast; I had no clue what he was saying. I hated him for putting me in this position to begin with. With all the others discussing who would sit where, I could not hear a thing. It had been decided that no one would sit shotgun. I had to be left alone so I could concentrate on the road. Some could say these people were considerate, but I still thought they were idiots and I was still freaking out.

"Don Kristiano!" I surprisingly heard from the left side. Who could that be? No one knew my name around here. I turned my head and saw my saviour, the man known as Pedro Sanchez, or Don Angel, was there in front of me. All of a sudden, his second name seemed very appropriate. I was so happy to see his smile and feel his confidence. My knight in shinning armour climbed through the opened window and sat beside me in the passenger seat, no one complained and everybody took their already designated place in the back. There were only three people in the box, so it would not be too heavy. We got on our way and exited the village, taking the road heading north.

"Alright Don Kristiano, rapido!" Pedro ordered nicely. I was surprised. I idiotically thought I would have to go slowly for the sake of my patient. I could not remember ever having so much pressure to perform behind the wheel, compared to this, my driving exam was inexistent. I had a pregnant woman on my backseat and I knew for certain how close *she* was, but I had no clue how close the *baby* really was.

Don Angel had said to go fast, but it was not all that easy. The road was still horrible: made of gravel, going up and down, left and right whenever it felt like it. There was the same amount of livestock and children strolling around. Further more, the man sitting with the woman on the back seat did not like to go fast, he was petrified that we would crash before our arrival. He kept signalling the slopes by pointing his hand downward. I did not bother with his hand gestures; there was enough stuff to think about.

The final slope was about a kilometre long and was ending with two serious curves. It all happened in a flash. I clenched my teeth and they probably all closed their eyes. I handled it so well, perfectly one might say, living the best downshifting moment I had ever had in my life. I passed from fifth to fourth gear during the first curve and then from fourth to third during the second. It was amazing. Some of them probably thought my last name was Schumacher. The wheels of the truck tossed a lot of rocks over the side of the cliff. People in the back were holding on for dear life. The woman cried in pain. There was a lot of exhilaration in the air, in the one I was breathing anyway. Don Angel looked at me in an indescribable way. He seemed concerned for my mental state of mind, maybe I was suddenly enjoying this too much.

A few moments later, we arrived in San Pedro. The villagers all jumped out of the way when they saw my truck with its trail of dust arriving at full speed. I came very close to killing a chicken, luckily for me it was not a pig. The bird ran in front of me and went right under the truck. No clue how it survived, it seemed too dumb to live.

Following the men's instructions, I drove to the *T* in the road and turned right. The second building was the hospital. I stopped the vehicle and everybody in the back jumped out immediately. I felt like exiting and jumping in the air, celebrating my victorious drive. I imagined myself on the F1 podium, with the American flag in the back, tossing champagne up into the air.

When I took a better look at the hospital, I realized how horrible it really was. I could not even find words to describe it. Somehow, the term *Stone Age* kept popping into my head.

A stretcher was brought to us and two men started helping the woman out of the truck. Even though she lamented as they moved her, she seemed to be able to endure a lot of pain. I did not know what she had, but I knew it was excruciating. There were no nurses around. I had no idea where they were or if the hospital had any for that matter. Perhaps they were on a coffee break.

The three men from the back box each grabbed a handle of the stretcher and the remaining one, although I absolutely did not want it, was left for me. The back seat man was already inside, directing the operation. Some other villagers, who had just arrived, took the woman and put her down on the mobile bed. This woman was now the village's center of attention. For a second, I wondered who she was. Was she an important lady, why were there so many people helping out here, would they do the same for anybody else of the area?

We started going in, Pedro beside me, coaching me out. I was glad he was there; it kept me from yelling at the three other incompetents holding the stretcher with me. The villagers saw me as an alien and rarely even looked at me. Most times, Don Angel was addressing his comments straight to me and it was very enjoyable. I did not think the others isolated me because they disliked my personality. Maybe they were just shy, embarrassed to meet me in such a crisis situation. Did this woman have a husband, where the heck was the father of the child?

We entered the building and had to stop quickly, we were blocked at the end of the first corridor. The only solution was now to go by the backyard and re-enter in the back entrance. To my great surprise, there actually was a tree just outside that was blocking the exit. I could not believe it. Why did somebody not cut that tree before? Were we the first ones to use this way out? I felt as if I were on candid camera. I was expecting some guy to pop up, laughing at me and my gullibility. Don Angel looked my way. "Let the other man take it alone Don Kristiano, go under and take it from the other side." Pedro instructed. I had to abandon my post so we could step outside completely, crawling under the stretcher. It was the only way for the others to position themselves better and allow us to keep moving.

We kept going for a bit until our next obstacle. The door of the room, supposed to be used by our patient, could not open. This time, I seriously searched for the hidden camera. Again, I had to crawl under and clear everything out of the way. It was essentially a bunch of chairs and a desk. It looked like office material. This hospital was a joke that could make a clown sob. Once we were in, we kept holding the stretchers while other men took the woman and put her on the bedspread.

The doctor finally appeared and started to discuss things with the first man who had asked me for the ride. I decided not to care and looked around for a while. The other patients of the hospital did not seem to have anything serious. I wondered what the pregnant woman had. She was clearly not about to go into labour, so what could it be?

Regardless, this place was a mess. The walls were dirty and the equipment was very representative of the building. Even in my country, it was said that hundreds of people died each year because nurses did not wash their hands properly, I could not begin to imagine what the rate here was. I looked around and tried to find myself a souvenir, but I could not decide on anything. There was not much of a choice, some scissors or gloves, but everything just seemed too valuable. It was weird because I did not see any of the usual things I was used to seeing in a hospital: no curtains in the windows, movable beds, solute, pressure-testing machines, towels, pillows, or telephones. There was no trashcan and I mean the regular kind, not the ones for biological wastes. There was no bell to call the nurse and come to think of it, I still had yet to even see a nurse. How could I take anything as a souvenir? I definitely would just have to remember this in my head.

"Time to go!" Pedro gave me a shout. When I turned around, he was already at the other end of the corridor. He seemed too far for him to have been the one to talk to me a second ago. Whatever, he was right, we had no more purpose here.

When I got into the truck, some guy came to bring a little bag of yellow liquid. He did not give any to Pedro. Maybe, it was a thankful gesture for my ambulance role-play. I was extremely thirsty so I tore up the top corner of the bag right away and started drinking.

We left, without waiting to enquire if anyone needed a ride back. Then, I rolled on some dog's tail and uneasily laughed when I heard him squeal like a pig. I needed to go back to Martin's house and relax for a while.

The weird juice I drank was excellent. "That's good stuff. What is it?" I asked Don Angel.

"Corn, milk, sugar and water!" He replied.

Once the words were out of his mouth I realized I would soon be in trouble. I had not thought properly, my mind had gone astray. I did not discuss it with Pedro, but I knew I would soon be suffering on the toilet. Bastards!

I tried not to worry about my lower back side too much and thought about the woman. It could have been cool to watch her deliver the baby on the backseat though. It was stuff that Hollywood was made of, it must happen sometimes in real life. This was insane, just wishful thinking. I was truly glad she was lying on a hospital bed, although it was not much of an establishment, it was surely the safest place for her at the moment.

Once in Cinco Pinos, I dropped Pedro in front of a path that went up in the mountain at the end of the last street. He started walking up and then came back down. "You did a very good thing today." He congratulated. "The baby should be named after you, in your honour. It would be a nice story for him to remember."

"Thanks, it'd be alright."

"Don Kristiano, lime is very good for diarrhoea." He finished with a smile, tapped the side of the door and left.

This guy was already reading my thoughts.

I went back to Martin's house and found him at his desk, slash table, preparing the upcoming visit of important people. Some journalist, ministers, and company presidents would soon come and observe our project. The idea was to bring as many suits as we could to find future financing. In my view, it was a load of crap, the same kind that I would surely soon dish out in the latrines outback. Men, chocked by their too-tight ties, would come and see what we decided to show them. It would probably be everything except a real day's work, theatre for money. Martin took it very seriously because he would stay here a lot longer than I. For my part, I would be there with a smile and an invisible tape on my mouth.

"I've saved a baby's life today!" I interrupted Martin's work.

"What?" He blurted out. "What do you mean?"

"I was waiting in El Chaparral and these people appeared with a sick pregnant woman. They asked me to carry her to the hospital, and I did." I told him with excitement in my voice.

"So you just drove her to San Pedro?" He dully demanded.

Since he seemed unimpressed with my story, I decided to cut it very short. "Oh yeah, that's right. By the way, I rolled on a dog's tail as well." I still added.

"Really, how did that happened?" He almost jumped out of his chair.

This guy was so weird. "Nothing, I just wanted to see if you'd react to it. A dog's tail isn't bigger than a chicken so don't worry." I said as I lay down on my mattress. Martin was too much in his work. Perhaps tomorrow, he would realize what I had just told him and be stunned.

I was able to relax for about fifteen minutes until my butt summoned me to the latrines. I jogged through the backyard and made it in record time considering that on the way there, you always had chickens, pigs or other animals blocking your way. The place was actually just a hole in a big wooden box. There were cobwebs everywhere. Personally, I never accepted to sit directly on the wood. I simply perched myself like a bird on a branch. In this position, it was easier to see the bugs crawling out of the hole. When I went at night, as soon as I would appear with my flashlight, I would see all the cockroaches walking around, coming from the darkness below. Disgusting seemed too weak of a qualifier to even use it. Furthermore, I felt that every time I went there I was getting closer to Juanita, the restaurant's cook. The reason had nothing to do with food. It was mostly because the walls of the latrines were very poorly built and had wide cracks into them. If I were able to see her, I was sure the opposite was also true. She was a great diplomat thought, always pretended not to notice anything.

Perched in the cabin, I went through hell for about ten minutes, my knees were killing me. Once I got back inside the house, Martin came to tease me. "Well, that was quick!" He said, with sarcastic reference to my trip to the latrine.

"How can I take my time with all those cockroaches?" I retaliated.

"You don't like cockroaches?" My partner asked, seeming genuinely surprised.

"Why the heck would I like them?"

"They're wicked creatures; you'd be surprised."

"Enlighten me!"

"They could be frozen for a week and come back to life, perfectly fine."

"I think they're pretty safe from any type of freezing around here." I replied. "I caught one and threw as far as I could." I invented just to get him angry.

"That was a waste of energy, they're indestructible, they can stand a hundred-and-twenty-six Gs, we humans die at eighteen."

"You're serious?" I was shocked. "You like the buggers; that's why your latrine's infested."

"They can flatten themselves as thin as a paper sheet." Martin answered.

"They don't need to do that to squeeze in your shit hole." I countered.

"Exactly!" He shouted. "All and all, did you enjoy yourself?" He added in a serious tone.

"Honestly no, if you must know. It ticks me off that I can no longer sit, read and relax when I'm doing a number two." I admitted out loud.

"Why do you need to read on the toilet?" He asked.

"I'll have you know that I get most of my knowledge from the books by the Bathroom's Reader Institute." I half-jokingly declared. Martin had no idea what I was talking about anyway.

Later, we went to eat at the restaurant next door. I ordered my food and went to get myself a *Fanta* in the fridge room.

"There's a thing I forgot at the house. I'll be back in a minute or two." My friend said.

"No problem, I think I'll just try out the hammock in there." I responded as I pointed to the freezer's room. Time passed, our plates came and strangely Martin was nowhere to be found. I started eating alone. A few minutes later, a truck that was throwing some huge think smoke drove by in the street. Since the restaurant's door was opened, it came straight into the room. The cooks ran outside in the backyard. My first reflex was to grab my plate and dive under the table, but it was not enough. I was forced to imitate Juanita and go hide in the backyard.

"It is for the insects." The cook said. "It helps to exterminate them."

"For an instant, I wondered if I could still eat my food even though it had been fumigated. I figured it would surely, well hopefully, be fine. Behind me, I saw Juanita's daughter looking in our backyard. When I copied her, I spotted Martin perched on the latrines' seat. This young girl could definitely give herself a show at my friend's hairy bum's expense. I laughed and went back to eat inside. With the wind, the smoke had cleared almost as quickly as it had appeared.

I rested on my mattress for the evening. I needed to decompress. I turned off the light and listened to my music. Martin was getting ready for bed. Between two songs, I heard him talking to himself.

"Well, I'm gonna go to bed now. Maybe if I'm lucky I'll have an erection." He thought out loud.

It almost made me feel good to hear it. At least, I was not the only one with deranged emotions today. I fell asleep about two minutes later.

CHAPTER 2.5

My three first days were the only ones with anything to write home about. The Nicaraguan routine settled in and things became stagnant. The days became long and slow, and I became quiet, simply walking around, alternating villages from one day to the next. I helped foremen to set people up and made sure they had everything needed to work a full day. Once it was done, I usually came back down to have breakfast with Martin at Juanita's restaurant.

The daily heat was torturing me. I was looking for shade the same way an ant would if a merciless child was chasing it with a magnifying glass. I came from the north and had spent all my life getting used to the cold. I had always preferred hot chocolate to the cold one. This everyday scorcher was absolute torture. I regularly wished there could be a solar eclipse in this Mayan country.

My days were full of little anecdotes that I would probably never tell anyone until I would be over sixty years old. Two mornings ago a spider had bitten me in the face as I was sleeping and I had totally freaked out. I had pictured myself inflating like a balloon and suffocating to death. How could I brag about this to anyone at home immediately after my return?

The Nicaraguan lifestyle I had been experiencing over the last few days had been entirely new to me. It was a complete change of pace from back home. Looking around, I realized I was not the only prisoner of a routine. The whole village seemed to be going nowhere. People were always doing the same thing, conversations never changed. Most men spend their day working down at the field or up in the mountains. Women stayed home and took care of the little ones. The bigger kids were sent to school until noon and then hung around for the rest of the day. Some were inside watching television. Teenagers were a mystery, the ones with whom I was unable to establish contact. They seemed to always be going somewhere, but also did not seem to be doing anything. In general, people were rarely alone. They always had a partner to be with. The only loner of the village was a drunken man, sitting on the opened front door of a random house. The others passed him by, ignoring him. The town drunk looked like he was lost, confused about this never-changing life. What they all do about it?

As for Martin and I, we had a good friendship. We did not always agree, but we could usually talk for hours without running out of subjects of conversation. I enjoyed our discussions. They were habitually filled with laughter. We generally spoke French, triggered by myself: it helped our privacy towards the others.

The work was fine. I did not really have to spend a lot of time checking, the workers were going way too slow for the quality to be poor. At this rhythm, they would almost have to do it on purpose. As time passed, the crew leaders became worthy of our trust and I was only going to the plantations to justify my salary. I was sitting, and even lying down a lot. Some people were amazed of how careless I was about getting my clothes dirty, not owning an electrical washer and dryer made them think differently. Still, it was good for the workers to see that I knew what was going on. I simply walked around the field, watching them in silence. My three-day beard and my sunglasses made me look lethal. The workers had no way of guessing what I was thinking. According to Martin, some of them feared me. If they only knew what was inside my brain. I was a front, a plain figure of power and that was necessary to keep them in line.

As days passed, I started to have a lot of fun with the villagers. Since money was not an object for me, I made bets with the workers. It always attracted a lot of people. It was stupid stuff like: I give you two dollars if you hit that tree with a rock. They were very rarely successful. I also taught them German, French or English words, making them say stupid things that we would all laugh at together a few seconds later. Truthfully, these Commies were a great public and I had become a great attraction for most of them. Who would have thought?

One morning, I woke up after having spent one of my worst nights ever. Dogs had had a barking contest right beside our door. My mattress was lying a couple meters parallel to the road. It was there to stop people from entering, but definitely not the sound. It was like they were woofing right in my ear. At one point, I could not take it anymore. I had taken a stick and gone outside to chase after the pack. Martin would have been cracking up to see the great puss in boots at three in the morning, chasing dogs with a stick, in his underwear. They stopped barking after about two hours, but the damage had been done, I had not slept until four.

Then at five, actually at exactly four fifty-two, there was a religious parade. I thought I was dreaming, but I also heard Martin complaining about it. How could they worship God so much and was it necessary for them to show their love for Him at this time of the morning? When I looked out the window, I saw these Communists carrying candles and singing a repetitive religious song. And I thought Muslims were fanatics? Please.

Luckily for me, the next day would be off. After all, we had to give the workers time to rest once in a while. I fell back asleep around five thirty and had time for one quick dream.

CHAPTER 3.1

My dream was disturbing that early morning; the night's distractions had definitely messed up my brain. I was climbing some stairs and came out to a balcony where there was a wounded animal. A light breeze was blowing gently, and then all I saw was an apple on the floor.

Even as I slept, I felt strangely depressed; my head was turning counter clockwise. My wits were not functioning anymore; thinking was no longer an option. In my dream, I looked at my face in the mirror and hated the image it projected. I could see my own reflection in the black colour of my iris and it was a sad one. My soul was in pain, tortured. As I saw it, I knew that it did not want to keep going. My spiritual core was covered with dark mud.

Then, I noticed it over my left shoulder. She was at the back of the room, suspended on a pipe that followed the ceiling. I had no clue what she was doing there, but she seemed to be beckoning for me to get nearer. She was attractive, simple, and beautiful. I wanted her to be mine. She was there to help me solve all my problems, end my misery. I got closer and touched her. She was long and soft. I loved to feel her dancing between my fingers. The contact from her tiny waves brought enormous pleasure. My body was shivering, slightly feeling her nearby. I would have enjoyed for her to touch my whole being. I wanted her to encircle me, to have our two skins communicating. I was becoming a positive victim of her attachment. Mostly, I wanted her to stroke my nape.

Without attaching any importance to the gesture, I pulled up a chair and took position on it. Seconds after, I put her around my neck. As she slowly caressed it, a small doubt came to mind, but it was too late: I could not push her away anymore. Suddenly, the chair moved. The rope snapped and so did my neck. Everything became black. There was not even the slightest sight of light.

I woke up in a flash. The room was bright and I was reassured at the sight of Martin's usual furniture surrounding me. I wiped my damp cheeks with my right hand and stared at the ceiling. I had forgotten about the dogs and the religious freaks.

It had been a while since our last day off and it was not even seven o'clock. I did not feel like getting up right away. I had a bit of time to waste, daydreaming about my day to come. Earlier during the week, Martin had suggested the beach of Corinto for a good swim. It was about two hours west, just passed Chinandega. According to him, supposedly, the seaside port had played a strategic roll in the war. It was where all the weapons were arriving through the Golfo De Fonseca from El Salvador. In the past, mines had been placed in the harbour and the oil refineries had been set on fire. This had ticked off some of the men in Congress and motivated them to do something about it. They had even sued, and had won against the United States in International court. My partner had lost me when he had said the US had never honoured the court's decision, as if they would have done that. Regardless of the political history, I was glad to have a beach decently closed by. Robert had also told me that the waves were a bit tricky, as if the ocean was no longer breathing properly. The sand was black, because of the volcanoes in the area and the water was warm; it was all I needed. Furthermore, there was a shipwreck a kilometre up north of the beach. Apparently, the spectacle was worth seeing. The day would be great and I would soon be all set to go.

In general, Nicaraguans did not really swim. There were rivers here and there, but I never saw anyone in them. I could not believe that even with this surreal heat, villagers did not feel the desire to get soaked.

Martin appeared in the door step with a serious look on his face. "You awake?" He asked.

"Hey why don't these people ever swim?" I questioned straight away.

He seemed confused and hesitated. "Pollution, snakes, I guess." He answered distantly. My partner kept going before I could start again. "I have big news for you my friend."

"Really, you changed your mind and decided to come swimming with me?"

"I wish my friend." He replied.

He had called me *friend* in both sentences, I knew he was about to ask me a huge favour. "Remember the pregnant woman?" He said.

It was my turn to hesitate a while, thinking he would ask something work related. "*I* do, but seeing the little attention you gave to the story, I'm actually surprised *you* remember her."

Martin ignored my crack. "Well, she had some complications and the San Pedro hospital isn't really equipped to treat her." He continued.

I so felt like answering a shockingly sarcastic response, but I decided against it. I was still sleepy and did not really understand where he was going with this.

Luckily for my thirst of knowledge, Martin kept at it. "You know ambulances are a rarity around here. For the moment, the only one there is has a problem with the gas pump and is in no working condition."

"What do people do then?"

"They manage." He shortly said and continued since he saw that I was hoping for more. "Just before you arrived in Nicaragua some guy came to borrow my bike to bring his wife to Chinandega."

"I guess you can't carry the pregnant woman on your bike, hey?"

"Not really. Besides, she has to be taken a bit further on up the road."

I delayed my response. "What do you mean? Where exactly *is a bit further* for you?" I suspiciously asked.

"Honestly, she has to go to the biggest, most sophisticated, hospital in the country and it's in Managua. Her husband can't afford to pay an ambulance to come from the capital." He stopped. "Do you even know who her husband is?" He then questioned.

I stared at him in his eyes. "No. How could I? Should I?" As I finished the question, Martin turned around and signalled somebody to come closer. It was the man called Antonio De La Vega, the most typical Sandinistas around, the person who if he knew about my birthplace would shoot me right on the spot. I could not believe it. I would now have to help *him*. Every single time I had seen this man, he had spoken dreadfully about my dear Uncle Sam and now he was asking *me* for help. Maybe I should just tell him the truth about my life, my origins. He would surely not want my driving skills anymore. How could this attractive young woman be married to this old dude?

We saluted each other, but remained silent. Oh well, saving his wife once was not enough. It was fine though, where I was born, that was how we acted; we helped those who were less fortunate than we were.

"Buenas Don Kristiano!" He said at last. The man looked sad. He had the eyes of a street beggar. He timidly stayed quiet and let Martin do the talking.

"If we do some serious post runs this morning, we won't really need the pick up truck for the next few days. I won't mention anything to the big head honcho back home. As long as he doesn't know you aren't here, you'll still get your full salary."

"Well, gosh I sure hope so. I don't mind helping these people, but I don't want to lose money over it." I severely responded in French.

"You won't have to, just gas up in Somotillio and put it on the tab. You'll have enough to go there."

I stopped him there. "Why can't you go instead?" I exclaimed.

"It may come as a shock to you, but I do have a lot of work to do here and you're the only guy available who knows how to drive." He replied.

"What? No one in this village knows how to drive?" I enquired.

"Some do, but they don't have my trust like you do."

"Why can't anybody learn?"

"It just costs too much money. Plus, your name's the one beside mine on the rental contract."

"And what about gas from there to here?" I asked.

"Antonio has enough money for you to fill the tank up once and make it home." Martin retorted.

"And the coffee plants, how will you move them around?" I demanded.

"We'll use horses and donkeys, everything should be fine. Don't worry; the foremen can now handle the job on their own."

I felt troubled to hear it; I had not realized that my colleague knew about my uselessness, and to top it all of, I was about to lose my only day-off. "Alright, I just have to go the capital and back, correct?"

"We hope so; you see the doctor is not sure what my wife has." Antonio jumped in.

"Does your wife have a name?" I asked annoyingly.

"Of course, sorry, it's Margarita-Anna."

"You don't know what sickness Margarita-Anna has." I questioned intriguingly.

"The doctor in San Pedro says it is some kind of infection. Well that is what he hopes anyway."

"Hopes?" I inquired.

"We do not hope." He hesitated. "It is just that it could be worst. She has some problems with her thyroid gland. There is a possibility that she could have what is called Graves disease." He finished.

With a name like that I could tell that one could die from it. "I have to admit that I've no idea what it is".

"It's quite normal, you're not a doctor and it's a relatively unknown disease. I mean it's not as old as leprosy." Martin said.

"Graves is simply the name of the one who first discovered it. For what I understood from the doctor and I am not even sure, it is a dangerously high level of hypothyroidism." Antonio clarified.

"I can't believe they can't do anything." Martin added.

"It's because you haven't been inside the San Pedro hospital." I replied.

"It is possible to treat it, but there are complications involving the late state of the pregnancy. Of course, the opposite is also probable, she may not be able to be cared for." Antonio said.

"How does your wife feel about all it?" Martin asked.

"It's Margarita-Anna!" I told my friend, but they both ignored me.

"She is in a state of total denial. It has taken a very long time for her to get pregnant again. She doesn't want to accept the fact that it may be her last chance." Antonio answered.

"And how come you guys just learned about it?" I inquired.

"The disease's symptoms are the same as a textbook pregnancy: fatigue, swelling, weight gain."

"So the only reason you have to believe that it's not just an infection is the doctor's opinion?" I questioned.

"That's right!" Antonio responded.

"I wouldn't worry too much about it then." I said carelessly, but then another thought popped into my head. "What if it is the disease, what do we do then?" I added.

"I truly don't know. We can only hope it will not be, but if it is, I will decide there and then." The Latino man said. "I would like to go even if it is merely a small infection. Last year, my sister's brother-in-law died of a trivial dental virus."

"Minor things can turn bad quickly around here." Martin included when he saw my facial expression of disbelief.

"What do you guys mean?" I asked.

"People don't have the money to go to the doctor's right away and the more they wait, the bigger the disease becomes." My friend paused. "Sorry Kristian, but they have to go now, not tomorrow, now." Martin said with authority.

"I know. I know. Hopefully we'll just go there and come back right away. I mean, after they confirmed it was a simple infection." I responded.

"I don't know what the people at the hospital will say, but keep a door opened for unpredictability. It's likely to pop at anytime up around here." My partner warned.

Strangely, I stayed very calm. I was sad that I had just lost my day at the beach, but our conversation proved there were worst things in life than losing a dip in the ocean. I wondered if it was karma getting her back, or was it getting Antonio back? Although he was not an easy man to read, his general story was right in front of me around his neck. The wooden cross symbolized where he came from and the gold chain was where he was now. It was as if the past and the present were uniting to take him further into the future. I figured this out, but what about his detailed past? Two villagers had told me he had been gone during the revolution years. Why was his wife half his age? How did he really become such a big land owner? The men had also mentioned that he had not inherited the land from his family members as he had claimed. He seemed like a good man now, but his real story was uncertain, just like his wife's future.

As they were chatting in front of the house, giving me some time to get up and get dressed, I called them back inside. "Is Margarita-Anna well enough to sit on the backseat?" I asked.

Martin looked at me and Antonio answered. "No. We will have to build a bed and install it in the back box. I will sit beside her for most of the ride. I would rather not leave her alone."

This was going to be a long trip. I hoped for them that the weather would remain nice.

Both of them left and I started to get ready to go get the posts. As I moved around the house, I realized I was getting more nervous with every passing second. I had a strange feeling it was not going to be just a simple ride.

As I looked in the fridge to get the bottle of chloride water, I heard a noise coming from the backyard. I stuck my head out and saw Don Angel, Pedro Sanchez, coming my way. He smiled at me as he passed through a flock of unperturbed chickens.

"Going on a trip?" He asked.

Geez! News travelled fast around here. "Yeah, I guess I am." I blurted. "Where have you been?" I kept going.

"I spent some time with my brother Felix." He answered.

"I don't suppose you'd want to tag along?" I half-jokingly asked.

"I would love to go with you if you think you need my help." He replied without hesitation.

"Are you serious?" I had to question because I could not believe him. "Would you really come with us?" I asked again.

"If you ask me nicely, why wouldn't I?"

He waited and I was not sure why. Did he really want me to ask in a nicer way or did he mean that I had already done it properly? Still, he waited. "Would you please come with me?" I finally dared to ask, again or for the first time.

"I would love to go with you Don Kristiano." Pedro said with his ever-present smile. He seemed so use to smiling, he could probably whistle at the same time.

Still, I was so happy, relieved. This guy was my saviour. I could now say good-bye to the long boring driving hours in front of me. I decided not to ask any more questions. I was happy about his decision and I did not want him to change his mind.

"I will be back soon." Pedro said and left from the same way he had arrived.

I decided not to even ask Martin or Antonio for permission, this was settled in my head. They were not the ones in charge of this expedition. I could invite anybody I wanted to since I was the one driving. I wanted to have some company and I would have it.

Antonio, Martin, and I worked on the posts until two in the afternoon and then returned home to prepare the trip. We parked the truck and I went inside to pack a small bag. I only needed clothes for two days, so I took some for three just to be sure. Martin checked out all the fluids under the hood and some men started to build the bed in the back. During that time, Antonio went back home with the mayor's chauffeur to get Margarita-Anna. The woman's condition was stable for the moment. The crisis she had had in El Chaparral had been her first and only. As for Pedro, I did not know where he was, I could only hope he would make it back in time to join the party.

I felt like Frodo at his departure from Elrond's house: I knew what I had to do and who would be with me, but I had no clue where I was going.

Later, Antonio arrived with Margarita-Anna and they came to see me right away. "I am really grateful for everything you are doing for us Señor." The woman started.

"Don't worry about it Margarita-Anna." I replied with my best public relation tone of voice.

"Please, just call me Anna from now on." She kindly demanded.

"I gladly will as long as you don't call me Señor anymore." I answered with a smile.

She gave me a look that assured me we had solid deal. Then, I caught a glance of Don Angel walking behind the house on the other side of the road. I was beginning to worry if he would make it.

At four thirty, the couple climbed aboard. They settled in the back and got comfortable as I chatted with Martin. "So you never told me, how's everything under the hood?"

"According to my mechanical expertise, it seems alright." Martin came back with.

"Do you have any mechanical expertise?" I questioned.

"Not really!" He answered and we both started laughing.

"Please do me a favour and tell Juanita I won't make it for dinner tonight." I demanded.

"Don't worry, she already knows." He said with a grin. "As we speak, the entire village, and maybe even others, know where you guys are going." My partner said.

I did not add anything; there was simply no need to. We shook and gave each other an honest smile. I turned back and I saw Pedro sitting in the truck. I was surprised, and very happy, to see him there. He was staring at the radio, probably looking for a good station to listen to on the way, just with that, I was already glad to have him with me.

I started going slowly. I could not believe how many people had come to see us off. It was not like we were leaving for a long time. Most of them waved and said encouraging things to the couple. If only I could have had their cheer as well. Over the last days, I had gotten to know some of these people, but only on a superficial level. The eyes staring at me seemed to beg me to save the couple. I looked at them in my rear-view mirror and they looked a lot further than they were in reality. I hoped it would not be the same for this adventure.

An instant later, all the villagers could see was the dust lifted by my wheels.

About thirty kilometres outside Cinco Pinos, I saw two people with shovels in the middle of the street. When they saw us arriving, they each went to a side and lifted a rope to create the weakest roadblock I had ever seen. "What are they doing?" I quickly asked Pedro.

"They are fixing holes on the road." He answered.

"Yes, I get that, but why are they blocking the way?" I enquired as we were getting closer to them.

"They hope that you will stop and give them money for their work." Pedro replied.

I hesitated a moment, not even knowing if I had some change in my pocket. I had been complaining about the holes for so long, I could not really ignore these workers. After all, they were doing it the capitalist way. I started to slow the vehicle down and Antonio's head appeared in the opened back window. "Don Kristiano, please we have no time to stop for anything. Just keep going." The husband said with a sorry, but serious tone.

"Well he's a real humanitarian!" I told my cabin partner.

Pedro looked at me. "Don't feel bad, these workers are also the ones coming at night to dig up new holes. Antonio knows that." He admitted.

"Lying bastards!" I was angry.

"It is what they have found to survive." He said in a sad tone of voice.

We drove for about an hour and stopped in Somotillo, the place of permanent heat wave. Antonio seemed to be known by everybody. There was a mixture of expression in the faces looking at him. Some liked him and others seemed to loathe him. We bought some food for the road. There was no way we were going to stop in restaurants along the way. We went into the same general store that Martin and I had been to on our first trip together. This time, there were also two kids staring at me like I was from outer space. It did not bother me. I totally ignored them and pretended that they were not even there. They would not have my sanity this time.

We finished our shopping, mostly fruit and vegetables, and all jumped back in the truck. The end of this first stop also marked the end of the gravel roads, hopefully for the rest of the journey. The paved way was still full of holes and no self-employed road-worker could do any good out here. A couple of times, I went straight into deep ones. I was looking at the scenery and Angel was always warning me when it was too late. A verb tense could change very quickly at eighty kilometres an hour.

Nothing happened between the first and second stop. The landscape remained the same for about an hour and a half. There was the temporary metal bridge over the river that had been placed there to replace the one that had been wiped out by Mitch. "How can the new bridge they're building look so cheap when the temporary one looks invincible?" I had to ask Pedro.

"They've borrowed it." He replied.

"From who?"

"You really don't know?" Don Angel responded.

"No reason, where did it come from?"

"USAID!" He shortly answered.

"What?"

"Why is it so hard to believe?"

"No, I guess I didn't expect to hear that answer. You mean that the US government paid for it, right?" I asked insistently.

"Yes, they did." He finished.

I was confused. I had been brainwashed to think the Americans were the baddies around here. I did not know what was going on, who to believe. In most front yards, I saw the red and black flag of the Sandinistas flying high at the end of a long pole. And yet, the States were lending out bridges.

We drove until Chinandega. It was still hot, even with the late hour of the day. At the first turn, there were about twenty strange little blue bags on the pavement. For about a block, I really wondered what they were. Then, I saw a vendor holding two or three full ones in his hand. They were filled with water, good clean water.

Nothing was going on. Our only distraction was a mentally-challenged child who pretended to be a rooster in front of our vehicle. When he saw us coming, he left the sidewalk and ran right in the middle of the road. He moved quickly, looking left and right with his head. About a hundred yards later, he decided to jump back on the sidewalk.

Every building looked the same. It was hard to tell the difference between a store and a house. The only one that came out of the ordinary was the Parroquier de Santa-Anna, a superb church, typically Latino. I could almost picture the little moustache over the door.

At Antonio's request, we parked right in front of it. He stepped out and started to chat with some guy who was wearing a green cape. It lasted about five long minutes before he finally came slowly walking our way. He went to check on his wife and came beside my opened window. "We will be spending the night in Chinandega." He said. "Anna can't stand it anymore. We will go at my brother-in-law's place." He completed.

Don Angel quickly jumped in the back seat as Antonio opened the front door to sit in the front with us. As we drove through the streets of the city, I realized that the husband knew a lot of people here. He waved to about twelve people in about eleven minutes, or the opposite. Since Pedro did not salute anyone, I had to ask Antonio. "How come you know all these people?"

"Most of them are originally from villages up north."

"Aren't they worried about overpopulation if all the villagers come down to the city?"

"Not really, many Chinandega natives moved to the capital so it all evens out." He explained.

It was strange how people always seemed to think it was better somewhere else. Maybe it was easier to succeed in a foreign land where no one knew you, after all, was Adolph not born in Austria?

The brother-in-law, married to Antonio's sister, was named Leandro. He barely looked at me when we arrived so I did not really pay any attention to him either. It was hard to read him at first sight. Well, all I knew for sure was that his T-shirt had been washed recently and it had been dried on a clothesline. I could not describe his attitude, except maybe that he was extremely arrogant. Nothing against arrogance, but you had to be able to back it up. The perfect example would be the Bambino with the final point of the nineteen-thirty-two World Series.

Leandro's house was small for the amount of occupants. He only had three children, which was pretty normal for an urban family. At some point, I had to go to the toilet. When I pushed the door open and turned on the light, I was relieved not to see any cockroaches running for their lives. In my opinion, it was the major distinction between the Nicaraguan city and the country side. The sewer system was terrible, but at least it existed and it was enough for me. I was also happily surprised to find a seat over the chubby white chair. The toilet seat was definitely a comfort that I used to take for granted, but not anymore. It was pretty understandable, because other than my summer camping trips, I had never been deprived of it. How could I have known?

Antonio did not seem close to neither his sister nor her husband. It was like they had seen each other just last week. "They're not the tightest family." I quietly declared to Don Angel.

He hesitated and then said. "I guess you're right. Most husbands are not the nicest they could be with their wives. It is sometimes difficult for brothers-in-law to get along."

"It's funny because honestly, I can't picture Antonio being a totally faithful husband." I admitted.

"You could be right, but that does not mean he does not condone it when it is done to his own sister."

"So it's okay for them to hurt their wives, but not their sisters?"

He looked around to make sure we were alone, which he seemed to do often, and then said. "It depends who does the deed." Don Angel paused. "Families stick together. In case of a separation, it is not rare to see the former spouse go live with a family member."

"Regardless of how they feel about each other, we will spend the night here." I expressed out loud to convince myself.

Antonio and Leandro took the bed out of the truck and put it inside, beside the kitchen table. The brother-in-law was a mechanic and owned a decent garage just around the corner. The women were left alone and the men decided to go hang out in the car-hospital.

As they left, I listened to the conversation going on between them, it was purely superficial. After all, he was a mechanic. Most of them could not be trusted; I preferred to stay away from him.

"You do not seem to like this guy?" Don Angel asked me.

"I don't mind him personally, I just distrust his profession."

"Why is that?"

"I'm not sure how things are around here, but back home all mechanics suffer from the same sickness: immorality." I made sure the brother-in-law could not hear me and carried on. "You see, they hold the biggest end of the wrench and they know it. Their work is easy, but it is very complicated for us. We have no clue what's going on under the hood. These people have the power to do whatever they want."

"Don Kristiano, some of them know that the world is what we make of it." He said with a slight hope in his voice.

"I'm sure some of them do, they're just not the ones who have fixed my car lately. Mechanics always want more money."

"Are you not like that? There must be times when you want to have more?" Don Angel asked.

I did not want to admit he was right. "Maybe, when I'm taking a shower back home, I always want more hot water." I paused when I saw his expression of confusion. "Surely you must be like that as well."
"I can not say, I have never taken a hot shower before." He admitted. "I think you are off the subject. Mechanics can not all be bad and you know it."

"I don't like to be had and they don't seem to mind doing it. Isn't the engine supposed to be dirtier than the guy fixing it?"

I waited for a response, he softly said. "There is no answer to that question." He stopped and then went on. "Don't take this the wrong way Don Kristiano, but maybe, and I do mean maybe, if your society was not so centered on money, this sort of behaviour would not happen." Pedro concluded.

Anna and her sister were sitting at the main table so I went to the back room. On the wall, there was a dart board with the word *Tacho* written in the middle. I had no clue what that meant, but I was not about to ask. The three kids were running around the room. Women here seemed to spend their whole life taking care of their children. What were their life pleasures? Was the satisfaction coming from raising little people great enough? These females required a sort of feminist association. I did not think they should go to the extreme as some do back home. Although women here deserved more and should definitely start asking for it, they should never aspire to be as equally dumb as men.

We left in the very early morning. Luckily, there was no traffic. I plainly hated to stare at the licence plate in front of me, waiting for it to push the car forward. I drove silently, the couple was still in the back and Don Angel was by my side. Things were quiet and it was just fine that way.

At some point I remembered yesterday's dart board. "What does Tacho mean?" I asked Don Angel.

"It's the nickname of the Somozas." He answered.

"Somozas, with an *S*?" I was confused.

"There were actually three; the third one was the worst."

"What's his story? How did he get to be badder than the other two?"

"If you really want to know, he studied in the United States at West Point Military Academy."

I was stunned by his answer. "You're joking, right?" I had to say.

"I am sorry, Don Kristiano, but it is a fact. Do not worry though, there is nothing saying that he would not have been the same if he had not gone to that school." He replied quietly.

"Maybe it would've been worst."

"Who knows?"

I did not to continue the discussion. It was too early for me to learn new stuff about American atrocities.

Just after a sign announcing the proximity of Leon, Antonio banged on the window. "Just keep going. Anna is sleeping and I do not want to wake her." Soon after, maybe because he guessed my disappointment, he climbed on the side and slipped himself inside the truck, through the back window. He did it with such agility, as if there was nothing to it. "I'm sorry if you wanted to stop. We have no business going there. Anna was not able to sleep very well last night and I think she can use the rest." I simply nodded and he kept going. "Did you know that Leon has the biggest cathedral in Central America?"

I knew he wanted to distract me and it was fine. "No I didn't know that." I replied. "I don't know much about Leon." I admitted, trying to make him feel guilty for not allowing me a quick visit.

"It's mostly a University city with a lot of students." He paused and seemed to ask himself if I truly wanted to hear about it.

"Go on!" I said, making it easier on him.

"During the dictatorial years, one of the only traditions honoured was that soldiers had no right to enter universities. Because of that, students could discuss anything they wanted. Of course, they did not talk about the weather, they got the Revolution organized. They convinced each other and it got things moving."

I could have told him about the trivial stuff discussed by students in our universities, but it would only have made us seem inferior.

"My personal hero studied here, you know. This is where Omar Cabezas started as a regular student and went up to train in the mountains. There, he became a great Sandinistas leader."

Was this going to be another anti-American discussion? Since I would never know by staying silent, so I decided to ask. "Did you ever meet him?"

"Our paths crossed once or twice, but we never spoke." He proudly, and also disappointingly, said.

"I can't say I really know what went on around here." I admitted without real interest. I knew a bit about the Contra, but had no clue as to what had happened before.

"Well, since we have time, would you like me to tell you?" He asked.

"Of course." I answered.

"It all began in nineteen-ten; the Unitedstatesians took over José Zelaya's government." He paused when he saw the expression on my face, but then kept going. I did not think he would start so early. I mean, why not tell me about the time Christopher Columbus showed up? With these thoughts, I missed the reasons why the Americans did it, but it did not matter, he went on. "This is when the first Somoza seized power. Since the Unitedstatesian President responsible for the coup could not trust anyone, he decided to leave his Marines behind. The first resistance appeared about ten years later. It was lead by a small Marxist man who thought of himself as a nationalist. His name was Augusto Sandino. This man was able to kick the Marines out with a promise to surrender when they would leave. Before they left, they trained what was called the National Guard. It was the same kind of military unit, only from Nicaragua and under Somoza's total control. Unitedstatesians departed, Sandino surrendered, and was shot almost instantly." Antonio told me.

I felt like I was listening to a movie summary. It all seemed so distant, probably because it was all so new to me.

He carried on. "A little later, the first Somoza dictator was assassinated at a ball by a poet called Lopez. The dictator's son, Luis, took over until he too died, this time of a heart attack. Then the third Somoza came to power, the one who sadly popularize the nickname Tacho, even though he was the second to use it. He went on a destructive rampage across the land. He did everything he could to get money. The National Guard became unstable; they too wanted their share of the wealth. Some of them could even be bought rather easily." Antonio paused a bit and went on. "Then somebody was assassinated and that did not please the Unitedstatesians government; they could not back Tacho up anymore."

"What happened?" I asked.

"It's a different story; I will tell you later." He looked out the window and started going with looking back in. "Since the beginning of the sixties, people had had enough. They had gotten organized and had formed the FSLN. I could tell you a lot about it, but the bottom line is that they fought until victory, until July seventeenth nineteen-seventy-nine when they walked in the streets of Managua to seize power."

I was a bit stunned by this premature ending. I thought he would go on for hours. "What about the dictator, what happened to him?" I at least questioned.

"When he was overthrown in seventy-nine, he owned about three quarters of Nicaragua's wealth. Tacho first tried to flee to the United states, but he quickly realized he would not be safe there. He decided to take refuge in Paraguay. The then dictator would accommodate every scum of the earth to hide in his country. Among other things, it was a paradise for old Nazis." Antonio stopped talking when a car came dangerously close to our left. "Somoza did not have much time to enjoy his exile. He was surprised by a bazooka rocket that entered his car, uninvited, and officially made it his last ride." He said.

"Who killed him?" I decided to ask, even though, it seemed like an obvious answer.

"Honestly, I'm not sure. I know it was not me. I have never officially heard the assassination claimed by anyone."

"Sandinistas?" I interrupted.

"That was also my first thought, but I doubt it. Somoza was no longer getting in the way; they would not have wanted to resurrect their enemy's anger. If you really want my opinion, the Unitedstatians killed him." My partner paused when he saw the expression on my face change. "Think about it, Don Kristiano. They never could have totally controlled the Contra army if the dictator had been alive. They needed him out of their way." Antonio finished. He then gave me a tap on the shoulder and went out back the same way he had come in.

I looked at the road ahead and thought about his story. "Rich folks must have been pretty angry when they learned that they would now have to share their wealth." I said out loud to myself.

Pedro took over. "It was no longer about money for the revolutionaries, it was surviving. Tens of thousands of people, poor ones mostly, died for a change of government, Don Kristiano." He answered in a sad tone of voice.

"You don't know exactly how many?" I questioned for the heck of it.

"Our country is not organized like yours. Some people up in the mountains do not have a birth-certificate, a health card, or a driver's licence to identify them. Many of them die unrecognized, without burial or even anybody knowing." Don Angel explained.

"You don't believe in the revolution? Didn't you participate in it?" I asked intriguingly.

"I managed to stay out of it, but I could not stay out of the Contra Revolution, even if I wanted to." He abruptly finished with.

I stayed silent and kept driving; it was a beautiful day.

CHAPTER 3.2

We arrived in the country's biggest city in the beginning of the afternoon. Antonio climbed inside his usual way and sat in the backseat. "Take the first street on your left." He directed.

"So, you know anything about the capital?" I asked the husband for the heck of it.

He hesitated a bit, not seeming to know what he should say. "Do you?"

Not really, but although not much, I had done a bit of reading before I left home. "When you look up the industrial productions of the capital, beer is listed first." I replied.

He briefly laughed. "Be serious, the city can be dangerous. People get killed for a watch." The husband advised.

"Really?!" Hopefully, it was just the villager in him speaking; country boys do get nervous when they come to the big city.

"Well, they get killed for other things to, but just be careful."

"I will!"

Antonio easily showed me the way to the general hospital and we parked right in front of the door. He and Anna went inside and told us to stay in the truck.

A few minutes later, Don Angel decided to go in to find out what was up.

Thirty minutes passed until Antonio came out with Pedro behind him. "They said it could take up to four hours."

"That's too bad."

"There is no reason for you to wait around. Why don't you go for a ride or something? Go see the Masaya." The husband recommended.

"What's that?"

"A volcano."

"Sure, why not?" I replied. I had always wanted to see a real one. "Is it safe?" Really, was there any chance of eruption?

"Do you have a watch?"

"No."

"Then you should be fine!" He managed to crack a smile.

I said goodbye and jumped in the truck. To my great surprise Don Angel also climbed in and tagged alone.

"They do not need me for this." He said with a grin.

"Do you know how to get there?"

"Not really, but I think we can find the way."

"Are you sure? Maybe we should ask for direction."

"Trust me, my intuition will show us the way."

"Your what?" I asked puzzled.

"Intuition." He repeated. "Maybe you should learn to listen to yours." He said.

"You're just too macho to admit you need help." I replied.

"It's amazing how wrong about me you can be sometimes. For the time that you have known me, what have I ever done to be considered macho today?" He almost sadly inquired.

"Nothing, I'm sorry." I admitted.

"Now let's drive and go check out the mamacitas on Main Street!" He jokingly ordered.

"Is that your intuition talking?"

"No, but seriously, you must let you insights resurface. You can control your subconscious mind." Don Angel said.

"Give me an example."

"Just think about when you have to get up without an alarm clock, you usually wake up on time, right? It is your sub-conscience. You could even set your brain to always look at your watch at the changing of the minutes and you would be successful. When it is cold outside, picture yourself on a beach with a nice breeze blowing in your face and you will be alright. All you need to do is believe." He finished as he pointed a road to turn on.

The more we were getting away from the city the more poverty was getting apparent. How was it possible to live this way? I saw, from my own eyes, a sixty-year-old woman walking naked in the street. The only thing hiding her was a cardboard plate that she used to cover her breast with. I was shocked by the scene, but it saddened me even more to realize that I would surely soon forget.

We made it to the entrance of the park without getting lost and bought ourselves some tickets. The girl in the booth made a mistake and only charged me for one person, I did not correct her. So what if one of us walked around the volcano for free, it would not take anything from them.

When she gave me the brochure, I learned that there were actually two volcanoes, the Nindiri and of course, the Masaya.

The road to go up was winding. There were some trees boarding it closely, leaving no room for a sidewalk. The pavement was a mixture of black and red, arguing on both sides of the yellow line.

When we arrived at the top, I parked the truck and some woman came straight for me. I thought she would ask to check our tickets. "Could you park your vehicle the other way Sir?" She simply demanded.

I did not answer out loud and executed her order. Still, I wondered why. Did I need to be ready to escape in case the volcano erupted?

We got out of the truck. There was a thick smoke elevating in the air, coming out of the huge hole. It was very windy. The facades were grey, brown and black. I had no clue why I was impressed. After all, it all looked like an enormous kettle. "We could walk up the stairs to the cross of Bobadilla." Don Angel suggested.

"Let's go!" I did not need a guide, I had Pedro with me and somehow he knew a lot about everything.

"This volcano erupted around the year five thousand B.C. and it created the largest eruption known to mankind. The Spaniards called it the mouth of hell. They are the ones who planted this cross during the sixteenth century." He explained.

"Why did they do that?" I asked.

"To exorcise the demon of fire."

"I guess it was more active in the old days."

"Before the Conquistadors, the indigenous people believed the eruptions represented the Gods' anger. Many people, mostly women and children, were sacrificed to calm down the anger of Chaciutique." He desolately said.

"Another perfect example of men's stupidity." I replied.

"I am not sure it is stupidity, Don Kristiano, it is insecurity, fear. Men simply need to believe they are safe."

"In my book, it's still sad to lose an innocent life to appease the fictitious wrath of a natural phenomenon."

"Sad, I agree, but it is important to believe in something."

"Even if it is not true?" I questioned.

"Even if it is not true." Pedro answered.

Once we were at the top of the stairs, the view was magnificent. We looked around for a bit. On the bottom part of the hill, we could see traces of lava. There was a huge trail of black little rocks crossing the fields after following the edge. The wind was still strong, coming from the north, forcing the vertical line of clouds to move south. I had to properly tie my cap so it would not fly away, with this ever-present sun, it would be a dreadful loss.

On my way down, I noticed that Don Angel and I were moving a lot faster than the other visitors. Maybe it was proving the fact that my job in the mountains had put me in great physical shape. "Look at those tourists, walking around like turtles." I made the mistake of saying out loud.

"They are going at their own pace, Don Kristiano." He retaliated.

I waited a while. "I don't really like tourists." I had to admit.

"Why not? They are opening their minds to different cultures, new ideas. What can be wrong with that?"

"I don't know. I see them taking pictures, hear them talking loudly and it disgusts me. You're right, they are opening their minds, but they're doing it for the wrong reason."

"You are generalizing."

"Maybe!" I agreed. "If you ask me, tourists can be separated in two groups: the backpackers and the baby-boomers."

"Is there one better than the other?" He asked with a hopeful tone.

"It's hard to say. The first ones dress like bums, but with quality clothing. They have greasy hair, but hold it with three-hundred-dollar sunglasses."

"And the second group?"

"The old ones can easily be spotted by the whiteness of their hair and running shoes."

"What?" Pedro said intriguingly.

"Most of them just buy their runners before leaving and only wear them inside the house."

"Why would they do that?"

"To break them in, so they won't get any uncomfortable blisters on their trip." I paused and looked at a bunch of horses in a faraway field. "They have a city map in the back pocket and a huge camera around their neck. They take pictures of everything and everybody, without asking permission."

"They just want some souvenirs and sometimes they take it clumsily, but they are only human." He defended.

"I just don't want to be compared with them." I finally admitted.

"These people want to see the same things as you. You look at the same attractions. Perhaps, the way they do things is different, but it is the same for every situation in life. It is not what you do that counts, it is how you do it." He preached.

We both kept our mouths shut for a bit and looked at the herd walking around the volcano.

"There must be a lot of tourism where you live. Can you not find anything good about it?" Don Angel asked.

"Of course I can: they bring in money. Talk about it to restaurant owners. Unlike me, they love tourists and it's not for their charming attitude. It's the same all over the world. It's not all bad; just look at the mountain gorillas in Rwanda or somewhere around there. The only way the government was able to stop poachers from exterminating them was to charge tourists close to three hundred US dollars for a safari. With the money, they were finally able to pay decent salaries to forest rangers and stop the extermination."

"I'm glad to see you can find some positive." Pedro said.

"Yes, they're financing a good cause, but they are still pathetic to me." I paused when I saw Pedro's disappointed expression, but I continued nonetheless. "The worst one I heard happens in Thailand. Many hospitals there don't accept patient with AIDS so they go die in some sort of camp." I took a breather. Pedro did not seem to know where I was going with this. "The camp operators need money to buy food for the invalids, so they actually let tourists in to watch these people slowly die. They probably bring their video cameras, Don Angel, for God's sake!" I exclaimed and then stayed silent.

He did not reply right away. "Do you know anyone who went to Thailand?" He asked.

"Yes, I do actually."

"Did they visit such places?"

"Not to my knowledge, no." I retaliated. "And they didn't take advantage of kiddie porn." I added. Now I was the one who did not know where he was going.

"What does that tell you?" He demanded with a serious tone. I did not answer. I knew that he wanted me to admit that there was always going to be bad ones and good ones, no matter what the human group was called. I stayed silent and acknowledged with a nod and apologetic eyes.

"I rest my case, your honour." He teasingly concluded.

Suddenly, some guy stepped out from behind the edge. Some guy, tall, with long curly brown hair tied in a pony tail. He was poorly shaven and seemed generally cool. He joined the group of tourists at the back, but did not look like he belonged there. He was probably Dutch or German, was there even a difference between the two? I felt like chatting him up. I wanted to prove my tourist-traveller theory to Don Angel. "Let's follow them!" I proposed.

The group took the right path and the traveler halted. He fixed his pony tail, destroyed by the strong winds and decided to hang a left. It was my occasion to join him. I had a feeling he could entertain me a bit; change my set of mind.

There was a paved road cutting the path in two. Curiously there was a sign to warn cars not to drive on it. I was glad the German had chosen this different path. The mountain on the left had intrigued me from the start.

As we walked up, a second sign announced a panoramic view at a hundred meters. Nothing spectacular seemed to be waiting for me where the indication had said. At best, it was probably a view over Lake Managua.

Later the *camino* ended with a tiny brick fence. The guy was nowhere in sight. I was disappointed, but I kept moving forward. The wall started to go down and the scenery behind went up. Right in front of our eyes, the mountain just transformed itself into a gigantic crater, full of magnificent trees with many different shades of green. Birds flew at the bottom of it, protected from the high wind. It was breathtaking.

The first volcano I had seen earlier was only smoke. It was a dead hole made of black and grey stones. I had forgotten the traveller and the tourists. I could barely see Don Angel beside me. We started walking on the path that surrounded the opening. I carefully followed the edge, falling down was not an option. My acolytes in the capital would be in big trouble if something happened to me.

Then, the European popped up in front of us. "Nice view!" He started very naturally, like he was waiting for me.

"Yeah, it's a great place!" I answered as we both looked around. I spotted the black, red and yellow flag on his knapsack: I was right, German. We then went through every little trivial travelling question, the typical custom-agent interrogations. "Well take care now!" He wished and just left.

Don Angel and I looked at each other with the same puzzled expression. He was first to break the silence. "I guess travellers do not have a lot of social skills." He joked.

"Not this one anyway." I agreed and looked back at the first volcano. "I love the Masaya. It's so alive. It's cool to see the white smoke coming out. It's like a giant kettle."

"Personally I prefer this Nindiri. It is like its death has given him another chance." Pedro joyfully replied.

I enjoyed the scenery so much I did not want to leave anymore. We started walking again for as long as we could. I then looked at my watch and realized we had been gone for almost two hours. It was time to make our way back. We could not take the chance to make the couple wait in the parking lot. I was not a tourist or a traveller. I was unique, somewhere in between, and it was time for me to go back.

When we arrived at the hospital, there was no sign of Antonio or Anna, only a bunch of kids running around, asking for money. I did not give them any. My little bills were all stacked up with the big ones and I did not want them to start begging for more. "No tengo, no tengo!" I just kept repeating. Just beside us, there was a cute little baby in a child's arms, her big brother perhaps. The tiny infant kept staring into the eyes of Don Angel. It was pretty wonderful to see the way their two pairs of eyes met.

Since, we still had about thirty minutes to kill, we decided to abandon the children and go for a ride.

We looked for the main street, but did not really find it. "Isn't there a center somewhere in this city?" I annoyingly asked Don Angel.

"Not really."

"Why is that?"

"I guess they never figured out where to put it exactly when they rebuilt everything after the earthquake." He answered.

"Geez, there was an earthquake as well..."

"It was a big one too; destroyed most of the city. Only two buildings out of ten were still standing." He pointed with his right finger to a street that opened into a nice square. "This is probably the touristiest place in Managua. It is called the Plaza de la Republica."

There was a magnificent cathedral by the lakeside and other beautiful buildings. I parked the truck and we went to sit on a bench close to a burning flame. I wondered why it was there, probably to symbolize the revolution. I did not feel like asking Pedro. I had had enough war stories and history lessons for a while. I wanted to relax and appreciate the moment. I remembered how this capital was supposed to be extremely violent. I personally did not see it. Maybe I felt secure because I was with Don Angel. Locals would not try to rob me with one of their kind beside me.

In front of us, there was a small child with a red t-shirt trying to sell some popcorn to a backpacker. Judging from the guy's hat, I presumed he was from Australia.

There were a lot of people coming and going. I would have liked to be alone to enjoy the square, in silence. "Do you see this building, Don Kristiano?" Pedro questioned as he pointed towards it. "It is the Palacio Nacional. If you want to know what Augusto Sandino looked like, you can go in and you will see a great painting."

"Not right now, thanks. Anyway, I've seen enough graffiti to give me a great idea." I paused and examined the boy with the Aussie. "Augusto was the man with the amazingly huge hat, right?" I continued.

"For you yes, but he was a lot more than that for Nicaraguans."

"I'm sure he was."

"There is also a portrait of Carlos Fonseca."

"Sorry, Pedro, but I'm not really in the mood for it at the moment." I looked in his eyes and saw disappointment. "I just don't feel like learning about the revolution. I'm worried about Anna." That was not entirely true, but I figured it would give me a break.

"Alright then, make sure you do not go into this building, it is the Museo de la Revolución." He said with his typical smile.

Then, we were spooked by some shouts coming from a gathering of people. Some policemen were having an altercation with a woman carrying a child on her back, surely a dangerous criminal. The mother was arguing with the officers as the baby was crying his heart out. People were looking on without interfering in any way. Why would I be any different? Don Angel got up and went to sniff around.

I was touched on the left shoulder with what seemed to be a very tiny index. When I turned back, the boy with the red T-shirt was standing right beside me. "Hey Yankee sir, want to buy me a bag of popcorn?" He offered as the baby stopped crying.

"I don't know, how much?"

"Thirty-five centavos."

I checked my pockets and I did not have any small bills. I realized I did not have to feel guilty for not having given anything to the children at the hospital earlier. "Do you have any change?" I asked the boy. He signalled no with his head. "Well I can't buy a bag, I only have twenty centavos." I said with the most desolated tone I could take.

"You must have more than that! I need to sell this popcorn or my mother will be furious." He explained with puppy dog eyes.

"It's not a question of spending the money, I just don't have it." I said, looking for an out. I thought about the Australian to distract him. "Did the man in front buy some?"

"He did not want to, he is very bad person." He explained as he pointed to the backpacker.

The kid was cute and intrigued me. "Does this mean that I'm a bad man if I don't buy a bag?"

He ignored my question and asked one of his own. "Do you have American coins? I would very much like to see one."

"I'm sorry; I don't have any, but wait a second." I looked in my backpack and found a few Francs. "I do have one from Switzerland though."

"Where is that?"

"It's in Europe." I answered as I turned around to look and see where Don Angel had wondered off to.

"Sure. I accept." He said and I showed him the coin.

"Since I can't buy a bag, you can keep this coin as a souvenir if you like." I finished.

He took the money and asked. "What is your name Yankee Sir?"

"Kristiano! How about you?"

"Osmar!"

"Do you sell your popcorn everyday?"

"Yes, everyday when school ends, until eight o'clock in the evening."

I felt bad for him. At that time, it was dark around here. "Please take these two ten centavos pieces. I don't need them; you'll find more use for them." I would have liked to tell him to keep it for himself and not give it to his mother, but I did not want to rebel his innocent mind. "I have to leave now." I announced.

"Where do you have to go?"

"The hospital."

"Are you sick?" He intriguingly asked.

"No, but a friend of mine is."

"Is he seriously ill?" Osmar said as he put his little hand on my thighs.

"It's a woman and we don't know yet. That's what I have to go find out." I searched for Pedro with my eyes.

"I want you to have a bag." He whispered and he put the bag right on my chest. It was so sweet the way he had spoken so softly, as if he had not wanted anybody else to hear him.

"No, I cannot accept. You keep it and you'll sell it to another customer." I replied.

"I want you to be the one to have it, not another customer. Share it with your sick lady friend; it will make her feel better." He insisted.

"Okay, I'll take the bag and when I'm finished at the hospital, I'll return and give you the money."

"That is fine, I have to go. There are a lot of other places for me to work." He paused, smiled and carried on. "Just accept the present and say thank you."

"I'm sorry. Thank you very much. I truly appreciate your gift, Osmar." I was in disbelief towards his generosity. He had nothing and yet he still managed to give. This boy had definitely taught me a lesson, now I just had to figure out what it was.

I walked to the vehicle and reflected on a few things. Pedro joined me. "I just proved that I'm not a tourist." I announced to him.

"Why's that?"

"Osmar gave me the evidence I needed."

"Go on."

"You see, I'm different from that Australian. I did not just reject this little boy with the red t-shirt. He was interesting to me, more than a part of the scenery. I listened to him and heard his words instead of simply taking a picture of him." I explained.

"Well good for you, you are making my country a better place." Don Angel congratulated.

"I'm serious, I feel like I have a purpose and this couple at the hospital needed my help." I said to convince him.

"You do not have to convince me, I am sold. I am just glad you are as well." He studied me for a bit and continued on with. "Did you hear it clearly, Don Kristiano?"

"Hear what?" I replied.

"Don't reminisce about the past or envision the future: just accept the present and say thank you." Don Angel concluded.

Funny, it was not the lesson I believed Osmar had taught me. "He was a cute boy, I wished I could have had more coins on me, or at least thank him in a better way." I confessed to my partner.

"Don't worry, you can always find someone else to pay it forward." My friend said.

I smiled and got into the vehicle.

We arrived, again, at the hospital and, this time, saw our couple sitting on a bench. Antonio came to join us and left Anna sitting by herself. "The first diagnosis is not good. We have to wait for a second, and better, one. I am really sorry, but we cannot go anywhere yet." He started.

"How come it's taking so long?" I asked.

"What do you mean so long? This is the fastest it has ever been." He said as he stared at me with a look of surprise. "We usually have to wait for days. I was able to get us in because one of the doctors is an old army buddy of mine." The husband carried on.

"I know what you mean. It's the same where I come from. If you want to receive healthcare quickly, you either have to know somebody or be somebody known. Of course, if you're a dog that goes to the veterinarian, you're on the operation table minutes after you walk in." I explained.

He ignored my comment. "We will stay here and wait."

"Would you like company?" I shallowly proposed.

"No, not really. Why don't you go and grab something to eat. You can come back in an hour and it should be fine." He counter-proposed.

"Sure!" I finished. They wanted to be left alone; all I could do was obey Antonio's suggestion.

A few blocks away, we found a little café and entered. The establishment was not great, but it would have to do for now. With the looks of its concrete walls and wooden tables, not much could be expected from its kitchen. It was obvious that Mister Hygiene had not been here for a few years; maybe he had never been here at all.

We sat down and I chose what I was going to order. Don Angel said he was not hungry; this meal would have to be enjoyed in solo. It was all very fast, the menu was on the table and the waitress, who was astonishingly cute, took my order right away.

"You should try the local rum; it's the best in the world." Pedro encouraged me.

If he had said the best in Central America I would have believed him, but the world was pushing it. "I thought beer was the specialty around here?" I teasingly enquired.

"Yes, but personally I prefer the rum."

The lovely waitress showed up and silently waited for our order. "Alright Señorita: a couple of rums to start with."

When she went away, Pedro said. "I'm sorry, I don't drink."

"What do you mean you don't drink? Why did you say you preferred rum? How do you know if this rum's even good?"

He seemed embarrassed. "Well, I used to drink alcohol a long time ago, but I stopped. If I still drank, I would prefer the rum that's all." Don Angel said.

"Fine! I'll just have both glasses." I did not usually drink rum, but I figured it would be a good opportunity for me to start. This way, every time I would drink rum in my life, I would remember this day, in Nicaragua.

The waitress brought the couple of drinks and gave me the most exquisite smile I had ever seen. She was so attractive, she made me regret the fact that I was only here for a few more hours. As she went away, Pedro caught me staring at her derrière and gave me a huge smile.

The girl brought my food plate and I quietly ate my meal, chicken, avocado salad and some fried plantains. It was very good, very filling, I could not even finish. The alcohol started to kick in. My partner stayed silent, simply looking around in his usual way. The waitress smiled at me from the end of the room. The whole situation was ticking me off. Why could I not meet a girl like that at home? I laid my lower arms on the table and pushed my hands down with my chin. I dozed off for a few seconds.

Suddenly, a tall glass of water was put in front of me and I heard Don Angel say a word that resembled: "bamosse". I drank the glass down without thinking of future possible diarrhoea complication and went to pay the *quanta*. As I walked towards the cashier, I realized that those glasses of rum had taken their tow, more than I had though they would. I felt dizzy, very dizzy. I probably could not drive for a while. I would have to teach Pedro or Antonio. I paid and asked for some coins to give to poor buggers... beggars outside.

My head was pounding like a hammer on my shoulders. I tried very hard to walk straight and not touch any lines on the sidewalk. Some underprivileged kids came running in my direction when they saw me arriving. Before they could reach me, I threw a few coins up in the air. When I saw the change flying, I had the feeling of repaying Osmar: the popcorn kid. It was as if I was helping them in their life struggle. After this thought, I felt pretty pathetic, a few coins in the air and I was their saviour? I was proud to give them spare change I would never use: my selfishness had no boundary.

When we re-re-arrived at the hospital's parking lot, the couple was still sitting on the same bench as before. Anna seemed dreadfully angry. It was weird for me to see her like this. I had never imagined her even raising her voice and now I could even see the muscles in her jaw jumping. Maybe I was hallucinating. My head was still turning. "Qué pasa amigos?" I initiated to try to lighten the mood.

They both looked at me and Antonio started to speak. "It is official now, it's Graves disease." He said with a depressed tone of voice.

"I'm truly sorry." I replied, trying to sound honest. Strangely, I was not sure I truly was. I did not really know this woman, and I was drunk. "What's going on now? Can they cure it?"

"There are some treatments available but..." The husband tried to say.

"I don't want them!" Anna interrupted.

I looked at them in confusion. "At this late stage of the pregnancy, the treatments could be harmful to the foetus, even fatal." Antonio put his right hand on his wife's left arm and carried on. "Iodine can cause major problems to the placenta, but that's not all. There is some kind of radioactive iodine that they have to use and this one can be catastrophic for the thyroid gland, the mother's and the baby's."

"Jesus!" This was way too much for my half-drunken state of mind. "So what's going on now?" I repeated my question.

"If the treatments are done, the child could have physical and mental damage." Anna irritably answered my question.

The husband looked at me with a sympathetic eye. I did not know what to reply at all, I was glad when he started speaking again. "They could always try to bring out the baby by caesarean, but they do not guarantee anything."

"They don't even guarantee we'll have a spot in the delivery room. How can they guarantee success of the operation?" Anna said angrily.

I stared at them, waiting to hear what was happening next.

"They cannot save the baby. They said they could the last times and they did not." She started weeping.

I was confused and Antonio noticed it. "We have expected other children over the years and they have never made it as far as this one." Antonio paused. "There also was some hypothyroidism involved. Graves disease usually comes after a pregnancy. We simply do not know if we can trust these Cubans anymore."

"Cubans?" I said.

"Sorry, I did not mean it in a bad way. It is just that before the Revolution there were not really any medical students in Nicaragua, most doctors used to come from Cuba." Antonio clarified.

"So we no longer need to stay in Managua?" I gently enquired.

"No, we don't." Anna said.

"Back to the village..." I said, but I cut myself off when I noticed two doctors coming out of the hospital. One went straight to his car and the other looked at us. He hesitated for a moment and then came our way. I could tell he was a true Nicaraguan by the looks of him. He signalled Antonio to meet him half way. The husband accepted his invitation and dragged me along. As I followed him, I was amazed at how straight I could walk. This intense conversation had definitely pushed most of the alcohol out of my system.

The doctor began. "Again, I'm sorry Franco, but there is nothing we can do for your wife if you are not willing to sacrifice the baby."

I was spooked, I had no clue Anna's life was in danger. And why was this guy calling Antonio *Franco*? The conversation was fast and almost whispered. There were also many technical terms that my knowledge of Spanish did not allow me to fully comprehend. For what I understood, the doctor was suggesting that we looked for *softer* medicine. I did not know what he meant and he noticed my puzzled expression. "Look for a Shaman." He straightforwardly said as he fixed me in the eyes.

"A Shaman?" I said and laughed. "No problem, I think I just saw one on the square earlier." I sarcastically told them.

He smiled politely. "A *real* one, not a trap for tourists like you." The doctor paused and studied me. He seemed to realized he had insulted me with his tourist comparison. "I think you know what I mean." He added.

"I'm not sure." I admitted. When we left the village, I knew what to look for, now it was becoming very different. "Where can they find a Shaman, in a cave behind a huge waterfall?" I asked to both men.

Antonio lowered his eyes to the ground and it was the doctor who spoke. "They don't usually hang out in the city. Governments pushed them away. Most doctors take a strong stand against them. Make no mistake about it, although they are very rare, they still exist. You will have to go south and search the farthest villages."

"It's like looking for a ghost." I said with a mocking smiled, after all we could always just go buy ourselves a ouija board. "That's fine, but where do we stop, La Tierra de Fuego?" I questioned.

Antonio lifted his head. "We will turn back before South America, do not worry." He replied in a serious tone.

Before South America, I came close to asking him if he was joking. Really, why not make it to Cape Horn, just to say we have been there? "I'm surprised you believe in them. I thought you said that doctors took stand against them." I sardonically declared.

The man in the long white coat waited a bit. "I am simply suggesting it to you." He answered.

Anna had gotten tired of standing alone. She had decided to go and sit in the back of the truck on her bench. I turned my head and looked at Don Angel in the car. Predictably, he had gone to sit with the woman. I wondered why he was not taking part in this manly discussion. "Is it really possible or are you sending us out to look for false hope, so we don't pack your hospital or your guilty conscience?" I questioned.

Antonio seemed to agree with me on this one. "Seriously, do you believe it is possible?" The husband asked.

"A Shaman will be able to help your wife. This I guarantee." The doctor declared and paused. He brought his two hands to his top shirt buttons and started to undo them. As he did it, I could see on his left wrist a little bracelet filled with white bones. He opened his shirt and showed us his heart. There was a strange tattoo painted over a thin scar. "Remember seventy-eight when you left me for dead in the jungle, Franco?" He asked Antonio. The husband's face turned to shame. "A Shaman was there for me." The doctor concluded with a solemn tone of voice. He pointed at both our hearts. "Now the question is: Do *you* believe a Shaman can help your wife?" He questioned.

"Okay, where do we start looking?" Antonio asked.

"I am not sure. The one I met has surely been dead for a long time. Your best bet would be to go south, away from big cities, and ask villagers for advice along the way." The doctor instructed.

"That's it?" I retorted. I could not believe we would seriously set off to search for a shaman.

"I know that one of my colleagues knows a guy in the San Jose Hospital that might know something."

A friend of a friend of a friend of a friend, what the heck was that about? "Does he at least have a name?" I asked.

"He is known only as Gael." The man said. "I wish you good luck!" He added, turned and walked away.

Well, it was now official; we were looking for needle in hay stack called Central America, only the needle had the form of a Shaman.

Antonio looked to the ground again. I wanted to ask him about seventy-eight, but even I knew it was absolutely not the right time. Still staring at his feet, the husband said two words. "Kristiano! Vamos!"

"What? Where?"

"South! Question some villagers." He explained.

"This could last forever."

"It could also last only a few days." He positively countered. "We must have faith." He concluded.

"Why don't we just go straight to San Jose Hospital and find that long shot Gael?" I asked.

"Because as you said, he is a long shot and San Jose is a long way away. Maybe someone will know something before. We do not know how long Anna has. If we make it to the Costa Rican capital, we will meet Gael, but he will not be our priority." He clarified and stopped.

"Kristiano! Por favor, vamos!" He repeated again, but this time with a pleading tone of voice.

I knew what we had to do and no matter how badly I wished we could have gone back to Cinco Pinos, I could not contest the decision. Anna's life was lying on an imaginary poker table. We were heading southbound, looking for a spiritual doctor who was hiding in a place called: somewhere. The task seemed ludicrous. Which road would I take? Would we simply stop and ask people: pardon me, would you happen to know where I could find a Shaman? It was absurd.

I had to call Martin.

I always thought a phone call was a simple thing to do, but not around here. I tried Martin's cell phone, but there was no answer. He would actually have to be on top of El Cero to receive a decent signal. Anyway, I tried the village pharmacy, the only place to have a telephone, and asked them to go get Martin. I would call back in ten minutes. Hopefully, he was not gone too far in the plantation.

I was lucky enough to have my old partner answer me directly with a loud and enthusiastic: "Kristian my friend, how are you?"

"I'm okay."

"You sure? Your voice sounds weird."

Geez, I didn't know it was that obvious. "I had a bit to drink."

"Well, I wasn't talking about that, but since you mention it: did you have fun with Victoria or Toña?" He questioned.

"I didn't drink any beer, I tried the rum." I admitted.

"Good for you, you know it's one of the best in the world?"

"Yeah, I've heard that." I quickly said. Maybe it was true after all.

"So, I thought you'd be on your way back already. How's everything?" Martin asked.

"I'm alright, but things aren't great for the couple. The woman officially has the disease and it can't be treated without sacrificing the baby." I replied.

"Ouch! How are they taking it?"

"I can't say for the moment. I think they don't fully realize it yet."

"Then, you guys are coming back home?" He asked with confidence.

Martin seemed so certain of our return; it felt weird to tell him what our plan was. I still did not really believe it myself and it would be the first time I would actually say it out loud. Perhaps it would help my approval of it. "Well," I hesitated some more, "you see, Antonio decided to look for a Shaman."

"A what?" He scornfully questioned.

"A Shaman! You heard me the first time." I retorted.

"And where the heck are you going to find him?"

"I don't know. We heard of this guy called Gael in San Jose, but it's only a possibility. He might not even know anything."

"Does Antonio know? To my knowledge, the only time this man left his village was to go running around the surrounding jungles with a rifle, he probably doesn't know either."

"So what do you think he should do, just come back to the village and let his wife die?"

"Who says she's gonna die?" Martin sceptically asked.

"Doctors! They said that if she didn't get treated, there was a solid chance she wouldn't make it."

"Why won't she have the treatments?"

"She really wants to keep the baby."

"Why does she cling on to that foetus so hard? They can have another one later."

"Do you know what happened to them?" I countered.

"The miscarriage? Yes, their neighbour told me."

"I think there was more than just one." I paused. "I can't refuse them, but if you want to get me out of this mess, you can always tell them you need the truck. Remember, you still have authority over me, when it comes to the job, just order me to come back." I said; it would save me a truck load of guilt.

"That's right, but now I'll be the one to have the culpability of Anna's death on the conscience." My friend said.

"It's not our fault." I answered.

He did not reply to my comment, but simply said. "Go ahead then, go look for your ghost Doctor."

"Do you think I want to be running around looking for a phantom healer? Don't say it as if it was my idea." I retaliated and let out a serious rum burp.

He was silent for a bit, I thought he would lecture me on drinking and driving, but he surprised me with. "You know that Antonio only had enough money to go to Managua and back, did he ask you to pay for it all?"

"Not yet, but I have feeling it's going to come soon." I retorted.

"You gonna be alright with that?"

"Well, my instant bank card works around here so it shouldn't be a problem."

"You do know that there's a chance you won't be paid back."

"What?" I exclaimed. "I thought Antonio was a big land owner."

"Exactly, he has land, not cash. He's worth more money than the other villagers, but that still doesn't say much."

"Well, he's gonna have to sell some land 'cause I ain't paying for his little adventure. If it was up to me, I'd be with you right now." I felt like adding: taking it easy, hiking around in the mountains, earning easy money, but I did not.

"I don't think he'll find buyers easily." My partner countered my proposition.

"Am I still getting paid at least?" I asked in a begging tone.

"If no one finds out you're gone, I won't be the one to tell them." He answered. "So cheer up, you're still making money, it's just that now, you're a chauffeur."

"Alright, I'm gonna let you go, all this financial talk made me realize that this phone call is costing me a fortune."

"Don't worry about it." Martin teasingly said.

"You're joking, right. I just told you all about the situation and the only thing you can finish with is *don't worry about it*." I said in uncertainty.

"I meant not to worry about Juanita; I'll tell her not to cook you dinner for the next few nights." He said with a laughing tone.

"Funny guy! I'll talk to you later."

We both hung up the phone. He probably walked straight out of the pharmacy, but I stayed in my cabin for a few seconds. I knew that as soon as I would step out, they would want to leave. There would be no turning back. I was immobile, thinking, reflecting on this trip to come. Where could they find a Shaman?

Soon, we would be heading southbound, a direction I had never taken in the past. It was all unknown from now on. I did not know if my head was hurting from the alcohol or from thinking too much. If I were home, I probably would not be driving for another hour. The Nicaraguan laws were unknown to me so, in a way, I had a right to ignore them. Perhaps I was fine after all. I decided to pick up some stones and juggle them into the air. It went great, I only dropped one out of three, it was a passing grade: the road was mine to take.

I entered the truck and looked at Don Angel. "Why weren't you involved in the big discussion?"

"The decision is not mine to take." Pedro replied.

"What do you think about it? Are you still okay to tag along?" I asked.

"You still want me to?" He answered with a question of his own.

"Of course." Although I did not express it out loud, I really needed him beside me.

"Then let's go." He concluded.

I was quickly relieved after the first few minutes of driving: the vehicle seemed to be going perfectly straight. Antonio was sitting on the front seat, Anna wanted to rest alone. Don Angel had taken the back without even a comment.

"If you don't mind, we have to find a pharmacy and buy some drugs for Anna." The husband said.

"Did your doctor friend give you a prescription?" I asked.

"No, I could not afford the proper stuff, but he told me the name of a cheap decent product I could get." He admitted.

I thought about offering him money, but decided not to. Where would it stop? Still, I could not leave it to that. "When we get out of the city, we'll find some dirt road and I'll teach you to drive." I said. Pedro just looked totally afraid and signalled me that there was no way he would do it. Antonio was just glaring out the window and did not even seem to hear me. "Did you hear me Antonio?"

"Driving?" He answered intriguingly.

"Yes, I would like you to learn how to drive. I can't be the only one if we'll be on the road for so long."

"We don't know how long it'll be really." He added uneasily.

"Exactly, so we need another driver if this thing drags."

"Are you alright to drive for the moment?" Antonio asked.

"I'm fine." I retorted. "You mean because of the rum I drank at the café?" I questioned.

"Si!"

"That was a while ago, don't worry." I paused. "I'm the first one to think drunk drivers should receive a more severe penalty. If they'd rather take the risk of killing innocent people instead of taking a taxi, they can't be intelligent enough to drive." I declared.

"Yes you're right; the price of a taxi is less than prison." He looked out the window and pointed at a small gathering of houses. "That's one of the good things about not having many cars in our village. People can drink all they want." He whistled. "Could you please stop here?" Antonio said when we drove in front of a drugstore and got out.

"You have to be careful though, the car isn't the problem: alcohol is." Don Angel said from the back. "No one pictures himself drinking and simply falling down stairs. A neck can be easily broken." He finished.

After a few minutes, the husband came back in. "They don't know anything."

"Did you get the drugs?"

"Yes!"

"And did they say anything else?" I asked.

"They said we should forget about it and go home." He replied.

"And what do you say?" I asked.

"They can stick it!" Antonio had an expression of defiance. "We will return home only when Anna will be perfectly at ease. Vamos!" He ended.

We were driving further away from the city; hills started to fill up the scenery. Of course, they all could have been volcanoes and I would never have known the difference. I was tired. My head was still pounding. Antonio had dozed off and Pedro was quiet. There was no conversation in the cabin, silence. No distractions came up on the road. I was almost starting to hope for an accident, not a big one, just a gentle bump that would give us something to think about for a while. I knew it would not happen, there were no other cars, not even any holes. Antonio had to learn to drive; he had to share the responsibility. I tried to wake him up with some small talk. "Hey Antonio!" I waited until he opened his eyes and carried on. "Why did that doctor call you Franco?"

"It was my old nickname, during the war years." He replied.

"Why Franco? Don't tell me it's because of the Spanish Dictator?" I dared to ask with a condescending tone.

He gave me a disapproving look in return. "It comes from *francotirador*, which means sniper in Spanish."

"Is that what you used to do in the army?" I pushed on.

"Among other things." He vaguely answered.

I could tell he would not give me any more details so I changed the subject. "What'll we do for food?"

It took him a while. "Well, we will have to go to the grocery store and buy some." He answered.

I was uneasy to bring it up, but I had no choice. "You see I didn't mention it before, because there's still some gas left in the tank, but we'll have to discuss money issues."

"Money is not an issue, my wife's life is." He replied.

I admit I did not really know what to answer to that one. He was right. He had probably not had time to worry about money. At that moment, I felt sympathetic. "I can lend you the money and you can pay me back later." He smiled, but did not answer. "Are you okay with that?" I insisted.

"I would appreciate it a lot if you could provide the money." He finally said. "Thank you very much Don Kristiano."

"So, what about food?" I asked.

"We will mostly go to grocery stores and buy some fruit and vegetables, rice and beans. Frijoles will become our travelling dish. We can cook for ourselves if we simply buy a cheap metal pot." Antonio replied.

"Where are we gonna cook?"

"We can't really afford to sleep in hotels. We'll have to camp out." The husband said.

I had so many questions. Where would we camp, what would we sleep on and in, who would cook, would we eat frijoles and rice everyday, and most of all, where the heck could we find a Shaman?

I was sleepy; my brain was probably still suffering from the fumes of the Nicaraguan rum. "I thought that Guatemala was south of Nicaragua." I admitted to my partners.

Antonio looked at me with a bit of disdain in his eyes. "It's north." He simply corrected.

"I thought that was Honduras."

"It's above Honduras and El Savador, under Mexico." The husband clarified.

"Did they have anything to do with your revolution?" I decided to ask.

"Not really, they had their own problems." He replied.

"Don't tell me the big bad CIA was active there as well?" I questioned in a mocking tone to the disapproving silent look of Don Angel.

"Actually they were. The CIA was able to overthrow Jacobo Arbenz in what was called Operation PBSUCCESS. So starting in the fifties, the US government supported Guatemala's army until the nineties."

"You gotta be kidding me?" I declared. Only Antonio was reacting, I sure would have preferred to hear Don Angel's more moderate version of the facts.

The husband was angered by my comment. "Look it up in your books if you don't believe me, you seem to like history. You'll love to read about the military Junta, the general strikes, the many coup d'état, or how the US Green Berets trained what was known as the Death Squads." He stopped and looked at me. "You want more? The war of repression, the guerrillas, the massacre of the Mayans and the Quiché Indians, the million refugees, the Civil War."

"It's okay; I think I've enough to keep me reading for a while." I interrupted him.

We all stayed quiet. I needed to change the mood and teach Antonio how to drive. I saw a little side road, it seemed perfect and desolated. The weather was great, sunny as usual.

I stopped the truck and asked Anna to get out for a few minutes. She agreed with me. Her anger seemed to have vanished for a while. "Are you sure about teaching my husband to drive?" She questioned. Somehow, she did not seem to have the same confidence as me that Antonio could be a good driver. I did not even want him to be good, just enough to get us through the small roads. I would handle the city ones.

Anna settled by a little creek with water that was surprisingly clear. There were some nice light-coloured rocks at the bottom. The husband soaked a cloth in the stream and gave it to his wife. She took it and pressed it against her forehead. He gently rubbed her big belly before standing back up. They looked like they had a strong union; hopefully it was not just a front.

Antonio went into the truck and took place behind the steering wheel. I looked back, before joining my apprentice. "Don't worry, everything will be fine." I heard Pedro tell Anna. He then signalled me that he would stay with the woman. I climbed aboard the truck, but this time in the passenger's side. I explained everything to my student. He had been observing my driving; he must be ready to do it himself. The road was winding, but still safe. "Don't worry, Antonio, like my mother once said to me: If everybody can do it, you probably can too."

"Did you take that as a compliment?" He asked.

"Not really, but it was encouraging." I retorted. "Listo?"

"Si!"

"Vamos!"

My apprentice declutched surprisingly well and we started rolling forward. My confidence in him disappeared as the first few meters were left behind. The man could not even steer properly. He was zigzagging all over the road. Every time he went on a side, he always overcompensated and it always brought him to the opposite side. I tried to show him how to steer and prayed that the road would always be ours totally. He stayed in first gear and even though he did not go over twenty kilometres an hour, it was still scary.

When Antonio finally got the steering down, he started to have confidence in himself. The road became a slope and some houses appeared on each side. The student now had an audience and it turned from bad to worst. My learner transformed himself into a kid who wanted to prove others that he could drive like David Coulthard. He did not care about anything, the pedals, the stick shift, and mostly the steering wheel, even the speedometer was no longer a concern. All that mattered now was the people looking on.

The situation became overwhelming very quickly. We were going faster, but we were still in first gear. The engine was turning at six thousand RPM. My apprentice realized his mistake, panicked, forgot everything and was doing nothing. We were going straight for the little ditch on the right, but he did not turn the wheel. It all happened so rapidly. "Bréké!" I screamed, but he did not react. I had to be the one to violently steer to the left. We were out of danger for about a second because unfortunately, there was a bigger ditch on the left: a cliff. "Bréké!" I repeated. I was shocked. Millions of questions were rushing through my head. Why could he not find the brake pedal? Why was he still pressing the gas pedal? We had accepted "Bréké!", that I shouted again, as the word signifying the brake pedal. Everything seemed to take place at two hundred kilometres an hour. I was so scared when I saw the edge of the cliff. "Bréké!" I screamed again as I clanged on to the steering wheel. I was powerless.

Thankfully, he finally pressed the middle pedal. We were able to stop. The front view was showing us an empty space. There was no more road to go on. "Don't even think about moving." I said, when it came out of my mouth, I realized I had said it in French, but I knew he had gotten the message. I put my head out the window and got the certainty that my front wheel was still on land, there were about ten centimetres in front of it. It was alright, I did not have the intention of going forward, not in this direction anyway. I pulled the emergency brake and looked at Antonio. His facial expression still had not changed. He did not seem to be able to move, I told him not to, just to be sure. I opened the door and got out. The area was desolated; no house or people could be seen anymore. I went around the back and saw Anna's bed upside down. Once behind the hitch, I puked my guts out in a single second. In a flash, the world's greatest rum was on the ground. I took a moment to myself, ignoring Antonio's questions regarding my wellbeing. Then, I slowly opened his door and put my hand on the concerned pedal. His right foot was now stuck to the thing, as if he could not take it off. It was about time. "You can remove your foot, Antonio. Let go, I have it now." He executed my wish and got out of the vehicle. I unhurriedly took place behind the wheel. I was scared that the ground under the front right wheel would give. I took a deep breath. I could not allow myself to let the truck roll forward. My apprentice went on the other side of the vehicle and hanged on to the opened window, ready to pull back. I had to get this over with or I would die of stress. I put the gear on the *R*, pressed the clutch, then the gas and let go of the far left pedal as I gave the emergency brake a break. The truck rolled back, dirt was thrown into the cliff and I never looked in front again. We were out.

Antonio got back in. "I'm very sorry, Don Kristiano." He apologized. I had to accept my responsibility, but I sure hoped he realized that impressing strangers was not worth the risk of killing yourself, and especially me.

We drove back to Anna and Pedro, silent reigned inside the cabin.

When we arrived, Anna was put in the box on her bed and her husband stayed beside her. When we started going again, I was back in the saddle with Don Angel beside me. I explained everything that had happened. "I sure could have used you." I declared.

"I know, but you also have to learn to fly on your own." He replied.

"Why do you think Antonio acted like this?" I then asked.

"I'm not sure. Some men feel the need to prove themselves."

"Prove what?"

"It does not matter what."

"He almost killed us. It would've been great for you guys to wait for us on the side of the road." I sarcastically supposed.

"It did not happen Don Kristiano. Let it go. We could discuss *what ifs* for a very long time." Don Angel said.

"I just can't believe he would do such a thing."

"Tell me, Don Kristiano, in your heart, do you really think this road was a good place to teach him to drive?" He questioned with a serious tone of voice.

I hesitated, but still admitted. "Maybe not." I stopped and looked to my left. "Time is a factor, I couldn't wait." Don Angel did not retort. He looked at the open road and gave a sympathetic smile. I carried on. "Alright it wasn't a good place at all."

"Not everybody can drive you know. It's a luxury that your people take as a priority." He turned and looked straight at me. "The fact that Antonio is unable to drive does not take anything away from the man he is." He said.

"I know; I understand."

"Do you really?" He questioned with honesty.

"I never told this to anybody, but back in Cinco Pinos, Martin had tried to show me how to drive the motorbike." His eyes widened, obviously hoping to hear more. "I was going way too fast because I wanted him to think I was a natural."

"And?" Don Angel asked with a grin.

"Well, I didn't get the principle of turning left without the accelerator going downward." I declared.

"So?"

"Well I had to jump off because there was huge ditch coming my way." I finally confessed annoyingly.

Don Angel laughed and then said. "No shame in that, Don Kristiano, you are only human after all."

I held back not to make fun of his cliché. "Perhaps it's in our human nature to show off?" I said.

"I would say it is more human tendency." He finished.

Right after my motorbike confessions, Antonio stuck his head inside. "Go on until we can find a remote village." He ordered. We kept on driving for about two hours on this small dirt road. Nothing was going on.

When we finally made it to the village, Antonio jumped out from the back and started his interrogation. I stayed inside the vehicle. Looking around, I was impressed by the graffiti on the houses. It was amazing to me how these communists had taken over the government; a Revolution was an incredible concept. "Hey Pedro, do you think they'll ever repaint their houses and get rid of those graffiti?" I asked.

"Maybe, but paint is expensive. It's also a part of their glorious history, why would they want to get rid of it?"

"Because the Revolution's over." I quickly replied.

"It has been over for quite some time, but there was still some fighting after." Pedro said.

"Don't you think the Revolution and the Contra are the same?" I questioned.

"Not at all." Don Angel blurted. The first one had a noble purpose. As for the second one, it was just a useless bloodshed." He finished.

I could tell I had made him feel bad so I started rambling on about my own country. "Something like this could never happen where I come from. We probably would have stayed under dictatorial rules for ever."

"Why do you say that?" He asked.

I was glad to see I had not vexed him too much, I carried on. "The government can do pretty much anything and get away with it."

"Why is that?"

"I guess because the majority of the people have a cozy life in their private little homes and that's all that matters to them. We mostly complain in our living rooms. There are very few demonstrations and when we do protest, they're simple walks just to show our disapproval, nothing is truly done about the problem at hand."

"But what does that solve?"

"Honestly, nothing. Things are discussed for a very long time, but rarely solved." I admitted.

"Maybe you guys still have it too good?" Pedro said.

"I know; it would take something humongous to truly anger the population. All we have to complain about now are high taxes and bad management. There are also modest abstract details that no one worries about."

Antonio jumped back up into the box and we were about to get going.

We entered the city of Granada with the idea of crossing it quickly. We went from street to street; everything was pretty much the same as in Managua. "So venerable guide; what can you tell me about this city?" I teasingly asked Don Angel.

"Not much. For what I heard the city is a nice place, literature plays a strong role in the social scheme of things. It is nicknamed *La Gran Sultana*. Don't ask me why. It probably has some old Spanish explanation. Also, the mountain you see over there," he pointed to it, "is actually a volcano called Mombacho."

Big woop-ti-doo!

We drove around for a bit, Antonio picked people randomly and asked them the question. Later, I saw a carriage pulled by a horse waiting at the street corner. It made me feel pity for the animal. The weather was incredibly hot. I could not believe the horse would have to pull the carriage all day. Its mouth was opened, seeming to be begging for water, but he received none. His master gave him a good whipping on the butt instead. I was glad to be in a moving truck and not have to interfere in this spectacle.

"I would like to find the hospital so we could question the people." Antonio yelled through the back-opened window.

We did just that, but it was totally useless. No one even took him seriously. They could not even pretend to care about Anna's sickness. It was as if they were so happy that we were not asking for a bed in their establishment, the rest did not matter.

We got on the way again, our only alternative left was to drive and find ourselves a free place to spend the night. There was a teenager selling little bags at the lights. "Would you like to buy some *Tiste*?" Pedro asked.

"No, gracias, I tried the stuff at the village and it gave me diarrhoea for two days." I answered.

"This is not the same; this one is made with corn and cocoa."

"What did I have at the village then?"

"It was probably some *posol con leche*."

"All sounds the same to me: a recipe for fast fiery fluid poop." I finished.

During the evening, we got back on the highway. We even had time to drive south for a bit before dusk. The great Lake Nicaragua followed our road for a time. "Do you know that this is the only lake with sharks in it?" Pedro rhetorically asked.

"I didn't know that, no." I admitted. How could I have?

"Yes, they are the only fresh-water sharks in the world." He concluded.

I was also totally ignorant to the fact that sharks could survive in non-salt water. "Are they dangerous for swimmers?" I questioned.

"I'm not sure, but sharks will always be sharks. It always depends when you see them or rather when they see you." Don Angel answered.

"Yeah, they scare me. Aren't they the only animals, with polar bears, to attack humans just for the fun of it?" I asked.

"I do not think so, but I do know that they should be more scared of humans. we kill up to a hundred million sharks every year."

"Don't they fight back?"

"They kill only fifteen people in return." Pedro explained.

He was right; humans were definitely the ones to be afraid of.

Later, in front of a sort of pub, there was some guy standing on a chair talking to others. At the speed we were going, he looked like he was preaching. "Did you see that guy?" I asked my partner.

"Yes I did." He replied.

I doubted his response because he seemed to be staring the other way. "Seriously, did you see him standing on the chair?" I repeated.

"Yes I did. He was reciting poetry."

"How do you know that's what he was doing?" I had wanted to tease Pedro about his preaching, but a poet was killing my gag.

"This area is famous for its artists." He looked at the lake and continued. "There is even a small group of islands called the Solentiname. It is renowned for its amount of poets and craftsmen. We will not see it, it is too far down south of the lake." Pedro concluded.

The highway was the same; there was still no sign of a decent campsite. I was getting nervous with this camping out idea. According to Don Angel, we were now in the region of the Pacific lowlands; there were about forty volcanoes in this area, what was to say one would not erupt? And how good could camping be so near the Mosquito Coast? We would probably wake up in the morning with bug bites all over our faces. I had had my malaria shots, but I did not think I should tempt my fate. Did not Alexander the Great die of malaria? Imagine that, conquering the world and then being killed by a tiny mosquito. Yes, I was feeling sorry for Anna, but this whole deal was getting me angry. How could we find a place to set camp? We were on a highway and we did not know which secondary road to take. The first and only one we had taken had led us right into a dead end. It would have been better just to look for a hotel in the next city.

"Take this road right there!" Don Angel ordered on the spot.

I executed his command. Suddenly Antonio knocked on the back window. "Where are you going?" He quickly demanded.

"I'm not sure, but it seems like a good place to find a campsite." I answered back with a little white lie. I looked at Pedro and he, of course, smiled at me.

A few kilometres later, we came to a small farm. The place was not in great shape, but it was still up and running. There was an old couple standing on some rundown front porch. We stopped the truck. "Why don't we ask these nice people if we could camp on their property?" Don Angel suggested.

Antonio jumped out and went straight for the couple. I could see them talking, but could not hear a thing. The husband turned around and gave me the thumbs up. I stepped out and went to introduce myself. Antonio and I both came back to the truck and he helped Anna out. "They offered to cook dinner for us, but we'd have to pay for it." The husband said.

"Sure! Go for it, can't be too expensive." I agreed.

Within ten minutes, we were all settled outback. Luckily for us, there did not seem to be many animals running around in our space. About ten other minutes later, a lady's voice announced dinner. She brought the plates outside. I was expecting us all to sit around the table and discuss trivial anecdotes of the farm; it was not going to be the deal.

The meal was really good, some kind of beef, beans and rice. There was also a cabbage and tomato salad with tortillas, definitely not something I was used to back home. What would a typical Nicaraguan meal be without tortillas? This little bread tasted good though, but if you asked me, it smelled exactly like poop.

After dinner, I went for a little walk. Although it was getting dark, the air was still hot. It seemed to be hotter around here than up north in Cinco Pinos. I could not believe how green everything was, thanks for the rainy season, even if it almost never rained anymore. The property was pretty big after all. The jungle trees formed a huge fence around the field.

Don Angel joined me and we started to chitchat. "Be careful where you go, Don Kristiano, there are a many animals in the area."

"Aren't I the one they should fear?" I joked. "I know you're right, but since we're about to sleep outside, I thought I could come and see what was out here." I replied.

"You do not have to go out there; I can tell you what lives within these trees. There are some pumas, jaguars, warthogs, ocelots, and spider monkeys. If you see any one of them, do not get close."

What the heck was an ocelot? "Anything I can get close too?" I asked to be smart.

"Well, if you see a sloth, it should be fine for you to approach it." He retorted with a smile.

We kept on walking around the field. The sky was dark blue. "Look up, Don Kristiano." Pedro quickly said as he pointed with his right index. "I think there is a quetzal right over there."

"What the heck is a quetzal?" I questioned out loud this time as I looked in the pointed direction. It was so far away, I could not distinguish anything, except maybe that it was mostly green with some blue and red. It also had a very long tail.

"It's the Mayan holy bird. It's very rare." Don Angel clarified.

It did fly very gracefully for a small bird. I did not see anything holy about it though.

A few silent minutes passed. I killed a mosquito on my forehead and almost hurt myself doing it.

"Every creature has the right to live, you know." Pedro preached.

I though for sure he was joking so I did not answer anything.

My partner was quiet for a bit, even though he looked like he was about to say something important. "You seem angry Don Kristiano." He finally let out.

I was not sure if he wanted me to answer. Was it a real question or a simple rhetorical one? Still, I decided to respond since he was not adding anything. "Of course I'm angry. I'm surprised you've just noticed it." I said.

"I have noticed it before, but I did not think it was the proper time to mention it."

"And what makes you think this is the right time?"

"Nothing, there is just never a perfect moment to talk about these things." He took a breather. "If I may be so bold to ask, why are you so irritated?"

"Isn't it obvious?" I replied.

"Obviously not, because I would not ask." He replied.

I knew he had his suspicions and he simply wanted me to say it out loud. "I'm not in control of anything here. I'm supposed to be in Cinco Pinos, spending the day hiking the mountains, dealing with coffee and coming back to Martin's house everyday, but instead I'm here, looking for a ghost Doctor." I blurted. "And we should have gone straight for San Jose and talk to Gael." I added.

"It is alright to be angry you know, but..." Pedro started saying.

"I don't need you to lecture me on this, okay?" I admitted.

"Pardon me, but I think I do. Do not worry it will be short." He said. "Perhaps you are making too much of all this. I think you are angry about more than just what is happening here, but regardless: just go with the flow, roll with the punches: you can not change the way things are going now. In a way, anger should become an imaginary friend, a kind of wild animal you are able to tame."

"What do you mean?" I enquired.

"Well, I can answer your question, but my speech will be longer than I predicted." He looked up to see where the quetzal was. "Should I keep going then?" He asked.

"Alright, go ahead." I permitted in an annoyed tone of voice.

"You can bring your anger with you if you want, but make sure it does not hurt anyone." Don Angel said.

"I don't get it."

"You do not have to understand it." He said bluntly. "What makes you so angry anyway, this journey, people in general?" He questioned.

"Sometimes people do, but I'm mostly okay with all those idiots."

"Which idiots, as you call them, are we talking about here?"

"All of them pretty much, I basically trust no one to be smart. I guess I just get fed up of seeing the six o'clock news filled up with immorality."

"I am afraid I can not understand, Don Kristiano, I do not have a television." Don Angel admitted.

I still could not believe most of these people did not possess the best invention ever. They could at least go watch it at the local hotel. What a bunch of clowns. "Whatever, I guess I just don't want to be like all of them, that's all."

"You are the only one responsible for your actions. Atrocities in newspapers should be like examples of what not to do."

"It's not just them, it's the regular Joes working nine to five; rushing home to quickly eat so they can have a free evening to advance themselves in their job." I confessed.

"You do not have to be like everyone else. It is possible to combine happiness with marginality and still be included in society."

I stayed silent for a while. In a way, anger was not the worst emotion to feel. At least, it was something I had in common with Dean, Lennon or Hemingway. Was it the key to their success? Possibly, but their fury caught up with them and killed them all. Car crash, assassination, and a hypothetical accident, were those the only ways to escape the wicked emotion? What about Ludwig? The German composer was able to create amazing symphonies with his turbulent emotions. Perhaps I could learn to make good usage of my anger. That was surely what Don Angel meant by taming the ferocious pet.

We walked back to the campsite. From a distance I could see Antonio folding a few blankets. "Where did we get the blankets?" I asked Pedro.

"The old couple brought them earlier and said we could keep them, minus a small fee evidently. All you have to do now is to elevate the corners and tie them to trees or little sticks planted in the ground." He answered.

"Why is that? Shouldn't I just cover myself with it?"

"You can if you are cold, but it is unlikely. My technique will make sure no little animals will walk all over you during the night."

I looked at Antonio again and counted only three blankets. "We couldn't get four?" I questioned.

"I do not need one. I prefer to just sleep in the truck." He replied.

We got up the next morning and said our goodbyes to the farm couple. We drove around for the whole morning, asking questions left and right, up and down. The same desolated paths for hours, I did not even know the country stretched so far west at this level. "Stay to the left." Don Angel ordered nicely.

He always was nervous in the curves so I did not argue. This time though, I was glad he was panicky, once we went around the bend, there were three huge cows on the right side of the road. We surely would have hit them.

The road system here was absurd, at some point it just stopped and we were forced to go back the way we came. There were no villages, nobody to tell us where a Shaman could be found. It seemed more than ever an impossible task. There was no way we could succeed proceeding in this manner. We were wasting time, time that I did not have, surely time Anna did not have.

About an hour later, we saw a small grocery store and stopped. The place was horrible; I never would have guessed they were selling food. We bought a stack of provisions that Antonio, to my personal surprise, paid for. We bought some rice and bread for our dinner. It was all rapped up in brown paper towels. We still had not purchased the cooking pot to prepare the meals for ourselves. We definitely had to get back closer to civilization, if I could call it that.

Darkness was upon us. We kept on driving, daydreaming about everything and nothing, searching for a safe place to spend the night. A few moments later, the husband climbed inside. "What's going on?" He asked.

"Not much, just wondering why some men are so violent, having affairs, abusing their kids." I honestly replied.

He did not say anything and seemed to wish I would not go on. "Would you like to hear about an affair?" Antonio questioned.

"Sure, why not, I have time to kill."

"I will tell you about the Iran-Contra Affair. Did you ever hear of it?" He demanded.

"No, I have not." I had to admit my ignorance once again.

"It is a bit complicated, so try not to get lost." He said with a grin and then kept going. "You see once there was a man called Ronald Reagan who had decided to stop communism around the world, by any means necessary."

Here we go again, I thought to myself.

"Evidently, this required a gigantic amount of money, and congress did not think Nicaragua was worth that much. During the same period, Ronnie also had problems in the Middle East where some of his compatriots were taken hostages in Lebanon. Beside this country, there was another war being fought between Iran and Iraq. At that time, the US mostly supported their good buddy Saddam, but Iran was a good friend of the Lebanese people and they also needed weapons to fight the Iraqis. So, they simply asked Ronald, who had plenty of missiles, to sell them some. In return, Iran would talk to the Lebanese and made sure some of the hostages were freed. Not to worry, they could always get some more in the future."

"What does that *affair* have to do with you guys?" I interrupted.

"I am glad you asked, because I am about to tell you. The money from the arsenal's sales was used to finance the Contra army. Millions of dollars did not make it to the US government and went straight into the mercenaries' pockets."

"Are you telling me that the US government financed the supposed mercenaries with weapons' sales to Iran?" I asked in shock.

"To Ayatollah himself." The husband let out a short evil laugh. "I could also tell you about Oliver North or Cuban-Unitedstatians selling drugs in the streets of Miami and sending the money to Nicaragua, but I think it would be a bit much for you to handle right now." Antonio added with a smirk on his face.

I reflected on it for a while. "How come I never heard anything about it before or seen it in a movie?" I asked naively.

"Maybe you just have not watched the right movies." He suggested.

"Maybe you're right." After all, I was a cheesy comedy freak.

"Be careful about what you learn in movies anyway." He added.

"What do you mean now?" I inquired.

"There are many examples, but just take Pancho Villa, the Mexican revolutionary. Do you know about him?"

"Go on!"

"He wanted the world to know his story. He invited a film crew to make sure his actions would not vanish. His revolution was filmed by the States and its facts were transformed for the general public's amusement. Do you seriously think a Hollywood movie gives an objective version of a story?" The husband questioned and continued without waiting. "Of course not, it is a show, a projection created to entertain and make a profit. It is simply *based* on facts. No one really knows what happened except for people who lived it."

I remained quiet. There was no way I was going to admit that he was making sense.

We finally found a place to stay about thirty minutes later. It was out of the main road and safe. What more could we ask for?

We parked the truck and settled in for the night. Darkness was fast to fall, the evenings were long. "So this Pancho guy, he overturned the government, lived happily ever after?" I decided to ask to get him back on the subject, kill time.

"Not happily no, he was defeated by another group." The husband started.

"Americans, I suppose." I guessed; I could see him coming from a mile away.

"No, Mexicans: Carranza." He first said and waited to observe my facial expression. "But Carranza did receive his weapons from the US and when he overpowered Villa, they recognized him as the rightful president of Mexico."

"That probably did not sit too well with old Pancho." I replied, wanting to continue the discussion, possibly just because Pancho was such a fun name to say out loud.

"You're right. He wanted revenge on the United States; he crossed the border and killed as many as he could."

It was weird that he made it sound like the heroic thing to do. "As angry as Pancho was, Pancho was probably killing innocent men, women and child." I assumed.

"Most likely." He simply answered in a tone of voice that proved me right.

"And was Pancho finally killed at least?" I asked with an honest curiosity.

"No he was not, but they sure tried hard."

"How's that?"

"Over one hundred and fifty thousand men were sent, tanks, airplanes, but Villa was always able to escape. One day, they just forgot about him. I guess they had no more money to spend on the matter. After all, there was a World War going on in Europe." Antonio explained.

I had no clue how his version differed from the real one, but it sure was entertaining. Antonio was not the most objective man, but what he believed to be true, he knew it well. At least, I had learned a few things tonight. How was he able to switch from the Contra-Iran affair to Pancho Villa? I simply lifted my cap to him and went to my blanket. There went another great anti-American tale; the worst part was that they unfortunately sounded more and more believable to my ears.

I did not say much during the rest of the evening. I was too exhausted to be ticked off anymore; I felt more like crying.

CHAPTER 3.3

Nothing happened for the whole day; we looked around from dirt road to dirt road. Every person Antonio asked for information either ignored him or laughed. We were able to buy ourselves a cooking pot in a city called Rivas. We ate frijoles twice during the day. Finally, we spent last night in a damp and horrible location by the side of the street.

I woke up with nasty back spasms. I was starting to feel a bit down. Yesterday had proven that finding a Shaman was a task close to impossibility. Good radio stations were getting harder to find and my own music was already overused. On small roads, there were many people begging me to give them a ride, some even blocking my way. It was bad enough that animals were constantly doing it; I did not need humans to join in as well. Antonio could not drive and my other partner refused to even try. Don Angel was always advising me on stuff. What did he know? Who was he to tell me all these things? He had spent his life in the mountains, sheltered from the real world, how could he know so much? Luckily he was here at times though, since the couple was mostly in the back box and kept to themselves. I had to face the fact and accept it: I was just a chauffeur, a man caressing the steering wheel and masturbating the stick shift.

We arrived at our first border on a depressingly cloudy morning. Although the weather was sad, I was happy to think that we would soon arrived in San Jose: home of long-shot Gael. At Penas Blancas, we parked the vehicle and went inside a small house. We first had to get an exit stamp and pay some kind of departure tax. Then, we got in the pick-up again and drove for a few seconds to the Costa Rican entry point. "Aren't you coming?" I questioned Don Angel before getting out.

"I don't have a passport, but don't worry, they won't mind." He assured me with a smile.

After asking left and right, we learned we had to go behind the gas station, close to the duty-free shop and get an exit stamp. Then, we walked to the next building and inside, there was a big line that started in front of big box sitting on a rectangle pedestal. No matter the country, customs were pretty much all the same: they were either a joke or a nightmare. "What's going on here?" I asked Antonio.

"Well, we get to the box and there will be a button with two lights. When you press the button, if the green one illuminates, you are clear. If it is the red one, you have to go into that office over there." He explained.

The people in front of us were tested one by one. I was last in line and when I pressed, I saw the blood red light turn on. How did this thing really work anyway, why was everybody else fine, was this a stress detector, was it all just luck, was there a big brother looking on from somewhere?

Since, I was just standing there, not moving, some agent came to get me and escorted me to a back office. I sat in a small room with about five other people. The man who had brought me in forced me to hand him my passport. I was reluctant to give it away. These little booklets could fetch a very interesting price on the black market. As for the people sitting beside me, they totally ignored my presence. It was like I had not even penetrated the room, I yawned twice and none of them imitated me.

After forty-five minutes, I ended up alone in the room. I tried to wait calmly, but it was very difficult. How could I calm down? I was told so many stories and had heard so many rumours about police in under-developed countries? I had no clue what was going to happen? Did I need a visa to cross over to Costa Rica?

I was finally called to a third room. There was a huge desk in the middle and a man sitting behind it. He had grey hair only around his ears; his forehead was going all the way back to the top of his neck. There was small black cap on the writing table. I wondered what had appeared first in his case, the baldness or the hat. This guy seemed so stiff; he would need a rule book to play heads or tails. He never even looked at me when I came in, staring at a piece of paper on his desk. Both of his elbows were on the surface. The man had a pen in his right hand and held his head with his left one, creating ripples on the skin of his forehead.

Everything was simple, nothing stood out of the ordinary and it gave my imagination many opportunities to run wild. The agent behind the desk still had not looked at me. I was starting to really freak out. I was also worried about the car battery that was in the far corner of the room. The booster cables beside it were too small to reassure me. I needed to know what was going on, I was about to lose it. I did not feel like being electrocuted, I hated electricity. At least my voltage paranoia had helped me to forget about the nightstick and the cuffs on the side table. Then, I saw Don Angel's face quickly pass in front of the window and it calmed me down.

After that, the original agent entered the room and gave my passport to the man at the desk. He started to read out loud. I heard, my name, my birth date and mostly: New Orleans, USA. As the man read this last part, his facial expression made me worried. It also made me nervous that Antonio could be at an easy hearing distance. The man waited for the other to leave and started to speak. "So Señor Imbeault, what is your purpose in Costa Rica?" He firstly questioned.

Evidently, I could not tell him the real reason. I doubted he would believe the fact that I was looking for a Shaman. That might be enough for him to stop me from entering his country. Even though I felt like punching him in the face, I had to play his game. After all, I truly needed to get in his third world homeland. "I am a tourist with Nicaraguan friends. They said that your country was really worth visiting." I nicely replied.

"Is that so? How much money do you have?"

"Honestly, I don't have much on me, but I do have a bank card and a credit card. I plan to get some more cash when we reach the capital." I explained, unsure of the tone he wanted to hear.

He basically ignored my answer and went on asking. "How long do you plan to stay?"

This one was more difficult because I had no clue. I needed to find a charming reply and quick. He lowered his eyebrows and stared right at me. I still did not know what to say. Suddenly, there was a knock a door. The door gently opened and, to the disappointment of my interrogator, the first agent entered again. He went to whisper something in the sitting man's ear. Almost instantly, my passport was given back to the first man. Then, the door opened again, this time with extreme authority. I was expecting Don Angel to appear, but it was Antonio who did. He immediately grabbed my passport out of the man's hand. He held it for a while as he spoke to both men. From out the door, I heard Don Angel voice telling me to get out of there. I got up and left without looking back. At that moment, Antonio the mediocre driver definitely was no longer in my head. He had seemed strong, powerful, and so intimidating. Then, I clicked that he still had my passport, what if opened it and saw my birthplace. During our first conversation together, I had denied the truth. How would he react if he learned now, would he leave me in here?

Don Angel was waiting at the door and we walked back to the vehicle together. "Are you okay?" He asked softly.

"Yes, I'm fine." Of course I was not, but I did not want to discuss it. I felt I had been treated unjustly because of where I was from and it depressed me. I had suffered from racism for the first time in my life.

"Whatever you say, Don Kristiano." He concluded.

Moments later, we made it to the vehicle. Anna smiled at me. "I'm glad you are here."

"Thank you. You know I wouldn't abandon you, right?" I said, trying to reassure her.

She looked uneasy. "I know you would not abandon us." She replied in a tone of voice that seemed to want to be convincing. I was just not sure who she was trying to convince, herself or me.

I sat in the pickup and waited for Antonio. I was nervous, in a different way than before, but very uneasy nonetheless. I was especially anxious to get out of here. When the husband finally arrived, I could tell from far away that he was not happy. The question was to know why. Was it because of the customs dudes or was my secret out: had he read my passport?

"Kristiano, vamos! We will talk later." He kindly ordered.

I started driving and did not slow down when we passed the gate. We officially entered Costa Rica at four fifty in the late afternoon.

I tried to clear my mind and forget about those agents. It worked for a few minutes. There were many trucks parked on the side of the road. Drivers were taking a break, chatting with one another. Most of them did not have a cabin and some drivers had placed a hammock between the farthest wheels. These people were sleeping under their huge metal box, sheltered from all weather coming from above. They were swinging with the wind, almost looking comfortable. I missed Juanita's restaurant in Cinco Pinos and its hammock in the freezer's room. When we passed by a bus, the compartment door opened and there was a man sleeping inside. Big deal! Had Antonio opened my passport?

We had to keep going for the evening. I needed to lie down on a nice comfortable bed. I had been mentally drained into that office. I could not help to think how we were meant to play many different roles in life. Antonio could not drive a car, but gosh, he could surely take care of business. Lord knows what could have happened if he had not shown up at the right time. These custom men could have done whatever they had wanted with me. Things could get pretty ugly when ordinary jerks got a position of authority. It was Peter's principle all over again, some community theatre actor had accepted to play an Oscar winning role.

Then Antonio climbed through the back window. "How are you?" He started. "I forgot to give you this back." He said as he threw my passport on the front seat.

I stared at the passport and wondered if he had taken a look. "I'm alright, thanks to you." I replied.

"Don't worry about it. You would have done the same thing for me." He answered, almost confirming that he had not seen my birthplace.

"What makes you sure?" I asked.

The husband began laughing. "I don't know; the fact that you are doing it now and you have been doing it for the last few days." He said with a smile.

"It's not the same."

"Maybe, but it is very close. We are compañeros, Don Kristiano. Anna's faith and mine are bound to yours." He paused. "I am sorry it took me so long to react. There were four guards with weapons that would not let me go in. It would have been wrong of me to just take them out, times have changed: I had to wait. I expected them to release you from one minute to the next. I hesitated too long and I apologized for it. Anna was the one to give me the final kick I needed." Antonio stopped and looked at me in the mirror. "Did they give you a hard time?"

Was he joking about being able to take them out? Who did this guy think he was? "Not really, I'm mostly the one who mentally tortured myself." I admitted.

"Sometimes, that's all they want you to do." He looked around, checked his wife lying outback, and then continued. "You can't blame them; they probably thought you were American."

I was not sure if I should answer this one, tell him the truth. "And what if I was?"

"What do you mean?" He questioned.

"You know me pretty well now; you think they would have been right to treat me like this if I had been American?"

"I would not have cared for anything they would have done to a Unitedstatian." He stopped, looked back at Anna again. "That is not the question though; they did it to you, and that, I care about."

"Whatever." I whispered. At least, one thing was for sure, he had not looked at my passport. "Why don't we just go directly to see Gael?" I dared question.

"Gael will come in his right time, keep the faith my friend. I still believe the people can help us." He said. "I am going back to my wife. If you see a village with potential answers, do not hesitate to stop. I will bang the roof if I do." The husband concluded and stepped out.

What was going on here? This man, who claimed to be my friend, would probably slaughter me if he knew my birthplace. "You've been awfully quiet!" I said to Pedro.

"I just thought you needed time to sort things out. Your anger seemed to have passed though. That's a good thing."

"I'm just too depressed to be angry." I answered.

"Why is that?" He asked.

"I don't understand why Antonio doesn't just want to go see Gael right away."

"Antonio believes in the villagers, in the people." He explained. "It can not only be what you are depressed about?" He added.

"These custom boys, and Antonio if I may add, think I deserve to suffer because they think I'm American." I confessed.

"Are you telling me they are wrong?"

I was not sure if he was asking about the fact that they were wrong about my birthplace or Americans should suffer; I stayed quiet.

"Are you telling me that you had no preconceived ideas during your first days in Nicaragua?" Don Angel asked.

I knew he knew; there was no point in lying. "Of course, I had some." I confessed.

"After all the time you spent in Cinco Pinos, are the prejudices still there?"

"I'm not sure, there's a lot of commotion in my mind." I confessed.

"And which way is this narrow-mindedness moving?"

"Definitely on its way out." I said encouragingly.

"Well, that is a start." Don Angel concluded.

We drove for a while, the road never changed. There was no difference between the old and the new country. The sky was totally dark, the lower blue had disappeared and since the light of day had been gone, it made it difficult to find a campsite. I was tired, anxious to stop and have dinner.

We finally did find ourselves a little spot by the side of the road. Nobody said much during the meal. Antonio and his wife had prepared some rice and beans over the camp fire, it all tasted like garbage to me.

We set up our blankets close to one another; Don Angel was still sleeping in the truck. "Please God, if you save my life and mostly the one of my baby, I will never ask for anything again." I heard Anna praying just before I fell asleep. I tried not to hear the rest and think of something else, but it did not really work. I wanted to go tell her to stop hoping, she could not gamble with God this way.

We got on the road after we quickly ate some mangos for breakfast. I drove quietly and transformed myself into a mean thinking machine. I had too much time for myself.

Our first major stop was in a tiny village. Antonio jumped out and started interrogating people from left to right. It did not matter who it was, young and old, short and tall, fat and small: they were all questioned. I simply walked around with Don Angel.

Near the end of the morning, Antonio banged on the roof. "I just saw a gathering of houses over there. Let's check it out." The husband said as he stuck his head inside only long enough to finish his words.

"What is this place?" I asked Don Angel.

"I think we are inside the Parque Nacional Volcán Arenal." He replied.

"These mountains are all volcanoes?"

"Most of them, yes."

We tried to cross a river and got stuck right in the middle. I helplessly tried to get out of it for half an hour. Water was coming in, my feet were soaking. My exhaust pipe was flooded. I got very nervous, I had no clue what would happen. I had never gone swimming with a pick-up truck before. Finally, Antonio went out to look for help and returned with an elderly cultivator.

"Wait here, I will be right back." The farmer said.

We had no choice but to wait. Still, *right back* meant over twenty minutes later. He appeared with an old tractor. He stayed ashore and I tied some chains under our truck. It took three times for his tractor to pull us out. Surely I had gotten myself in deeper every time I had moved back and forth.

When it was all over, the farmer chatted with us for ever. He only left when I clicked that he wanted some money for his troubles. I gave him the equivalent of five bucks and we got on our way.

For dinner, we decided to eat in a restaurant. I was fed-up of beans and rice. Pedro was against the idea and chose not to come with us. We sat down and ordered right away, none of us asked for frijoles. There was a TV in the far corner of the room and I stared at it like there was no tomorrow. "Do you like football?" The husband asked me.

"Heck yeah! I'm European." I replied, half-lying. In reality, I was the only Swiss in the world that referred to the sport as soccer.

"We play it too you know?"

"Has Nicaragua ever been to the World Cup?"

"Of course! Has Switzerland?"

"The last time was when it was played in the States and we did pretty well." I declared with confidence.

"If you ask me, the United States had no right to host the World Cup." Antonio said.

Big surprise! "Why's that?"

"For one, they're the only ones in the world to call it soccer."

"Canada does too, you know."

"Bunch of followers." He teased in a good way.

"Are Central Americans real fanatics?" I questioned.

"We take it pretty seriously." The husband confessed and made his wife giggle.

"Not like that guy in Columbia who was shot for scoring in his won goal in ninety-four I hope." I said.

"Is the World Cup in the United States the only one you know about?"

"Of course not." I totally lied. It was in fact, the only one I had ever watched on TV.

Anna surprisingly joined the conversation. "That's not the worst though: Honduras and El Salvador went to war for a week because of an incident at a football game. They called it La Guerra Del Futbol." She told me.

The husband seemed to disagree. "There were problems between the two countries before it erupted." He defended.

"Like what?" The wife dared to ask.

"The Honduran government blamed a lot of the economical problems on illegal immigrants from El Salvador. There were also disputes as to where the official boundaries were." Antonio replied with a smile, keeping the argument a friendly one.

"Don't listen to him, most of it started because of a riot before a World Cup qualifying match." Anna went on. "Yes, Don Kristiano: men can be that stupid." She laughed.

"So what happened?" I wanted them to finish.

"The next day, war was declared. The Salvadoran army crossed over and attacked Honduras. They did well at first, but it did not last. Nicaragua helped out; the OAS imposed a few sanctions, political stuff you would not be interested in." The husband explained.

"How did it end?"

"El Salvador was forced to pull out its army, Salvadoran illegal immigrants were expelled, thousands died, and the two countries have been on bad terms ever since." Antonio replied.

"Gotta love football!" I stupidly said. We had more important issues to deal with anyway, like where would we sleep tonight.

The rest of the day went alright; nothing made me feel any happier or worst. We found ourselves a place to stay for the night just outside the city of Liberia. There was a forest that was too little to be called a jungle.

Anna fell asleep right away and since Pedro had gone for a walk, Antonio and I had a short, but important conversation. "Why don't you guys accept the treatments? You could always try to have another baby later." I started by saying.

He waited a while, as if he knew the conversation would take a long time, or be painful. "This is surely our last chance to have a child. Anna is still relatively young, but I am over fifty." The man replied.

"Have you ever tried before?" I asked.

"Anna had many miscarriages over the years. It is as if her body was psychologically afraid to have a child."

"What do you mean?" I invited for him to continue.

"I had children before you know." Antonio said.

I was surprised by this revelation. "What happened?" I questioned.

"It is an old story, demons I would rather forget."

"C'mon! We have nothing else to do around here. What happened?" I insisted politely.

He looked around and then started talking. "Anna is not my first wife, I had another one before. I once had a family, right after the Revolution." He said and paused for a bit. "As I told you, I fought the original one. When the Contra came along, I was uncertain about joining in, I had done some stuff in the war that I was uncomfortable with. So I enrolled myself in the army only as a medic. One day, I was returning home after spending two days patrolling the mountains and as I walked up the hill, I saw pieces of my house on fire in the middle of street. I discovered my wife's body, pierced with bullet holes. Her clothes had been ripped apart, blood all the way down her legs. The remains of our dead boys' bodies were lying inside what was left of our home. Their faces covered with ashes, the smell of burning hair was intolerable. My daughter had disappeared, kidnapped and I never saw her again." He rested and swallowed his emotional saliva.

I felt horrible. "What did you do?"

"I fell down, kneeling on the paved street, screaming my heart out. I took my gun and put it in my mouth, but when I pressed the trigger, nothing happened, the chamber was empty." A teardrop fell from Antonio's left eye.

I had no clue what to say. "I'm so sorry, I had no idea."

He went on. "No, no, I'm sorry. Maybe I should not have told you this story. It is just that you do not know anything about us. I wanted you to understand what we went through, what we are still going through. You probably see us Nicaraguans as violent revolutionary whiners; we are not Don Kristiano. We are simple human beings who were dealt a shitty hand in the game of life." He explained with passion.

I waited, took a breather. "I had no idea, I apologized for my indiscretion." I said.

"Why do you apologize? I should apologize for bringing this on you."

"No, it's okay, don't be silly."

"That very night, I crossed the border for the first time. I located an enemy camp, found myself an elevated position where I could easily snipe as many as I could. I opened fire, and did so until I was out of ammunition." The husband admitted with a tone of voice that meant business.

"El francotirador hey?" I said with compassion and continued. "How many kids did you have?"

"I had three." He sighed deeply. Anna moved around in her sleep and he looked at her. "I am a man hunted by his past and it is not always pleasurable for Anna. I have decided to forget about war and live a peaceful life. Still, I was never able to give this amazing woman the title of mother. This is our only chance and we have to succeed. I am grateful for what you are doing here." Antonio finished and went to check up on his young wife.

It was unbelievable how he had told me his story almost as if it were par for the course. I now completely understood his hatred for the CIA, the United States. I was certain Antonio was disappointed when the Nicaraguan government decided to take off *Yankee, enemy of humanity* from their national anthem.

I had to get away, go for a walk, find Don Angel or be by myself. I had the choice between the side of the road or inside the forest. I decided on the shelter of the trees.

Darkness was complete. I went forward with great difficulty. There was no path and I had to wrestle with branches coming from every direction. I stopped and closed my eyes. Scorpions and lizards were far in my mind. I reflected on Antonio's story, picturing him holding his dead family. Tears came to my eyes, but none of them had the courage to jump out. Since, I was alone in the dark and did not fight them. I encouraged them to roll down my cheeks, but it was unfeasible. I tried to shut my eyelids as strongly as possible. I would have liked to nailed them shut and never see the world again. I started to push down as hard as I could. I wanted my eyebrows to touch my cheeks. I pressed down for too long. The strength deployed had reversed my vision. My eyes were closed and everything was white. The light was mesmerizing, pierced by rays of energy that disappeared after a while. I attempted to redo it and succeeded only once. When I tried a second time, the light did not have enough intensity.

When I opened my eyes, I could not see anymore. The scenery had vanished, as if I had fainted. I had to bring my hand in front of my nose to realize that there was hope. My palm seemed to be surrounded by an aurora. I moved it from left to right, following with my sight. The trees started to appear in the background, they were represented by long fuzzy lines. My hands were flying, turning on themselves like ballerinas. This tiny jungle had become magical, enchanted. I felt strangely weird and I realized I needed some sleep.

I walked back to the campsite and lay down. I reflected on my life back home. I missed my bed. I felt hungry and remembered last winter when my stomach once had felt the same way. Pathetically, I had been happy because it had meant I would lose some weight. Now it was different, I definitely could have used a hamburger, or two, or even three.

We got up the next day in the early morning; it was not even five o'clock. I had breakfast with the couple while Don Angel was sitting on the back bumper, silently throwing rocks into the trees. We ate fruits and disgusting leftover bread. Antonio acted like last night's conversation had never happened. After a bunch of small talk, the man turned to me. "So, do you like Costa Rica Don Kristiano?" He asked.

"I guess so. Honestly, it isn't too different from your country." I replied.

"You are right; the two countries have a lot of similarities." He said.

"What are they?" I had to question.

"Well, both were struck by Mitch in ninety-eight." He started.

"That's too bad, but you do get USAID to fix the damages now, don't you?" I courageously, or stupidly, retorted. Regardless of his poignant personal story, I wanted to let him know that I could not be easily fooled by his propaganda. "What about Americans, are they well perceived around here?" I cockily continued, since he never answered my question.

"They do have a history, but it is a lot older than ours." The husband said.

It was a bit early for that, but I was curious. "Really what did we... *they,* do this time?" I asked.

"In the middle of the eighteenth century some adventurous Yankee called William Walker came here to seize power. Actually, he had already done it in Nicaragua and had even become President of our nation for a short time. The political party of the time had asked him to be their leader to topple the government. Once it was done, he continued to try and annex other Latino countries with his American army and some newly captured Nicaraguan slaves by his side." That last part sort of shut me up, and Antonio saw it in my face. "The Costa Rican president, a retired farmer, was able to create an army of civilians and defeat the Yankees."

I did not reply anything. I wished Anna would say more. I sometimes had a hard time dealing with Antonio's negativity.

The couple settled in the back as Pedro and I entered the cabin. "Why did you change the pronoun of your sentence?" Don Angel questioned.

"What?" I asked. How could he have picked up on it? Perhaps I should have admitted about my birthplace, but it did not feel right. "I don't know what you're talking about."

"The cat will have to come out of the bag someday Don Kristiano."

"I don't see any cats around here, Pedro!" I blurted out. "Let me be." I finished.

The afternoon seemed endless; I did not feel like talking. Luckily for me Don Angel gave me some space and did not say much either, just enough to keep me awake when it was needed. It was like he knew exactly when to speak to make sure I would not fall asleep. There were only so many things I could do to keep my eyes open. I sang with the radio and picked my nose, but it was not like I could open the window for some cool air. At some point, I started staring at the yellow line and let my hemispherical vision do the rest. I thought about those poor workers who were forced to paint this never-ending line. What about those people who cleaned the seats in humongous stadiums? There were so many boring jobs in the world; it was depressing to think about it. When the line became dotted, I used a squished bug in the windshield and transformed it into a slalom champion. He was so good that I baptised him Tomba Junior. I had to start up a conversation with Pedro, but what subjects were left?

Don Angel turned my way and was about to speak, but was abruptly interrupted by Antonio who hit the roof and stuck his head inside. "There seems to be a few roads up ahead, make a right turn." He shouted.

This pretty much summed up the rest of the day. We spend our time driving from village to village, always getting the same unhelpful answer. We did get close to some city called Monteverde, but we did not even go into it.

My deliverance came when we finally stopped and found ourselves a decent campsite by the side of a beautiful lake. It was only about five o'clock, but tiredness killed me as soon as I turned off the engine. I was mentally drained. I had not really conversed all day. Anna had had some cramps and Don Angel had spent most of the afternoon outback. My brain had overheated from thinking too much.

We ate dinner, same menu as always. When it was over, I wiped my plastic plate and went to the beach. I knew I was not alone, but I still felt abandoned. My thoughts had become my friends and that was not a good thing. I was far from home and wished I could have just clicked my heels three times to return to it.

The lake's water could definitely never be drinkable, even with the finest filters. There were two couples on my left. One was sitting on a dock that probably would not support them for very long and there was a second one sitting on a trunk that laid on the sand. All four of them looked so happy. Unlike me, they were all smiles and I envied them deeply. They were home, in the arms of a person they loved. They knew where they belonged and that seemed to be the greatest possible feeling. I considered myself lost and even if I had known where to go, I could not go there tonight.

I probably would have been better off going to bed, but I decided to continue my walk. It was too early and I could not find the strength to call it quits. I felt like taking my clothes off and going for a never-ending swim. I could have kept going until fatigue came to pull me down to the bottom. This sand was keeping me grounded, but I longed to feel free. I could not stay stationary. I needed some motivation and get moving, quickly.

I simply stood there for many long minutes, thinking. It was all useless. The same question popped back every passing second: Where could they find a Shaman?

Just as darkness was about to totally fog my brain; Don Angel came to see me. "I do not mean to bother you, but you seem to need some company." He said.

"Honestly, I don't think I do." I contradicted. I was not even good company for myself, so I doubted I would be for others.

"You should get some rest, you drove all day."

Pedro was a good guy. After all, he was always there when I needed him. "I know, I'm just thinking a bit before I go to sleep." I answered. I could not just drive, eat and sleep. It still was not dark yet. "Do you seriously think a Shaman can help Anna?" I questioned Pedro.

"Personally, I'm not sure. What is important is that Anna and also Antonio believe it. We are just here to help them, give them hope." He retorted.

"Will the Shaman be able to give them more than that?"

"Who knows?"

I have always hated that kind of reply. Of course no one knows. I mean when sixteen-year-old Jack Daniel bought the local preacher's distillery for twenty-five dollars, he could never have predicted what was about to come his way. "Do you know anything about Shamans, Don Angel?" I asked annoyingly.

"Some things, yes. They can seize cosmic energy. They can hear and see things we can not. They can also talk to the other side, to the spiritual ones."

"Talking to spirits, that's pretty farfetched." I exclaimed.

"You'd be surprised." Don Angel said.

"What do you mean?"

"Nothing."

"Anything else Shamans can do?" I demanded.

"Some say they can predict the future and even take animal forms." Pedro went on.

"Alright, that's enough for me. Please don't tell Antonio that crap; he'll start asking racoons and monkeys to save his wife's life." I said, forgetting about the foreseeing nonsense.

"Don't be ridiculous Don Kristiano. I am only telling you what I have heard. You make the choice to believe or not."

"Well, I definitely decide *not* to believe. I also decide to end our conversation and continue my little walk alone, if you don't mind."

"Of course not, I will go back to the site, check on the couple."

Where did he hear all that stuff? I always thought Shamans were old farts dressed with feathers who danced around campfires. Even if the description Don Angel had given was half truth, it was impossible to find such a person. We could be going in a straight line to Gael, but we were going in circle, just for the sake of keeping hope and burning gasoline. Luckily for me, this whole expedition had not cost me too much yet, but if it dragged, I would spend all the money I had earned.

I sat on the ground; the idea of going swimming came back up to surface. My mind was clogged. Was it better dark or blank? Often in the past, I had wanted to be someone else; today I would have liked to be somewhere else. I should have gone to bed. I was so tired; my brain could not command my limbs to move. The sky started to express itself, a nice sunset was beginning to settle in. The surface of the lake made the scenery double its personality. The red flames of the top reflected on the black waves of the bottom. My right was lighting up as my left was filled with darkness. Rain was definitely present on the other side of the lake. I did not mind, I had not seen it for so long. The west was sunny, the east was rainy and a rainbow appeared to split them in harmony. The arc was taking characteristics of both sides and was making it its own. The couple on the dock quickly disappeared, taking refuge from Mother Nature's possible future fury. The second duo lasted a bit longer, but left just the same. I thought it was weird how people did not seem to take pleasure in the same things as me. Why were these couples running away? Was this sunset not amazing and worth watching? I knew the clouds were grey, but so what? We had not seen rain in such a long time; it would only be a pleasure to feel it on our faces. It was as if these people were still angry at the sun for being so hot and cruel during the day. I saw this finale as an apology, a symbol of peace. I was confused, tired. I simply did not understand why I always seemed to be doing something abnormal. People worried so much about washing their dishes properly, how come I was the only one to think about the germs in the drying cloth?

My mind was too busy reflecting. I should have gone to bed. There was no need for me to torture myself this way. The sun was useless to me and the clouds were too far to bother us tonight. I stood on the beach alone, full of confusion. Why did I want to go to bed anyway, simply to be in top shape for tomorrow's driving day? This woman's sake was now my only reason to live. I should decompress and enjoy the show that Mother Nature was putting out for me, but I could not.

Why was I so stressed out about going to bed? Who ever said I needed over seven hours of sleep to be in good form? Did I even need sleep for my well-being form or simply to have a relaxation period, an escape from reality? Why did I look at my watch and count the hours I had left to sleep? Why did I think about all the hours of driving I would have to do tomorrow? All these interrogations were impossible to answer at the moment. I needed order in my head. Structure lead to wealth, but wealth did not lead to wisdom. And since I was questioning myself, let's not forget my favourite: where could we find a Shaman?

I stood at the border of the water and sand. The little waves tried to grab me and pull me in. I needed a change, something that would clear up my mind. Out of the blue, or should it be: out of the black, I decided that swimming was a great idea. Strangely I no longer wanted to sink to the bottom, simply to enjoy the water. I was not going to go to bed so might as well do something with the last remaining rays of the sun.

I took off all my clothes, my shoes and my watch. It felt good to detach my bracelet. When I saw the tan line, the white bracelet still printed on my wrist, I felt free, as if time had just stopped. I was ready to go in the water. I was butt-naked and felt as light as the breeze.

As the water reached my ankles, I was relieved that my feet were still touching rocks. I had no desire to sink into mud and discover new bugs I had no clue existed. I kept going forward. The waves separated in half and allowed me to advance. The surface was ever changing, but always similar.

Once the level of deepness was sufficient, I dove forward and started to fly. I was so happy to be free as the wind, in a place that did not contain any. I tried to stay underwater as long as possible. It was all so quiet, so peaceful. There were some little rays of sun penetrating the surface. I swam and tried to catch them with my hands. Their beauty was spotless and would remain untouched.

I was swimming with my head out and my back to the sun. I was spitting water out of my mouth, creating myself my own personal rainbows. Since the huge one in the sky had disappeared, I was the only one to see this miracle of nature. I could distinctly see the seven colours when light pierced the drops I was spitting from my mouth. I had taken the rainbow from the sky and made it my own. This almost made me cheerful. I neglected everything else: the fact that I should have gone to bed or that I would not have a towel when I would come out. I ignored time, my watch was quietly resting inside my left shoe and that was just fine. There was no need for it at the moment.

I started dolphining again. It so was great to swim above and under, I wanted to enjoy it before total darkness fell upon me. I splashed all over, made little fountains with my hands, tried every possible swimming style I knew and even invented some.

Then, my feet touched the bottom and I stared at the horizon. It was so beautiful, so different from what I used to see back home. The mountains, or volcanoes, were stunning. Even with the blue night sky, I could see how green they were. There was now a small fog floating on the surface. This ghostly sheet brought me back to my reflecting mood. I stood there with my arms in the air and my hands on my head, probably looking like a guy who was peeing. I looked at the surface and saw my reflection. I stared for a few seconds until a wave came to slap me. I got spooked. Had I been slapped by my inner conscience wanting to remain secret? I walked up closer to the shore and looked at my reflecting self again. Once the water level moved from my shoulders to my belly button, I could look at myself longer, longer definitely, but not as clearly. I paused for a while and watched the mountains turn to complete darkness. Had I just discovered the meaning of life? I should definitely go to sleep.

I got out of the water and looked at the stars appearing in the sky. Strangely, none of them seemed familiar. I was lost between the Big Dipper and the Southern Cross. I got dressed and put my watch back on. My wet feet full of sand slid into my shoes and I started walking towards my blanket. No matter what my problems were, they would have to wait until tomorrow. Their solutions were out there, but tonight they were out of reach. I was philosophising too much. What was supposed to be a simple walk on the beach had turned out into a pathetic truth-seeking essay. Don Angel would probably tell me to float with the waves and not cut them in half. Everything would become a lot easier when I would go with the current and not against it.

I walked back to the campsite. They had made a little campfire and the three of them were silently sitting beside it. "So how was the walk?" The husband asked.

"Alright, it wasn't as relaxing as I wanted it to be, but it was good anyway." I replied.

"Why don't you join us?" Pedro offered.

"I think I'll just go to sleep right away." I declared.

"It's only seven thirty." Antonio retorted.

"Perhaps, but what time are we leaving tomorrow?"

"I would like to go around five thirty, if that is alright with you?"

I was actually very surprised that he seemed sincere in his demand. He had been such a dictator ever since we had left. Maybe, his stress level was finally starting to go down. "Five thirty is just fine, Don Antonio. You take care of Anna. Good night to all of you." I concluded.

All my inner questions disappeared once I lay down. My day was finished, even though it was still early; I yearned for a dreamless sleep. I wanted the world to forget about me for a night. It would all be there when I would wake up tomorrow. Then the same questions would pop up: where could I find a Shaman?

I woke up in the middle of the night when I heard a scratching sound on my blanket, probably some little animal that wanted to see what was inside. I was glad to have protection. Bugs were enough for me, I had so many bites I did not know where I could put an extra one.

Antonio woke me up with his usual little kick to the shoulder. We had breakfast and left right away, it was not even five thirty. The same story again: roads after roads after roads, all of them made of dirt. I longed for a paved highway. Poor Anna in the back, those holes were probably merciless for her condition. I truly wished we could have the chance to talk more often. If only I could ride in the back and someone else could drive. She was becoming a sort of hero to me, an unknown one, but one nonetheless. She never complained. She was mentally so strong that she could hide all physical and mental weaknesses.

"What are you thinking about now, Don Kristiano?" Pedro, who had probably noticed my over-reflecting state, asked.

"Anna." I simply replied.

"And what about her?"

"It's strange. She's just different than all the other sick people I have seen before. Back home, everybody almost seems happy to have the flu or something. I mean, they get the day off and if they're lucky, they'll have a chance to lose a few pounds."

"Sickness is kind of similar to a bad deed: it's attractive and repulsive at the same time." Don Angel said.

"I guess you're right. In a way, people are scared, but they almost wished they could be sick so they could stay in bed."

"Do you mean that a virus brings justification to laziness?" He asked.

"Yes. Finally, they have a reason to do nothing all day and get served by others. All of a sudden, everybody is so interested in the temporary patient."

"If what you say about other people is true, maybe you should tell them not to take their health for granted. Folks with real sicknesses like cancer, diabetes, or Parkinson would give their right arm for a day of good health. The people you mentioned earlier are glad to be sick simply because they know it is for a short period." He paused and looked behind. "If they could see Anna in the back of our pick-up, they would get off their butts and get back to work with their box of tissue." Don Angel said.

"You're right." I replied. "I wish I could get to know Anna better. After all, I'm here for her and we almost never speak." I added, slightly changing the subject.

"I know, but her battle is different from yours." He answered in low tone.

"What are you talking about? I don't have a battle to fight." I said.

He hesitated a moment. "Of course you do, we all do. Maybe you just don't want to admit it." He smiled. "Yet!"

We covered a lot of ground during the day. We even had to gas up twice. Evidently, I was the one who put his hand in his pocket. We would soon have to reach the capital for a bank, the funds were running low.

We drove through the city of Puntarenas at the end of the morning. We asked a thousand questions to all its inhabitants. The city was everything but abnormal for a Central American one. It all went well until we stopped at a stop sign and were almost taken hostage by a group of youngsters. There was about fifteen of them and four were standing right in front of the vehicle so I could not go forward. It started gently, but quickly got crazy. They were buzzing around the truck like bees around honey. From the back, I could hear Antonio trying to reason with them. I had no clue what to do. I observed the scene from my rear-view mirror. I saw one of them touched Anna and he received the husband's punch in the face the following half-second. The man fell flat on the sidewalk. I could not believe how destructive Antonio's blow had been. This aggressive retaliation drastically heated things up; people started yelling from all sides. Antonio was no longer trying to calm them down, he was screaming back. Both of us in the cabin stayed quiet. I sure did not know how to react. Don Angel just kept very still and tranquil, observing every participant. When one tried to climb in the back, things really got out of hands. Antonio started hitting from side to side. He used karate chops to the throat and other kinds of hit that made sure the receivers stayed down for the count. I was astounded by my partner's fighting skills. He was an unbelievable killing machine, able to keep them all from coming up.

"Don Kristiano, you will have to make a choice. We have to get out of here. You have to push these people out of our way or we could be in serious trouble." Pedro suddenly announced.

I had no time to waste. I heard Anna scream and then Antonio started banging the roof. I hit the accelerator and closed my eyes. I felt something hit the bumper. I began to get some speed and feel free. When I looked in my side mirror, I saw two guys lying on the ground. One was holding his left leg. Perhaps I had rolled over his ankle. The second one was not moving yet; hopefully I had not killed him or anything. There were about ten of them running after us, but there was no way they would catch us. Thankfully, I saw the second guy moving, relieving my conscience of his possible death. I hit the gas, prudently burned two red lights as we exited the city.

"Thank you Don Kristiano. Now please just drive for a while." Antonio said through the back window, breathing heavily, trying to calm himself down.

My hands were shaking and my gut was killing me. "No problem. Are you guys alright?" I replied.

"Yes we are." The husband concluded.

"Are *you* alright?" Don Angel asked.

"I'm fine, why shouldn't I be?" I answered to sound tough.

"No reason." He said with a sorry look on his face.

I stayed quiet for about ten minutes. "How can these people turn into animals like that?" I then questioned.

"I don't know." Don Angel answered.

"Sometimes I feel like human beings shouldn't be allowed to regroup together." I declared.

"Some people need it to feel secure." Pedro answered.

"And you see what happens? Gangs are cradles of hatred and violence!"

"Try not to generalize, Don Kristiano."

"C'mon, you know it, the more people get together, the crazier it gets."

"What about birthday parties and Christmas celebration, isn't that a group of people?" Pedro asked.

"That's not the same. Don't joke around. There's a difference between a friendly gathering and a gang like we just saw."

"The idea is the same; it is just the purpose that differs. Remember that many people can not bear to be alone. The only time they can really feel safe is when they are with others."

"I'm very often alone and it isn't that bad."

"Perhaps it is because you are stronger."

"Yeah, right!" I replied incredulously.

"Alright then, it may be because you are used to it. Still, some people need to be directed. There are leaders and followers." He said.

"I believe we can be both, depending on the situation."

"You can only speak for yourself. Some are simply not able to make the switch." Pedro contradicted again.

"I think they choose not to."

He hesitated a little. "Just like you choose not to admit the limitations of others?" Don Angel asked.

"The point is that gangs like that refuse to see other people's opinions; it's pathetic. It's as if they had no desire of understanding anything else than what they believed to be the truth." I blurted out aggressively.

"I know what you mean; it would be like a capitalist arriving in a village like Cinco Pinos and judging its inhabitants according to their Sandinistas beliefs." Don Angel concluded with half a smile.

I could not answer to that one. I tried not to become red and let my shame visible. How did he know, was it so apparent? I concentrated on the road and kept my mouth shut. Who was I to tell him that judging was immoral, he who had accepted me from day one: I was a sad excuse for a human being.

We drove through the city of Alajuela and asked a few questions here and there in surrounding villages. Once we were out, I stopped the truck to have a chat with Antonio. "This is ridiculous. We won't find any answers; these are ignorant peasants and who don't know a thing." I quickly challenged.

"These villagers, peasants as you called them, know a lot more than you can ever think." He answered.

"Maybe, but that's not the point!"

"What is the point then?" Antonio questioned.

"Well, we're out of money. These little towns don't have bank machines and if you haven't noticed, we've been spending a lot lately. We have to get to San Jose, if not for Gael, then to get some cash."

The husband did not answer anything. He looked like he was ashamed not to be able to financially support this expedition. The balance of power was shifting. I felt it. He felt it too, only he did not like it.

"Let's go see Gael and the Doctors at the capital's general hospital, they might have some answers." I tried to persuade once more.

"Okay, but I do not believe in modern medicine anymore." The husband replied shortly.

"I don't mean to offend you, Antonio, but Costa Rican doctors might know some stuff that the Nicaraguan ones don't. Maybe they'll have an alternative to this Shaman nonsense."

He looked at his wife's reaction and signalled me to take some distances. I felt bad that I had expressed out loud my negative thoughts. "You are the only one that it sounds like nonsense to." He paused. "Doctors are all the same. We will go to the hospital, but only to question Gael." He stopped talking when I stared at him in a defying way. He looked straight at me and hesitated for a bit. "I will not subject my wife to a bunch of tests again. She is done dealing with powerless doctors. From now on, she only hears good news. Got it?" He concluded with a very low tone of voice.

I smirked and looked at the woman. "We got ourselves a deal." I finished.

We arrived in the capital in the middle of the afternoon. We looked around for a bank machine, but it seemed just as hard as finding a Shaman. At some point, we did find one, but my card did not work in it. Already, I felt like the day was long. I still had not gotten used to the very early mornings. We went to the Central Mercado for a cheap and late lunch. It was almost scary to eat there. There were so many live animals. I thought one would attack me to get revenge for all his slaughtered companions. The husband asked his question to everyone he met. I spoke with this amazing looking man that looked like a voodoo priest. I though for sure he was a Shaman. All he said was to drink some venom from a freshly killed cobra. With the laugh he gave out following his sentence, I simply stared at him and started to walk backward. He was wack!

We drove around in search of the main hospital. The city stank. All this carbon dioxide could not be good for Anna's lungs. Luckily for her husband, she was always so quiet, never complained. It was sad to witness the hopeless fight she was leading. "I'm sorry," I said to a weird looking pedestrian, "could you tell me where I can find the general hospital?"

"You a Yankee tourist?" He questioned.

I did not answer.

"Forget the hospital." He said and then pointed at the building across the street. "This is the museum of Jade."

I could not believe this idiot. "I don't need art right now; I need to know where the hospital is." I replied angrily.

"Are you sure? It is the biggest collection of jade sculptures in the world." He said.

Did he not have any care for Anna in the back? Although she was hard to see, I knew for a fact she was not invisible. I decided to get him off my case. "Sorry, but we don't even have any cash for the time being."

"Don't worry about that, there is an instant-bank machine right there." He finished as he pointed to it.

I was saved. "Well look at that!" I exclaimed out loud. "Thanks man, I definitely owe you one." I drove off and went to park the truck. Minutes later, I was taking out all my savings and was stashing it in my two front pockets. Strangely, there was a lot more than I had expected. Very weird, but I was not complaining.

As I walked back to the truck, Antonio gave me a big smile.

"You're a good guy Don Kristiano. You will fully be repaid for that." Pedro said.

I climbed inside. "I doubt it." I sadly disagreed.

"I don't.' Don Angel concluded.

We drove around for about twenty minutes until we finally found the hospital. We parked and I got out with Antonio. We quickly entered and went straight to the counter. "We are looking for a man known only as Gael." My partner interrogated the lady.

She did not answer right away and looked a bit sad. "Is it an emergency?" She asked.

"Well, not really." I quickly responded, as the husband gave me a disapproving look.

"I'm sorry; you will have to make an appointment." The woman said.

"If we schedule a date, how long will have to wait?" Antonio demanded.

"I can give you a rendezvous in December."

"When!?" I exclaimed. "We only have a quick question. We can't wait that long." I insisted. The woman did not move. "December is in over four months from now!" I yelled, hoping to get a reaction from her.

"We are sorry sir, but that is the best we can do." She robotically replied.

Antonio pushed me aside, gently, but with a lot of authority. He bent down over the counter. He signalled for the woman to approach and he whispered something in her ear. It was a thing of beauty to witness her expression change, within five seconds, her face of nonchalance transformed into one of horrifying terror.

"Walk down the hall, it is the fourth door on your left." She explained.

"Thank you, we will be quick." Antonio said. "Let's go Don Kristiano." The husband ordered.

I simply followed and did not dare ask what he had said.

Few seconds later, we arrived at the door and Antonio knocked quickly. He did not wait for a reply, as if he was afraid of being arrested by security. He pushed the door open and locked it behind us.

There was an odd looking man with glasses standing beside a bunch of disorganised shelves. It was impossible for me to say what his job was. "Gael?" My partner asked.

"Si!" He replied with curiosity in his eyes.

"We will not take much of your time." Antonio assured.

"Can you tell us where we could find a Shaman?" I interrupted and straightforwardly questioned.

He did not say anything right a way. Staring at us, probably trying to figure out what a white boy like me was doing with an older Latino dude like Antonio. "A Shaman, who sent you here?" Gael demanded.

"A friend of a friend of a friend." I answered with an annoyed tone that meant business.

"Doctor Geraldo Olmos from the Managua Hospital. Please, my wife needs help. Do you know anything that can help us?" The husband cut in nicely.

He hesitate some more. "I was once saved by a Shaman in the Osa Peninsula." He stopped when he saw our looks of interrogation. "It is by the Pacific Ocean in the southern part of the country: a dense tropical rainforest" He clarified.

"Where exactly in the Peninsula?" I asked.

The man looked apologetic. "It was so long ago."

"How long ago was it?" I questioned again.

Gael waited a while. "Just over ten years." He replied.

It hit me like a hammer. Ten years? If I believed what they said on the news, half the forest could be gone by now. I stayed immobile. I wanted to shout and start throwing things around. At least our haystack would be narrowed down to a Peninsula. "Thanks a lot." I said honestly and lead Antonio out of the room.

"Was the Shaman old?" My partner asked as we were about to get out the door.

"Not at all." Gael answered with an encouraging tone.

We both crossed the corridor, the woman from the booth had gone away, probably needed a well-deserved break. We exited the building and silently walked to the truck.

When we arrived at the vehicle, Antonio went to talk to his wife in the back box. Don Angel caught my eye; he was walking around, staring at rocks on the ground and analyzing them.

"Don Kristiano!" Antonio called and got my mind off the pebble analyser.

The husband simply gave me an interrogating look. "So, what's the plan now?" I asked.

"The plan remains the same. We head for Osa, but we keep asking people on the way." He stopped and looked in Don Angel's direction. "Let's go, we are wasting time" Antonio commanded.

Although we all heard him, none of us seemed ready to move.

"Did you ask to see a doctor?" Anna lightly inquired.

"The earliest we could have gotten was December." Her husband answered gently.

"I don't understand how it can be that long." I expressed with sorrow.

"It's normal." Anna said with a sympathetic smile.

I remained speechless.

"You think this is bad? In Nicaragua, it is not abnormal to see a pregnant woman give birth in the hospital's parking lot because they have no room inside." The husband informed me.

And I thought my country was terrible. "How can that be? The pain must be excruciating without the drugs." I said.

"Do not fool yourself, Don Kristiano; even inside, drugs are not a luxury that Nicaraguans can afford. All women go through childbirth naturally." Anna clarified.

Incredible! I wanted to go back to the village and easily earn my money, but after this slap in the face, I could not refuse anything they asked for. "Well alright then, let's just keep going." I paused and waited for a reaction, but I got none. "We're heading south!" I swiftly ordered.

Antonio took out his map and stayed silent for a bit. "Yes we're heading south, aim for the Osa Peninsula." He concluded.

"Vamos!" I encouraged. I had absolutely no idea where that was, but I would have time to ask on my way there.

Our little stop in the capital had cut our routine in half, but it returned very quickly. We drove on similar dirt roads and started to ask the same question. At least, we now had money. I had taken everything out of my account. I was still wondering where the extra money had come from.

Antonio banged on the roof. "Don Kristiano, please stop by that restaurant. I would like to talk to these villagers." The husband said.

I executed the demand and the interrogator went on his lonesome way. "I'll be into that store over there." I shouted to Antonio. I needed some extra clothes, our trip was not supposed to last this long and we rarely had time to do a wash.

Anna stayed in the truck and Don Angel came out to watch over her. He was always so nice to her, telling her reassuring comments.

I entered the store and made the wooden chime sing over the door. A nice old lady came to greet me. "Do you need anything Señor?"

"I don't presume you would know where I could find a Shaman?" I surprised myself asking. I figured since I was there, I might as well join the inquisition party.

She was stunned as well. "Pardon me?" She asked very incredulously.

"It's okay, I don't need help. I'll just have a look around." I replied.

She went away and left me browsing on my own. After a while, I saw a nice white T-shirt. "Could I try on this one?" I called to the lady.

Without a word, she came to me and handed me a dark blue T-shirt. "You can try this one." She countered.

I did not know what to say. Why would she not let me try the white one? I did not like the fact that there was a huge sign on it. It was probably some cheap local brand. There was no questioning the fact that I was stepping out of the crowd around here. If they wanted me to advertise some cheap hometown trademark, they should pay me money. She insisted with her right hand, pushing the T-shirt on me and her left hand pointed at the changing room. Then I clicked, the lady surely thought I was too dirty to try on the immaculate colour. "That's fine; I'll simply buy it without trying it." I said as I grabbed back my white one. I left without saying thank you.

As I arrived to the truck, everyone was back in position, ready to leave.

Everything went well for the rest of the day. The afternoon was quiet; we crossed the city of Cartago, that was it. I felt guilty about not calling home and reflected on it a lot. Perhaps, I should even call Martin again and give him some news.

Antonio banged on the roof. "Please turn left at the next intersection, Don Kristiano."

I did what Antonio wanted and kept on driving mutely, not knowing if I should start chatting with Don Angel. He was looking out his window and I had no clue if he was mad at me. Maybe it was my depressing state of mind that was messing up my brain. Ever since I had met him in Cinco Pinos, I had found myself believing in him. Was I being well guided or being well fooled?

We found ourselves a nice place to camp for the night. "What is wrong Don Kristiano?" Pedro questioned.

"What do you mean?"

"Why are you so sad?" He asked.

"I'm not sure." I replied with a more serious tone.

"It does not tell me anything." He paused and looked around. "I will ask you again and now try to think of something better to say." My partner teased with a smile.

"Forget your question because I have one for you. How long do you have to be down to be considered on an official depression?" I asked.

"What?"

"This is all too much for me right now." I finally confessed.

"Tell me honestly, after everything you have seen here, did you ever, in your entire life, go through a *really* rough period?" Don Angel asked.

It was the first time I did not feel any compassion from my friend, it was all relative. "Of course!" I fibbed. I knew very well, he was about to tell me that my pain was nothing compared to some of the people's around here, but I did not care about them. Out of the corner of my eye, I saw him smile, as if his lips were telling me to get over myself. After all, maybe he was right. I never really had it rough. My parents had always helped me. It was not like I ever had to warm up my hands over a boiling pot of noodles. They had always made sure we had no financial problems. My parents were surely the reason why my bank account had gotten bigger. I had not even called home since I had left Cinco Pinos; they were probably worried out of their minds. For them, putting money in my bank account was always a good way to make sure I was fine.

"If you are so sad maybe you should just cry it out."

I did not know if he was sarcastic or he literally meant it. "What?! What good would crying do?" I shockingly asked.

"A lot. I saw you express your joy in the past, why can you not do the same with your sorrow? Perhaps if you let your sadness out, you could fill your heart with happiness again." Don Angel explained with compassion.

It made sense in a weird way, but I was not going to admit it. "Whatever! I don't need to hear it right now." I replied.

"What else do you have to do?" Pedro mockingly asked.

"I have to drive, I have a woman to help and for that, I have to find a Shaman, so keep your guidance to yourself. I don't need it right now." I said swiftly.

I went to sleep.

The next days went alright. I would try to describe them and nothing, absolutely nothing, would come out. We went through Quepos, San Isidro, and many other cities not worth mentioning. It was all totally boring.

The road was long and seemed endless. Always the same two lanes separated by a yellow line and boarded by tall green trees. "Antonio, get in here!" I shouted through the window.

"What is wrong?" The husband questioned as he settled in.

"Nothing, I'm bored. You have a story for me?" I asked. "Why don't you tell me about the great Christopher Columbus?" I randomly chose.

"I don't know about great, maybe for you Europeans he was, but not for us."

"What do you mean?" I was shocked.

"Why would he be considered great? He showed up uninvited, settled in, saw a few gold chunks and thought he could make a fortune. He captured indigenous, went back to Europe to show them off and also lied about the amount of gold he had seen. He returned to Guanahani, the Bahamas, with close to twenty ships and over a thousand men. Since there was not enough gold to quench his thirst, he captured Natives and turned them into slaves. He made them search for gold, and those who did not reach their quota had their hands cut off, slowly bleeding to death. The Bahamans were so afraid of getting caught that they committed group suicide by poisoning, they even killed their own children so they would not be captured."

"Alright, alright, I get the picture." I stopped him.

Antonio laughed out loud. "Columbus a hero? Please. Do you really think we celebrate Columbus Day around here?" He questioned.

"I think you should go check on your wife. Thanks for nothing." I finished. I knew I should have asked Pedro instead.

Hours passed: we went too far down to Golfito and had to come back north to find the road to the Osa Peninsula.

We drove around the Peninsula for a whole day. We had no leads. There was no way I could see how we would find anything. We barely saw anybody to talk to. The forest was thick and almost impenetrable. Where should we go? Should we start hiking? Which trail should we take? I knew I had thought this before, but this was truly nonsense and hopeless.

After the sunset, we set up camp in a remote area where no one could ever find us. We ate some leftover fruits for dinner and quickly went to sleep. I was exhausted and fell asleep on the spot, ignoring the six thousand types of different insects flying around.

I woke up in the morning with about a hundred bites on the face alone. We did not have breakfast and left right away. Our drive was cut very short by a pick-up truck blocking our way. Some kind of agent got out and came our way. Antonio quickly jumped out of the back box and met him before he could reach me. My friend gave me a nod and I joined the party. "Where are you going?" The man asked.

We did not answer. I certainly was not going to admit the truth to this stranger.

"This is a National Park and I need to know your purpose here." The ranger said nicely.

"A National Park?" I blurted.

"Yes, this is Corcovado Park" He clarified and since we were too surprised to speak, he carried on. "It is the best in the country. We shelter the biggest population of scarlet macaws and over fifty types of nocturnal bats." He proudly explained.

Did I give a hoot about bats? We just stared at him with puzzled expressions on our faces. Antonio was surely like me, wondering if a Shaman could live in a National Park. Unlikely. "Is the whole Peninsula controlled?" I questioned.

"Pretty much, I have worked here for over twenty years. I know it like the back of my hand." The park ranger answered.

"Do you know if we could find a Shaman here?" My friend interrogated.

The man, rightfully, seemed confused. He reflected a second. "Are you serious?" He asked, probably just to be sure he would not make a fool out of himself by answering.

"Yes, we are." I assured him.

He looked at the truck and spotted Anna in the back. "There was a tribe with a Shaman about fifty kilometres from here, just outside the park."

"Why are you using the past tense of the verb *to be*?" I cut in.

"These people were relocated about three years ago when the land was sold to a private owner. I'm really sorry. I have no idea where they are." He admitted.

I was boiling inside and by the looks of him, Antonio was ready to explode. Was the tribe relocated or *dislocated*? "Why was the land sold?" I asked, as my friend stayed quiet.

"So the wildlife could be protected." The ranger replied. "There was a lot of pollution created by gold mining over the century. People are simply protecting animals nowadays."

"But what about the people? The people?" Antonio questioned angrily.

The man did not say anything for a time. He simply stood there, looking sympathetic to our cause.

Antonio walked back to his wife and left me alone with the chap. "Do you have any idea where there could be another one?" I asked.

"I do not think you will find one around here. Panama is your best solution." He answered.

Damn! Why could he not have said Nicaragua? Why did he have to be south again? "Thanks!" I concluded, and went to tell Antonio about our next destination. Keep the faith.

Finally, we arrived in Paso Conaos where we easily crossed the border. We changed all our money into US currency and went on our way. After Nicaragua and Costa Rica, I added the Panamanian stamp to my passport.

CHAPTER 3.4

Again, the country's name had changed, but the scenery mostly remained the same. "Are all countries similar around here?" I asked Don Angel.

"It depends on the way you look at it." He answered.

Frankly, I was getting ticked at my friend's vagueness. There rarely were any straight answers. It had to be something deeply annoying that I needed to be interpreted. I stayed silent, ignoring his comment.

At that moment, Antonio came in through the back window and sat inside. "So, Don Kristiano, you want your history lesson?" He rhetorically questioned, in a nice way.

"Shoot your lesson! Who else is going to give it to me?" I said as I quickly looked at Don Angel. "You're going to give me an objective history lesson or your usual anti-American rubbish?" I dared to ask. He stared at me in the rear-view mirror and did not seem to know what to reply. "Forget what I said, I'm just tired. Please, I need to know some stuff about this land before I get further into it." I added encouragingly.

"First of all, early inhabitants were destroyed by some disease brought by the Spanish explorers."

"Damn Columbus!" I interrupted. "Sorry, do go on."

"The Europeans used the Pacific Coast to organize their invasion of Peru. This recent immense wealth coming in the Caribbean area attracted pirates from all over. It became very unsafe. The nation deteriorated and then became a province of Columbia." Antonio explained.

"They had control over Panama?" I asked.

"Yes, and they were the ones who granted the US the right to build a railroad across the Isthmus and even defend it by force if necessary."

"So Americans aren't the bad boys here?" I asked. I did not really want to be disrespectful, but for some strange reason, I felt like goofing off. I did not need to hear a Sandinistas version of Panama's history.

"I'm not finished yet." He replied.

"Sorry. How did the States get the canal?" I interrogated.

"The Yankees had wanted to build one for a long time. They had even tried to dig one in Nicaragua, but my country was too big and resistant." He proudly answered.

"So they simply asked for one here and the Panamanians said yes?"

"Actually, it was the French who first received the right to build a canal near the end of the nineteenth century. Panamanians never had anything to say, it was Columbia who gave permission."

"And what went wrong for the Frenchies?"

"Twenty thousands workers died from yellow fever and malaria. The French businessmen all went bankrupt and sold their never-ending rights to the Unitedstatians, regardless of the Columbian objections."

"How did the Panamanians feel about all this?" I asked.

"I do not know, but I can imagine they were getting tired of not having anything to say about what was going on in their own country. It got to a point when they were so angry that they decided to take arms against Columbia. They got their independence shortly after all the fighting was done, but it was too late; the canal was already out of their reach." The husband replied.

"But not anymore, right? The US did give it back?" I pointed out.

"Yes, they did." He admitted.

"Didn't you say that it was a never-ending deal?"

"Yes, it was supposed to be." He shyly said.

"Why did they give it back then?"

Antonio looked out the window, trying to find a way to get away. "It's complicated, I'm not sure."

I laughed out loud. "What happened?" I insisted.

"I am honestly not sure, and now I have to go back to my wife." He finished.

He started climbing out the window, but I stopped him. "Don't tell me you'll be forced to admit that the Americans might have done something good?" I laughed.

He did not answer and continued to climb out.

"I'm sure he knows." I told Don Angel.

"Maybe, maybe not." He replied.

"Well, if he doesn't know it's surely because he decided not to, probably the knowledge did not suit him." I alleged. "What is he so afraid of?" I questioned.

He took his time to answer. "Some Nicaraguans have beliefs that go beyond what you can see." Pedro replied.

"Could you add another sentence and be a bit vaguer?" I sarcastically asked.

"You do not know what Antonio went through in his life. Give him time." He explained.

"You also took part in all this and you don't hold a grudge that huge."

"Our situations are very different. My involvement was short and almost painless. Although it is hard to measure mental pain, I think Antonio suffered a lot more than I did."

"Still, I don't get him sometimes." I admitted.

"Who says you have to?"

"No one, it'd just be nice to understand him a little better."

"Tell me, Don Kristiano, do you understand *me* completely?"

"No way!" I blurted out.

"That does not mean that you can not appreciate me." He said and paused. "Do not worry; perhaps someday you *will* understand all of us very well.

"How's that?"

"Sometimes it is just easier to see when you are further away." Pedro concluded.

I had no reason not to trust Don Angel on this. Whether I liked to believe it or not, he was, almost, always right. I had to give both of them some time.

When I thought about it, Don Angel's story was not clear either. He was too busy giving me advice that he never told me exactly what had happened to him. I wanted to ask, but could not do it as directly as before. For the first time in my life, I was learning to deal with very delicate subjects.

We drove around all afternoon in the province of Chiriqui. The region was beautiful, surrounded by picturesque mountains. There were cattle everywhere we went. We also saw some coffee plantations that made me wonder how ours was doing. Even though we stopped everywhere and Antonio never got the answer he wanted, it was a pleasant day.

We found a place to camp for the night around the city of David. Nothing came out of the ordinary. We started the campfire and got ready to cook. I was surprised at how little Don Angel helped out. Perhaps it was why he barely ate anything. He probably felt guilty if he took food he had not paid for. Maybe he thought we needed it more than he did.

Once dinner was done, we set up our blankets and Pedro stayed in the truck. I joined him for a bit while the couple was relaxing by the cracking sound of the burning branches. I laid down on the front seat since Don Angel had taken the back one. "You alright Don Kristiano?" Pedro predictably started.

"I guess."

"This trip is taking his toll on you, is it not?" He asked.

"You could say that. I never thought it would last this long. I feel like I'm starting to lose it." I admitted.

"Lose it... what do you mean?"

"Like my mind is going. I think too much. I have a hard time focussing on the road." I paused. "I would hate for anyone to know what is stuck inside there." I added as I pointed to my forehead.

"I'm not sure I am following."

"Exactly!" I hesitated a bit, but decided to share it all with him. "When I'm driving, I daydream so much, I don't even know if I'm awake or not. I feel like every day lasts twenty-three hours, as if I'm on a train going west at fifty kilometre an hour. I'm lost and don't know which way to look at things anymore." I admitted.

"A concrete thing can also be abstract if it is viewed from a different angle. You are far from being unique." Don Angel encouraged.

"What do you mean by that? You think I'm an ordinary Joe."

"That's not what I mean. I simply mean that a lot of people are lost and confused. Did you ever think about going to see a psychologist?"

"Yeah, right!" I shortly replied in a negative tone of voice.

"Why not? You complain and admit that you can not find the answers on your own, why should you not go and ask for help?"

"I don't need a psychologist, I have you." I said with a smile and a strong laugh.

"The day that you will be able to say that out loud, without laughing, I might actually believe you." Don Angel concluded our conversation as he turned around to fall asleep.

I stepped out of the vehicle and went straight to my blanket. The couple was already asleep, peacefully. I felt bad about what I had said to Pedro. Well, it was not really what I had said, but mostly how I had said it. So it came out the wrong way: shoot me.

During the night, I woke up with a strange feeling. The sky was pitch-black with bright white clouds. There was a gentle rain falling down. The drops seemed to be rocked by a light tender wind. It was as if the breeze was helping them to safely fall on the hard ground I was sleeping on. The drops reflected the light of the night. Many of them came to give me a warm kiss on the face and helped me to fall asleep again. I had the intention of making a long blink to the hidden moon before the short sunrise ahead.

The day started early and, as usual, we got on the way after our morning fruit. We arrived in the city of David in the middle of the morning. It was big, but definitely not one that would attract a lot of tourism. I bought four little bags of water at the street lights. Don Angel refused his, pretending he was not thirsty. Evidently, the couple in the back, sizzling under the hot rays of Mr. Phoebus, gladly accepted theirs.

We asked people all over, but did not even bother stopping at the hospital. I think the one back in Costa Rica had left a bad taste in our mouths. At some point, Antonio decided to run off and ask his usual question in some back alleyways. Personally, I really had to go to the toilet and since we were in a city, I was looking forward to sitting on a nice comfortable seat. Don Angel assured me he would keep an eye on Anna so I peacefully left in search of a decent ceramic chair.

Once it was all over and I had thrown my paper in the bucket beside the loo, I stepped out and ran right into a young man wearing a red T-shirt with the white cross. "Are you from Switzerland as well or you just liked the shirt?" I questioned.

"Born and raised in Geneva." He proudly answered. "You?"

"Grew up in Luzern." I retaliated. "Are you always wearing the flag on your clothes?"

"No, no, but it's easier, people around here always assume I'm American."

Yeah right, as if they knew that it was the Swiss flag. I just nodded: What an idiot.

"Hey! What are you doing in this part of the world?" He loudly questioned.

I was stunned and did not know what to answer, or if I should even bother. "Probably the same thing as you." I finally replied.

"You're a university student doing a master's degree in political science?" He retorted with a cocky smile.

Once again, I made a facial expression that answered his question. He had me there, we were so far apart it was not even funny, a university geek wearing his country's flag on his shirt.

"Would you like to sit down for bit and chat? I haven't spoken French in so long, I could really use a Spanish break." He pleaded.

"Don't you have to use the men's room?" I asked to get away.

"I've been using it ever since I've arrived, I can wait a little while."

"Hold on, give me a second." I said to gain some time to figure out an excuse. I looked out the door and saw Anna in the back, Don Angel's silhouette beside her and Antonio was still nowhere in sight.

Unfortunately, I had a few minutes to spare. I nodded to the guy and he invited me to sit down at a table.

"My name is Arnaud. I just arrived two weeks ago. I came for my studies, but I also bought myself a board to surf the best beaches around. So far, I only heard about Santa Catalina Beach in the Azuero Peninsula. Did you see any cool beaches around?" He asked.

From the length of his introduction, I figured I would not say much. Did I look like someone who knew where the good beaches were? Did I look like I care? "I just arrived here as well; I haven't had the time to check out the beaches yet." I replied to be polite.

"I was thinking about going tomorrow, would you like to join me?"

"Sorry, no, I can't make it tomorrow." I simply declined. "So, what's your thesis on?" I questioned in an attempt to change the subject.

"The difference between our country and Panama, the way the two governments are doing things."

I felt like screaming. University was over for me, I had my degree in my back pocket and I had been sitting on it for the last two months. Suddenly, I had a thought and I expressed it out loud. "Hey, you know about politics, why did the States give back the canal?" I asked the book worm to conclude what Antonio and I had started.

"I'm not sure. In the past, there were many manifestations because the original agreement was clearly favourable to the United States. The Panamanian government never had much to say about all this, I believe. Theoretically, the people had the right to be angry. I mean, I know the US paid for Panama's independence, but it doesn't give them all the rights for ever."

"What?" I questioned, a small detail that Antonio had forgotten to mention. "The US paid for Panama's independence?"

"Yeah, in nineteen twenty something, the American government compensated the Columbian government with twenty-five million dollars for the umbilical cord to be cut."

"And they simply gave the canal back on New Year's Eve two thousand, free of charge?" I asked for specification.

"I think so, but we can never be sure." Arnaud replied.

"You're right about that." I concluded as I looked outside and saw the husband stepping back into the light of the square. "I gotta run. It was nice talking to you after all." Arnaud made a face when I said that last part. "Enjoy the beaches!" I wished to make him feel better. My tête-à-tête had just officially ended.

I walked back to the truck.

We were heading south towards Santiago, not the one in Chile, but the way things were going that one would probably be a destination later. "How will I find a Shaman?" I only moved my lips to the question; no sound came out of my voice.

"Don't be troubled, Don Kristiano. Our wish has been expressed; the solution will present itself someday." Don Angel said.

"When?" I asked.

"That's the beauty of it all, no one knows. We can only be patient and wait for it."

I held back not to argue with him about his choice of vocabulary word: *beauty*. "Why not just sit tight then and wait for it here?"

"Unfortunately it does not work that way." He concluded.

I turned the radio on and looked for a Rock station. "Leave it there please!" Pedro asked as the sound of ABBA appeared.

"You like Fernando?" I intriguingly questioned.

"Love it!" He shamelessly admitted. "I like all this new kind of music." He then said.

I thought it weird that he classified this old disco Swedish quartet as new. Maybe Nicaragua was not getting the music as fast as we did back home.

We stopped for the night on the side of some desolated road between the city of David and Santiago. It was a place with no name where Antonio had just stuck his head inside and had asked me to call it a day.

"Why are we stopping here in the middle of nowhere?" I asked Pedro when we exited the truck.

He glanced around the place, before answering. "If you separate that word *nowhere*, it makes *now* and *here*. And that is all that matters for the time being." Don Angel peacefully said.

I prepared myself for another boring evening. It was always the same. The couple would stay a bit afar and I would not want to disturb them, I would end up taking a walk by myself or with Don Angel: talk about excitement in Panama.

The next morning, we awoke and realized that there were no more fruit in the bag. "Let's just go right away, we'll find something on the way." The husband suggested.

I looked at Pedro with a puzzled stare, hoping he would argue, but he was not going to say a word. "On the way where, to Neverland?" I teasingly asked Antonio.

The husband just looked at me with a bit of desolation in his eyes. "We're heading south, same as yesterday." He said.

"And tomorrow." I added.

"Do you have a better idea?" Antonio demanded with irritation.

"No, I don't." I paused and looked at Don Angel, who moved away towards the truck. "But I hear that if we wait long enough, the solution will simply magically appear." I said with a big grin.

"Perhaps you are right, Don Kristiano." The husband almost cheerfully replied. Then he stopped and came closer so no one else could hear. "Can we please get going? My wife's life is a stake." The man expressed in a very dramatic tone.

We started rolling and my brain started to go crazy again. I stupidly imagined stupid things about every stupid subject in this stupid world. Why was I not able to lick my elbow?

Antonio took me away from my thoughts as he knocked on the back window. "Pull over at the grocery store coming up on my right."

We drove around all day and as we approached Santiago, I saw three crows going through the garbage on my right. They fitted well with the scenery. Then, two of them started fighting and flew up into the air. Evidently, the scene was useless for everybody else but me. Why did they have to fight? The other one quietly stayed on the ground, eating away. Was there not enough garbage for both of them to share? Why did they not quietly stay on the terra firma? Was the sky's battlefield more suitable for them? At last, they perched themselves on a tree. The branch bent with the weight of their small bodies. They seemed destabilized in front of this new problem. The third one left the ground and flew right in the middle of the other two, forcing them to separate. They all left the tree. One went back to the ground and the two others flew away towards the clouds. Which one was better, was the one on the ground considering this a victory or was it the one in the sky who was happier to be free?

I realized I was spending way too much time thinking about this, maybe because, for some reason, any couple I saw reminded me of Antonio and Anna. Regardless, they were far gone. I had to get my mind back in the present and forget about the now infamous Santiago Crows.

We spent a quiet night in a nice little location. Some old lady had accepted for us to sleep on her property. She even took out some old disgusting comfortable foamy mattresses. I went to bed early, thinking about the five o'clock rude awakening of tomorrow morning.

Strangely enough, Antonio woke me up with a nice friendly tap on the shoulder. He was kneeling beside me when I opened my eyes. "Wake up, Don Kristiano." He had said in a very paternal tone of voice. How could I refuse him?

Once we were on the road, we stayed quiet for a long time. Although I kept on getting a bit sillier every hour, ennui came to fetch me. "Okay, I'm bored." I expressed to Pedro. "Is there anybody else I should know about? I heard of Sandino, Somoza, Guevara, Columbus and Pancho Villa. Who else's left?" I asked.

Don Angel grinned. "My favourite: Simon Bolivar." He then quickly replied.

"Great, who's that?"

"He is the general who took care of the Spaniard's occupation in many parts of Latin America. They called him *El Liberator* or, you will love this one, the George Washington of South America."

That one made me smile. "I like that indeed."

"After many battles for many long years, the Republic of Columbia was formed. It included Panama, Venezuela, Columbia, and Ecuador. Evidently, Simon Bolivar was the first president. Later, he was also dictator of Peru."

Now that one surprised me. "Dictator?" I inquired.

"Yes, Don Kristiano. The term dictator simply means that he has absolute control, which by the way was offered to him by the government in place at the time. It does not necessarily mean that he uses it oppressively. He was every Latino's hero." Don Angel explained.

"That's why we see the name Bolivar almost everywhere?"

"You are exaggerating." He contradicted.

"Hey, they even named a country after him." I implied and Pedro stayed quiet. At that moment, Antonio hit the roof and we turned on some dirt road, again. The conversation ended.

The day flew by so rapidly, we rolled around from village to village and finished our day near Penonomé. It was all quiet. The spot was worse than yesterday, but probably better than tomorrow's, no one could complain. We were all used to it by now.

In the heart of Penonomé, Antonio started asking questions around and I was left by myself. I walked around for a bit. All these new sights were great, but they all remained the same. I would have liked to be allowed to go hiking or doing any entertaining activity.

A window caught my attention; it was a kind of tourist agency, displaying activities on a big poster. There was some hiking to be done at La Iguana. By looking at the pictures, the trail followed a superb canyon made of strange rocks. There were natural pools and lovely waterfalls. The other hiking was done at Barringon and it seemed even better. On the picture, there was a huge waterfall where people were swimming at the bottom. At the moment, I would have given my right arm to go swimming: to be a tourist.

As I was looking at the advertisement, some man came to tap me on the shoulder. I first thought it was Don Angel or Antonio, but it was not. It was a white man with a thick greyish beard and long brownish hair. "The human kind is dying and you're doing nothing to save it." He blurted loudly.

I stayed silent.

"See? You're doing zilch and so is the rest of all of these morons." He continued.

He had an accent that I could not identify. "You're not from around here are you?" I questioned.

"From Wales!" He almost screamed. I think he saw the puzzled expression on my face. "In the United Kingdom!" He clarified even louder, but then stopped and hastily looked right behind his shoulder. He spooked me as he did it so quickly.

"What's wrong?" I asked.

"Nothing!" He said, but then he turned again in the exact same manner. "Did you see them?" The man demanded hastily.

"See who?"

"Forget it." He said and took a breather. "The world is going down; we're on self destruction mode."

"What's your name?" I asked.

"Plato!"

"Is that your real name?"

"It's the one *they* gave me." He retorted.

"*They*, meaning your parents?"

He checked around, as if he wanted to make sure we were alone. "No, the Battery-Mongolians." He then admitted.

Well, that did not seem strange at all. "Who?" I had to ask.

"The Battery-Mongolians." Plato simply repeated as if everything was absolutely normal.

And I thought *I* was losing it. "Okay, and who are they, if I may ask?"

"Aliens who look human, they have the power to alter their physical appearance. They can take whatever size, height, or even face they want."

"I understand, Plato." I thought I should say to be polite.

"I'm not sure you do." He contradicted me. "They use effects to do it." He added.

I was afraid to ask, but decided to anyway. Antonio was probably still playing detective, I had time to kill. "Effects?"

"Yes, how else could they change their physicality like that?"

"Yes indeed, how else?" I agreed. "And they are good guys?" I questioned honestly.

"Not at all. They use their power for evil." He turned around swiftly for a third time and spooked the heck out of me, again. When his head came back my way, he looked afraid of something. I too checked behind him, but there was absolutely nothing. "When I returned from their home, I realized that I had brought their magic with me. Don't worry mate, I will fight them." The man added.

"Do you take drugs?" I interrogated without shame.

"Battery-Mongolians poisoned me." He yelled accusingly.

"So what's your plan now?" I asked.

"I wanna know who they are and why they're after me. I want some answers and I don't care if people think I'm ridiculous because I ask an unusual question."

"I think I may understand how you feel."

He looked straight at me. "Hypocrisy is a sickness that humans suffer from. Don't be a fool and join me in the healthy world."

Somehow it did not seem too crazy. "I think I will, Plato, but for now I have to go." The trio was probably waiting for me. "Farewell and good luck finding the bastards." I wished him for encouragement and started running towards the vehicle. Perhaps I should have asked him if he knew where I could find a Shaman, but I would never have trusted his answer anyway.

A little later, I met Antonio and we both walked back to the truck together. "So, any luck?" I asked.

"None."

"Did you talk to anybody?"

"I did have a nice conversation with Bishop Ashley." He replied.

I was going to tell him about my meeting with Plato, but I did not. "You spoke with a bishop?" I questioned with a surprising tone. "Yes, I just passed by the church as he was standing in front, dressed like a simple priest." He finished.

At that moment, we arrived at the pick-up and climbed inside. We left, I would never find out what Antonio and the bishop had discussed.

In the middle of the afternoon, we entered the city of San Carlos. We drove around for a bit. There was this dirt road that led us to the ocean, a place called El Palmar. The waves were incredible. I wished I could have had a way to reach Arnaud and tell him. There were two guys surfing on these beautiful waves. One of them was just amazing; he made me wonder if his last name was Hamilton. I heard them laughing and screaming of pleasure. They were so happy, as if they were above all the troubles of our world. They did not seem concerned about anything. I wished I could have stayed with them. Antonio banged on the roof. "Vamos, por favor!" He shouted.

"I wouldn't mind going for swim." I dared to say as I stepped out of the vehicle.

"We don't really have time." Antonio replied.

Anna looked at him in shock. "We will make time and take it, Tony." She said to her husband with authority.

"I'm sorry, Don Kristiano. Go right ahead, we will wait here for you." Antonio gave me permission.

"I promise I won't be long!" I said enthusiastically.

And so I went swimming, it was unbelievable. I body-surfed the waves and almost got hit by one of the real surfers. I could have stayed forever, but only took about ten minutes. I jumped back in the truck and got going right away. I felt rejuvenated: all gassed up and ready to go.

Back in town, we parked the truck in a nice little green area that could almost be called a park. "I'm going to go for walk in the city and quiz some people." Antonio told to us.

"Fine, I'll do the same." I replied.

"You mean you will just go walk around?" He asked intriguingly.

"I may ask a few questions on the way." I admitted.

He did not add anything, simply made a surprisingly happy expression. "Will you be alright?" The husband asked his wife.

"Of course, do not worry about me. I will just take a little nap. I will be perfectly fine." Anna blew a kiss to her husband who pretended to catch it in mid-air. I thought it was cool to see the romance in the couple; I was even more impressed by Antonio's display of public affection. "I am happy you will also be searching." She said to me.

I wanted to tell her I had been asking once or twice before. "The pleasure's all mine, Anna." I started walking, stopped and turned around. "Soon, we'll find somebody who knows something. It'll be alright, Anna." I encouraged, even though I was not sure to believe it.

"I know; I feel it inside." She admitted and smiled. I wanted to add that Pedro would be there to watch over her, but I figured it was unnecessary. It was a pretty obvious thing, no one even mentioned it.

I walked all over the city. It was not that big and I felt like I had quickly seen it all. There was a man on the sidewalk, standing beside a bathroom scale. He was charging money to people who desired to know their weight, but did not have the finances to own one at home. "How much?" I asked.

"A quarter!"

"American?"

"Of course, what else?"

"Alright." I was curious to know how much weight I had lost over the summer. I stepped on and was shocked to learn that I was more than twenty pounds lighter than before. Man! My mother who kept complaining about her weight, all she had to do was to come down here for a few weeks.

I went back to the vehicle and saw that Antonio had not returned. Anna was still in the box and Don Angel was lying under the shade of an enormous tree. "Hey, how's it going?" I quickly asked.

"Good, any luck?" The woman answered.

I simply moved my head from left to right. "Did you see Antonio?"

"Yes, he returned and brought me some food. He said he was going to keep looking for about an hour."

An hour! "Maybe I'll just go get myself some food as well then." I looked around in vain to find a restaurant. "Guess I'll have to go off again. You need anything?" I questioned as a formality because I knew she would not dare ask.

"No thank you. I will be fine." She predictably replied.

I got closer to her. "I know you will." I tenderly said with a smile.

I walked for about ten minutes and found a restaurant that seemed cheap enough for my tight budget. It was sort of a counter with Asian owners. They could barely speak Spanish or English. I had no idea how they did business. Probably costumers were required to point at the illustrations on the back wall. I designated the chicken pieces and fries with my right index and hoped that they understood. As I opened the door to get out, a weird looking man entered the establishment. "Do you know where I could find a Shaman?" I asked, ignoring the obvious bad timing.

"Piss off!" He rudely answered.

What could I answer to the stupidest of rudest remark of all? A part of me wanted to hit him, but the Don Angel part of me was saying that it was not worth it. Scarily, Pedro was rubbing off on me.

I stood in a discreet place of the sidewalk and ate my chicken. I was unable to finish it, so I started walking with my paper bag under my right arm. About five minutes later, some bald Latino dude stopped me. "Hey! Where are you from man?" He joyfully asked me in perfect English.

"America." I decided to say.

"You here on vacation?"

Why would a tourist come here? He looked suspicious and I had no clue what he wanted from me. "Yes I am." I cautiously answered.

"How long are you here for?" He continued.

I gave him an interrogative stare instead of a response.

He seemed nervous and he often slowly glanced around. "Do you like drugs, man?" The cat finally came out of the bag.

I had had enough of this guy. "No, but do you like chicken?" I returned.

He looked confused. "Yes." He then answered.

"Well, there you go." I said as I gave him the bag. I took advantage of the fact that he was exploring the content to walk away. I considered myself lucky to have been in contact with this freak and come out entirely safe and sound. Why did these dudes always come to see me? I was thinking about Plato and even Arnaud. Leave me alone, I am not on vacation.

We entered the capital city during the morning of the next day. I was not impressed at first, but it changed slowly. It was cool to see the ocean and all the buildings. "Pull over please, Don Kristiano." Antonio ordered through the opened back window.

I executed the order and we stopped in some little park by the water. There were some really nice trees and a few benches. Pedro and I stayed in the truck while the couple was getting down from their box. Facing the bay, when we looked to our left we could see the tall modern buildings of Panama; to our right, there was the old dirty city. In the middle of the park, there was a great monument; four men were holding hands to support the earth on their backs. There was some kind of conquistador on top of our planet. He was holding a flag that was covering his shoulder in one hand and a sword pointed to the sky in the other. Everything was white, except for the man on top. The statue seemed so clean, contrasting with the grey clouds of its background. "Who's this guy?" I asked Pedro.

"Vasco Nunez Balboa." Don Angel answered.

"And what did *he* do?" I questioned. He surely was not related to Rocky.

"He was the first Spaniard to see the Pacific Ocean."

"So he's not a friend of your Bolivar?" I teased.

"I am sure they would not have been if they had lived during the same period." He concluded.

Then Antonio called for me. "What's up?" I joined the couple who was now sitting on a bench.

"I think we should spend the night in the city." The husband announced.

I stayed quiet, waiting to hear some more.

"You could take some time off and go be a tourist for the rest of the day. We believe it would be good for you." Anna continued.

"That's sound really cool." I had to admit.

"There is a lot of activity going on here and it will take a long time to do my interrogations. First, I would like to find a hotel and then you would be free to roam around." Antonio said.

"Won't a hotel room be too expensive?" Anna asked.

"Most unlikely; there are many cheap ones. I am hoping we could get two rooms for around twenty dollars." The husband answered.

"Would that be alright on our budget?" The woman inquired.

"It'd be fine, Anna." I reassured to make her feel secure. Really, I had no clue. I still had no idea why there had been all the extra money in my bank account. It made me think that I should give my parents a call, reconnect with my old reality. I also should phone Martin, see how the coffee was going.

"We should go up that way. It seems like the older part of Panama; we will have better chances of finding something affordable." Antonio suggested.

"Okay, vamos!" I encouraged.

We all got in. "You never say much during our little meetings." I told Pedro.

"I told you before; it is not for me to decide. You guys are in charge of this expedition, not me. I am just here to help." He answered.

"Are you in good terms with Antonio and Anna?" I questioned.

"Of course, I am. Why do you ask?"

"I don't know. You guys don't seem to talk much."

"You are not always around, Don Kristiano. Besides, I have known them for a very long time. After a while, the need to speak becomes less necessary." Don Angel concluded.

Finding a place to stay was not so easy after all. I pulled over for a minute. "Do you know where I could find a cheap hotel?" I interrogated some guy on the street.

"Why don't you go to the Central?"

"Because I have no idea where it is." I retaliated too quickly. By the sound of its name, it was surely in the center of the city, but where was that?

He waited. "It's inside San Felipe, a block passed the Presidential Palace." He said.

"Okay; and where is the Presidential Palace?" I asked.

"Ah! You're a tourist?" He rhetorically asked. "You will love the area. It is full of old colonial buildings." He added.

I held back. "Please, just point us the way and we'll manage." I almost begged. I could see Antonio smiling in my rear-view mirror.

"Continue on this street; take a right, then a left, and then a right. You should see a square with a cathedral; the Central is right in front." He finally spat out.

"Well, thank you very much for your help." I said. I looked at Don Angel and tried to express my feelings with a grimace.

"Good job, Don Kristiano, short and sweet." Pedro teased.

We found the hotel as indicated, beside the square in the old city. The couple went in to get some information, but I stayed outside. The square seemed to have a history. There were great tall trees and even a gazebo. There were a lot of people; some kids were playing soccer with some sort of wooden ball. The church was the most amazing of all. The façade was brown and everything else was pure white. Cars were surrounding the square, making it safe. Great old buildings were adjoining the four streets. There was an edifice full of French flags. "It's nine dollars for a room." Antonio yelled from inside.

"Fine!" I agreed.

Don Angel got my attention with a fake cough. "You know, this hotel was probably once considered a very luxurious one." He assumed.

"It's falling apart now though." I replied. I had no clue how many stars it was given, but it surely was not many. "It's great that it is inexpensive, luckily for the owners because no fancy tourist would stay here." I added.

"Perhaps, but during the first construction of the canal, the big French head honchos surely slept here." Don Angel said.

"How do you know that?" I questioned, but then I clicked as I remembered the French building right beside. "It's fine, don't answer." I warned him, not wanting to be taught another obvious lesson. Still, I was anxious to sleep in a real bed and maybe even take a good shower.

The inside of the hotel made me think of all the pictures framed in my Dad's study. There was an inside courtyard surrounded by decrypted balconies on every level. It was like a big square hole in the middle of the building. I was so happy, as if I was visiting New Orleans.

We settled in: the couple in a room and Don Angel and I in another. We had great French doors followed by a small balcony with a view over the cathedral. The ceiling was high with a slow turning fan. Everything was perfect. Well, perfect for people who had been sleeping under the stars for such a long time. "Okay, I'm gonna get going now!" I announced to Don Angel. "Are you coming?" I questioned to be nice.

"No, you go and have fun. It's good to be alone sometimes." He retorted.

"It doesn't matter; I'm alone too often at home."

"Excess is never good, but this time it is different." He paused. "Go and enjoy, the city is yours." Don Angel concluded.

I walked to the truck wondering what Anna would do all day, waiting for her husband to return. I could not believe her strength; the physical pain must be unbearable. The cheap drugs we had bought in Managua were long gone. Antonio also had his demons, some more hidden than others, he dealt with mental suffering. I wondered which one was worst. Regardless, no pain was enjoyable, it would be against the term's definition. I tried not to think about them, this town needed to be painted and I had a big brush in my back pocket.

I walked across the street and entered the square. I looked around and almost ran into a phonebooth from lack of attention. I took that as I sign that it was high time for me to get in touch with Martin, my parents could wait a little longer. Some little boy came to offer me to shine my dirty runningshoes. I politely refused his offer and started dialing up.

It took a few minutes, but I finally got through to the Cinco Pinos pharmacy. Like the last time, I hung up and asked them to go and get the village's only white boy. I now had about fifteen minutes to kill before I would call back.

"Shoe-shine Yankee?" The same kid asked once more.

"Sorry buddy these are *running* shoes, I don't need them clean and don't call me Yankee." I answered and asked in a nice way.

"I could give you a clean up job" He insisted.

"No, no." He reminded me of Osmar the popcorn boy in Managua. "What's your name?" I questioned.

"Carlos!"

"I knew a Carlos back in San Francisco, in Nicaragua."

"You have been to Nicaragua?"

"Of course."

"What is your name?" He asked me.

"Kristiano!" I answered. "Where do you live?" I questioned in return.

"About a ten-minute walk from here." He replied.

There was still a bunch of kids playing soccer over the other side of the square. "You don't play soccer?" I asked.

"What is soccer?"

"The game with the ball." I explained as I pointed towards the children playing.

"Oh, you mean football." He replied and gave me a disapproving look. "Of course I play, but now I can't, I have to work." He continued.

"How many hours a day do you work?"

"All day." Carlos replied.

"You don't go to school?" I asked again.

"No, not anymore."

"Not anymore? How old are you?"

"Ten." He answered and then looked at me from top to bottom. "How old are you?" He questioned.

I realized that it was the first time somebody had ask me my age in a long time, no one around here knew. "I'm twenty-two years old." I admitted. "Well, listen, it's been great talking to you, but I gotta make an important phone call."

"Have a safe trip!" He wished.

I thought it was so nice of this ten-year-old to think of my safety. As I was leaving, my back to the boy, I looked in my pocket and search for a dollar. Unfortunately, all I had was a five, but I did not want to repeat what I had done with Osmar. I turned back. "Take it Carlos, I don't really need it." I gave him the five-dollar bill. Although I had not counted, I surely had enough in my pockets, in my bags and even some locked in the glove-box of the truck.

Carlos took the money and his eyes popped wide open, almost out of their sockets. "Gracias, Don Kristiano." He shouted and got up. The kid ran away and started playing soccer, football, with the others. I had probably just given him enough money to take the rest of the day, maybe the week, off.

I went to the phone booth and called Martin again. After five attempts, I finally heard the ringing sound and Martin picked up. "Hola Señor!" He greeted in Spanish.

"Don Martin! Que tal?" I played the part.

"Not bad; where the heck are you?" Martin straightforwardly asked.

"Panama City."

"What! What's going on?"

"Well, we're still looking for a Shaman." I told him.

"You're joking!"

"What else do you want us to do?"

He was speechless.

"Don't worry I'll probably be back soon." I said. I doubted there was a road that crossed to South America. I had always pictured it very swampy in that area.

"Yeah, it's okay." He said uneasily. "So, did Antonio decide anything, is he going to keep going until Cape Horn?"

"Man, I hope not. It's impossible to go by car right?" I asked.

"Why wouldn't it be?"

"No reason." I said, forgetting about my swampy imagination.

"You'll just have to take a ferry or something."

"I'm getting tired of all this. I can't wait to return. Is everything alright? Anything new I should know about?" I questioned.

"Kind of, I don't know if you've noticed but there's probably a lot of money in your bank account." Martin said.

"I did notice. I thought it was my parents who had put some in." I answered. "But wait a second, how do you know that? Wasn't I only supposed to get paid at the end of my contract?"

"Remember when you called me from Managua, I said: if no one finds out you're gone, I won't be the one to tell them. Remember that?"

"Vaguely, yes."

"Well, Mister Jordan came for an unexpected visit. He decided at the last minute that he wanted to be there for the meeting with the journalists, ministers, and company presidents. There was no way I could hide your absence. I even said that you were off to work with Carlos in San Francisco, but he really wanted to see you. I'm sorry, I had to confess everything."

"Did you get in trouble?"

"A bit, but not enough to bite." He admitted. "It doesn't matter anyway. Regardless of his over-developed sense of business, he's a good man. He agreed to pay you from the start to the time when he personally realized you were gone."

"Why's that?"

"There was no way for him to determine when you had actually left."

"All he had to do was to quiz you?" I said.

"I'm sorry, but I don't remember when you left. Didn't you know about my short-term memory loss?" He jokingly replied.

"And the villagers didn't say anything?"

"Strangely, none of them even remembered your name. It kind of made Mr Jordan realized that you had done a lot more than just take care of coffee, you had succeeded in gaining the trust of the crowd and that's worth gold in the mind of a business man who wants to stay here for a long time. We'll talk about it some other time."

"So, that's why I have extra money in my bank account." I said.

"You're not too disappointed about losing the rest of it?" Martin asked.

"That's alright I guess, it's just money." I could not believe I had just said that out loud.

Martin stayed quiet; I could feel his shock about my last comment. "Will you have enough for the trip?" He shyly asked.

"I'm sure I will, but let's just hope that this journey is close to the end, my credit margin isn't the biggest." I retorted. "Well, I'm going to let you go now. This is costing me a lot. Does Juanita miss me?" After all, the old cook had lost half of her revenue when I had left.

"Of course she does."

"I sure do miss her cooking that's for sure." I admitted with all honesty. I thought about getting into my rice and beans diet, but I did not want Martin to feel any worse than he already seemed to be. "Seriously, are things okay with the coffee?"

"Things are going well enough. Don't worry about us. Go find your Shaman!"

"I will. Take care!' I replied. "Ciao!" I finished before I hung up.

I climbed into the truck and tried to let my jobless situation sink in. I wondered if I should really take the vehicle or I should just walk around; it would be cheaper. "Sorry sir, how long would it take me to walk to the canal?" I asked a passer by, in a flash.

"Just the canal can be seen everywhere around the city, but would you like to go to the touristy lock?" He kindly answered.

"Honestly, I'd love the touristy thing." I confessed.

"Well, it would take you about seven hours."

"To drive there!" I exclaimed.

"I'm sorry; I thought you wanted to know how long it would take you to *walk* there. To drive would take you about thirty minutes, maybe." He finally informed me.

"Thanks. Now, how do I get there?"

"Just follow the signs. You'll be fine."

And so I would.

It took me about twenty-five minutes to get to Miraflores Lock. Some guard came to see me as soon as I parked the truck. I thought he was going to ask me to pay or to turn my truck around, ready to leave in case of a catastrophe. "Hurry! The ship is coming!" He warned. Soon after everyone started running and took place on some little tier.

"Thanks a lot!" I replied. He seemed so enthusiastic about it. What was so great about this lock?

When I made it there, I noticed some little trains, on rails parallel to the canal, pulling the huge ship. I could not believe how enormous it was. They stopped the boat and the water level started to go down. When the two levels met, the doors opened and the ship slowly crossed to the other side. It was pretty impressive after all, but probably not something I would remember for the rest of life. Then again, who was I to know?

Before I left, I entered a little house where all the tourists were going in and out. Inside, there was a great scale model of the canal. Now, that was interesting to be able to visualise it in its grandeur. Amazing, the amount of time and effort it must have taken the workers, for the real thing, not this scale.

I left for the city centre, but then saw a sign that pointed to Panama Viejo. It seemed very touristy and was just what I needed.

There was no hesitation in my mind. I drove about two miles and ended up at the entrance of a bunch of old ruins. There were two cute female backpackers walking the opposite way. "Hello!" I simply greeted.

"Hi." The blond one answered right away.

"Is it worth going in there?" I questioned.

"It's absolutely amazing." She said with a sexy voice.

"If you like old buildings and a bunch of rocks lying on the ground, go right ahead." The brown-haired one added.

"Don't listen to her, she's just grumpy 'cause I made her walk all the way here." The first one excused.

"Yeah, well don't listen to her 'cause she's just a geology freak who loves anything that's comes from the earth." The second one retaliated.

The blond one had such a killer charm that I decided to side with her. "Thanks a lot, I think I'll take a look." I said. "If you guys want a ride back, I shouldn't be too long." I finished.

"Thanks, but we should be alright." The cute blond replied.

"Yeah, we're used to walking." The other concluded.

Their cuteness put a smile on my face. I made it to the booth and bought my ticket. "So is this place worth visiting?" I asked again.

"It's great!" The man in the booth said.

"What is it?" I wanted a summary, a general idea, because I sure could not afford a private guide.

"It's the first Spaniard settlement in the Pacific Ocean."

"Cool, when was it?"

"Fifteen-nineteen."

"Good year!" I faked, thanked him and went on my way. Had he said the Pacific Ocean? Was it not the Atlantic on this side? Oh well. There was a paved road crossing a beautiful green field. The ruins were grey, standing here and there in no particular order. The best one was an amazing cathedral with big bell tower. There also was a bishop's house that was pretty impressive. Regardless of the redundancy of it all, it was a great escape from reality. I walked around for a bit, thinking about the history, imagining pirates sailing in the bay. Next to the ocean, there was a bunch of craftsmen selling their works of art. I thought about buying a few souvenirs, but figured that I should save my money until this journey was over.

I finally came back in the city, without seeing the two cute female backpackers. I parked the truck and started walking around. I did not really want to know where I was going. The streets were noisy, they looked exactly like the ones from San Jose and Managua, but yet, they managed to be a little different.

I watched three innings of a baseball game played on the beach and literally in the water. The man on the right field had salt water up to his ankles. Maybe the tide was coming in and nobody wanted to stop. It was funny because it seemed like a well organized league. They had shirts and decent equipment. I noticed that when they switched offence to defence, every field player gave their glove to the other team. All the trash from the beach had been cleared away and put to the side. Baseball was definitely a great game of good clean fun.

Two hours into my walk, I stopped on a park bench to rest. On my right, I heard loud voices speaking English. It was as if they wanted the whole country to hear. I turned around to see two Americans chatting. They had just finished discussing their return to Costa Rica. Still, I decided to relax and keep listening for a while. "Hey, you know what your new nickname should be, man?" The first one asked.

"No."

"Yeti Boy!"

"Why is that, Dude?" The second demanded.

"Just 'cause you're so huge, man." The first closed.

The short one was right; the Yeti guy was really tall. He had his head shaved and wore a plaid shirt opened to his belly button. He had the hairiest chest I had ever seen, almost certainly one of the hairiest in the world.

Then some new member arrived as happy as he probably could be. He had a big bag under his arm. "Dudes, I got twenty cheeseburgers for the road!" The third one said.

The two others just cheered triumphantly. Surely there was a special on cheeseburger at Raunchy-Ronnie's. I would have killed for a gigantic hamburger.

"Dudes, they even had to call the manager to approve my order." The third one announced.

"No way!" The two shouted in harmony.

"At one point, the manager gave me hell and I told him I would stick his twenty cheeseburgers up his ass." They all started laughing. "Wow! Look at the time, dudes; we gotta get going if we don't want to miss our bus." The Cheeseburger guy then warned.

They all got up and started walking for the coach station. I would not want to be beside them during the whole bus ride. They reminded me more of the three stooges than the three musketeers. It was true that I did not observe them for very long; perhaps I was totally wrong about them, but how else could I react in front of such walking stereotypes? Were they the real Americans of the time, the ones who had evolved with their country?

There was another man sitting on the park bench opposite the one where the stooges had been. He too, was definitely American, but not for the same reasons. He was as big as the Yeti Boy. He had too much body fat, even though you could tell it was covering a lot of muscles. The guy appeared to be astoundingly strong. His grip looked so tight, he could probably hold a fart in and it would not smell. Anyway, he stared at me and it made me think that he had been doing it for a while. He had surely noticed the disgust in my eyes when I was observing the three walking stereotypes and their cheeseburgers. I knew he had read my obvious facial expressions. For a short moment, I was scared that he was going to beat me up for the noticeable way I had stared down his co-citizens. There was only one thing to do to check the terrain. "How you doing?" I asked with my best Pedro grin.

He smiled back, and by that simple movement of his lips, it made me feel a whole lot better. "Pretty good, yourself?"

"Not bad." I did not know if he wanted to say more so I kept quiet.

"My name's Scott, what's yours?" He surprisingly questioned.

"Kris!" I chose to say, sounded more American. "Are you from the States?" I asked.

"Of course I am. Aren't you?" He returned.

"Yeah, just like the song: I was born in the USA." I happily affirmed.

"And a Springsteen fan to top it all off." He calmly said.

I was glad that he had recognized my quote. "He can sing the grandeur of America like no other." I decided to allege.

"What?" He said. "The Boss sings about America's truthfulness, not its grandeur. Did you even listen to the song's lyrics?" He asked, but I did not answer. "To me, it sounds more like war protest than and hymn to greatness." Scott continued.

"Well, I guess I'll have to sing the Yankee Doodle from now on." I went for the most patriotic song of all. "Stuck a feather in his cap and called it macaroni." I sang out loud and proud.

Scott gave me a disapproving stare. "Have you ever heard of the Macaroni Club in England?"

"No." I shamelessly admitted.

"It was a group of men who wore stupid continental hats they thought to be stylish. The British made fun of them because of how silly they looked. They also sang that song to laugh at our troops during the revolution."

When he finished his last sentence, he seemed ready to leave, picking his stuff up, uninterested by my stupid comments. I think he saw I was a fraud. I had to change the subject quickly. "Are you a tourist?" I gently questioned.

"Not really." He replied.

"A traveller then?" I insisted.

"No, no, I live here."

This guy made me curious. "Why do you live *here*? Is it for work?" I asked.

"Not anymore." He blunted.

He was starting to bug me, why was he so reserved? He had asked me for my name and now wanted to be left alone? What did he have to lose by telling a strange man details about his personal life? Of course, he was probably thinking, what did he have to gain, but it did not matter. I chose to play the honesty card. "Alright I admit it, I'm curious. Please tell why an American like you would chose to live in a Central American city like this one? Are you like a criminal who can't go back home?"

"Wow!" He softly exclaimed in a low tone of voice. "You're pretty good."

I was shocked as well. "You mean you committed some crime in the States?"

"No, I did my crimes right here." He answered. "That's why I'm staying." Scott clarified.

"The government of Panama won't let you leave the country?" I interrogated.

"Why does it always have to be somebody else? I'm the one who decides what I do and not anybody else." He said aggressively. "I gotta go." The man tried to conclude as kindly as he could.

He started to walk away, but I followed him. "I'm sorry if I offended you, I really am." I apologized as I caught up to him, a little voice inside me was telling me not to let him get away. I really felt like I needed to know more about him. Don Angel had said to trust my intuition and for once, I had the time to do it.

"I'm going to work, but it's a bit of a walk, you can tag along if you want." He explained and offered nicely.

"Cool, what kind of job do you have?" I asked.

"I work in a medical clinic by the docks." He said. I stayed silent and waited for him to say more. "I used to be in the Army and came here with Operation Just-Cause."

"What is that?" I questioned.

"Jesus! How old are you? How can you not know about it?" The ex-soldier cried out.

I felt so ignorant. It was Cinco Pinos all over again. I was close to admitting I had not spent my childhood in the States, but I could not speak, I simply lifted my shoulders.

"Do you even know who General Manuel Noriega is?"

"Yeah, but remind me again." I lied.

"He was a dictator who took control of Panama in the mid-eighties. The guy was bad. He killed political rivals, sold drugs and laundered money. He did things his way and didn't worry about anybody else. Basically, he nullified democracy. Since we couldn't let that happened, we decided to move."

"You invaded the country?"

"We would never; we just cut Panama off from our loop, that's all."

I was thinking about all the regular folks who had probably suffered from that US decision based on the actions of one bad man. What a shame. "And what finally brought you guys down here, then?" I asked.

"In eighty-nine, Noriega lost the election so he annulled the results and stayed in power. The day after, the dictator declared Panama at war with the US." Scott explained.

"That's why you came?" I cut off.

"Not only that, that same day, an unarmed American soldier dressed in civilian clothes was gunned down in the street. When we learned the news, we couldn't stay put any longer, twenty-six thousand troopers were sent to bring that tyrant to justice. It got ugly."

"It got ugly like in Nicaragua?" I asked. It sounded like a lot of soldiers for only one dead body.

"I'm glad to see that you know about Nicaragua." He said as he gave me the thumbs up. "Yeah, it was kind of the same as when we took Somoza out."

"No, I meant in the *Contra*-Revolution." I dared.

"We were never involved in the Contra." He retorted.

I did not want to offend the guy so I did not say anything to contradict him, but please. We kept on walking; strangely the streets were almost deserted. "How did it end for Noriega?"

"He took refuge in the Vatican embassy, but we were able to bring him out the American way."

"How's that, with force?"

"No man! With Rock n' Roll!" The man joyfully answered.

"What do you mean?" I questioned.

"Well, we put out a whole bunch of speakers and pointed them at the building. For six days, we blasted loud music, some a bit devilish I'll admit it. Maybe Manuel was willing to endure it, but we were pretty sure the Vatican boys wouldn't."

"So where's Noriega now?"

"He's enjoying the Florida sun inside a jail courtyard with over thirty years to go."

"They sentenced him for crimes against humanity?"

"No, for money laundering." He replied.

We kept on walking silently for a bit, nothing happened. I could see the bridge of the Americas on my left. "What was your part in all this?"

"Noriega's escape routes had to be cut off. I was part of a SEAL team that was supposed to take care of Patilla Airfield so he wouldn't get away on his Lear jet. Resistance was violent: we lost four men, eight more were injured."

"That's too bad!" I declared with sympathy. "Why don't you go home, Scott?"

"Remember when I said things got ugly during the operation Just-Cause?" Without waiting for my answer he continued. "I feel responsible for some of that ugliness. I chose to stay for a while and repair some of it."

"How long do you figure it's going to be?"

"I have no clue for the moment, but I'm certain that I'll know when it's going to be the right time. I don't want to go home and be spat on like the Vietnam veterans were."

"You can surely go home now; no one cares about what happens in Central America." I told him.

"Do you know that for a fact?" He asked.

"I'm living proof of it." I finished.

We kept on marching; his military past was almost obvious just by looking at the way he took each step. "D'you sometimes feel like Americans get a bad rap for no reason?" I asked him for no reason.

"Most of the times yeah. I guess that in a way we're punished for being too good." He said very seriously.

"Is that possible, being punished for being too good at something?" I questioned sarcastically.

"Sure it is." He paused and searched for an example. "Just look at the Bee Gees."

I was surprised about his answer, but when I thought about it, it kind of made sense. "They weren't too good; they were too popular, overplayed. There's a difference." I contradicted.

"Not in those days, you couldn't be popular if you weren't good. This was before the industry replaced good music by image." He argued in a lighter tone.

I was wondering what I was doing here, following this unknown man.

"This is it." He spontaneously said. "This is where we part, unless you'd like to come in?" He then offered.

"Sure, why not." After all, this was a medical clinic.

When I entered, I was shocked. It was even worst than the hospital in San Pedro Del Norte in Nicaragua. There were tiny rooms with bunk beds jammed into them. There was not even any space beside them; people had to get in and out by the front.

The patients seemed happy to see Scott. His imposing stature probably made them feel very secure. We came into a small room with a little desk and the big man sat down behind it. "See? These people need me. I'm respected. Back home, unless I stayed in the army, I could barely get a decent job. At least here, I'm making a difference." Scott explained.

I was thinking about something good to reply, but then, I looked out the door and he appeared in the hallway. There was a bare-chested man with ragged hospital pants walking my way. He had the perfect indigenous style with long tattoos across his back. "Who's this guy?" I quickly asked Scott.

"The Nurse calls him Sey. For what I was able to understand, because he speaks with a strong accent and sometimes unknown vocabulary, he's from the deep southern forests. The man arrived two days ago, saying he had an unknown disease." Scott told me.

"What's this disease?" I asked.

"We aren't sure yet. It's most likely to be some kind of cancer." The American explained. "The indigenous said that he was out on a pilgrimage since his illness was something that even his tribal doctor wasn't able to fix."

"Tribal doctor?!" I screamed. "You mean a Shaman?!"

"Something like that I guess." He paused when he saw the hopeful expression on my face. My skin had probably turned to green when I heard him say the words. "Why? What's going on?" He questioned.

"It's a long story, but could you find out where exactly Sey is from and is there really a shaman there? Please, it's extremely important!" I quickly demanded.

"I'm on it." He said in an inquisitive tone and went into the room where the indigenous had entered. He stayed there for five long minutes. I tried to be patient and looked at the stuff on the walls, but I could not fix anything. It was like watching a huge 3-D poster. I heard their voices as if they were further away.

Finally, Scott stepped out of the room and looked at a young female nurse who was coming our way. "Get me the map file!" He ordered to her.

About three minutes later, both of us were staring at a map of Panama laid down on the wooden desk. He could not let me leave with the map so I was concentrating really hard on the directions he was given me. I made myself a home-made plan on a blank sheet of paper. From now on, I would have to step up to the plate and take full control of the operations. Antonio would no longer be the captain who always guessed where to go next. "You have no idea what this means to us." I said.

He seemed intrigued by my choice of reflexive pronoun at the end of my sentence. Still, he stayed quiet. "There're other people involved, Scott. Trust me, if this location can give us what we want, you can definitely tell yourself that you have repaid some of your debt. I owe you one."

"I doubt we'll see each other again, so make sure you pay it pack to someone else." He said.

Suddenly, there was a loud Wilhelm scream coming from one of the rooms in the back. Two nurses ran down the hall. Scott got up. "Well, it's time we part!" He extended his hand and we shook. "I gotta go, Kris." He concluded.

"My real name is Kristian." I admitted as our hands were still hooked to one another.

He started running as another shout was heard from the back. "Suits you better!" He smoothly yelled.

There was nothing left for me to do but to walk right back to the hotel and spread the good news.

CHAPTER 3.5

I ran all the way back to the hotel; I had to tell Anna and Antonio as quickly as possible. The expectation of their smiles was giving me the energy to keep a fast pace. My legs were on fire, my breath had left me and my whole body was covered with sweat. The streets were full of bad drivers and I crossed them with excitement. I made my final sprint in the old pedestrian street; it was a total adrenaline rush. I sliced through the people like Moses through the Red Sea. "Out of my way!" I warned people as if I was the hero in a Hollywood movie.

I ran alongside the cathedral and crossed the square. I entered the hotel and climbed the stairs three by three. I knocked on the couple's door and waited. Finally, Anna answered. I could tell I had woken her up. "Don Kristiano, you look exhausted, is everything okay?" she said in panic at the sight on my sweaty body.

"I have great news!"

I had talked with Anna for about thirty minutes. As always, Antonio had returned depressed as heck, but once I told him the news, I had never seen a man so happy. They had held each other and then, Anna had given me a hug. We had talked for about forty minutes and I had decided to make my exit.

I had stopped by to see Don Angel, but the room was empty. Too excited to stay indoors, a walk had seemed like a great idea. I had to get the truck back anyway.

Everything was dark. I walked towards the bay area without looking around too much. I was recapping my meeting with Scott, but then I was interrupted by a man. He stood right in front of me, all dressed in black, carrying some kind of machine gun. The sight of his weapon scared the crap out of me. He meant business and very dangerously stared at me. To his eyes, my wimpy physic could only be a disguise. It was great to be taken seriously. "You can not pass here!" He robotically informed me.

"Why not? I'm just a tourist who wants to see the sea." I explained with a submissive tone of voice.

His expression was non-existent. He did not care about my desire. "This is the Presidential Palace, find another way." He harshly ordered.

I had totally forgotten about the palace. I did not insist; it would be a bad timing for the couple to lose their driver. It made me feel much better to learn that this soldier was no criminal, even if around here, it sometimes was a very thin line between the two. I simply nodded and went on my way. I was not going to argue. As I walked away, I heard him use his walkie-talkie. At the next corner, the same man seemed to be there. Of course, it was simply another guard in a similar costume. Again, I nodded and the only reply he gave me was a tighter grip on his gun.

I wondered what day of the week it was. I had lost count so long ago. I did not know how long our trip had lasted so far and it was probably better this way. There were many people outside. Up ahead on the sidewalk, there was bunch of drunken men sitting on little chairs. Life seemed to be alright for them. When I got closer, I realized that on the opposite side of the street, there was a TV set on top of an old car. They were watching pro-wrestling, coming straight from the US. There were pretty funny to look at. One big man got up and approached me. Was he going to practice some moves he had just learned? I knew wrestling was scripted, but it definitely looked painful at times. "Hey Gringo! *La Roca* is fighting next, would like to watch?" He offered as he pushed out the worst beer breath I had ever smelled in my life.

"No, but thank you very much. You are a very kind man." I brown-nosed just to be sure he would let me go peacefully. I wanted to hear the sound of the waves and see the moon reflect on the ocean's surface. I kept on walking.

I finally saw a little wall about a hundred meters later. I was only three blocks from the hotel. I wished I had known how close it was before I had started. There was a man sitting on it with his feet swinging in the emptiness. To my great surprised, I realized it was Don Angel. He did not look as cheerful as he normally did. He lifted his opened hand to the sky, towards the moon and left it there for a long time. He seemed to try and seized its energy, calling to it for aid. When he saw me coming, he put his arm down and stood up. "Buenas tardes, Don Kristiano!" He greeted as the smile came back to his face.

"Buenas! Are you alright? What are you doing here?" I asked.

"Nothing, really; I am just looking at the sea, listening to the sound of the waves, enjoying the beauty of the moon's reflection on the water."

I stayed silent, thinking about the similitude of our thoughts, maybe we had been together for too long. Still, it felt good to be here, watching the infinity of the dark ocean. The sound of the waves was slowly racing through my brain. It was amazing to think that the wall I was leaning on could have been built by the Spaniards over four hundred years ago.

"Do you regret getting involved on this trip, Don Kristiano?" Pedro asked.

"Not anymore, not after what happened today." I answered.

"What do you mean? Your time off in the city?" He questioned.

Somehow I thought he knew and was just playing dumb. "I found a village where there's a Shaman." I replied, smiling all the way to my ears.

He did not say anything for a bit and simply imitated my giant smile. We stayed silent for a while. "And how do you know this will not be the same as with Gael and the Osa Peninsula?" Pedro challenged.

I hesitated a while. "Because I feel it." I answered with assurance.

Don Angel smiled at me. "Why did you say, *not anymore*, did you regret it before?" He then asked.

"In a way, yes; I had to quit my job in the mountains, my easy time with Don Martin and my cosy little life in the village. It was hard at times for me to see the light at the end of the tunnel."

"No matter how long the tunnel, there is always a light, Don Kristiano."

"I know that now; I just didn't know how to react."

"And how did you react?" He wanted to get me to admit.

"I got angry, sad and then I kind of lost it." I confessed, probably to his greatest pleasure. "I'm sorry!" I added for some strange reason.

"Don't be sorry."

"Honestly, I'm not really. Right now, I'm just happy to be."

"That's a perfectly normal reaction."

"Perhaps, but it's all new to me, I never had a person's life in my care before. In my country, our biggest fear is to miss our weekly TV shows."

"Well, if you say you know where the Shaman is, the trip is coming to an end and we will all be able to go back to Nicaragua. Don't worry, there is still a lot of coffee to plant." Pedro said.

I stayed silent and looked at the sea. "I got fired."

"What do you mean?"

"The big boss noticed my absence and terminated my contract. I can't go back. Once I head back to Nicaragua, it'll be to pick up my stuff and fly home." I sadly replied.

His face made the most respectful and understanding emotion. We both turned to look at the ocean. "We found a Shaman, Don Angel, that's what counts for now. Right?" I said, searching his approval.

He turned and smiled at me. "Absolutely!"

"Please don't tell the others about this, they have enough worries." I demanded.

He did not answer, looking immensely proud of me.

I stared at the waves that were lying themselves one by one on the beach. "Vamos Don Angel!" I decided to go to sleep. He followed and we both walked back to the hotel, side by side. The wrestling fans were no longer there, although one was sleeping on the sidewalk beside the car that was holding the TV earlier.

When we made it in front of the hotel, I decided to stay out in the square for a few minutes. Pedro simply went inside and left me to my own thoughts. I had to look around one last time, the striking buildings, the astounding cathedral; it would all be gone tomorrow morning. I walked where the kids had been playing ball. I kicked a beer can that was on the ground and then decided to put it the trash can.

Soon after, I went inside, crossed the lobby. "Buenas tardes!" I heard coming from behind the desk. I answered and started to climb the old wooden staircase. I thought about going to see the couple, but they were probably asleep. I entered the room and saw Don Angel lying on his bed. He was over his covers, feeling the air from the ceiling's slow fan.

"Are you okay?" Pedro asked.

I looked at the French-doors slightly opened. "Just fine! I'll go sit on the balcony for a minute or two." I replied. Evidently, there were no lawn chairs so I simply stood and leaned over the rail. I observed the dark empty square, enjoying the silence of the city.

I had no clue what time it was, probably not that late. Regardless of the hour it was, it was time to go in. I was one foot away from a nice comfortable bed.

CHAPTER 4.1

"Wake up, Don Kristiano!" Pedro said softly. I opened my eyes and immediately put a smile on my face. I went straight for the bathroom and relieved myself of a small diarrhoea burden. Sitting on the toilet, I remembered that I had a weird dream last night. I was not sure about believing in dreams' interpretation, but this one was way out there. I sure hoped it did not mean anything.

There was bag on the floor and just as I was about to look what was inside of it, I got stung by a bee. I put a bandage on it right away. All of a sudden a mummy appeared and handed me a trophy.

Then everything went black and I saw this man walking my way. He started talking and claimed he had been cheated beyond belief. I stayed silent, confused, and honestly, uninterested. He later said he was from Vinci and was Leonardo's biological father's ancestor. He wanted money for all of his family's predecessor's accomplishments. Then, music could be heard and he started dancing the exact choreography from Michael Jackson's Thriller. He had it perfectly, the side to side claws, the little right shoulder pop, and the dragging feet: it was a thing of beauty. Suddenly, the man unfortunately stopped dancing and looked at me with a smile. He said something like: Make up Ton Krispiano. I had no idea what he meant. Afterwards, my eyesight became all brown. The man repeated his request and at that moment, I realized that it was Don Angel. "Wake up Don Kristiano!"

Once my job was done on the toilet, I flushed and went back to lie down. I wanted to let my poor vertebrae feel the comfort of the mattress for a little longer. I was staring at the fan; it looked like a plane propeller on vacation. This thought made me smile and reminded me that I was in no hurry. Through the French doors, I could see the rays of the sun were just beginning to touch the cathedral towers. I sure would have liked to have more time in this room.

I got up to take a shower, so good, so refreshing. There was even some sort of water heater fixed on the pipe. Unfortunately, as I was soaping my underarm, I touched it and slightly electrocuted myself. I screamed soprano style, just like the self-proclaimed king of pop. I could not believe this hotel would plug an electrical device inside a shower.

I heard three bangs coming from the other side of our door. "Are you ready?" Antonio spoke to me for the first time today. Strangely, he did not seem as happy as he should be.

I opened the door. "What's up?" I asked.

"Nothing, we have to go, that's all."

"I know, but you don't seem to be in a good mood."

"Why do you say that? I am in my usual mood." He replied.

"That's exactly what I mean. You do remember what we talked about yesterday?"

"I'm sorry. Anna is not feeling well at all this morning. Of course I remember what we talked about, but I will be happier when we actually get there. Millions of things can still go wrong. Vamos please." He concluded quietly.

I simply nodded and went back inside to pack up the little stuff I had.

The clerk behind the desk said goodbye and I exited the Central for surely the last time in my life. I was surprised to see the couple already in the back of the pick-up and Pedro in the front seat. My vacation was over, time for me to get back in my chauffeur mode. I was no longer a tourist; we had a job to do. There was a weird looking man on the square, he was dancing around, singing and throwing bones onto the ground. He was asking people if they wanted to know their future. We could say that we had found a Shaman; it simply was not the right kind.

We started heading south, rolling without buckling up again. Funny, I simply never thought that we would come this far. Had I not primarily agreed to drive them to Managua? It seemed like such a long time ago.

We saw a sign that indicated the Isla de Taboga. "What is it?" I asked Don Angel.

"It is a historical island. It has a nice beach and a rain forest. Plus, it is probably the place where you will see the most brown pelicans in America." He replied.

"So, it's place for geeky nature-lovers?"

"There is more to it than that; there was a Spanish settlement there before the one in Panama City. There is also the second oldest church in all Americas."

"Wow! That's cool." I said, but I was intrigued how he could know about this. Had Pedro left his village and travelled all across Central America, or even the whole planet, before? "It's too weird. I thought you had stayed in the mountains your whole life. Tell me, how do you know all this?" I decided to interrogate.

He hesitated a moment. "You're not the only one who had a day-off yesterday. I too, walked around the city and gathered information from left to right." He simply said.

I felt stupid. "I'm sorry, you're right." I laughingly admitted.

We drove for many hours without stopping. The temperature was the highest it had been since we had left the village. Evidently, I always felt that way, but this time it seemed to be truer than before. Even Antonio had installed a tarp over Anna's body for her to have some shade.

"Hey, you know that driver in front of us is gay," I declared, proud of my observational skills.

"What makes you say that?" Don Angel replied.

"Look at the bumper sticker." I clarified, pointing the rainbow flag.

"That is not the gay flag." He contradicted "That is the Huipala: the Inca flag." Pedro corrected me with laughter.

I stayed quiet and just answered with a puzzled expression. I knew he was probably right. Was there a difference between the two flags? Were all the Incas gay?

"Did you get yourself any souvenirs?" Pedro asked and changed the subject.

"Not really, I didn't want to spend any money." I explained. "I sure would've liked to get one of those Panama hats, though." I admitted.

"You know, those hats actually come from Ecuador." He told me.

"Then why are they called that?" I laughed.

"Because it is what many Ecuadorian gold seekers were wearing when they came to Panama in the nineteenth century." He clarified.

"So they came for the gold and lost their hat: serves 'em right." I joked. "I sure would've liked to have one, though." I repeated.

Things were great, the scenery was good and so was everybody's spirit. The highway gave us a great look at the Lago Bayano. I observed everything with an opened mind; there was no use for double entendres. It was like my mind was reading poetry diagonally. Finally knowing where we were going took the reflecting load off my shoulders.

I was looking at the map that I had drawn with Scott. The turn would probably appear tomorrow afternoon. I was trying to go fast at a slow speed. Anna seemed to be in great pain and the roads had not yet improved, getting worst, depending on the area. Following this thought, Antonio banged on the roof and asked me to stop for a pause. It was good to know that there were no more people to look for and ask questions.

"I saw a nice river over that slope when I was standing in the box. I need to go for a dip, does anybody want to come?" The husband announced as he got down from the back.

I hesitated, I felt like it, but did not want to leave Anna alone. Somehow I felt like I had to stay and keep her company. "No I think I'll pass. Go and have fun! We'll wait for you here." I replied. It felt very different from when I had had permission to go swimming in the ocean.

"Anna's forcing me to do this you know." The husband defended himself.

"It's either that or seeing you passing out because of the heat." His wife explained herself. "Be careful you're not much of a swimmer." Anna warned.

Don Angel came my way. "If you don't mind, Don Kristiano, I will go with Antonio." He quietly said to me.

I simply nodded in approval. It would be good for them to spend some time together. I then allowed myself to climb in the back-box and sit beside Anna, a thing I had never done before. I had so many questions. I did not know which one to start with or if I even had the right to ask them. We smiled at each other and I put my right hand on her left arm. "So where did you Antonio first meet?" I questioned.

"I do not really know, I can not remember a time when he was not part of my life. I had immense admiration for him when I was a little girl. He was a friend of my oldest brother." She paused and took a breather. "I know my husband told you about his family during the Contra. Well, when his first wife died, we became really close. Over the years, marriage seemed to be the perfect option. Luckily for us, both our families approved, it could have been a lot more complicated."

"Are there still arranged marriages?"

"It happens, but it is rare. You have to know that people living high up in the mountains do not have a lot of choice. We are forced to choose among the people that we know and sometimes there is not much to choose from." She said with a little laugh.

It felt great to hear her talk freely. I was finally getting to know the woman behind the sickness. "So what did you like about Antonio that made you want to marry him?" I interrogated.

"He was by far the funniest man I had ever met in my life." She replied.

I was waiting for her to laugh, but she did not. It was so strange, because for me Antonio was a lot of things, but *funny* was definitely not one of them. "Really?" I had to exclaim.

"Well, before his wife and children died of course. When I was little, he made me laugh so hard. I know in my heart that I have been in love with him since the day I was born. Unfortunately, he spent a lot of time away." She said, gently rubbing her belly.

The conversation was great, but it was all about her husband. I wanted some answers from her and I was afraid that I would run out of time. "If I may ask, why did you refuse those treatments?" I questioned, unexpectedly to my own self.

"I don't think you can understand." She said after a brief hesitation.

"Probably not, but you could always try me." I replied, and after all the driving I had done, she could not decline my request.

"I have felt that foetus growing in my belly for over seven months, how can I harm it?"

I could not answer to that so I stayed silent.

"There is more, though, Señor Imbault." She paused and it allowed me to express my sympathy with my speechless face. "I have never been able to have children. I have made seven miscarriages over the last fifteen years. Sure, we are wealthy compared to others in our village, but wealth is not simply a question of money. This is the only baby that has held on for so long. Now that he is strong and almost ready to come out, these doctors say that I should hurt him, risk killing him to save my own life. No man can understand the feeling that carrying this child is giving me every single second of the day." She explained.

I felt stupid "I'm really sorry. You're completely right; I can't understand any of it." I admitted.

"All I want, my dream is to hold him in my arms, hear him laugh, hold him when he cries, heal him when he is sick, feed him, dress him for school, play with him, read him stories before he falls asleep and look at him sleeping, hoping that he has joyful dreams that light up his long dark nights." She finished.

I waited a while and looked around to see if the men were on their way back. "You know Anna, maybe I do understand a bit, because for the first time ever in my life, the idea of having a child sounds good to my ears." I confessed.

She smiled warmly. "I'm very glad to hear that. You will make a great father someday." She added.

"But don't worry, we now know where we're going. You'll be fine, soon we'll be in front of a Shaman and I'm sure he'll be able to help you." I tried to convince her.

"It's very nice of you to say, but I feel good about my situation now."

"Really? Great!"

"During our night in Panama City, I got up around eleven at night, and went to the cathedral. The place was totally empty. I sat down and prayed for a long while, long enough to lose track of time. I thought about my life and my present battle. I felt like it could be the last one and something convinced me that it was just fine. Strangely, I agreed, my situation was out of my control. It was in the hands of God. All I could do was to have faith." She paused and seemed to wonder if she should continue.

"Please go on." I pleaded.

"That is it. I got up and left the cathedral. I stopped in the middle of the square and breathed the air of the city. I longed for our village with its cold breeze. I looked up at the clouded sky and felt like someone was watching over me. I climbed up to my room and slipped back beside my husband. He was snoring his nose off, as always, but it was still giving me a feeling of comfort, knowing that he was there beside me."

Suddenly, Anna had severe belly-ache, our conversation ended. She started to lament quietly, but I knew that she was holding it all inside. I gave her my hand to hold and she nearly crushed it to pieces. She was moaning in absolute pain and I was powerless to stop it. I felt so useless. I wanted to tell her to let it all out, to scream in agony. I stood up without letting go of her hand to look for her husband, but he was no where in sight. "Antonio!" I screamed.

She pulled me down. "Do not, please." Anna told me.

"I'm sorry." I apologized. Where the hell was Don Angel when I needed him? Knowing him, he probably did it on purpose so I would learn to solve my problems on my own.

Minutes passed and her pain went away. She calmed down and kept her eyes closed. I had no idea if she was awake or asleep, was conscious or had fainted. Then, she opened her eyes. "I am terribly sorry, Señor Imbault."

"Please don't..." I started.

"I'm sorry!" She cut me off.

"Two things: first don't call me Señor ever again, my name is Kristian. Second, and most important, do not apologize for anything. Just rest, your husband will be back soon." I tried to reassure her.

"Please do not tell him anything. I do not want to trouble him." She demanded, as she slowly recovered.

I could not believe her, she was the one suffering and yet, she was still protecting her husband. "What just happened here?" I asked.

"It's normal, even the doctors in Managua had mentioned that it could happen. This is the second time." She stopped when she saw my jaw drop and almost touched my chest. "It also happened yesterday when you were touring around Panama City. I'm sorry; we did not want to worry you." She concluded.

I waited a while and looked at her with a smile. "Please, stop apologizing." I said.

Anna fell asleep, or fainted, I stayed beside her, holding her hand. She was mistaken, this one was the third; the very first one had been when we had met in El Chaparral. Soon, I would have the Shaman in front of us.

Don Angel came back before Antonio. He was already dry, although with this scorching weather, it was not such a difficult job. "So, how was the water?" I softly asked not to wake Anna up.

"I did not swim. I decided to go bird-watching instead." Don Angel replied with a guilty look on his face.

When the husband came back, he was still wet. "How did it go?" I asked.

"Not too bad, I swam for a bit." He stopped and glanced at his wife. She woke up as soon as she heard her husband's voice. "But, I lost my balance at some point and started to sink in. Strangely, I was able to come back to the surface." He said with an expression of disbelief.

"Why is that strange?" I asked.

"You have never seen him swim that's why." Anna said drowsily. "He can barely keep his head out." She added, pretending she was in top shape.

I was intrigued. "Well, how did you do it this time?" I questioned.

"I can't say. It all happened in a matter of seconds. I really panicked at first, but then I quickly popped back up." He paused and waited for comments that never came. "So everything went alright, here?" He asked.

"Perfect!" The wife said, as she looked at me.

"Okay then, we are ready to go." The husband exclaimed and without waiting for a reply, moved towards the cabin.

We finally called it quits in the early evening. We were about a hundred kilometres from the city of Yaviza. We stopped before because it was supposedly not a recommendable place to spend the night. It was also where the highway stopped. From there, we either had to take a boat, which we would not do, or drive on very secondary roads, our only real option. It was already dark and quiet when we stopped by the side of the road.

We walked for a short while and found ourselves a decent spot beside a charming little creek. There even was a tiny waterfall. The surface was so beautiful, reflecting the moonbeams. Small dancing lights were shooting back up to the heavens. The water seemed so light, as if it could fly away, but stayed to watch over the bottom rock-bed. The black of the liquid, transformed itself into snowy-white, becoming pure by the motion of the brown rocks. The upstream part was slow until it decided to speed-up and dive into the falls of life.

It was all so lovely, so à-propos. I stayed for about fifteen minutes, letting Antonio and Anna prepare dinner together. I felt like they needed the time alone and evidently, I had no interest in cooking. It was as if I needed to see that the creek's beauty was not temporary, that it would still be there if I were to return next week or even next year.

"Your frijoles are ready, Don Kristiano!" Anna called.

I felt like puking just to hear what was on the menu again. Just tell me who I would have to kill to get some cheese fondue.

At least Anna had called me by my name and that, made me happy.

CHAPTER 4.2

We crossed the city of Yaviza in the early morning. We did not stop. My Gosh, I never drove so quickly in an urban area. Everybody looked like they were ready to jump us. Even the police looked at us in a crooked way. We saw some strip joints and bars. Antonio was standing in the back, ready to strike. I could only imagine the look he had in his eyes. One thing was certain, the street thugs did not see Antonio the driver, or the swimmer, but the real thing.

We started going on small dirt paths that could not even be called roads. The pace slowed down to less than twenty kilometres an hour. The jungle was so dense, I could not believe it. Luckily for us, everything was dry. Our four-by-four could not have done anything if these trails had been wet with mud. "I think we are now officially in the Darien Gap." Don Angel announced after about three hours of the worst driving I had ever done in my life.

"What's that?" I questioned.

"It is a jungle of ten thousand square miles, separating Central and South America, a legendary impenetrable rain forest that not many people have visited." He added.

"Are you shitting me?!" I blurted. Where the hell were we going?

"The legend says that it is impossible to cross, but do not worry."

"Why's that?" I interrupted.

"Because our objective is not to cross it." Pedro clarified.

I was speechless. Was this for real? Hopefully this had been invented by the Columbian drug lords so that no one would try to cross their border by way of land. Legendary impenetrable Pedro had said, but what did that really mean? Maybe it was one of those made up legends, like elephant graveyards which were in fact poachers' waste disposal site.

It was during the early afternoon that I finally saw it. "There! According to the map, this is the road where we have to turn!" I yelled for everyone to hear. It was nothing like Scott had explained, I was expecting a street light or a stop sign. Never had he mentioned this obscure Darien Gap.

Anna now had difficulty breathing. She had barely been able to sleep the night before because of her heart that had not stopped pinching. Her condition had deteriorated since yesterday's stroke. She seemed to suffer, but I could never be sure, she kept it all inside. I simply hoped that she would have the strength to be courageous. Had she decided to stop fighting now that she had accepted her fate, now that we were so close to our goal?

We started rolling on the worst dirt-road yet. We could not go faster than ten kilometres an hour. I would have liked to go faster and speed up. I wanted Anna to get better, at least to stop living this uncertainty. There was not enough space for two cars. Hopefully no one would come the other way. It was like a long soft half-pipe where I did not have to hold the steering wheel, even Antonio could have driven. I felt like I was inside a locomotive.

I kept going forward, without really knowing, or seeing where we were heading. The jungle was growing thicker and higher with every passing kilometre. There were now impenetrable green walls on each side of the road. I had to roll up the window, branches were wiping me pretty badly. I was lucky to have that option, I felt awful for the couple in the back. The trees were getting huge, always so dissimilar from the ones beside them. "This jungle is mind-blowing, if only it could be human-saw-proof." I said to Don Angel.

"The region is not really in danger. There have been plans to build a highway to unite Panama with Columbia since the early nineteen-twenties. I do not think they will ever do it. The forest is too precious. Indigenous tribes are now well politicized. They will not be chased out easily." He explained.

"Yeah, tell that to the tribe from the Osa Peninsula." I retaliated, as the truck fell into a huge mud hole.

It took us a few minutes of rocking back and forth before we could finally get out. Things were getting worse and worse. We drove for more than three hours. I started to get nervous, and angry. Where was this road going? It was stupid of us to keep going, especially with Anna's condition. We could not even turn the truck around if we wanted to. It would take me forever to drive back in reverse. Although, it was difficult to see, it felt like we were going up. This road was bringing us higher in altitude, closer to the sky. We crossed two creeks and a river and every time, I was looking for something to come out, a sign. The man at the clinic had only giving us the indication to this road. We had no clue where to go, but to follow the road. The problem was that this path did not go anywhere.

Finally, we saw something, or rather someone. In fact, we almost hit him with the truck. We turned a curve and there he was, standing in the middle, already staring in our direction. "What's this guy doing here?" I asked Don Angel in total shock.

He did not answer right away. We had not spoken for so long; perhaps he simply did not expect a comment. "How should I know?" He answered with his big smile. "Go check it out!" Pedro encouraged.

I difficultly stepped out of the vehicle, pushing the door against the branches. Antonio and I walked up to the aboriginal dude. I admit I was a bit intimidated. This man was beyond strange. First of all, he was almost naked, wearing only a loincloth. He held a stick in his left hand, either a walking staff or a spear, I was unsure. He did not have an ounce of fat, just small muscles that looked incredibly firm. Although, his body amazed me, it was when he slightly turned around and I noticed his back that I was truly spooked. He had the exact same kind of weird tattoo as the guy in Scott's clinic. I felt relieved; we were unquestionably on the right track.

When Antonio and I arrived at the man's side, he seemed just as shocked with me as I with him. He stared at me as if he had never seen a white man before. This guy surely spent his days hunting or fishing. The lack of tourism in the area gave him full right to gaze at me, but hopefully not forever.

"Hola!" Antonio greeted. "My name is Don Antonio De La Vega and this is Don Kristiano Imbault."

I was impressed at the official level that my friend was taking for this conversation. The man stayed quiet and appeared to be very much at ease with our presence. There was a remarkable absence of stress in his eyes.

"Could you please help us?" Antonio added.

The indigenous then turned to Antonio. "What do you need?" He asked, as he slowly bent his head from left to right.

The man had a strange accent that I could not fully understand. It would surely take me some time to get use to it.

"We really need to see a Shaman." The husband admitted.

The aboriginal hesitated a bit. "Come!" He then simply said.

"Great, we need to get my wife and then we will be ready to go." Antonio exclaimed.

"Is it far?" I asked.

He looked at me. "It will take us a day to get there, we will have to camp for the night. The great sun is about to set." He clarified calmly.

"What's your name?" I decided to question.

"Ley!" He then presented his left arm in order to shake my hand. When I gave him mine, he took my lower arm instead of my palm. It was strange, but very cool.

"We need to park this truck somewhere." I yelled to Antonio.

He jumped out the back and grabbed his machete. "I will take care of it." My friend started to hack through the jungle like a bulldozer. He was a mean cutting machine. In less than five minutes, I had a nice little parking space; the only thing missing was the parking-meter.

In about ten minutes, we were all ready to go. Anna's bed became a stretcher, reminding me of the first time I had seen her. Antonio and I were carriers and Don Angel was closing the march. We started walking in the forest at a pace that was way too fast for us all. We were out of shape, used to sitting in the truck for too long.

"Please wait! We can not walk with the stretcher at this speed!" The husband told our guide. He was right; losing him was definitely not an option.

"Give me your machete, I will clear the way for you." The indigenous answered and suggested.

"Thank you!" Antonio and I said in total harmony.

The jungle was dreadfully dense; I could not even feel the wind. The trees were astonishing, never had I thought such a variety to be possible. Several trunks were covered with leaves half-way up, others were tied with a vine, like a boa on its pray. Some got rid of their bark so they would not get tied up. Leaves were huge, like my mother's plants, but a hundred times their size. It was hard to walk, branches tried to grab us and pull us down. Being the man at the back, it was difficult to advance because I could not see where I was putting my feet. I was glad to hold the stretcher, though; it was an assurance not to get lost.

During a short well-deserved break, Pedro and I sat by a nice creek, I decided to kill the monotony of this jungle with a question to my buddy. "You think this Gap will be able to stand forever? At some point, someone will come and split it in half."

Don Angel snapped out of his quiet mood. "It would be unfortunate. There are many indigenous tribes still living around here. It is hard to say if they will be able to stay this way forever. Many great civilizations have come and gone: Incas, Mayas, and Aztecs: who knows?" Pedro answered.

"The Aztecs weren't the brightest, if you ask me. I mean, why did they welcome Conquistadors in such ceremonial fashion?" I asked.

"They did not know they were narrow-minded gold hunters. I believe the ceremony you refer to was the one given to Hernán Cortés when he first arrived."

I was not even sure. "Yeah! That's the one." I decided to confirm anyway.

"Well, just so you know, the Emperor Montezuma thought Cortez was the Feathered Snake returning." He stopped when I turned around to look at him in an interrogative way. "Quetzalcoatl was the main Mexican God, creator of all life, who had gone away and had promised to return." Don Angel explained.

"And they thought it was Cortés?"

"Well, the Spaniard arrived exactly on Quetzalcoatl's birthday. Furthermore, he arrived with eleven ships and over six hundred men, horses and banners flying in the wind: trust me, it must have been a sight to see for naive indigenous farmers." Pedro clarified.

"And they all died because of their gullibility, didn't they? They should have fled for their lives the second they saw the ships coming." I declared.

"Don Kristiano, everybody deserves a warm welcome, at first." Pedro preached in conclusion, minutes before we got back on our feet.

Darkness was upon us, although Phoebus was still present in the sky. The tree-tops were forming an impenetrable ceiling, blocking the light of the falling sun. It was now impossible to see where the trees ended and where the sky began.

Then, we came up to a river and arrived on a beach made of exquisite white sand. "We will stop here for the night. Soon all light will be gone. The jaguar sun is setting behind the distant mountain, getting ready for his fight against the lords of the underworld." The guide declared. He turned and looked in my direction. "Nothing to worry, he will successfully return tomorrow morning." Ley concluded.

No one argued, we were simply too tired. That stretcher was going to be the end of me and judging from Antonio's amount of sweat on his back, he too needed the rest.

We sat down and relaxed for a bit. Our guide did not rest with us. Right away, he was gathering wood for the fire. Suddenly, we heard a loud whistle coming from the jungle. I got really nervous, but tried not to let it show. What kind of birds could be so loud? Then, I saw Ley, who had just returned close by, make the same bird sound. He was answering. Surprisingly, four men stepped out of the jungle. Why did they have to make bird sounds? Who were they trying to fool? Why did they feel the need to get me all nervous and a bit angry, I might add?

Ley and the quartet had a long conversation that I could not hear and probably could not have understood anyway. Surely our guide had to explain why he was hanging out with a bunch of weird-looking people like us. In this jungle, in the company of these natives, even Antonio seemed out of place.

The four newcomers all looked alike, exactly like our guide, almost butt-naked. The difference between them and Ley was that they were armed. They all had a homemade knife tied to their waist, also a bow and arrows. Two of them had carried a long pole, holding a dead animal, tied by his four legs, inevitably falling down. I first thought it was a little bear, but when they put it down, I realized it was a tapir.

One of the two non-carriers looked at me in a strange way. He came closer and then really stared me down, observing every detail of my body. The man kept gazing into my blue eyes and took out the weird knife that was hanging from his tiny belt made of rope. "Are you hungry?" He questioned.

I was so nervous that I barely understood his question. I thought, he was about to offer food, but he stayed motionless. I was trying not to look nervous and irritated. What did he want, why was he not moving, did he really need me to reply? Of course, I was hungry, if that truly was the question? "Yes I am." I apprehensively gave it a shot.

He smiled and walked back beside the dead animal's carcase. In a very swift move, he cut a chunk from the back thigh and he showed it to me. It all seemed surreal, this man was holding a piece of tapir, black and red, and was inviting me for dinner. Then, all of a sudden, he threw me the meat. "Let's eat!" He declared while it was still in the air.

I caught it and walked up to Ley. "Are these guys just here to cook our meal?" I asked him, waving the thigh in his face.

He did not reply.

"How did they know we'd be here?" I turned toward Antonio.

"We have our ways Master Kristiano." The guide interfered. "Do you like tapir?" He continued.

"I've never tasted it before." I politely answered. How could I have, the animal was on the endangered species' list. It was illegal to kill it, let alone eat it. Still, they were so happy to bring us unlimited meat supplies and it would be such a great change from our usual rice and beans. I could not refuse. I put the thigh back beside its previous owner and waited for them to do the rest.

I was starved. Today, lunch had only been made of carrots. Luckily, there was plenty of meat for tonight. I just hoped we would not deprive anybody else of their tribe from eating. They did not give the impression to mind, so I was not going to bother either. In a way, I was glad to be in the jungle, restaurants were no longer an option. The money was almost gone. I should have counted better, plan some sort of budget. The way things were going, we would barely have enough to pay for the gas back.

Two men worked on the fire while another prepared the meat. They were all humming a tune together as they worked. Strangely, the melody sounded familiar.

The first man from before came back to see me with a stick in his hand and presented it to me. I saw a couple of ants running back and forth. Perhaps he simply wanted to explain to me what a tapir's dietetic habits were. I was about to tell him that I knew what tapirs ate and that this branch was too small for the fire. "Eat!" He then ordered.

I was shocked. "You want me to eat the stick?" I questioned.

He smiled. "No no, these are lemon ants. They are very good, very nutritious." He added.

I could not believe it: lemon ants. Or had he said lemonade? He took one, put it on his lower lip, his tongue quickly came out and brought the insect straight into his mouth. I had a shiver in my stomach. No way was I doing the same.

"Try it!" He kindly insisted.

I could hear Antonio, and even Anna, laughing in the background. "Come on Don Kristiano, they are lemon ants!" The husband encouraged.

"I don't care if they're lemon, grapefruit of even chocolate; they're still ants to me!" I retorted a bit angrily.

"Ahh! Don't be a tourist, be an adventurer!" Antonio dared.

He knew exactly that it would get me going. Annoying man, I thought to myself.

"Eat!" The first man insisted again.

"Another annoying man!" I whispered so no one would hear. Maybe, those were the required appetizers to have the right to the main dish? Why could we not at least kill them before? And I thought my big dilemma would be to decide if I was going to eat an endangered animal. I was dying for something to happen, a storm, or caimans coming out of the water. What kind of peaceful jungle was this?

Finally, the man made another gesture with his hand for me to try the darn lemon bugs. It reminded me of my father, trying to get me to swallow cough medicine as a child. Finally, I took a deep breath, closed my eyes and brought the branch to my mouth. When would I have another opportunity to taste some ants, especially lemon ones? I stared one of the insects straight in the eyes and gave the branch a strong lick. I felt the bugs running in my mouth, surely looking for an exit. I tried really hard not to spit them back out. Amazing! They did taste like lemon! The tribal men, and especially Antonio, were cracking up. My lips started to burn, the food was fighting back, biting me, punishing me for not swallowing them more quickly. That was enough for me. In a flash, I spat them all out. Everyone was laughing, even Anna was giggling.

I was disgusted. What had I done? I needed water, and fast. I searched for it like a madman. I looked through our bag and found nothing but an empty jug.

"Ley, can you help the man out?" Antonio asked our guide.

"Sure!" The indigenous replied. He stood up and walked next to a long vine. Then he signalled me with his right index finger to join him. As I was coming towards him, he slashed the vine in a flash. Liquid came out of it. The vine had transformed into a long wooden straw. Ley blocked it so there would be some left for me. I drank; it was the purest water I had ever tasted in my life.

"And how did you like those lemon ants?" The husband asked.

"Not bad, it's definitely not something I'll have the chance to try again so it's cool." I answered. "Did you try some?"

"Me, are you crazy? My bug-eating time is long gone my friend." He retorted.

I was proud of having done it. I would have regretted it if I had not. Plus, these indigenous probably had gained some respect for me. I had gotten a few laughs. Distractions were good at all times, entertainment was always a pleasure.

It was great not to wonder where I could find Shaman. Now, all I wanted to know was where my plate of endangered tapir was?

Dinner went relatively quickly. I had been anxious to witness how they would make fire from nothing, and was disappointed to see Antonio lend a pack of matches. In this darkness, there was no time to waste hitting two rocks together. Our tapir was served to us, already cut into small pieces, on giant leaves. I liked the big leaves instead of plates, eating with our hands, no dishes would need washing. The meat was hard, but still very juicy. I wondered if I could go to jail for this, would people judge me back home, would I have to keep this a secret for the rest of my life? Who would believe anything that happened to me out here anyway?

The atmosphere around the campfire was amazing. The indigenous spent the whole meal time laughing, the most sincere laughter a man could hear. This simple life-style unquestionably had its advantages. Surely the fact that none of them had to go to work the next day helped a lot. No one worried about paying the house, car, electricity, groceries, telephone, cell phone, or cable. They did not own much, but it also meant they did not have much to be concerned with. Earlier, I had been happy to give them an opportunity to laugh; boy was I wrong when I thought it was a rare occasion. It felt great to see Anna and Antonio join in and enjoy themselves.

The aboriginal people set up a shelter with huge tree branches for Anna and Antonio. A little later, the five jungle boys disappeared in the forest to sleep in its secure arms. As for myself, I put my blanket on the beach beside the fire. I was a bit too close to the water for my liking, too many unknown types of snakes and caimans could come out and kiss me goodbye during the night. Still, luckily for me, Don Angel was right beside me, proving that my idea was not so stupid after all. I was sure I would be alright. For what I had read as a kid, caimans and alligator, could not stick their tongues out anyway. At least it would not be a French kiss.

It was amazing to be spending the night here. The stars were bright and the Milky Way was reflected in the mirror of the river. It was all superb, even the firefly doubled their brightness in the water. I could see the black silhouette of the trees on the other side. Birds were replaced by frogs and crickets in the soundtrack of the night. They would not rest and I would have to ignore them in order to fall asleep. Everything was great, everything except maybe the little rock under my left shoulder.

In the middle of the night, I got up to go relieve my bladder. It was great to feel the sand between my toes. I went to the far side of the beach, right by the timber line and let it all out. Once it was done, I stayed up and smelled the fresh air. Everything was so peaceful.

Then, it arrived without warning and gently landed on me. Holy Jesus, I thought to myself. It had the size of a normal cricket, but this bug was nothing ordinary. It was astounding; it had two little lights on top of its head, a pair of minuscule balls that lit up in a florescent green colour. When it flapped its wings, its belly lit up as well, but it was more than just light, it was a bright orange zigzag. I had never seen anything like it, how could I have? I could understand fireflies, but this was beyond belief. This insect was so full of energy; I was surprised it did not explode. It was unreal, dreamlike, illusory, and mostly, out of this world.

It flew from my shoulder and stepped into the jungle. Since I was awake and had nothing better to do at that time, I decided to follow it. Without regards for my bare feet, I painfully walked into the jungle. Seconds later, a branch made me regret my decision, but I kept going. Luckily for me, the bug was still in sight, waiting for me to catch up. It even came back and started going in circle around my head. It was probably observing me, wanting to know why I was pursuing it.

It was special. I simply could not go back to sleep. I wanted to think it was more than a simple bug. It seemed out of place, like it was an alien trapped on earth, hiding in this deep jungle land. Did not the Incas scriptures talk about the great Gods coming from the sky? Was this insect on a reconnaissance mission, or maybe it was a Battery-Mongolian? As I finished this stupid thought, it came straight in front of my nose, stayed there for a second and then flew away, never to return.

I found myself alone, in total darkness. There was no moon for the time being. I stood inside and inkwell made of leaves and branches. My eyes slowly started to get use to it. The bug's enlightenment was slowly disappearing from my vision. The sun's little sister slowly made her way through a whole in the clouds. She was showing me three quarters of her splendour. Light clouds, more like a mist, masked her quickly and then she came back, stronger, clearer and more beautiful than before. Her beams lit up the leaves surrounding it. A positive force was finally penetrating this dark jungle. Strangely, I did not even feel any fear or nervousness. Frogs and insects still played their greatest hits. My dizzy body, with my head looking up, rocked to their music. I was ready to go back to my blanket.

Back on the beach, through the dispersed clouds, I stared at the stars. After a few minutes, one came flying, shooting through the others like a comet. My desire could only be Anna's recovery. Once I wished it, I was ready to sleep.

"Are you okay, Don Kristiano?" Pedro asked in a whisper.

I was a bit surprised; he had been different this last day. "Yes, I'm fine. But I should be the one to ask you though. You've been really quiet since we've entered the jungle." I expressed in a higher tone of voice than his careful one.

He hesitated a bit, as if he did not want to worry me. "You are right; I can not say I enjoy this forest hike." He confessed.

I did not push my interrogation; surely he had a good reason. Perhaps it had something to do with the war. Although, he had said he had only played a small part in it, a small part was all that was needed to have some psychological problems. "Pedro, do you believe in intelligent alien life form?" I decided to ask for a refreshing change of subject.

"Of course!" He rapidly answered.

"How can you be so sure?"

"No one has tried to contact us." He jokingly replied.

"Seriously, how can there be life on other planets?"

"How can there not be? Could we be the only living beings in such an immense universe?" Pedro retorted.

"And how easy is it to answer someone else's question with another question?" I sarcastically asked.

Don Angel smiled. "I am sorry. The truth is that there is no proof to the question. In a way, it is like having faith in God. You have to feel it inside yourself. How can you discuss something that there is no argument except what other people have seen or heard? There are always going to be people to ridicule the ones who accept it as fact. The choice to believe or not is entirely yours, Don Kristiano." He advised.

"Before tonight, I did not think life could exist on other planets, but now I'm not sure." I admitted.

"Why is that?" Don Angel asked.

"I saw something in the jungle, a bug that was so remarkable, special. It had to be from another planet." I paused and my friend obviously waited for more. "It was this big." I said as I showed him the size with my thumb and my index. "It had green lights on its head and a zigzagging light on its belly." I added.

"Ah! You mean a click beetle?" Pedro plainly said. At that moment, I came back to earth. Don Angel saw the deception in my face. "Do not be disappointed. It is still an incredible species, and very rare, you should be happy you have seen one."

"But it's just a bug from our planet." I replied.

"The fact that it is from earth should not take away its splendour and radiance, on the contrary. Granted, we sometimes have to look very hard for magnificence, but do not worry, it is always there." He concluded.

CHAPTER 4.3

I got up the last one, the sun was barely up and Don Angel was nowhere in sight. "Wake up, Don Kristiano! We will have to go soon." Antonio declared.

"Thanks, I'll be ready when *soon* comes." I answered.

"Did you sleep okay? I heard you talking in your sleep." My friend said.

"Really?" I questioned.

"Oh yeah, you were having a whole conversation with yourself." He said laughing.

"Oh well!" I finished. As I stood up, when I looked to the far side of the beach, I saw a dozen butterflies on the spot where I had urinated last night. I preferred to ignore what they were doing.

We had some cold leftover tapir for breakfast. The indigenous quartet had already left. I went beside Ley. "So, ready for the hike?" I said for the simple pleasure of shooting the breeze.

"We are no longer walking." The guide answered as he pointed to a long pirogue by the water.

We all climbed inside and found ourselves a spot, the stretcher taking most of the space. Weirdly, Don Angel sat right beside me even though there was an empty seat. He stayed very calm. What was his problem, was he afraid of being swallowed by the darkness of the jungle? I did not ask him anything. I figured if the roles were reversed, he would give me the space I needed. We pushed the river bed and started moving with the current.

Antonio and Ley were the only ones with paddles; they were sculpted in tree trunks. I would have liked to have one, keep me occupied. All I had to do was relax and enjoy this stunning boat ride. The water was brown, but very clean. We were too far away from civilization for it to be polluted. The surface perfectly reflected the scenery, until our boat split it in half. The swirls were shinning with the early light of the sun. Everything was so quiet, the birds and the sounds of the two blades gently splashing the water.

I had no clue which direction we were taking. The river was winding, but seemed to know exactly where it was going. The only thing we could do was to go with the flow. The scenery was great, but always similar. Different types of trees bordered the liquidly way. Some were straight, some curved over the water, some furnished, some naked, some lit by the sun, some hidden under the shady leaves. There were hundreds of shades of green, but regardless of their differences, they remained identical. However exceptional and out of the ordinary this trip was, my bum was hurting, and sleepiness was about to get me.

Nobody really spoke; it was not only Don Angel. In my opinion, our guide was not going fast enough. I wondered if Ley was worried about Anna. He did not seem to trouble himself too much. Perhaps he knew that she would be cured once we reached his village. Or was it the opposite? "How far is your village, Ley?" I decided to ask him.

"Not far!" He simply replied.

I felt like asking how far was *not far*, but did not. Every time Anna was moaning in pain, I felt a little sadder and sadder. I had a friend in need here, how many hours was this boat tour going to last? Too bad my watch had stayed in the glove box.

I saw unbelievable birds during my half-asleep state. They flew in front of our pirogue, almost touching the water's mirror; their reflected image followed them as long as possible until it flew towards the bottom. With the sun getting higher up in the sky, it was becoming a lot hotter. I wondered if I could swim in this river. Were there any piranhas? Why could I not see any mammals on the land? Why were the toucans' noses not multicoloured like the one from the cereal box? If only the atmosphere was more relaxed, I could ask all these questions to Ley.

We finally got off the boat and on to the mainland. Judging by the sun, it was probably half-day, but I had had no lunch to prove it. "How long is it to your village now?" I questioned our guide.

"Not far!" He again answered.

Why could he not give me a straight answer? Antonio came to see me, noticing that this guy was starting to get me down. "Relax, Don Kristiano, this man probably does not have the same conception of time and distance as you do. What do you expect him to say, two hours and twelve minutes or five and a half kilometres?" The husband excused him.

"Maybe you're right. I'm sorry." I felt like I should apologize.

We started hiking again. The bed was once again transformed into a stretcher. The air was fresh, just like in our forest back home, but a bit sweeter, more sugary. I was in front and Antonio had taken the back. I was impressed at my own strength for carrying Anna so long without needing to pause. I only had to relax my brain, enjoy this remarkable chaotic forest, and make sure I did not lose sight of Ley. The terrain was more mountainous than before. Luckily, the trail was never going over them, it was going around the great big bumps. Another positive thing was that trees were now more spaced out and let us by more freely. The bad thing was that Ley did not have to use his machete anymore and was going a lot faster. The ground was muddy, as if it had once been the bottom of a great sea that had decided to pull back with time. My running shoes were dirty beyond recognition. There were no rocks, only dead leaves that would probably serve as fertilizer for the next generation of plants. I tried not to touch anything. There were so many types of foliage, how was I to know which ones were poisonous? Green made me feel secure, but I did not want to get in contact with anything red or yellow. It would have been great to know which vine to cut for water, which mushroom was venomous, or which fruit was filled with juice and not with worms. Sadly, I was very far from my good buddy Collin Webster.

We walked at a steady pace and I was getting tired. Anna looked paler with every step we took. "We're almost there!" I kept repeating to myself, hoping that it would give me hope and soon be true.

Then things got uglier, vegetation got denser and our guide had to get back to work. Branches were wiping us badly. Some little bushes had needles that would grab hold of us. My pants and Anna's left sleeve ripped under the insistent pressure of a little tree. It was depressing; I felt so bad to see the red skin on the woman's arm. We were following some creek that we constantly had to cross. My only choice was to try to take pleasure in the sounds that our shoes were making as they escaped the mud's suction. Ley did not mind getting wet, but I would have preferred to stay dried. The sun had disappeared behind the clouds a long time ago. There was very little light crossing the leafy rooftop and making it to the ground. This jungle seemed endless. "We're almost there!" I said to encourage the troop's spirit.

Suddenly, everything got really dark. I felt a chill. It all happened very quickly, the air started to feel cool, humid. Birdsongs paused. Seconds later, the clouds burst and rain slowly started to come down.

At first it was tolerable because we were protected by the leaves of the trees, but our natural shield did not last very long. Antonio took out a blanket and put it over his wife. We had to keep going since our guide, sure as heck, was not stopping.

Then, the rain got really angry. We got drenched in a matter of seconds. Ley was still walking, impervious to the water. "Come on! Not far now!" He turned to us and encouraged in vain.

Why was this storm coming down on us? Probably some stupid butterfly in China had flapped its wings one time too many. I felt like dropping the stretcher and starting to cry. "We can't go on like this, we have to stop!" I yelled.

"Ley! My wife is going to catch pneumonia. Please!" Antonio begged.

Finally, I got what Don Garcia was so afraid of back in San Francisco. Ten minutes ago I was sweating, now I felt cold, freezing.

Ley simply turned and nodded to us. "There!" He said as he pointed a spot between two huge trees.

What did he mean? We still listened to the man and placed Anna right where he had indicated. As for our guide, he was cutting the biggest leaves he could find and also a few long vines. He joined us and put the branches along the trunk, facing up and tied them. When he let them go, they came down at a ninety degree angle to form a perfect umbrella. Antonio and I helped him for about ten others and our shelter was completed.

The noise of the rain was massively powerful. It was like a gigantic circular wave surrounding us, coming our way with speed. Leaves everywhere were dancing to the wind's violent music. We all took out our blanket and wrapped ourselves. Don Angel was still as quiet as ever and I did not bother him, nobody did. As for our guide, he did not even seem to mind the weather. Ley walked around looking for fruit to eat. The guy was amazing. He seemed to feel no physical pain. It took him about ten minutes and we all had enough to eat for lunch.

An hour later, the rain stopped. We were ready to leave, hike to dry ourselves off. Anna even got up, painfully, and walked to get rid of the wetness, but it was useless. She had to lie back down in her drenched clothes. How could she get better in these conditions? Why had we not stopped before? Antonio looked at her with courage, trying to hide his concerned mind. They were both trying to conceal something so obvious.

We walked again for two more horrendous hours. The clouds had vanished and the sun was now trying its hardest to dry us up. The leaves now shone with the light of the sky. The jungle had become brighter. Anna started to cough, and always wiped her mouth with a handkerchief. I turned around a few times to see if there was blood on the hankie, but she kept it locked tight in her hand.

Then, I turned around when I heard the woman badly coughing. Antonio and I stopped the train to give Anna time to feel better. Seconds later, when my head came back to the front, Ley had disappeared, vanished. I had become the leader of our group. It was easy to see extremely far ahead. Still, he was nowhere in sight. We all stayed silent. For Don Angel, it was not difficult, but Antonio and I were stunned. Where had our guide gone? What were we supposed to do? "Let's put the stretcher down." Antonio suggested.

"And then what? Where the hell did he go?" I blurted.

Antonio just looked at me. He did not know what to say. The scenery was the same as always. We were on the side of mountain and there were trees everywhere. Anna looked so nervous; I had to calm myself down. We were totally alone and it scared the shit out of me. I searched around looking for our guide. We had been so close to him at the moment when he had disappeared. "Patience." I heard one of the two men say.

Good idea, but until when? We were screwed now. Would this guy ever come back, magically reappear? We should have never trusted this indigenous stranger. Anna started to cough her lungs out. We could not go back. There was no yellow brick road to show us the way. We were lost, trapped inside this jungle jail. We still could not talk about it, refusing to admit the situation. The husband took care of his wife. I still looked for Ley. Don Angel observed everything from a distance. "Wait!" Someone said again. I was so messed up, it could have been me talking and I would not have known it.

Suddenly, in a flash, a door opened through the mountain. Ley came out of it. He resurrected in our lives like a saviour from the sky. I remembered Martin who had once told me I was a hard man to impress. Well, in my entire life, I had never been so impressed.

CHAPTER 4.4

Our guide Ley was followed by two men from last night's quartet and also by a fourth one, a different one, unique. The man was old, slowly walking with a weird-looking staff. He had thin snowy hair and an almost inexistent beard. He wore a bandanna on the head and some sort of skirts covering him from the waist down. He bore a strange necklace made of bones around his neck. It was his face that struck me, such peacefulness, such kindness came out of his eyes. Regardless of how the old man looked, I was certain of one thing: we had him, he was a Shaman. We had found what we had searched for during these last few weeks. Where could they, we, I, find a Shaman? The answer was now known: in the middle of the Panamanian Darien Gap, obviously.

The healer knelt down beside Anna and observed her. He closed his eyes and looked heartbroken. The old man placed a hand over her forehead and the other on top of her bellybutton, hovering over her body. Anna opened her eyes and softly smiled at him. The sage stood up and with a slow hand gesture, ordered the men to carry her inside the heart of the mountain.

Antonio followed them, but I stayed behind with Don Angel. I needed to decompress, a minute ago I thought I was going to die in this jungle. We both silently looked around, trying to understand what had just happened. It all seemed so normal; there was no way to know what was inside. Pedro pointed at the mountain. "Look!"

"What?" I asked. He did not answer right away and as I was about to ask again, I noticed little triangular sculpted rocks on the mountain's bank. Everything was lined up together perfectly. Judging from the size this huge hill, I knew that these stones were only the tip of the iceberg. I did not say anything, just stayed there with my mouth opened. Then, I saw two birds fly out of the mountain, probably from small windows. They resembled peaceful missiles shot into the forest. "What do you think?" I questioned Don Angel.

"It's hard to say." He replied.

I felt like teasing him, he who always knew all the answers. "What's your best guess then?" I insisted.

"Well, we are in front of a mountain that is hiding what seems to be a very old pyramid." He said.

"Maya, Aztec or Inca?" I asked.

"Maybe, maybe none of them, there is no way to be sure. Everything is possible and exceptions are always a probability." Pedro added.

We both stared at this wonder in total astonishment. Time allowed this pyramid to become a mountain. It looked so much like a regular one with all the dirt and the trees. It was totally indescribable. People lived in there unnoticed, perfectly sheltered from the rest of the world. Birds freely kept coming in and out. I was positively suffering from a severe case of horripilation, having goose bumps in front of this spectacle. I stood in the boiling jungle and I could not stop shivering.

Neither of us seemed ready to walk in. "Isn't this Inca country?" I questioned to avoid taking the first step inside.

"At one point yes, it was."

"Do you know anything about them?"

"They measured time by how long it was taking to cook a potato." He answered in all seriousness, until I gave him a look and he started to laugh. "They are descendants of Manco Capac who came out from the depths of Lake Titicaca with his wife-sister." He told me.

"What was so great about them anyway?" I kept it going.

"They had a well-organized system: government, education, technology, astronomy, mathematics, art, and more."

"If they were so great, why did they lose it all?"

"The conquistadors and Francisco Pizarro, they had riffles, canon, and horses. Atahualpa was no match for them and their treachery."

"What do you mean by that?" I asked.

"You are only curious to avoid going inside. I accepted it for a while, but we can no longer stay here, we have to go in."

"You're right!" I agreed. I would have preferred Don Angel to be in his normal frame of mind, so he could go in first and I would have simply follow. I would have liked to stare at his back and let him be the first to meet people. The folks inside the pyramid surely all had that weird accent.

The minute we entered, a man with crooked eyes came straight towards us. "Follow me!" He calmly ordered.

We took a few steps inside and all exterior light disappeared. The tunnel was dark, lit up by torches hung, stinking of weird sugary oil. The grey walls were full of hieroglyphic carvings. Everything started to move very slowly; perhaps it was all too much for me to digest. It was as if I was watching a movie in slow-motion. I could even see the weightless dust coming from the man's footsteps in front of me. How was it possible, was it my head that had blown a fuse, was it the change of temperature or the claustrophobic air inside this mountain? I seemed to put the brakes on my movements, but I was effortlessly following the indigenous.

Then, the first tunnel ended and we penetrated a giant square. There was a fire in the middle of the place, probably the exact center of the whole building. Maybe this was the only heating system in the building. Darkness surrounded this square. I could not really distinct where the roof was.

There were a lot of people, most of them tattooed and half-naked. Needless to say, I had never seen such a crowd. Some women had a golden nose ring and much jewellery. The female were all very small. I noticed two guys with sharp teeth, as if they had sharpened them with a file. They were writing some weird letters on a piece of bark. I even spotted an albino; he was easily perceptible, with his white hair, among the black ones. I had no clue what they were all doing, most of them were simply chatting. Maybe this was a market of some kind. They all looked very peaceful; barely noticing us walking by. Had they ever seen a white man before, did they know anything of the world outside this jungle? They had probably never seen a telephone, a television, a telegram or any other *tele* I could think of. For all I knew, they probably still thought the earth was flat.

We crossed the hall and entered another tunnel. I did not really like this claustrophobic sensation. I thought the jungle was bad with its trees, but now it was worst, I was walking inside a rocky mountain. I had a desperate need for windows in this absolute secret place. At least, the second passage was shorter than the first one.

We hung a right and accessed the room in which Anna was lying in the middle of. Then, things in my mind started moving at the proper speed again. She was naked and unconscious. Her belly had gotten so much bigger since the first time I had seen her in El Chaparral. It was incredibly hot, I could barely breathe, surely the reason why my female friend had passed out. Surrounding her, were four weird-looking stoves with hot stones. A man poured a little bit of water on them and steam flew up in the air. The Shaman was kneeling beside Anna. He now wore some kind of indigenous top hat with a few feathers. His back was straight and had his hands placed over her. He was whispering strange non-melodic incantations.

Don Angel did not say a word and moved himself out of the picture. Antonio was on the other side of the old man, kneeling, praying. There were five indigenous men in total, two on each side of the door and three on the door-less walls. Once the Shaman was done talking, they all started singing, in harmony, it sounded like some Gregorian chant. The husband got up and came to see me. "The baby really needs to come out. There is a strong chance they both will die." He painfully told me.

"So why are they just singing and not pulling it out right away?" I questioned.

"They tried, but it did not work." He said in a desolated tone. "They are now singing to calm the Goddess Muu down." Antonio added quietly.

"Who?" I had to ask.

"The Goddess Muu! He repeated. "According to the Shaman she is a protective spirit that inhabits the woman's uterus." My friend explained.

After what I had seen today, I was not shocked by any nonsense I would hear. "If she's a protective spirit, why does she need to be calmed down?" I asked.

"It seems that since the foetus was sick, she took special care of him and now she does not want to let him go." He made clear.

I stayed quiet. It was definitely something I had never thought I would ever hear in my life.

"The song tells the story of the Shaman against Muu inside the tunnel, fighting for the baby's freedom." Antonio said.

In a way, it made me think of all those divorced couples back home, fighting to have custody of their kids. Still, how could the Shaman be inside this woman's uterus? Then, the tune changed and became more upbeat.

"The singers are now asking Ix Chel's aid." He paused and before I could ask. "She is the Goddess of childbirth and healing." He explained.

These stories gave the impression to be taken straight out of a comic book. If I had not been in the interior of a pyramid, hidden under a mountain, watching it with my own eyes, I would have thought it to be bogus to implore all these divinities.

"I will pray some more." Antonio excused himself. He knelt down and started to recite the Our Father.

I waited a while. Why was Anna suffering so much, some murderers and rapists lived to be eighty years old, why could Anna and her baby not do the same? Surely God had a plan.

Nothing changed in the room; these people held their position. Then, Don Angel came beside me. "What are you doing, are you okay?" He whispered very softly.

I did not want to get into anything, so I simply nodded with a facial expression that was telling him not to be concerned.

"Do not worry, the only thing we can be sure of, is that things will go according to God's plan." Pedro said.

How did he do it? It ticked me off that I could never seem to keep anything secret from him. "How do you always know what I am thinking about?" I asked him so quietly that no one else could hear.

"I do not always know what you are thinking. I just said that because I was looking at Anna, I felt powerless to just stand here and do nothing." He explained. "Let's pray, Don Kristiano. You can be like Antonio and kneel down, recite prayers to God in heaven or you could be like the Shaman, asking help to Itzamna in his house of lizards."

I did not think too much about it. I simply knelt down and started reflecting. Did Anna and her baby deserve this? Perhaps the mother and child were paying for something they had done wrong in a past life or earning their next one. Actions were already planned and consequences could only follow. There was no such thing as coincidences. I could barely accept what was happening here, life would take its course no matter what. If Anna had to die, then so be it. I could only wish that it would happen peacefully and painlessly.

Although I had seen him for only a few minutes, this Shaman was the most astonishing man I had ever met. Strangely, I felt satisfied and had hope for Anna. I had faith that things would be alright, so I decided to get off my knees and leave the room. As I was walking towards the great hall, I felt bad and thought that perhaps I should have stayed, but I felt like there was nothing I could do in there.

Soon after, I arrived in the square and entered without being noticed. I looked around, bent down and sat on my ankles with my back to the wall. I felt a bit guilty for feeling at ease. Was I still deranged, should I be nervous? I did not need to think so much anymore. So what if I did not understand what was going on. I closed my eyes. I felt like I was sitting beside myself. I dozed off for a few minutes. I was totally exhausted.

Margarita-Anna Lorca died in the evening of July thirty-first. "And the baby?" I asked with already watery eyes.

"Gone as well." Don Angel answered without a smile. "The boy came out without crying, snooped around and decided that he was not ready."

"What happened?" I questioned as I fought to keep the tears inside.

"Anna softly smiled and tenderly held him in her arms. He fell asleep, secure, had time for a quick dream and then they went away, both at the exact same time." Don Angel gave me time to breathe. "He simply went back to where he came from and convinced his mother to follow." He added.

"What if she didn't *want* to follow?" I contradicted, trying to control myself.

"You know that she was ready for that eventuality." He replied.

"Maybe, but..." I could not finish, my throat clogged up.

"She is lucky. They went together, Don Kristiano, hand in hand. You know how difficult it is to do things alone. We should not be sad. We should wish them luck on the great voyage they are beginning today. The baby knows the way, he will show his mother. The destination was changed, the roles were reversed. It will be a lot easier if they go together. Sometimes, leaving is a lot harder than it can sound. Death confronts you with the highest form of insecurity." He put his hand on my shoulder.

I think it was the only time he actually touched me. "Please leave me. I'll be fine." I pleaded although his gesture weirdly made me feel a lot better. There was no way I could find the will, mentally nor physically, to stand up. My knees wanted to explode. I threw myself on the ground and connected with the earth. It was as if I became part of the sandy floor. It was the first time that somebody I knew had died. I stayed on the ground, using my right arm as a pillow. All the thinking I had done since I had left Cinco Pinos, it all seemed useless right now. Why could this not be a daydream?

Don Angel was still beside me. He stood there in perfect silence, waiting for me to be ready, respecting the fact that I needed some time.

"Get up!" An unrecognizable inner voice told me. I could not listen; it would have to wait and be very patient. I was going to lie here for a while.

People walked by and did not even look at me. I wondered if they cared about me, about us, about Anna?

"Get up now!" The strange voice repeated, but I still ignored it.

I would miss Anna, although I had not known her as well as I would have liked to. Our conversation by the side of the road had helped me to understand a few things. This woman was the reason I had gone through so many things over the last weeks. She was responsible for turning a boy into a man.

I was looking up, still trying to see the ceiling of this pyramid. The smoke from the fire was getting lost in darkness. Where was Anna at this moment? Had her soul already gone away? Probably, she had been ready for sometime now, since the cathedral in Panama City. Suddenly, the flames became out of focus. A tear slowly came out from my right eye and fell, licking my cheek on its way down to the ground. The drop was quickly followed by three others. They relieved me and also made me feel horrific. I had waited for these tears for so long and strangely, they did not really make me feel sad.

"Get the hell up!" The strange voice repeated once more. This time, it sounded angry, I had to listen. I recognized it and realized it was my own. I simply was not ready to hear it before. I put my back up against the wall. I now had to get all the way up. Pedro would not help me with this one. Surely, the strength to obey my inner voice could be found somewhere inside me.

I was about to give the final effort when the Shaman arrived, promptly and unhurriedly. He looked at Don Angel who was still standing in silence and knelt down beside me at the speed of a ten year old. He stared into the fire. I stayed quiet. What was I supposed to say: Wazzup?

"What's your name?" The old man initiated.

"Kristian." I said. Somehow, I did not think I should transform it the Spaniard way.

"I only want you to know that Anna went peacefully and so did her baby, do not be saddened, Kristian." He said in soft melodic voice.

I hesitated before I spoke, turning my tongue seven times in my mouth, making sure I would not make a complete fool out of myself. "That's easier said than done." I finally replied with honesty.

"No it is not, there are both the same, only different in your mind." The indigenous doctor said.

If he had been anybody else, I would have bluntly told him that he was quoting Master Yoda, but with this Shaman, I simply could not. I stayed silent, trying to have a receptive attitude.

"Don't worry for too long. You don't need all your questions to be answered right away. Be patient, you will not run out of time." The Shaman explained.

He made a lot of sense. Were the answers simply waiting somewhere, which one came before, did the lighter not appear before the matches? Regardless, I felt like I was listening to one of Don Angel's preaching session. Still, the moralizing speeches had been good for me. I knew that when I would go back home, things would be different. It was as if I had spent my time in a dark room, looking at the night outside the window. Then, I had turned on the light, everything outside became black and I could finally see around me. "I think I understand." I admitted.

The old man stopped staring at the fire and looked me straight in the eyes. He had the eyes of a wolf, a minuscule black dot surrounded by different shades of grey. "Do not waste your time living emotions that do not need such attention. Do not seek to have material possessions. Do not be bothered by anger, sadness and insanity. Just be the best person you can be." He said. "This is where true happiness rests." The old man advised slowly.

"Thank you."

The Shaman got up. "You took great care of him, but you will have to let go soon." He instructed Don Angel who seemed uneasy with his request. Then, he left as quickly as he had appeared.

I got up right away, forgetting all my physical pain. The Shaman had read me like an opened book. How could I be so obvious? This Shaman was even worse than Don Angel who always seemed to be able to guess my thoughts. I needed to get out of here and get some fresh air, like the imperceptible roof would soon collapse on me if I did not leave this building immediately.

I was standing tall, my back still to the wall and I had nowhere to go. Where was Antonio? My brain was messed up. Even my vision had started to come and go. It sometimes seemed inverted, I felt like I could see inside my head. I located the initial tunnel's entrance and started to put one foot in front of the other. I crossed the great square and did not look back.

In a matter of seconds, I was outside, gazing at the clear dark sky through the gigantic trees, smelling the sweet leaves of the jungle.

I stood there, taking deep breaths, trying to calm myself down. I looked up at the stars, searching comfort in this dark part of the world. Then I took a look at the mountain. It was impossible to imagine everything that was going on behind this magical shield of nature. I could not believe everything the earth was able to swallow. Things were definitely not always what they seemed. I started to think about climbing up to the top. What was it like to be standing on an ancient pyramid? What would the view be like? I decided to stop questioning and go get some answers.

I started climbing, grabbing a hold of the many trees that stood on it. I felt bad about stepping on the precious shielding dirt, but it did not seem to cause too much damage and I needed to get to the summit. It took about fifteen minutes to make it. I was breathing heavily and sweating like a pig. The first thing I saw was the earth's satellite. It reflected enough light for me to see far into jungle land. There was a huge clearing at the bottom, behind the mountain. There were agricultural fields and some kind of big round reservoir beside.

I could see the Milky Way. The light of the night hit the leaves of the trees with such loveliness. It was purely beautiful, reminding me of back home when the full moon illuminates the freshly fallen snow. Whether it was because of Anna, because I was exhausted, or because I was surrounded by such beauty, the result was the same: I sat down and cried my heart out.

I made my way down and ran into Don Angel at the bottom. I surprised him, or he pretended, when I appeared from the mountain. "What are you doing out?" I questioned.

"I needed some fresh air." He answered. "Where were you?" He asked at his turn.

"I've been to the mountain top."

"And? Have you seen the other side?" He questioned with a smile.

I smiled as well. "Yes, I believe I did." I replied with relief.

"That's good." Pedro shortly said.

We stayed quiet for a bit. I did not want to think about Anna's death. I had to start an unrelated conversation. "So, how are you holding out?" I asked him.

"Good, I will be fine." Pedro answered in a positive tone.

"I know you will, but you have to help me out here."

"Sure, that's what I'm here for." He replied.

"I know I'll be pushy and you don't have to answer if you don't want to, but I'd like to know why you've been so quiet ever since we entered this jungle." I cautiously said.

He hesitated a while. "I am not sure why I have a weird feeling. I guess I do not like being in a forest, it just reminds of bad memories from back home." He admitted.

"Cinco Pinos?" I questioned.

"No, San Francisco." He corrected.

"That's right. Please go on." I gently insisted.

"I do not think I have ever told you this, but I was present the day of the massacre." He explained.

That was an unmentioned detail indeed. "Stop anytime you want, but you saw it from close?" I questioned, not caring that I could barely see Antonio and Ley ahead of us.

"Honestly, I'm not sure what went on. I heard gunshots flying around, people running and screaming, and then all of a sudden, I fainted. Everything went quiet, a mixture of black and white." He told me.

"Then what?"

"I woke up in the middle of the jungle nearby the village. I was dizzy and my vision was blurry. I was scared and started running, wanting to get out of the forest. It was crazy. I had grown up in the area, but I could not find my way back to the village. I yearned for the comfort of my home, but when it finally happened, I never felt safe again." He finished.

"Is that why you moved out of San Francisco?" I questioned again.

"After the carnage, things were no longer the same." He said and took a breather. "I sometimes wished I had stayed. I still consider San Francisco home, it is where my heart is. I was never able to definitively cut the umbilical cord."

"I heard Don Garcia's story about the massacre and I can only imagine your pain. It must have been horrible." I said with real compassion.

"I could not bear to see my family and friends so sad all the time: I had to leave." He admitted.

I could not believe what I had just heard. He, out of all men, could not deal with a situation. Right then, Antonio came out. His eyes and face were red like an apple. "We will eat now, they organized the most amazing meal for us." He told us and walked right back in.

"No thank you. I can not eat at a time like this." Don Angel told the widower as he was walking back inside. "I'm not hungry. You go ahead." He then said in my direction.

"What do you mean you're not hungry?" I asked in shock. Did this guy ever eat? Perhaps I had been used to always eating the extra bite, he had not.

"I had some food when you were on top of the world." He justified. "Do not worry; you can go on without me." He said in a serious tone.

I hesitated a bit, trying to see if he was lying to me. "I know." I decided to simply say.

We had dinner. I was sitting at one end of the table and Antonio was at the other. He was not going to eat anything. The Shaman was in the middle, surrounded by about thirteen other indigenous people, including our guide Ley and one woman. The food was great. We had some tortillas and were invited to put anything we wanted on it. There were some red hot chilli peppers, brown rice, green beans and even squashes. Furthermore, there was a diverse variety of unknown pieces of meat. Surely, half of it was on the endangered animal species' list. I did recognise the tapir, but the rest was barely discernible. Was guinea pig edible? Regardless of the look, size or colour, I ate all I was served. There was no way I could refuse anything. The serving I had in front of me was probably more than what these people ate in a week.

I was given a bed in a room and spent the best night since I had left Cinco Pinos. I did not dream, nor did I wake up for probably fifteen hours. It was Ley who had come to wake me up. "Don Kristiano, it is about to begin." He had announced through the door.

I had no idea what was about to start, but I figured that if Ley had been sent to get me, it must have been important. I got up, got dressed, checked my shoes for bugs and got on my way to the main square.

Everybody was there, all in one big circle. The fire had been removed and a large altar had been placed in its place. Anna's body lied on it and they had put the baby in her arms. Her body was covered with a white sheet and surrounded by candles. The Shaman was standing right beside her. The old healer started to speak some incomprehensible words. He mostly moved his hands over the body and raised his arms up in the air from time to time. No one was talking, they were all listening. Death seemed to be of great importance; after all, none of these people knew Anna.

The speech lasted about fifteen minutes and then it stopped. A noise was heard coming from the imperceptible ceiling. Tiny pieces of dirt glided down to the ground. All of a sudden, a sunbeam came straight down from the roof and struck Anna's body full blast. A gong was hit four times and my body shivered every single time. I wondered how that beam could have happened so quickly, maybe someone had simply opened a trapdoor at the right moment the sun had reached its peek. Was it already noon? Illumination hit Anna's heart for the last time, because shortly after, the opening was closed and the light died off. The scene was very emotional and I could not wait for everything to end. I wanted to turn the page, get rid of the ball stuck in my throat.

"Hola, Don Kristiano." I softly heard from my left.

"Hey!" I simply answered.

"Are you okay?" Don Angel asked.

I nodded positively. I saw that there was movement at the altar. "What's going on now?"

"The Shaman will put some food and a little rock in her mouth."

"A rock?" I asked.

"Jade." Pedro replied.

The Shaman signalled four men, including Antonio, to get closer. The husband ripped off the cross and gold chain around his neck and he placed the wooden part in his wife's hand. Anna's was then rapped with many pieces of cloth. Once it was finished, the Shaman bent down and seized some sand that he spread over her mummified body.

The four men each took a corner of the higher part of the altar and lifted it in the air. Four different men joined them carrying a torch. All of them started to move towards the far corner of the square.

"What's going on?" I asked Don Angel.

"Anna has asked her husband to stay here forever. She said that she had felt at peace in this pyramid and did not want to go back her village." Pedro explained.

It was good to learn they had had time for a final conversation. "Are they going to burry her outback?" I questioned.

"No, these people believe that Xibalba can only be reached from an underground cave or a natural well. She will be placed in the basement of this pyramid in catacombs."

"And what is Xibalba, if I may ask?" I said in a gentle, but annoyed tone of voice.

"Heaven. Do not worry, I do not have absolute knowledge, I simply overheard them earlier when they explained it to Antonio." My partner answered.

We looked at the torch's lights slowly fade away. This was it. We would never see Anna again; memories of her smile would be the only images left. It was time to move on, go back to home, to Cinco Pinos.

CHAPTER 4.5

We said our goodbyes in the early morning and started going back to the truck. Ley was our guide once again and it was a very good thing because we would have been totally lost. We did not really talk much, Antonio was saddened, crushed, by the loss of his wife and Don Angel still seemed petrified of the jungle. The indigenous was almost jogging in front of us. We were able to hike quickly, since we unfortunately did not have to carry a stretcher.

Once, Don Angel and I fell behind. I had to change my mind, talk about something else or I would not make it out of here. "Who were these people inside the pyramid? Were they Mayans?" I questioned.

"I do not really know, I did not ask. Maybe they were simple Panamanian Indigenous people. They might have been Cuna Indians for all we know."

"Who are they?"

"People living off the islands in the Pacific." Don Angel retorted.

These Cuna were surely great, but I had never heard of them so I decided to change the subject. "Why did the Mayans disappear if they were so advanced? Did they all get killed by the Conquistadors? Did they follow the extra-terrestrials or rejoined Atlantis?"

"Actually, they did not vanish at all; I do not know why some people seem to think so. There are over six millions Mayans living around the northern countries of Central America and although it can no longer be considered an Empire, their old dominance lasted six times longer than the Roman Empire's." He explained. "One of them even won a Nobel peace prize in the nineties." He added.

"But they were a lot more before, how did their number diminish so much?" I asked.

"Some people say there might have been a long drought. I have also heard that an enemy tribe started a long war with them. All the men had to leave their great cities and fight. The women and children were left alone and were unable to maintain their majestic lifestyle. They had to move to smaller houses on the countryside. All the technological advancement they had once had was lost." Pedro made clear.

"So, fighting instead of creating, even I can see the lack of logic in that." I concluded.

"You are right." Pedro agreed.

"Though, we might be wrong. No one knows for sure." I said with a smile. "You think these people inside the pyramid were Mayans?" I asked again.

"Honestly, I doubt it, but who knows, everything is possible. They could be distant relatives." He finished with a smile. At that moment, I heard a noise behind and saw what seemed to be a jaguar. It was hard to distinguish in the shade of the trees. Then, we saw Ley and Antonio who had thankfully stopped to wait for us. Our conversation ended there and we went back to our quiet ways.

We walked the whole way and finally made it to the truck in less than seven hours. The pirogue had not been used. It was probably too difficult to go up against the current. We were all very glad to find the vehicle exactly where we had left it. Ley made a fast retreat. I heard a little cracking-sound behind us and saw the jaguar walking the other way. Luckily I was by the truck, safe. Although I did not feel like driving, it would be better than walking. The path back to the first city was a challenge I did not feel like facing. After the endless fresh air I had breathed, even the paved roads would be difficult to get accustomed to. "You ready to go?" I asked Antonio.

"Yes I am, but if you don't mind, I will ride in the back for a while." He replied.

"Sure! No problem." What else could I say? I still had Pedro who would probably start chatting again.

I started the engine and let it run for a few minutes, reminding me of the cold Swiss days. I turned the vehicle around with great difficulty; Antonio even had to cut down a few trees by the side of the path. We got going.

The road was just as slow as before. There were over one thousand kilometres from here to the village in a straight line; we no longer had to stop. It would take the rest of the day and tomorrow. We had enough money for gas, but food would have been a problem if the indigenous had not given us some provisions for the ride. I could not wait to get there, wash up properly and sit down. "So you gonna start talking again?" I asked Don Angel.

"Of course, you know me. I always have something to preach." He answered. "Are you okay about Anna and everything?" He then questioned in a comforting tone.

"Yeah, I'm fine. I'll find a way to deal with it." I admitted.

"Why don't you write a book about what happened here?" He asked lightly.

It might have been a simple remark for him, but it really made me think. "Maybe the idea isn't so bad, but why would people be interested?" I questioned.

"I'm not sure, perhaps because most readers are people who like to stay home in their pyjamas. It would give them a chance to know what else is going on in this part of the world." Don Angel said with hope.

"They'd probably think it'd be pure fiction." I answered shortly.

"It does not matter. It would be an entertaining story, maybe helping them to learn a few things."

I hesitated.

"Seriously, you do not think you could write a novel?" He repeated intriguingly.

"It's hard to say, I've never tried. It'd probably be full of sentences following each other in no particular order, like cars stuck in traffic in a one way dead-end street." I negatively assumed.

"I think you are selling yourself short. There are so many empty lines waiting to be filled with your words."

"That's the problem; why couldn't I say what I want with only *one* word. Everything gets so complicated between the capital letter and the period." I joked.

"That's just a risk you will have to take." Pedro said half-seriously.

"Yes, but I'm not ready to take it. It takes many years to write a book. What if I never get published? If I wanted to make money, I should open a bookstore instead. I heard they get forty percent of the earnings while authors barely get ten." I argued and continued. "Do you know that only two percent of manuscripts make it to bookstore shelves?" I asked.

"You are lucky. In Nicaragua during the Somoza days, publishing houses did not even exist. Authors had to go get published in the surrounding countries." He retaliated.

I did not say anything about his remark.

Two and a half hours later, we finally hit the highway. I noticed that there were some strange trees in the middle of the field. They were all bended towards the east, as if it was only sunny in the morning or that the wind only blew form the west. "Our story would not compare to what writers publish today. They'd probably laugh at me." I weirdly decided to carry on our conversation about literature.

"Since when do you care what famous writers think? Don't worry, chances are, they will never read your book."

Well, that was encouraging. "You're right; they don't matter much to me. Things have changed a lot over the years. We have replaced Hemingway by Grisham. At this rate, dogs will be publishing books in fifty years." I joked as my friend gave me a disapproving look. "I guess I could always write our story for my personal benefit and not for the money." As I finished the sentence, Don Angel gave me a huge smile. Right then, I understood that it was what he had meant all along. It was probably some therapeutic method that he was suggesting; publishing had never been on his mind. He stayed quiet, so I continued. "Book buyers are a dying breed anyway. They go get it for free on the Internet. Plus, most readers simply do it in their bed to help them fall asleep. Ironic isn't it? Writers stay awake all-night for years in order to create books that will become substitute to pharmaceutics sleeping pills against insomnia." I alleged.

"You are being a bit too hard." Pedro expressed.

"Who knows what to write? Who knows what to read? Which questions deserve their interrogation points? Which comma can allow itself to cut and which semicolon can pretend to have the right to tear apart? Which exclamation point truly belongs at the end of a sentence said to be expressive? Which period has the right to put an end to it all?" I philosophised.

"And who could listen to all this and not think it was a total waste of time?" Pedro cut me off to ask in a funny way. We both started laughing. "Just do it for yourself, Don Kristiano." He suggested.

"I don't think my imagination compares to yours." I countered.

"You would be surprised!" Don Angel concluded.

In a way, I was a tiny bit disappointed about going back up north. South America would have been nice to discover. Things could not have been so different down there though. It was probably richer in some places, but dictators and poor people were surely no strangers to reality. Antonio would have taught me about Pinochet and Peron, while Don Angel would have taken care of Pelé and Evita. I would not know now, but perhaps someday. I was heading north, back to where my Latino life had been born.

The scenery remained the same forever. I had never realized that cutting off in little dirt roads was killing monotony. Now, I simply followed the two endless yellow lines and tried to keep my eyes open.

By the very end of the next day, we unnoticeably rolled into Cinco Pinos.

CHAPTER 5.1

Things were quiet; it was passed eleven o'clock at night. The village was asleep. "Well, this is it!" I said as I turned off the engine for the last time.

"Yes, it is." Don Angel said, but did not move.

I stepped out of the vehicle at the same moment as Antonio. We met beside the truck. "I think I will just walk home. I have asked way too much from you already." He said and waited a while. "I can not find the words to thank you right now; I will do it later though." He added and went away before I could insist on giving him a ride. Although he probably had done it many times before, I could not believe he would walk all the way to San Pedro.

I turned and saw Don Angel. "You alright?" I asked.

"Yes Don Kristiano! I think I am ready to go now." He announced with seriousness, as if he had just taken the most important decision ever. "But perhaps I will come down for a short visit in a day or two." Pedro added with his usual smile and left by the backyard. I wondered where he lived, how high up the mountain it was. I would be curious to visit his house, maybe someday I would.

"I'll see you tomorrow buddy. Sleep well!" I wished and walked up the stairs of Martin's house. I tried to open the front door, but it was locked. I knocked a couple times. "Martin!" I shouted four times. Damn! I could not believe it. I drove all this way, made it so close to my mattress and now I was going to have to sleep outside again. "Martin! Wake up!" I walked around a bit, the lights were off. Where was this guy? I looked around the house and found an opened window to climb inside. I searched a bit to see if Martin was sleeping somewhere, but he was not. Things had not changed that much. He had found himself a poster of Fidel Castro and JFK shaking hands. There was hope after all.

I jumped on my bed and fell asleep right away.

I was in my bedroom, wearing jeans with huge pockets, there was a bath with a bed in it. When I looked around, I noticed that I was inside an igloo.

Later, I was walking around a small village of the Bavarian Alps. Everything was so simple. It was fall and trees were showing their greatest colours of the year. The sky was filled with thick grey cotton-ball-like clouds. There was a small northern breeze lifting up my hair. There also was a great church surrounded by small white houses. Many chimneys made of rocks were spitting a gentle smoke. People were slowly walking up and down the main street. There was a wonderful lake where boats were lined up along the dock. This was the perfect place to be.

It must have been a Sunday, everything was so peaceful. I was hiking on a gravel path and was not worry about anything. I was just glad to be happy, not knowing why, I felt great.

Then, I realized something. I simply looked at the end of my own hand and there she was. Inside my hand was a palm, belonging to an attractive young woman. Our thumbs touched while my index and middle finger surrounded her little. Why had I not noticed her before? Had she been there all along while I was staring at the scenery? She was pretty. Her eyes were sparkling with a pale blue colour. Her hair was light brown, uncertain whether to be straight or curly. There was something special about her, about the way she moved, and about her way to be.

We walked together side by side, in perfect harmony. There was a small waterfall and we stopped to feel its cool wind. We were silent, delighted to be a couple. I wanted her to know me by heart, the real me, with all my little secrets. I desired to be hers, belong to her, like lightning to thunder or salt to pepper. I desired to be inside her heart and soul. Suddenly, I felt a pressure between my legs that had nothing sexual. It started to hurt. Then, everything became yellow. I did not want to wake up. My vision faded. I told her I loved her, wishing she could truly feel what was inside my heart, hoping those three common cliché words would be enough. The girl turned to me and smiled. There was deception in her eyes, but her lips gave me hope. Without opening, I could sense that they seemed to be telling me: see you soon.

My eyelids opened and everything disappeared, everything but the pain between my legs. I got up and ran to the backyard to pee.

As I walked back inside, I heard the front door open. "It was a duck damnit!" Martin shouted at the top of his lungs as he tripped on my backpack. We both burst out laughing and shook hands, both of us too uncomfortable to hug each other.

He was drunk, returning from a party in Somotillo. We talked for over two hours. I told most of the story, but not in details. My friend could not believe how blessed I was to have seen everything I had seen. Regardless of the mental suffering, dirtiness, endless driving hours, starvation, and lack of money, I had been a part of something amazing.

I went back to sleep, thinking how I had missed this village more than I had realized. It actually felt good to be back.

The following day, all I did was rest. I did not really leave the house, except to cross next door and go eat some of Juanita's best, decent, cooking. I rediscovered the joy of shaving with cream. I poured thousands of water buckets on me, trying to get clean. My back was covered with red zits, probably due to sweat and the hot car seat. I sat at Martin's desk, enjoying the music on his laptop. I also tried to write everything that had happened down in a little notebook. I even tried to draw the truck, the beautiful lake, the cathedral of Panama, our guide Ley, and the Shaman. Maybe it would be nice to remember all this in my old age.

Martin was working, I barely saw him during the day. Antonio had gone back to San Pedro and had not returned yet. This morning, a message had come announcing that he would come for a visit tomorrow. As for Don Angel, I had not seen or heard from him. I wondered where he was. Strangely, I missed his preaching.

The villagers' attitude had changed a lot while I was gone. They remained the same people, but they now fully accepted me. I was no longer looked upon as a stranger. My role in the journey had made me a part of their gang. The main ones all came in for a visit, Chale, Diego, Esteban, Emilio, Paco, Romaro or Armano or was it Ramiro? It seemed like a great honour for the villagers to offer me to try their bike or even their horse. People came to chat for the simple pleasure of talking. We discussed their country and mine. They asked many questions and my answers were always vague. I was no longer pushing for the Occidental grip to grab a hold of them. They all wanted to look for America, but with their foreign accent it sounded more like a *miracle*. I was glad about their attention, but wished they had acknowledged me before, for me, and not because I had helped out Anna and Antonio. Perhaps the voyage made me what I was. Was it possible to accept someone for his abstract inner mind or did humans always required something more, something concrete? It did not really matter, I was leaving the day after tomorrow and everything here would soon become memories, souvenirs.

Life was simple here. I had found a peaceful place in the heart of a Sandinistas country. There were no sign, no advertisement to eat food, go see a movie, rent a car, buy drinks, or merchandise. I truly felt free. The village's breath was soft and lovely. Was it really better up north? I did not know anymore. Suddenly, the idea of staying here for a little longer did not sound so bad.

It was weird to think how many people in North America were unhappy with their reality. Perhaps it was just that they did not know any other and it was so fun to criticize. If only rich folks from back home, sitting in their three hundred thousand dollar secondary residence, could see Juanita working, slaving in her kitchen everyday. The problem was that her restaurant was not on any tourist itinerary.

CHAPTER 5.2

During the afternoon, Martin and I had lunch at Juanita's. She tried to make us some hot-dogs with black pudding. The thought was there, but definitely not the positive result. "So you're not bored staying at the house all the time? Why don't you come with me? The workers are asking about you." Martin proposed.

"I don't know. Why should I go when I'm not even paid for it anymore?" I retorted in spite.

He looked at me in a weird way. "Don't bullshit me. You don't believe that and you know it." He paused and saw the expression on my face that made him right. "Do you have any plans for this afternoon?" Martin decided to ask to change the subject.

"Well, I was wondering if I could borrow your camera and take some pictures around the village." I said.

"Sure! I have a fresh roll, take it. You can even have the truck, I got used to not using it."

"Good, that's what I'll do then." I agreed.

"And... if you feel like hiking a bit, you know where to find us." Martin added.

I first walked around Cinco Pinos and took a few shots. I photographed Martin's house, the restaurant, the pharmacy and some people on the streets, ladies washing clothes, old men playing cards, young children in the streets, dirty cats and dogs, students coming back from school in their white and blue uniform, and many other things.

Then, I decided to go to San Francisco, give my regards to Don Garcia and take a few pictures. I drove there without any problem from the rivers.

When I made it, there was no one in sight. They were working in the fields and the others were probably inside, hiding from the heat. I drove to the massacre's site. I knocked on the door of the house in front of the gates, but no one answered. I observed the surroundings for two minutes. Since there was still no one, I decided to climb over the gate. I ripped my shirt on the way down. Again, I gazed around to see if anybody had noticed, nothing had changed. I strolled in silence, looking at the fifteen victims' graves. I photographed a bunch and then concentrated on the monument in the middle. I took a few shots from different angles and even a close-up of the plaque. Although these fifteen names were not much compared to the tens of thousands who had died during the revolution, these fifteen *heroes y martires* were fifteen too many. It felt weird; there were strange vibrations in this park. I left right after the last picture was taken, drove straight back to Cinco Pinos, Don Garcia and his men were surely too far up the mountain for me to wave goodbye.

Back at the house, Martin was nowhere to be found, but Antonio arrived seconds after I did. "Can I come in?" He had started to ask.

"Sure, sure." I replied. I was happy to see him. I had definitely suffered from the Stockholm syndrome during this journey.

"Do you mind if I close the door?" He questioned.

I simply motioned my agreement with my hand.

"I can not pay you back the money, Don Kristiano." The widower confessed.

"I know." I shortly said. Antonio did not react. "What is it?" I then asked.

"I do not have cash, I have land. I thought I could sell some of it, but no one has the money to buy it from me." He paused. "I am forever thankful and I want to repay my debt. I have decided to give you the most beautiful lot I own." Antonio offered.

I hesitated before answering. What was I going to do with a farming field in the northern mountains of Nicaragua? That would surely be my most useless possession. "Are you sure? I'm returning home and chances are I'll never come back here again." I said truthfully.

"I know, but the land is truly magnificent. There is a small lake with a river that runs beside a charming little shack that I built there a few years ago. It would be the perfect escape for you, your friends and family, if you ever wanted to get away for a holiday." He explained. "I have to be honest with you, my friend. I possess a lot of terrain that I bought at ridiculous prices from families of people who had died during the Contra. In a way, I took advantage of these people's misery and it was wrong of me to do so. Most of the families I took the land from have gone away." Antonio came clean with shame. "At least, let me do something good with it. Please, just accept it, Don Kristiano." He pleaded.

I stayed quiet and then decided to go for it. "Why did you purchase land in such ways?"

"I suffered so much during the Revolution. I just wanted to take care of my family. I wanted us to have it all." He admitted. "The land was given freely by the government. When men were called back for the Contra, and did not come back, the remaining family members had a hard time managing it. This was where I came in, easily acquiring lot, after lot, after lot." He confessed.

The Antonio I had gotten to know was simply not the same person he was describing. "I don't think you should worry about the man you once were, he doesn't exist anymore. I mean, you're helping us with our coffee project. In my opinion, you are being too hard on yourself." I told him.

"The land issue is not the only one, Don Kristiano." He insisted.

"Why don't you tell me what happened to you, Antonio?" I boldly asked. "It will be your way of repaying me." I added to give him a way out and a great story for me to hear.

He did not speak for a while. "Before our journey together, I would have never even considered answering your question; no one knows the truth, not even Anna. Strangely, I feel different now. My second wife has passed away and I am alone once again, only this time it is truly finished, I am too old, I will not restart all over." He stopped and looked around. "You see, the Bishop in Penonomé told me that a wound needed fresh air to heal; it can never do if it is kept inside. Maybe I can reveal my secret to you. After all we went through, there is no doubt in my mind that you are worthy of it." He paused again. "The only thing I ask is that if you decide to tell others, make sure you are back in your country." He ended with an embarrassed smile.

"I will do as you wish." I retorted.

Antonio hesitated. "Would you mind taking a walk?" He asked.

"No not at all. Where would you like to go?"

"The *campo*, the baseball field, beside the school will be fine." Antonio suggested.

"Let's just take the truck, it will be faster." I offered.

We rode in silence, both of us in the front. He was probably reflecting about how to say his future words and I was simply wondering what they would be.

We made it there and stopped the truck. We both got out and sat on the tail gate. "You see, I told you that I fought during the Contra, but I never gave you any details about my revolutionary days."

"That's fine. There are things about me you don't know as well; we don't have to give each other every single detail." I replied in a sympathetic tone.

"I know, but no one has ever helped me the way you did."

"Circumstances made me do it."

"No, no, you could have turned back anytime you wanted. You stayed and went until the end." Antonio sincerely retorted.

"As if I would have abandoned you and Anna out there."

"Don't be so modest, the choice was always there for you."

"Anyway, let's get back to your story. What have you done?" I asked directly.

He smiled at me for turning the subject around so clumsily. "You see, when I was really young, the revolution slowly started, it was taking form. I got interested in it after an evening in front of the television at a neighbour's house. I remember it like it was yesterday." He first started saying.

"What do you mean?" I questioned.

"Once, the National Guard ambushed a man inside a small house. That man was Comandante Julio Buitrago. He was alone, a soul survivor of his unit, surrounded by Somoza's henchmen. The dictator blocked off the streets, brought in TV cameras. The tyrant wanted to show the Nation what happened when peasants defied him. Unfortunately, it did not go as planned. Buitrago resisted for hours. There were soldiers, tanks, helicopters and even planes."

"Wow! How did he escape?" I asked.

"He did not. The Comandante came out charging, shooting, and dying heroically." Antonio passionately explained.

"You saw all that live on TV?"

"Not live, Somoza was stupid enough to show it over and over, thinking it would discourage people to stand up against him. It did the exact opposite. When Nicaraguans saw Buitrago fighting against the odds, it proved that the Guard could be beaten."

"I'm not sure I understand why you are telling me this." I admitted to him.

"You see, this man made me want to join the fight. I felt like I was cowering in my village while he fought and died to get rid of the bullies that oppressed us all. So, I did the whole training, went straight up in the mountains as a boy with a wooden walking stick and I came down as a man, with a riffle in my hand."

I could not believe it.

"As time passed, I became second in a command of a small special squad." He went on.

"What was this special squad?" I interrupted.

"We were not really special; there were tons of other small units like us. The FSLN was split in three and we were in the Terceristas, the most active group of all."

238

"I didn't even know there were three groups."

"Yes, there was a big break-up when the great leader Carlos Fonseca was assassinated." Antonio explained.

"The dictator was probably very proud of this killing." I implied.

"Maybe for a while, but it made us stronger. Our fallen leaders became martyrs, pushing us to go to the end."

"Were there many of them?" I questioned, not knowing if he would answer or simply go on with his story.

"Yes, a few important ones like Carlos Aguero or Pedro Arauz. Although it was Buitrago who had started it all for me, for most of the population it was when Joaquin Chomorrow was killed. The execution of a journalist proved to the people that no one was safe. He was the editor of a newspaper, financed by the CIA, called La Prensa. He was by far the most outspoken critic against the dictator. Some say he was the one who would replace Somoza, if they could get him out. After his assassination, the Unitedstatesians slowly started to pull back. An amazing uproar began. People came down to demonstrate, whole cities were closed down. A few months later, all three FSLN sections were reunited and fighting alongside each other. Even though we never officially entered Managua, we were in business, fighting for all Central Americans. In August seventy-eight, we captured the National Palace, holding three and a half thousand people hostage."

"What were you asking for?" I questioned.

"We forced Somoza to release Sandinistas prisoners." He explained.

"That's incredible!" I exclaimed. I could not believe that the man who had been sitting in the back of my truck for all this time had such a history. "What happened to your squad exactly?" I asked.

"We were mostly sent in different parts of the capital, doing the jobs that organized soldiers could not officially do. Our faces were always painted red and black and we unleashed hell on whoever did not support our cause."

I stayed quiet, giving him room to express his thoughts freely.

"So the war went on for a long time. We were getting closer to our goal with each passing day. Once, we were in Managua and, by accident, we came upon a Unitedstatesian who was interrogated by members of the National Guard. We took cover and observed the scene from a nearby rooftop. The man in white clothes was forced to the ground. We stayed quiet. Obviously, it was looking badly for the Yankee. Still, there was no way to be certain. Usually a man caught in the city was sent to prison, executions on the spot mostly happened in the countryside. The wind was strong, blowing smoke from a small fire nearby. We realized he was a journalist from a TV station. Even though at that time, we had no love for Unitedstatesians, we hated the National Guard more than anybody else. The reporter was lying in the dirt, probably pleading for his life, explaining his noble journalistic purpose in Nicaragua. There was only a soldier interested in him; the six others we could see were walking around, patrolling the area. When the journalist received a solid kick to the gut, we got ready to take action and relieve the world of the soldier and his acolytes. Our three snipers were in position, they were about to shoot when I noticed a new player. Down the road, there was another man in the picture and this one was heavily armed. He did not have a machine gun or a bazooka over the shoulder, but a video camera, pointed straight at the scene. When I saw the cameraman, I thought about Buitrago's televised death and the impact it had had on me and my countrymen. Everybody in the squad knew that the reporter would not survive if we did not intervene, but it came down to my dilemma: I either helped him and kill a few guards or I sacrificed him and let the whole world finally know what Somoza was capable of. It may seem like a tough choice, but I did not even hesitate. Although everything happened in a second, it was all so cleared to me. I automatically signalled my snipers back. Two seconds later, the main Guard held his machine gun in his single right hand and shot the reporter. Immediately after, the cameraman started running the opposite way. I remembered closing my eyes, slightly smiling, happy that the video had gotten away safely. In a way, I was immensely satisfied of being responsible for the journalist's death. I ignored his children, parents, and friends. They had nothing to do with our war, they knew nothing of it. I was proud of what I had accomplished. I could almost envision the six o'clock news and the Unitedstatesians' outraged, screaming for Somoza's head. It was so obvious that they would now help us in our fight. They, who had personally installed the National Guard so many years ago, were now being killed by their own creation. At the time, the reporter's life seemed priceless in a way and worthless in another." He explained with a total absence of pride in his voice.

"Did it work at least?" I asked expressionless.

"Soon after, President Carter stopped supporting Somoza. He still did not want to see the FSLN in power, so he formed a commission to help the Frente Amplio Opositor. A party that was more moderate, less efficient, but as long as it was not Somoza, we were happy. I was happy. The people stayed behind us. They knew we were the only ones who could get things done to the end, to the very end."

"I guess you can't make an omelette without breaking any eggs." I said to be nice to my friend, wondering if the expression also made sense in Spanish.

"I did think about that reporter as I rolled into the Plaza de la Republica on top of a tank, slowly cutting through the crowd of thousands of people celebrating our victory. I saw all the cameras, journalists and photographers there. I knew I was part of history. Images taken here would be seen all over the world. We had done it and my decision had definitely played a big role."

"TV, hey?"

"Yes. Is it not strange? I have never even owned a television in my life." He paused and looked around the field.

"What did you do when Sandinistas took office?" I questioned.

"I came back to the San Pedro and, for a time, I was able to forget all about the people I had killed and we had a great life. Then, the Contra came and I lost everything except my land. I have been the immoral and unscrupulous landowner ever since." He stopped and reflected. "You know something, Don Kristiano? When you decide to hurt another person, the first one to pay is yourself. When I look back, the Revolution, although necessary at the time, was not a profitable move for either of us. There was just too much misery everywhere. In general, Nicaraguans are just peasants. I cannot even blame the ones who fought on the wrong side during the Contra war. They simply played the cards, shitty ones, they were dealt to the best of their abilities." He paused again.

I had no idea what to say.

"I have been very close to death a few times and trust me when I say that witnessing the death of people you truly love is a thousand times worst than living it yourself. Now I understand I was wrong to let that reporter die. He was someone's son, maybe even someone's father. I killed that man and God knows he did not deserve it. He had come to my country to cover the revolution, show the world what was going on here. My wife and child died a few days ago and I feel like I am being punished for what I have done."

"You couldn't have known back then." I comforted. What do you say after a story like that?

"Do not be fooled, I heard the inner voice telling me it was not right, but I still went along with my plan. I chose to ignore my intuition and that, was a very bad decision."

It sounded familiar, but I had forgotten where I had heard it before. "And what happens to Antonio De La Vega from now on?" I asked.

"Who knows? Good things I hope." Antonio answered and did not say anything else for a while.

"I'm sure of it." I agreed with a smile. The man had suffered enough; he had to be done.

We stayed quiet for about five minutes. There were four kids running around the yard, playing for fun, and a man who was jogging. "Would you like to learn to drive?" I asked.

"We tried that before and you know very well what happened." He countered with a smile.

"Yes, but this time will be different because you're different. Besides, there are no cliffs around here." I jokingly said. "Vamos, let's give it another try." I persuaded.

We climbed inside the truck and the widower took the driving seat for the second time in his life. I explained everything again, from the pedals to the steering wheel.

"Listo!" He expressed.

He started without hesitation, and this time, it went great. Antonio took it slowly. We turned in circles around the baseball field, waving to the runner as we passed him by. Perhaps my friend had mentally practiced during the trip. He even allowed himself the time to shout at the kids to get out of the way. At some point, I showed him how to shift it into second gear. He was good, succeeding where he had failed in the past.

We continued for about fifteen minutes. A flock of birds landed on the field, right in front of us. They were the exact same kind as the one from the San Juan's Day. "Do not worry Don Kristiano; I will not hit the ducks." Antonio said.

I started laughing, they were ducks after all. "I know. Concentrate on what's in front of you." I said.

The sun was starting to set; it would be dark in less than an hour. We both knew that when he would turn the engine off, it would be over for us. We went around the field one last time and he slowed down. "Bréké?" He asked with a smile.

"Bréké." I softly answered.

Antonio decided to walk to Martin's house where his horse waited his return. I watched his silhouette get away for the last time. As he was leaving, Don Angel appeared. When, the two of them passed each other, they did not stop, but I was glad to see that Pedro said something to him. Antonio then turned around and waved. Of course, he might have been waving at me, so I waved as well, just in case. "Buenas tardes, Don Kristiano!" Pedro greeted me.

"Hello my friend, you've been to your home?" I questioned.

"Yes I have. I must say it was a bit strange at first, but it felt very good once I got used to it." He said. "Are you ready to leave tomorrow morning?" He was nice enough to change the subject.

"Yes, I'm all packed up." I answered.

"I was not talking about luggage." He specified.

"Yes, I'm mentally ready to go home." I annoyingly replied.

"Things will probably not be different when you get there."

"I know, that's fine with me. Don't worry; I've heard every word you said over the course of the journey. If I ever decide to go see a psychologist, I hope he'll be exactly like you." I said with a grin.

"Thank you!" He looked around. "Did Antonio finally learn to drive?" My friend questioned.

"Yes he did." I shortly answered. "And by the way, I am now the owner of a piece of land in the mountains somewhere. We might see each other again. And we also had a very long discussion." I added.

"Was it a good final conversation?"

"Yes it was. At long last, I can say I know the true Antonio." I replied.

"Well, truth can be okay sometimes." Pedro said with a smile. "And does Antonio know the true Kristiano?" He asked.

"What do you mean?"

"Your origins! After what he spilled on the table, you still did not think he deserved to know the true you?" He questioned.

I hesitated a bit. I was petrified of Antonio's reaction. What if that simple detail took away all his gratitude? "I'm not even sure it's worth mentioning anymore." I confessed.

"Do not be troubled. You are who you are, regardless of where you are from geographically." He said.

"I know it, but does he? I don't even see the United States in the same way anymore."

"I know, but so what if you learned a few bad things over the summer. People here gave you a different view and people over there will repeat your old views. It always depends on who you listen to, which paper you read or which TV station you watch. Who is right, who is wrong? It does not matter: the question now is what do *you* believe to be right or wrong?" Don Angel added.

"I'm not sure." I repeated once more, as an old man sat on the player's bench.

"And that is just fine, there is no time limit. Take all the time you need." He answered. "One thing remains though, if you want people to like you for who you are, you must be honest with them." Pedro explained.

It was a simple detail and Antonio was worthy of receiving the same honesty that he had given me. "Again," and probably for the last time, "I have to acknowledge that you're right." I admitted. There was no used doubting Don Angel, the man was never wrong. After all, you cannot be wrong when you quote life and forget about other people's sayings. "Any final thought to rap it all up?" I then questioned before leaving.

"Just be happy and make sure that everybody you meet is happier for having been in contact with you. Most of all, be at peace here," he advised as he pointed to my forehead, "and here." He added as he touched my heart.

I stayed quiet for a bit. "And how do I do that?" I jokingly demanded.

"You will figure it out." He said and stared at the children who were now lying in the grass of left field, laughing.

"You see those kids?" He interrogated and continued right away. "They've been playing with dandelions ever since we arrived." Pedro said.

"So?"

"Most adults consider dandelions like bad weeds that need to be eliminated." He went on.

I was not sure where he was going with this, but I looked at them for a few seconds before Don Angel started again.

"See the old man sitting over there, how peaceful and undisturbed he seems? If you are unhappy, relearn to enjoy life's simplest pleasures like kids do and aim for an old man's serenity. It will be a good way to start." He said.

"I hope we see each other again." I declared.

"I know we will, but it will take a while though." He answered and started walking away. Then, turned around, looked at me straight in the eye and smiled in a way that filled my heart with happiness.

Once his silhouette was out of sight, I jumped in the vehicle and took the road to San Pedro. After about five minutes, I caught up with Antonio. I beeped the horn and pulled over to the side of the road. I got out and he got down from his horse. We met and shook hands. He was unquestionably surprised to see me. "There is something I forgot to tell you." I paused and looked him straight in the eye. "I was born in America." I blunted out.

"So was I." He answered back, not knowing if he truly wanted to know what a really meant.

"No, I mean I was born in the USA." I repeated. "In the United States of America." I made very clear.

He stayed quiet, staring at me. He seemed to recapitulate every action we had done together. "Why did you not tell me before?" He then questioned.

"Isn't it obvious? During the whole trip, all I heard from you was anti-American stories. You think Americans, Unitedstatians, are the worst people on earth." I nervously said.

"Well, maybe war brings out the worst in people." He answered.

I tried to calm down. "Face it Antonio, you hate all Unitedstatians." I alleged quickly, but coolly.

He stayed quiet again. "That is unfair, Don Kristiano, you are wrong." He said with his eyes to the ground.

"Why is that?" I dared to question.

"I do not hate them *all*." He stopped and then looked me straight in the eye. "As a matter of fact, I happen to like one of them very much." He clarified as he extended his right hand in friendship.

"Well, that's a start!" I then said as my hand joined his for a solid grip. We shook and he pulled me closer to give me a hug. It was the first time a man ever hugged me, including my father. I heard him sniff before he let me go and then he got back on the horse.

I got in the truck and rolled back to Cinco Pinos.

I parked the truck and took a little walk around the village. Then I entered Don Martin's house and saw the light on the back porch. My friend liked to read there at night when the electricity permitted it. He had no idea I had entered. "Gosh! Are the neighbours cooking turds?" He exclaimed out loud.

It was true that it was never easy to live between two sewer canals. "Oh honey, I'm home!" I jokingly shouted.

CHAPTER 5.3

In the early morning, Don Martin and I had breakfast at the house instead of Juanita's. We had cereal. Miraculously, the power had not run out and the milk was still fresh. "Maybe I could stay a bit longer." I said between two spoonfuls.

"You can't!" He answered with desolation.

"Why not?"

"Your plane ticket is today that's all."

"So? I can get the date changed."

"Not really, the big boss said to make sure you left on the appropriate date. He even said I had to go find you where ever you were if you weren't back." He explained. "I'm sorry, Kristian." He added. There was nothing else to say.

We finished our bowls and got ready to leave.

My goodbyes were quick. Most villagers came to Martin's house and the others who did not, made sure they were by the side of the road to wave me off. I was saddened to let them go, but deep down, I knew it was the right time.

The truck started going for my last ride. My friend was driving and I occupied the passenger seat. When I bent my head towards my left shoulder, I saw the villagers in my review mirror; they seemed exactly where they belong, no closer, no further.

We stopped for a Fanta in Somotillo. Again, we went to the general store and kids were staring. As Martin paid for our drinks, I picked up two oranges and started juggling them with one hand. It attracted three more little boys and they all started to cheer me on. It made me laugh to hear their chant. They all sounded so happy, it could only bring a smile to my face. Then, the oranges banged together and dropped to the ground. Boys ran for them and handed them back to me. A tiny little girl also gave me an apple. They all asked for me to start again, which I did without hesitation. Funny, I was always told never to mix apples with oranges, but this time it did not matter. Some were now clapping; even some adults were looking at me from a distance. I juggled for about a minute until I heard Martin from the back. "Time to go, Don Kristiano!" He said with laughter.

"Did you pay for the fruit?" I asked as I kept going.

"No, I didn't."

"Could you?" I said without dropping any.

"Sure!?" He replied with confusion. "Put these on my tab!" He ordered to the clerk.

I caught all three fruits and gave them to the kids. "Make sure you share them okay?" I told them as they thanked me many times. It truly was a joy to hear their goodbyes ringing in my ears.

We gassed up in Chinandega and Martin made me notice that there was an American submarine counter. "Do you want to go for a sub?" He asked.

"No thanks! I'm not really hungry." I admitted. I had been used to starving for so long, it seemed useless to eat lunch. Plus, I did not feel like spending over five US dollars on a sub. Who, in this three-dollar-a-day land, could afford a sandwich at this price?

It was exactly noon when we arrived at the Managua airport. "Well, I guess this is it." I declared.

"Yes it is. Don't worry, after all you went through, you should be fine by yourself."

"Funny guy!" I smiled. "You don't have to walk me in, Don Martin."

"I wasn't going to. I have an appointment at the bank in fifteen minutes." My friend excused himself.

I felt relieved, I never liked long goodbyes.

"It's time for you to return to your normal life." Martin said.

"How can I return to my normal life after all I've witnessed? I can't un-see everything I've seen. You know I won't ever be the same." I explained.

"Maybe you're right." He answered. "You'll be better." He added.

"You sound just like Don Angel!" I told him.

"Like who?"

"Forget it!" I retorted. I did not feel like telling him he was preaching too much, so I preferred to stop it there.

"And you'll get to see your American compañeros in Miami." My friend insinuated.

"I'm not sure about them anymore either." I admitted.

"Don't worry so much. All you've learned here doesn't change everything you knew before. Maybe you've just switched from being a Republican to a Democrat." He laughed.

I did not know what to say; I looked at birds feeding on some crap in the parking lot. "When will you go back home?" I asked to change the subject.

"I'm going back this evening."

"I meant back to France, idiot." I clarified.

"Oh! I don't know exactly, my contract finishes in two and a half years." He stopped talking so we could both stare at a beautiful woman walking beside us. "Thanks for everything you've done here." Martin said.

"I haven't done as much as I would've liked. Those coffee plantations aren't doing too well." I replied.

He hesitated a while. "You weren't only brought here for your coffee expertise. We were told by the friend of your friend, the one you helped renovate his house, that you were a great guy and a great entertainer. The truth is that we would have hired another guy before you, but he was as dull as a spoon." Martin difficulty admitted.

I was speechless and my partner noticed it.

"Don't take it the wrong way, Kristian, but there was more than one reason for your coming, it wasn't *only* coffee."

"What do you mean?"

"The Nicaraguans needed to approve of our presence here for the project to succeed and trust is a difficult thing to earn from entire villages. What you did for that couple gave us total agreement from every single person. You're a big reason why this plantation will go on. Even if not a single coffee plant grows this year, we're in and that's thanks to you." Martin said.

"I helped you guys manipulate these poor villagers?" I asked in shock.

"Not at all! We're not here to make profits. We're here to really help them out." Martin justified.

"So you haven't lied to me, you guys are still here for good reasons?" I almost begged for reassurance.

"Yes, you helped us help them." He finished.

I reflected a few seconds. "That's fine. I also helped myself doing it."

"I'm trying to give you a great compliment, Kristian. We needed you for people skills because I don't really have that much. It's a lot harder to deal with people than to deal with coffee. This plantation will survive in big part because of you. Although your Capitalist attitude made me very nervous at the beginning, it was mostly your actions that made these villagers involved in our project. You made them believe in us, not me. You don't know this, but while you were gone, things got tougher, a number of workers probably would have quit if it hadn't been for your performance. Some of them can now feed their families because of you. You can be damn proud of what you've done here. These people

248

will never forget you, and neither will I." He paused and looked me straight in the eye. "Need I talk about the couple: Anna and Antonio?" He added.

"No you don't." We shook hands. I heard an announcement from inside the airport and it made me nervous about my flight. "I gotta go." I said in an uncertain tone of voice.

We parted without adding anything. I probably should have thanked him, tell him that I was glad he had been there, or ask him what the heck he was talking about when he said he had no people skills. Regardless, I had good memories of the conversations we used to have at his house and hoped he did too. I entered the airport as I blew on a mosquito that was about to bite me on my left arm.

CHAPTER 5.4

I took care of my tickets and went to sit down. I had about an hour to kill. I observed people. Strangely, they were all exactly as they were when I had first landed in this airport.

I noticed a sign in a window that said they developed pictures in under sixty minutes. I decided to get mine done right away. Then, I walked around as I waited; found a little store, not too expensive. I counted the money I had left in my pockets. When I calculated everything, it was ironic to realize that my total earnings came to about three dollars a day. After about two minutes of hesitation, I decided to exterminate the rest of it and buy some souvenirs.

I paid for everything and went to sit back down in front of the departure gate. Hopefully planes would feed me, because I did not even have enough money for a coffee. I searched into my bag and took out my book and my music. It had been such a long time since I had had the pleasure of relaxing in their company. I was anxious to lift up in the sky, see the wonderful green lagoon inside the Apoyeque volcano.

We landed in Miami, Florida. The USA, the birthplace I had once been so proud of and longed to return to.

I had six hours to waste before my connection. I thought about going Downtown, but chose not to. In some weird way, I felt like I would betray my Sandinista friends if I enjoyed it too much. Maybe someday I would return, but now was not the time. I could not compare the two continents so different from one another. It was black and white, yin and yang, totally useless to try and measure. They probably completed each other in some weird way. Why would you compare fire and water? Both of them danced on a similar kind of music. One laid on a soft bedrock bordered by a long wooden fence. The other one stood up on suffering branches and was enclosed by hot stones. Both were fascinating, hypnotizing. I could almost hear Don Angel's voice in my head: there is not one better than the other, they are *different.*

"I got it Pedro!" I actually said out loud, causing two people to turn around and stare at me.

People seemed so rich and carefree. I would have liked to tell them about everything I had seen and make them realize how lucky they were. I did not even need to know them personally to see that they were taking their wealth for granted: the big house with the pool, the remote control for the giant screen, the toilet seat and its paper, the milk in the fridge. It sounded all so trivial to them, but so amazing to others. The worst part was that they did not even need to search very far. Inside their own country was about a quarter of the population that was living below the acceptable poverty level. I felt like taking a megaphone and scream to them to share their wealth. I could see myself preaching my Nicaraguan illumination that they would probably not understand: it had to be lived.

Rain began falling, Mother Nature had decided to spare me, maybe she felt bad about the jungle incident. I observed people, these Unitedstatians. They were beautiful. I just needed to look at them from a newer point of view. Who could blame simple suburban people for their government's actions? They had nothing to do with it. After all, at election time, they were only given two choices. They did not pick the best, but rather what they believe to be the lesser of two evils. A country's population and its government were two very different things. Antonio talked about the Nicaraguan people all the time, but never about the government. The people!

Rain made the dark pavement reflect every single little light. It was almost lovely. The raindrops were violently hitting the window, but I was safe. I crossed my arms, pressing them on my chest, pushing my dry sweatshirt on my bare skin. Following the plane's acceleration, the wheel kissed the UnitedStatesians' ground good-bye. Seconds passed and land became a reduced model, perception instantly changed. The black clouds of the night made the ground look like a giant jigsaw puzzle. We shot through the cumulus like William Tell's arrow, the plane shook and it stopped raining. I finally started to decompress, it was time for me to go home.

CHAPTER 5.5

I woke up and took off my earphones. I looked outside and there was a line of clouds full of electricity in the sky. Lightning formed themselves inside, prisoners of the night. They moved around at high speed, but could not escape. Every lightning presented a new shape, a new face. Some came alone, others in group. I could not take my eyes from it all, expecting the lights of the future. I did not fear the time when our plane would cross inside the electric storm, maybe it would never come. So many things could change and for now, stars were shining over my head.

Everyone, especially Don Angel, had taught me so much. Now, it was time for me to put it into practice. The Shaman had curiously been a key player. I needed to accept things more quickly, the old healer had said to me. So what if I sometimes had a deranged state of mind, misunderstanding of human immorality or misguided society. I did not need to question myself about it, I only had to try. At least, this way, it would all seem a bit more possible.

I now believed in the hitchhiking phases of life, that every situation was formed of three main stages and that these stages were enclosed by normality. In my view, life was a circle made of anger, sadness and insanity, preceded by a need to have and enclosed by the will to be.

I looked at my pictures once again, remembering all those moments very clearly. I stopped on the one from the monument of San Francisco's massacre: the Héroes Y Martires. There were so many names. Aside from the Nicaraguan flag, they were the only things in white, separated from the red and the black. I read Don Garcia's father-in-law's name. There were two Espinal, Justo and Victorino. Considering what had happened to them, the term *just* and *victory* did not feel very à-propos. There were also three victims with the last name Espinoza, probably coming from the same family. I noticed on the right row that Felix had lost an *I* and that his last name was Sanchez. Then another one really came to my attention, at the bottom of the first row, there was another martyr with the same last name. I shivered to see it there. Did *P* stand for Pedro? I could not believe it. A thousand thoughts came into my head, but they were all ridiculous. I knew it could only be a coincidence. There was no way he could have been a spirit, a true guardian seraph. After all, Angel was a very common name in the Latino world.

www.ingramcontent.com/pod-product-compliance
Lightning Source LLC
Chambersburg PA
CBHW052030020726
47501CB00004B/1333